Danica Winters is a multiple-aw[...] author who writes books that g[...] ability to drive emotion through suspense and occasionally a touch of magic. When she's not working, she can be found in the wilds of Montana, testing her patience while she tries to hone her skills at various crafts—quilting, pottery and painting are not her areas of expertise. She believes the cup is neither half-full nor half-empty, but it better be filled with wine. Visit her website at danicawinters.net

Addison Fox is a lifelong romance reader, addicted to happily-ever-afters. After discovering she found as much joy writing about romance as she did reading it, she's never looked back. Addison lives in New York with an apartment full of books, a laptop that's rarely out of sight and a wily beagle who keeps her running. You can find her at her home on the web at addisonfox.com or on Facebook (Facebook.com/addisonfoxauthor) and X (@addisonfox).

Also by Danica Winters

Big Sky Search and Rescue
Helicopter Rescue
Swiftwater Enemies
Mountain Abduction
Winter Warning

STEALTH: Shadow Team
A Judge's Secrets
K-9 Recovery
Lone Wolf Bounty Hunter
Montana Wilderness Pursuit

Also by Addison Fox

Wyoming Warriors
Renegade Reunion

New York Harbor Patrol
Danger in the Depths
Peril in the Shallows
Threats in the Deep

The Coltons of Owl Creek
Guarding Colton's Secrets

The Coltons of New York
Under Colton's Watch

Discover more at millsandboon.co.uk

RODEO CRIME RING

DANICA WINTERS

COLTON REUNION

ADDISON FOX

MILLS & BOON

All rights reserved including the right of reproduction in whole or in part in any form. This edition is published by arrangement with Harlequin Enterprises ULC.

This is a work of fiction. Names, characters, places, locations and incidents are purely fictional and bear no relationship to any real life individuals, living or dead, or to any actual places, business establishments, locations, events or incidents. Any resemblance is entirely coincidental.

Without limiting the author's and publisher's exclusive rights, any unauthorised use of this publication to train generative artificial intelligence (AI) technologies is expressly prohibited. HarperCollins also exercise their rights under Article 4(3) of the Digital Single Market Directive 2019/790 and expressly reserve this publication from the text and data mining exception.

® and ™ are trademarks owned and used by the trademark owner and/or its licensee. Trademarks marked with ® are registered with the United Kingdom Patent Office and/or the Office for Harmonisation in the Internal Market and in other countries.

First Published in Great Britain 2025
by Mills & Boon, an imprint of HarperCollins*Publishers* Ltd
1 London Bridge Street, London, SE1 9GF

www.harpercollins.co.uk

HarperCollins*Publishers*
Macken House, 39/40 Mayor Street Upper,
Dublin 1, D01 C9W8, Ireland

Rodeo Crime Ring © 2025 Danica Winters
Colton Reunion © 2025 Harlequin Enterprises ULC

Special thanks and acknowledgement are given to Addison Fox
for her contribution to *The Coltons of Arizona* series.

ISBN: 978-0-263-39716-1

0625

This book contains FSC™ certified paper and other controlled sources to ensure responsible forest management.

For more information visit: www.harpercollins.co.uk/green

Printed and Bound in the UK using 100% Renewable Electricity at
CPI Group (UK) Ltd, Croydon, CR0 4YY

RODEO CRIME RING

DANICA WINTERS

Thank you to all my readers.

It is an incredible feeling to know our worlds meet,
even if it is only for a moment on the page.

Chapter One

The smell of cows only meant one thing to Cameron Trapper and his Montana family on the West Glacier Cattle Ranch—*money*.

The bigger the stink, the better they'd weathered the winter and the larger the operation could grow. He rolled down the pickup's window and let the wind pour in. This summer, the air smelled too much like roses.

In the distance sat the shiny green bailer. Last summer, his father, Leonard, had taken out another note of credit and purchased the newest model, complete with heat and air-conditioning. It was one heck of a step up from the swather and the tall, log beaverslides Cameron had grown up using on their ranch when his grandparents had been running the place.

His father had never been great with money and, even though beef prices were higher than ever, he'd found a great way to drive the ranch into the ground.

He thought of the old beaverslides. They had been so fun to play with as a kid. His family had used the tractors to move the cut hay to the elevator-style lifts that cranked the hay up the slide and dumped it into large, fenced piles. When they ran out of room in one fence, they'd move the huge slides to the next spot with the tractor and start the process all over again.

It was old tech, and an even older tradition, but it worked better than the new bailer his father had purchased. It used less gas, plus it also kept wildlife like deer and elk from grazing on their family's much-needed winter hay supply for the cattle. Not only had his father cost them the note, but he'd also tripled their gas bill and they'd ended up having to buy hay for their herd last winter.

Cameron was so mad at Leonard that he could almost cuss.

Modernization might be their ruin.

It was a Montana tradition and possibly a tale as old as the state itself—multiple generations of hard work and sacrifice brought down by one bad trustee.

He would put a stop to it, dammit.

His couldn't be like every other family who'd worked hard for their brand—like the P Lazy J and the D◊H—who'd then watched them become nothing more than a decoration hanging on their living room walls.

Yet, Montana was being hit by a land grab like he'd never seen before, perpetuated by deep pockets. The worst part about it was that the ranch was sitting at its epicenter and his father wasn't ready for the war.

When he rolled up to the barn, Leonard was sitting on the ground by the back tire of his pickup, his arms over his chest and his hat tipped low. Cameron didn't understand how his father could have been sleeping on a day like this, one with plenty of work that needed doing.

He pulled his truck next to his father's and made sure to slam the door a little extra hard to jerk him awake. His father didn't stir.

Trying to control his rage, Cameron walked to the barn

and slid open the door, the caster squeaking as loudly as it had since as early as he could remember. Ginger was in her stall and she stuck her head out and nickered as he walked into the damp, musty-smelling barn. They needed to open this place up and get it dried out and ready for hay.

"How's it going, old lady?" he asked the blaze-faced mare. "You gonna play nice or are you feeling a little hot? I saw you looking at that young roan stud yesterday. You better not be getting any ideas." He gave the horse a loving, gentle scratch behind her ear as he chastised.

The bay mare closed her eyes and dropped her head as he rubbed, and they both seemed to acknowledge that her glory days as a brood mare were past. Now, Ginger was devoted to him and the occasional neighborhood kid who came through the barn during baling season.

His father's paint, Bessie, came sidling up to the other stall's door and gave him the side-eye like she could read his feelings toward her rider. "Don't worry, he'll be along. Or do you want me to saddle you up, too?" he asked Bessie as he grabbed the tack for Ginger.

The paint blew snot at him as he walked by her carrying Ginger's saddle.

She was definitely his father's horse.

Ginger was an angel, even exhaling as he tightened the saddle. Bessie, on the other hand, held her breath and puffed up when he tried to tighten the cinch.

"If you don't watch it, you're going to the glue factory." He didn't mean it, but that horse really was something else.

He walked them out of the barn before he stepped into Ginger's saddle and grabbed Bessie's reins. As she moved, the paint let out her breath and the saddle on her back shifted to the left. It couldn't feel good on the mare's back, but his father would have to tighten her up when she got over her attitude.

He rode over toward his resting father. "You getting up, lazy bones?"

There wasn't an answer. His father must have really tied one on last night.

"Hey, old man, you awake?" he called over the crunch of the horses' footfalls on the gravel in the driveway.

Bessie let out a huff and a nicker, throwing her head like she was trying to pull the reins out of his hands and head back to the barn. Instead of letting her, he held on tighter and gave them a little nudge. Bessie stopped and refused to budge, leaning back into her haunches.

"Are you freaking kidding me? You old pain in the..." He gave the reins another pull to get her moving, but she leaned back even farther. She turned her head and the whites of her eyes were showing—he didn't know why, or of what, but Bessie was afraid.

He dropped her reins and before they even touched the ground, she spun on her back hooves and raced toward the barn. She disappeared into the barn and away from them. Ginger looked back at him like she was hoping he would lead her away as well, but had a cool enough head to wait and not get into an impromptu rodeo.

She would be getting an extra flake of hay tonight.

He nudged Ginger forward. His father could deal with Bessie in a minute. First, he needed to figure out what was bothering the animals.

His thoughts moved to his father's note. They couldn't handle any more predation or losses on the ranch. Not if they wanted to be in the black.

Ginger took a tentative step toward the pickups, to where his father had been sitting.

"Dad?" he asked once more.

Again, no answer. Maybe he had run inside or something while Cameron had been saddling up the horses.

Ginger moved forward, but only thanks to his goading her with the press of his thighs. She drew in a long breath and exhaled hard, nickering. She didn't like her task, but she plodded forward, dragging her hooves.

As he neared Leonard's pickup, where Cameron had last seen his father resting, Ginger snorted and threw her head. "Whoa, girl. It's okay," he cooed, trying to calm his spooked mare.

She took another step but then stopped and refused to be urged another. Horses were smart—smarter than cows and definitely smarter than most people. If Ginger was spooked, something was very wrong.

He gave her a pat on the side of her neck and she looked back at him, concern in her eyes, as though she was trying to tell him what he was clearly too stupid to already know.

The last time he'd seen her act like this they had edged up on a rattlesnake in the Red Rocks. The way she was acting now—there was something deadly and darned close.

A griz had been skulking around the ranch the last month or so, but it hadn't posed a real threat. Hopefully, the bear hadn't decided to start causing problems. The last thing they needed was the game wardens coming out and poking around.

That was to say nothing about the wolves who had gotten to five of their calves this spring. Even though they had insurance on the cattle and their losses of the calves had been a stipend, it didn't cover the real losses of possible sales prices—at least with the price of beef being what it was.

He backed his horse up and turned her away from the truck. As he had her move, she seemed to relax under him.

Whatever was wrong was by that truck and near where his father had been.

He stepped down out of the saddle and looped the reins over the edge of the truck's tailgate. Ginger wouldn't take them and run; for her, the idea of being tied up was enough for her to stay put. Unless things went totally haywire.

Though he considered calling out to his father one more time, Cameron stopped himself. If his father was still out here, he would be in no shape to answer, or he would have spoken up already. He steeled himself as he walked around the pickup. Leonard's boots came into view in exactly the same position he'd seen them when he'd first arrived.

The world dissolved around him as he stared at the tip of those boots. They were so dirty and caked with muck that they were nearly black except in the places where the muck had dried and turned gray. A piece of hay stuck out from his heel. For a long moment, Cameron just stared at the piece of grass. It was faded green and moldy, folded in the middle, like his father had just happened to pick it up on his heel while he'd gone around his morning chores.

It was so *normal*, but he couldn't help fixating on the little thing as he comprehended the reasons why his father wouldn't have been answering—or moving.

He pushed forward, goading himself like he had his mare. She had been right; things were fifty shades of wrong.

His father's face was partially hidden by his black cowboy hat, but now that he was closer and not just rolling by, Cameron could see that his father's skin was an eerie shade of gray—the same color of that dead calf's lips and tongue, the tint of bloodlessness.

There was a silver-and-elk-antler hilt sticking out from under his father's folded arms, which looked like they were resting on the object. His dad had carried a Ruana knife just like that one on his belt every day of his life—except when he'd put on his Sunday clothes for churchgoing.

Cameron squatted down beside his father and put his finger to his leathery neck, though he knew exactly what he'd fail to find.

Part of him half expected his father to sit up and exclaim some stupid thing like this was some sick joke, but he remained still and his arms stayed folded over his chest, resting on that damned knife.

Without thinking, Cameron took out his phone and dialed 9-1-1. While he talked, he started taking pictures of his father's body and the area around him.

Questions raced through his mind about what had happened to the family's controversial patriarch and how. But one thing was certain—his father was gone.

The crown he'd left behind would be almost as heavy as the family's loss.

Chapter Two

If Emily Monahan had known the Glock 19 she'd bought at the ranch supply store would be the gun someone would try to murder her with, she would have never made the purchase. The one thing Emily Monahan didn't have was the knowledge of what the future would bring

She tapped at the gun tightly wrapped in the bellyband around her center mass. The handgun was a little too big to be totally concealed, even though she and her chest were larger than the average woman, and the end of the magazine could be seen if she breathed just a little too hard.

Truth be told, she liked the fact that if someone was really paying attention, they would know she was carrying a concealed weapon in addition to her service weapon. It was the people who would notice who were truly her enemies or her allies.

She definitely had plenty of enemies—in the small town of West Glacier, just outside Glacier National Park, people could be incredibly kind or brutally cruel. As a sheriff's deputy for six years running, she had seen more than her fair share of the latter.

She stared out at the courthouse as she prepped her squad car for the day and took a sip of her coffee. The white building stood in stark contrast to the snowcapped mountains in the background.

As of late, cruelty wasn't just something she was facing at work. Her divorce from Todd had been the stuff of nightmares—mostly thanks to the shared parenting plan they were trying to renegotiate. Though they had been divorced for two years, Todd was now contesting the parenting plan and was demanding they revise.

At the beginning of her exit from their marriage, she'd promised herself their daughter, Stacy, wouldn't be put in the middle. Yet, no matter how hard she'd tried to keep her five-year-old safe and out of lawyer's offices, they would have their third meeting with the mediator this week.

A sickening lump formed in her stomach at the thought.

Until recently, Emily had never really wanted to commit a crime, but she'd be lying if she said she hadn't considered taking her daughter and making a run for the Canadian border. If they just ran, this nightmare could come to an end.

Todd Monahan hadn't been a bad man when they'd met. He'd seemed pretty good, actually. He'd opened the car doors, said all the right things; he'd been working a stable job as a pharmacy technician. On their first date, he'd shown up with flowers not only for her but for her mom, who had been alive and staying with her at the time. Her mother, Julie Moore, had taken an instant liking to him.

Before the wedding, Emily could still recall the moment over the bathroom sink, in her wedding dress, when she was trying to catch her breath between sobs. Her mother had put her hand on the center of her back, her touch cool against Emily's sweating skin. She'd told her mother she wasn't ready, that she couldn't make the walk down the aisle, but her mom had told her that those kinds of nerves were normal and *to be expected on a girl's wedding day*.

Thinking back, the fact that her mother had called it a *girl's* wedding day should have been one of many clues that she had been far too young and not nearly experienced enough to understand the choice she had been making.

To this day, she wasn't sure she knew what true love was—except when it came to her daughter. She'd do anything for that little blond nugget. She smiled as she recalled this morning's tiff over whether Stacy would wear the pink Minnie Mouse bow in her hair or the red Mickey one. In the end, Emily had given up and let her wear both. She couldn't really blame her. At five years old, no colors clashed—there was only what she loved with a dash of something else she adored—and damn if it didn't end up looking completely adorable.

Maternal love was chemical and, for many women, undeniable. It was as natural as the rain and just as critical for a child's healthy development.

The kind of true love she couldn't understand, or believe in, was the kind that came from a partner. When she'd initially been with Todd, she'd thought she'd known what love was—at the time, she'd assumed it was promises of a shared future and fidelity. It was dreams of rings, houses, children and everything down to a little white dog. It was a future of easy choices, *shared choices*, which would be rationally discussed and agreed upon. Then their lives would be beautiful, all the way to their perfectly matching dinner plates and immaculate lawn.

Now she knew that when love was easy and beautiful… that wasn't the true love she had envisioned. With Todd, "easy and beautiful" had meant he had been staying silent to keep the peace and seeking the gritty challenge that came with another woman.

True love in a partnership was a lie.

By the time she'd found out about the other woman, or rather *women*, her mother had passed away from breast cancer. It was stupid, but there were nights when she wanted to rage against her mother's ghost and tell her how wrong she had been to try to mollify her daughter over that sink on the day of her wedding. In fact, her mother would have been better off putting Emily's face in the water, rinsing off the paint that masked the features of the young girl, and helping her to run away.

Emily would never put her own daughter in a situation where she felt forced.

Then again, she had told herself she would never put her daughter in the middle of the fight with Todd—and look where that had gotten her.

Never was Fate's call to arms. Maybe, just maybe, one of these days, she would figure out a way to say never and actually be able to keep the promise.

She instinctively touched her ring finger with her thumb, looking for the band that had reminded her far too much of a handcuff. There was an indent in her skin where it had been up until the day Todd's lawyer had asked to have it returned.

She'd thrown it on the floor at the attorney's feet. If Todd and his team were to be so petty, then she had been fine with them hitting their knees to pick it up.

She cringed at the thought of attorneys. By and large, she would be fine with every last one of them enduring a slow death.

And that was to say nothing of the defense attorneys she ran into on a regular basis in the office. Some of those lawyers were slicker than an oiled-up serpent and far less likable.

Coffee...she just needed coffee and to remember to take

one moment and one day at a time. She was in control of her life and her emotions. The second she allowed anyone else to dictate her feelings was when she'd start losing what mattered to her the most.

Emily glanced down at Stacy's picture that was stuck in the corner of her dashboard. Her daughter was smiling up from the paper, one of her front teeth was missing and she was holding a dollar bill like it was some kind of prized fish.

The call log on her computer screen moved as another call popped up, requiring her attention. According to the dispatcher, there was a report of an unwitnessed death on the WGC Ranch. The dispatcher noted that the man was seventy-six years old but, aside from that, there wasn't any more information about the decedent.

As she was the acting coroner for the Flathead County Sheriff's Office, it fell upon Emily to handle this situation. Being the coroner on call gave her a leg up at the office, allowing her to gain more Peace Officer Standard and Training or POST Certifications, but it did little for her social life. Few of her friends really wanted to talk about dead bodies, not really. Sure, they had a morbid curiosity, like many, and they could handle hearing about the latest death or interesting case, but when it came right down to it, she wasn't about to tell them the truth about what she saw out there while working.

No one wanted to know what pets did to a human body after a person died. It was safe to say that while she liked them, she was not going to be owning a cat any time in the near future. She had simply seen too much.

She let the dispatcher know she was en route to West Glacier Cattle Ranch and then flipped on the radio and listened to the latest country music. Though Dispatch had posted the address, it was unnecessary; she drove by their front gate more often than she cared to admit during her days on patrol. The ranch sat just off Highway 2 East and was tucked into one of the languid bellies of the glacial moraines of the Lewis Mountains.

It was the location that, she had to assume, kept the Trapper family ranching. By and large, most of the rest of their sleepy little town was being swept up in the scurry for land deals by out-of-staters who wanted to make the picturesque town into their personal playground. It was rare these days to see any parcels larger than a handful of acres. Taxes were getting too high for a working ranch to survive, even with the agricultural breaks—or so she'd read in the *Daily Interlake* and heard from the few old timers who were left and still frequented the out-of-the-way diner, the Coffee Cup.

The diner had been around even longer than Emily and she had grown up drinking out of the heavy brown mugs that she was sure the owners had bought sometime in the 1970s. Once in a while, when she went there in the early morning hours, she would still spot one of the mugs float by on a waitress's tray, but these days, most of them had been replaced by the cheaper white ones. Seeing those chipped and fading brown mugs saddened her though she really couldn't explain why.

The entrance to the ranch was coming up, complete with the log archway decorated with the company's hanging iron brand. As she turned, the brand listed in the wind and, as it moved, she spotted a smattering of rust eating away at its black surface.

She had grown up in Kalispell, the biggest city nearest to the little town, but besides playing sports and a couple of dates with a receiver from the area, she hadn't known many of the people who had lived in West Glacier—at least not when she'd been growing up. Now, she had a few places that she frequently visited, thanks to either tumultuous romantic partners, family feuds, or criminal behaviors, but most callouts to the area were for minor things.

People usually kept to themselves, and when she did have to make traffic stops, she was usually treated with kindness and deference. Though there were outliers to every generalization.

As Emily slowed down and turned onto the road that led into the ranch, she spotted two saddled horses munching on grass on the inside of the cattle guard that sat across the end of the driveway. The bay looked up at her and swished its tail, almost as if waving hello, but the paint turned its back as she approached, and she noted that its saddle was sitting lopsided. The cattle guard sat across the end of the driveway, keeping them from getting hit by highway traffic but little more.

She liked horses, but since they were so far from the barn, untied, and not being used, it told her that they had probably been at the epicenter of some major drama. No cowboy worth his Wranglers would ever leave a horse out like those two. If left too long, the paint would get sores from that saddle, and that was the least of their worries if they decided to take a jump over the guard.

She was tempted to stop the car, grab the horses and lead them back to the barn, but this wasn't her ranch, and maybe these horses had been out there for some reason. She needed to take care of business first and then she could come back for them.

Then again, if that paint had been carrying that lopsided saddle for a while, it might have been hurting. She hated seeing animals in pain. Besides, she was out here to pick up a body and if she didn't get there in five minutes, it wasn't like they could get *more* dead.

She pulled her car over to the side of the driveway and stepped out. "Hello, babies," she called in a singsong voice.

The bay started to walk toward her, slowly, as if trying to decide whether or not she was to be trusted. The paint didn't even acknowledge her and instead continued to graze on the green grass and move in the opposite direction.

She walked toward the more amiable horse and took hold of its reins, gently scratching it behind the ear. The mare had a beautiful saddle, its leather worn and darkened with time and age, but it had been oiled and well maintained over the years.

"You're a beautiful girl," she said, leading the horse to the white fence. She looped the rein around the top slat. "You go ahead and wait here, babe, and I'm gonna go and try to get your comrade over there all fixed up. Okay?" She gave the mare a gentle pat and made her way toward the paint.

The paint took a step away from her, swishing her tail and pinning her ears back in Emily's direction. "Hey, beautiful," she cooed, trying to move slowly so as not to spook the horse.

The horse huffed.

"Yes, you know I want to take care of you," she said, trying to keep her voice soft but authoritative. She stepped around the paint and took hold of the horse's reins. The paint tried to throw her head, but Emily applied a slight bit of pressure and checked the horse. This one didn't need to think it was in control.

She stepped toward the fence. The horse didn't want to move her feet at first, but Emily wouldn't take no for an answer and, finally, the horse took a couple of tentative steps in the right direction. "Good, girl, we've got this," she said, trying to reinforce the desired behavior.

There had been many days like this on her grandparents' ranch on the east side of the state. They'd had a five-thousand-acre ranch on the outskirts of Havre and near the Rocky Boy Reservation. Every spring she would come up and help round up the cattle for cutting and branding. She hadn't been there in the last ten years, ever since her eldest brother had taken over the ranch. She missed it, but she wasn't about to work with her brother. That man had a mean streak a mile wide and a mouth dirtier than any sailor she had ever met.

She would never understand why her grandfather had chosen her brother to inherit the place. Then again, her brother was one of the hardest workers she had ever met. There was nothing that man couldn't fix and no cow that could slip his rope. It just gnawed at her that as the younger and female member of the family, she hadn't been considered to take over the family's business.

In all reality, she couldn't complain about where life had taken her. She loved her work in law enforcement. Besides, if she had taken over the ranch, it would have been expected that she would have had to get married and let her husband take the helm—at least, according to the unspoken generational rules handed down by her German great-grandparents, who had come to this country in hopes of changing their and their children's futures. In some ways, the only thing they had done was change their familial location. Many of the toxic behaviors had come right along with them and had been passed down.

Everything had been conditional on her playing by the rules. She had never been very good at being told what she could or could not do; as such, maybe it wasn't such a mystery as to why her brother had been selected to control the family's legacy.

The paint nickered and blew out a little bubble of snot. "You feel okay, pumpkin?" she asked, wrapping the rein around the fence before stepping back and readjusting the saddle. The horse exhaled hard, letting her pull the cinch tight. "There you go, that ought to feel better." She pulled the leather rein free of the fence and climbed up into the saddle.

She nudged the paint in the direction of the bay and, taking the rein off the fence, she led the bay back toward the ranch. The house was at least a mile away from the road and where she had parked her squad car. When they came into view of the barn, the paint started to speed up. The horse made her smile; it had one heck of a personality. She wasn't a horse that would be good for someone who didn't have a ton of experience in handling.

For so many reasons, the beautiful horse made her miss having her own.

The barn was bright red with white trim, and it looked as though it had been painted in the last year or two. The family must have been doing well, or they were up to their eyeballs in debt. She hoped it wasn't the latter. Ranching was a fickle business, and everything could change in the blink of an eye or a springtime hard freeze.

Her brother had told her he had been forced to sell off most of his cattle last year because of a dry summer, which had led to an even drier fall. Every crop that had managed to make it through the hard scrabble had then been gobbled up by hordes of grasshoppers. According to Josh, they had only managed to make pennies on the dollar—and that was before they'd had to pay the cutters.

There was a collection of dented-up pickups, all of which

were covered in mud and bits of grass. A couple of the trucks that were parked nearest to the barn were so old that she wondered if they were even capable of turning over or if they had become lawn ornaments. A man with a white cowboy hat and a red-flannel shirt had his back turned to her as she approached with the horses. There was the distinctive Copenhagen can mark in the back pocket of his jeans, the wear mark that was as much a part of cowboy culture as beer and buckles.

The horses' hoofs crunched on the gravel and the man turned. Even under the brim of his hat, she could tell he had blue eyes that were almost the same tone as the sunny sky. His hair poked out from under the band, making a swoop at the nape of his neck. It was a little long, but he was the kind of cowboy that could make any hairstyle look good.

His chin had a patch of dirt where he must have rubbed the back of his fist against his scruff. In his hand was a cell phone and he had it pressed against his ear. He was a strange juxtaposition between the old ways and the new, but something about him and the way he looked made her want to know more about the mystery of him.

"I gotta go," he said, his voice was as gravely as the driveway. He clicked off the phone and gave her an acknowledging tip of the hat as she slipped out of the saddle. "Glad you could make it." He looked at his watch. "I called you guys over an hour ago."

She wasn't sure what to make of his icy greeting. Sure, the guy was having one heck of a day, but that still didn't mean he had to be less than civil. "It took me a little longer than expected. I found these two roaming close to the highway," she said, playing nice in an attempt to give the man the benefit of the doubt about whether or not his attitude was situational or habitual. "This one here," she said, motioning to the paint, "nearly had her saddle upside down."

He sighed, running his hand over his face. "Thanks for grabbing the runaways. Last time I checked on them, they had wandered around the back of the barn, so I don't know how they got out there. I thought they were all right. I appreciate you looking out for them." He walked over and took the reins of the bay from her, their fingers grazing against one another, and the simple action caught her so off guard that her breath hitched in her throat.

What was wrong with her? Since when did a man inadvertently brushing against her on a death scene cause this kind of reaction?

She was distracted by that little can mark in his jeans as he walked the horses to the barn and disappeared inside. His momentary absence was welcome; it gave her a moment to come to her senses and remember exactly why she was there.

Brushing her hands over her hair, she tucked a wayward piece behind her ear as she took a look around. In the distance, she could make out the siren of an ambulance.

There were the sounds of footfalls behind her. "Do you want me to take you to him?" Cameron asked.

She nodded, not daring to look back at the man out of the fear he would see the confusing mix of feelings displayed on her face.

Following him, he led her through the mix of trucks to an older model Ford with mud caked over most of its body and wheels. "I found my father like this," he said, motioning toward the back tire.

As she stepped around, an older man came into view. He looked like he was taking a nap—except for the antler-handled knife protruding from his chest. When Dispatch had called, they had told her it was merely an unwitnessed death. She had been led to believe the man had likely died of natural causes and this was little more than a body retrieval. But what she was looking at was far from a natural death: what she was looking at was murder.

Chapter Three

Cameron couldn't believe how quickly two other cops had shown up at the ranch. Sitting inside a squad car was a deputy who looked to be no more than in his early twenties, with dark hair that was a little too long and a patchy clump of chin hair. Standing near his father's body was a heavy-set detective who looked like he had a baton taped to his spine, or maybe placed somewhere else.

He glanced toward Deputy Monahan, or as he'd heard the older Detective Bullock call her, Emily.

She was standing by the detective and staring at him, and as Cameron caught her looking, he expected her to turn away, but instead they locked eyes for a long awkward moment. She had been looking at him weirdly ever since she had arrived. She must have thought he'd had something to do with his father's death, though that couldn't have been further from the truth.

Sure, he and Leonard had had their fair share of friction and fights, but that didn't mean he'd wanted the man dead. If anything, he would have just wanted his father to retire and get out of the way so the ranch could stand a chance to make it in a world that seemed hell-bent on turning it into a strip mall.

Deputy Monahan said something to Bullock and walked

over toward him. She had her thumb jammed under her utility belt and her palm resting on the grip of her pistol. Something in the way she stood made him wonder if she was uncomfortable either with the belt, with the gun or with him. Her brows furrowed as she glanced up at him. "You okay?"

He nodded. "Just thinking about all the chores that need to be done. We were planning on moving the other half of our cattle out of the spring pasture and up onto the range." He pointed toward the mountains behind their ranch where they always let the cattle freely roam during the summer months.

"Will they be okay for another day? You have enough feed?" she asked.

"Another day won't break us, but I was hoping to get them out of the spring grounds so we can get it ready for them to come back in the fall. The less we have to hay, the better."

"I understand." She rested her other hand on her utility belt and he couldn't help but notice the roundness of her hips.

She had the silhouette of his perfect type of woman. Not a woman who was out running marathons for fun maybe, rather one he could hold in his arms and take comfort in her softness. All he really cared about, though, was finding a woman who understood what it took to be with a rancher and love him for who he was.

His ex had told him that she'd understood the long hours and the crazy responsibilities from cleaning stalls and pulling calves to tuning up carburetors. Yet that had proven to be nothing more than pretty old promises pitted against an ugly modern reality. Now, not only was there the coming and goings of ranching, but there was also the paperwork.

The modern farmer and rancher had to have someone on their team who knew how to apply for government grants and programs to help ensure that when times were lean, they were covered against financial ruin. His ex wasn't the first woman who had come to learn what it meant to be a rancher's wife and then hit the road.

"Yeah, thanks." He sighed as he considered the state of the place and what had just fallen on his plate. He almost felt guilty for thinking about the business at a time like this and that even earlier that day he had *wished* to get control. This hadn't been how he'd wanted to gain power. He'd only wanted his father to retire.

"Were you working with your father full-time?" she asked.

He nodded. "I was his right-hand man. Well... I was his primary hand anyway."

She studied him as though she was trying to translate what he'd said. "You guys close?"

He shrugged. "I don't know how many ranching families you know, but if you've been around a few, I'm sure you know that closeness can be a curse as much as it can be a boon. Every little thing can get under your skin."

"That doesn't really answer my question. Or are you telling me you didn't get along?" she countered.

"That's not it," he said, waving her off. "We had our knock-down-drag-outs, but at the end of the day, if either of us needed anything, we knew who we could rely on."

"Any knockdowns lately?"

He didn't like where she was taking these questions. "Look, my father and I butted heads, but I didn't want him dead and, like I've told the detectives, I didn't have anything to do with his death. I found my father out here perched like this. And no, I don't know anyone else who would have wanted him dead, either."

"Have you talked to your mom and told her about your father? Is she around?" she asked.

He shook his head. "She passed away a few years ago. Cancer. She is buried in Sunset Memorial." He motioned toward town.

Deputy Monahan pinched her lips. "I'm sorry to hear that." She paused. "What about siblings?"

He knew she was doing her job, but he was so tired of answering all these questions. "I have a brother who lives out of state. Last I heard, he was rough-necking in North Dakota, but who knows if he is still there. I haven't heard from him in the last year. I also have a sister who is in the wind. She was in Burbank, doing something in Hollywood. And there's my other sister on the rodeo circuit, a barrel racer. Once they left, none looked back." He tried to check the anger and resentment caused by their abandonment from flecking his voice.

He couldn't be angry at the fact that they had seized their chances to get out and away from the prison this ranch had become.

She looked at him, but he didn't want to let her meet his gaze out of some weird feeling that if she did, she would be able to see right through him and she would know all the things he was thinking and feeling. No one needed to know how he felt—feelings were for the weak and in this world only the strongest survived.

"Anyone else work on the ranch, or is it just you and your father?"

He noticed one of the deputies had made his way over and was listening to their conversation even though he wasn't facing him. Cameron was tempted to just tell the guy to turn around and join the conversation, but one questioning him was enough.

"We have managed to keep on a skeleton crew." As he said the word *skeleton* he cringed. "I mean, we have me, my dad and a hand named Trevor, whose been living out at the bunkhouse for the past year, but he's worked at the ranch since he was eighteen. Soon, though, we will hire some kids to come in and buck bales and move irrigation for us." He pulled out his phone and texted his best friend and hand, Trevor Band. "I texted my main guy, but he said he had his kid this morning."

"*Had* his kid?" she asked.

"Yeah, he and his ex-wife share custody." There was a pain in her expression as he mentioned custody, making him wonder if she had her own battle there.

"Do you think he might have seen or talked to your father?"

He shrugged. "I doubt it, but talk to him."

He didn't mean to come off curt, but he didn't know any more than they did about it.

"Do you have anyone else living on the ranch besides you guys?"

He nodded. "Not right now, but soon maybe we will. Like I said, teenagers and cowboys rounding up cows and bucking bales. Low-budget jobs that no one else wants to do and no one sticks around after they've done them."

She pointed at the main house. It stood in stark contrast to the freshly painted barn. The house was the kind that had probably been extraordinary when it had been built in the early 1900s, but now looked as dilapidated as the Sears catalog the model had probably been bought from with its sagging roof and half-missing gables. "Just you and your father live in there?"

He shook his head. "I live in my own house, just down the road." He pointed north.

In Montana speak, *just down the road* could have meant anything from two houses down to two hundred acres away. Time and space didn't really exist in this state; they were more suggestions and reminders.

"Have you been in your father's house recently?" she asked, an air of judgment to her question.

Did she think he was some kind of delinquent son for not wanting to live with his aged father? Was he the bad guy for wanting his own place and some sense of independence from the chaos that was his father?

He instantly felt horrible for his thoughts—he couldn't think badly of his father, not when he was sitting there not a dozen yards from him, dead as a doornail.

Gah. Cameron nearly made the sound aloud. *I'm a monster.* He ran his hand over the back of his neck as he chastised himself for his callousness about his father's demise.

No matter how he had been feeling about the man, he was always his father—dead or alive.

"I haven't," he said. "He didn't keep it locked though. Do you want to take a look around? I'm sure my father wouldn't have minded." He strode past her as he made his way to the front door of the house and he could make out the sound of her footfalls in the gravel as she followed behind.

He heard her say something to the detective, but the wailing of the ambulance on the highway as it passed by drowned out her exact words.

As the sound grew faint and the ambulance moved farther into the distance, somehow their departure saddened him—maybe if he had noticed his father earlier, he would have had a chance to save him. Instead, he'd been so focused on the task at hand and the work that had to be done that he had failed to notice the gravity of the situation.

He was complicit in his father's passing.

Guilt rattled through him, striking every rib and settling deep in his heart, right next to the grief he still held for losing his mother.

No matter what anyone said, some pains never went away—instead, they only waited to be compounded and refreshed.

The front door of the house swung open and he was hit with the metallic scent of blood.

"Hello?" he called out, trying to make sense of the smell when his father lay outside.

"Stop," Emily ordered, unholstering her weapon. "Hey, Sergeant Bullock, we've got something going on in here!" she called to the detective.

The detective rushed over, waving at the kid in the squad car to take over custody of the scene outside. "What's going on, Deputy?"

Emily pulled in a breath. "Do you smell that?" She gave the man a knowing look.

Over the years, they had lost a number of cows to natural causes and disease. The scent of death was unmistakable.

Oddly enough, he hadn't smelled it outside on his father, but standing here inside the doorway of his father's house, it hit him like a mallet.

Death was waiting for them.

"Stay here, Mr. Trapper," the detective said, taking out his gun. He motioned for Emily to follow him.

As the door swung open, Cameron stared down the hallway that led into the main room. There was a long, bloody streak and a handprint near the doorway that led toward the bedrooms. From the direction, it appeared as though someone had walked in and struggled down the hallway.

Had it been his father's killer?

Had his father put up a fight and hurt the person who had killed him?

He felt some comfort in the idea that his father's murderer had been injured and that they possibly lay dead somewhere in the house.

As the two officers made their way inside, cleared the hallway and moved toward the main room, they stopped. Emily said something to the detective Cameron couldn't quite make out.

Cameron wanted to follow them, to go in and find out exactly what had happened and who had played a role in his father's death. He had to know. He had to know who had wished to destroy his family and the ranch. However, he did as the detective had ordered and he stayed outside. In order to see inside, he rushed to the right and the big bay window that looked into the main room. He pressed his face against the glass. Emily was bending down over a man's body. There, lying dead in his family's living room—where he had spent dozens of Christmases opening presents and celebrated a hundred different birthdays—was his roughnecking brother, Ben. His lifeless eyes caught his and, for a long moment, Cameron couldn't look away from the azure that had started to cloud with death.

Those eyes... The last time he had been looking in them, his brother had been telling him he was leaving the ranch and never coming back. Ben had never wanted to step foot back here. He'd never wanted to speak to his father again. Now, both were dead.

Cameron was the last man left alive in his family.

His thoughts swirled, but one rose to the top... No matter how hard he tried, he couldn't understand why his world was suddenly filled with the ghosts of his past—ghosts that would now undoubtedly come to haunt his future.

Chapter Four

Emily stood up after confirming that the man at her feet was, in fact, devoid of a pulse. There was a loud rap on the front window of the ranch house. The sound made her jump, but she tried to cover up her surprise by calmly wiping her fingers on the leg of her pants as she turned in the direction of the jarring sound.

She was met with Cameron's wide eyes and his hands pressing against the glass. His fingertips were almost as white as his face. He was saying something but his voice was muffled and she couldn't make sense of his words.

For some strange and almost primal reason, the fear and pain in his expression made her want to rush to him, but she held back. She had a job to do. Now wasn't the time to give in to any baser instincts and fall for some unnecessary pull from unspoken places in her belly.

Detective Bullock huffed as he looked at her. "Why don't you go talk to your buddy out there? See if you can get an ID on our vic, here."

She nodded as she tried to keep her footsteps at a normal speed as she exited the ranch house's living room and made her way outside.

Cameron hurried toward her as soon as she stepped outside and he put his hand on her arm. "That's my brother. Ben. That's Ben." His words came out in a single breath.

She put her hand on his. "This is your brother?" she repeated, hoping to see something in his face to give her a sense of their relationship, but she was only met with shock.

He nodded.

The human part of her wanted to ask the handsome, shaken cowboy if he was okay, but the law enforcement officer part of her brain held her back. This was an active crime scene and Cameron was now at its epicenter.

His hand tightened on her arm slightly and she caught his gaze. "He...he hasn't been here in years. This doesn't make sense."

She wanted to ask him questions, but she didn't want to step on Detective Bullock's toes.

Inside the house, through the window, Bullock was taking pictures of the scene and tapping away at his phone. He seemed to have relaxed with her outside the room, evidenced by his belly now pressing hard against his shirt, testing the tensile strength of his buttons.

Detective Bullock had never been the type of man who swayed from protocol, and he wouldn't want her doing so, either. In fact, he was so linear and composed that even his gig line was always rigidly straight. To see him waver from perfection and relax when he thought no one was watching made a smile creep over her lips. It brought her some hope that he was at least a little bit human.

As it was, she wasn't sure she would ever come close to measuring up to this man who had a career record that was so long and distinguished that she was surprised it wasn't chiseled in stone outside the courthouse where the sheriff's office was located.

Something about the simple moment helped Emily find

her courage. If Bullock found fault in something she did or didn't do, she would ask for forgiveness later. Though she had come to this scene as a coroner, she was still first and foremost a deputy for Flathead County. She could take a statement just as well as anyone else on this scene. She had been the first one here; she had the right. If nothing else, it was better to act now than to get armchair quarterbacked later and called inept or incompetent.

As the only female deputy in their office, she was constantly scrutinized more than anyone else. Sometimes that was okay because, if someone was to let her off without such analysis, there would have been another person in the office who would be only too happy to wonder if there was something untoward happening between them in the bedroom.

It may have been a modern world, but sexism was still alive and well in this little corner of the world—and it wasn't being aimed at her by just the men in the office but also by the female staff members.

The only thing she could do was what she did best, push her chin up and ignore the chatter. If someone didn't have direct control over her life, then they had no right to levy their opinions onto her psyche.

Though she was good at putting up a brave front, she was insecure enough on her own without stopping to add the weight of what everyone else thought.

She turned to Cameron and readjusted her utility belt slightly. As she moved, the Glock in her bellyband pressed hard against the front of her shirt and she noticed his gaze flicker down to the gun.

"Cam," she started, truncating his name in an effort to instantly gain some bonding ground, "why don't you and

I step over to the barn?" She tapped his hand on her arm, motioning him to release.

As though he hadn't noticed his hand upon her, he let go. He opened his mouth, like he was about to start apologizing, but then stopped himself. "Yes." He turned from her, walking onto the gravel driveway and toward the barn.

Deputy Vetter gave him a tip of the head as Cameron walked past the young officer's car. Vetter would be there until Detective Bullock released the scene or another deputy came along to relieve him in the chain of custody. She waved at him to follow just in case she needed him to stay with their man here.

"Cam, can you tell me a little bit about your family?" He looked at her for a long minute as though, for the first time, he was seeing her as his enemy. She didn't like the feeling. "Don't worry," she added, trying to make his expression disappear. "I just have to ask you a few questions for the detective. He will want to know more about your brother, I'm sure."

He seemed to relax, but it didn't really assuage the feeling in her stomach, which made her feel a bit like a fox in the henhouse.

"He is an oil worker out of North Dakota. Thirty." He rattled off his birthday. "He hasn't been married, but he always seem to have women around him."

"Do you know of anyone who he would have considered an enemy?"

He thought about the question for a long moment before shaking his head. "He and I weren't close enough for me to know something like that. To be honest, you would probably be better off going to social media to find anything out about his private life."

She nodded. "I have a sister like that, I completely understand. She and I never speak, not after my divorce."

His eyebrows shot up and, as soon as they did, she wished she could have reeled in her statement. This man wasn't her friend, she didn't know why she had said anything personal to him. He had no business knowing anything about her—it had been inappropriate of her to speak as she had. Why couldn't she seem to remember who she was around this man?

The last thing he needed to know was that she was damaged.

Never mind that thought. Just because she was divorced and had a history didn't mean she was damaged; it could have just meant she had boundaries—what did he know? She adjusted her utility belt and dabbed slightly at the tip of her nose as she tried to reaffirm her composure.

Thankfully, Deputy Vetter came to her rescue. "How can I help you, Monahan?"

"Would you mind standing here with our friend for a minute?" She put her hand on Cameron's shoulder, like he was her friend—one she was trying to keep just close enough to remain communicating but far enough to keep the strange pull at her core from becoming too strong.

Vetter nodded. "Sure, no problem."

Cameron exhaled as she dropped her hand from his arm, but she tried not to read anything into the sound as it could have meant nearly anything.

Before her thoughts could run away, she smiled. "I'll be right back. I just want to talk to Bullock." She hurried to the house, knowing she could have merely texted him the vic's identity instead of telling him about the information in person.

Whatever, though, it wouldn't hurt for Bullock to see her.

Making her way inside, she was hit with the coppery scent of blood once again. It made her wonder how long it would stay in the house before it would turn into one of fetid death.

Emily tapped on the doorjamb to get Bullock's attention. He sucked in his stomach as she entered the living room. He ran his hand over waxed hair, smoothing what was already perfected. Like he noticed her watching him from outside the front door of the house, he motioned to her with a flick of his finger. She hated that he beckoned her and that she answered like a well-trained pup, but in her job, he was her master—there was no getting around their hierarchy.

"Detective?" she asked, coming to a stop before him.

He peered down his nose at her, the tip was so large that she wondered how he could even fully see her. "Did you get a name?"

She nodded. "It is the son of the man outside. A man name Ben Trapper."

Bullock frowned. "Any idea what the relationship was between father and son? I'm assuming Cameron is his brother?"

She nodded. "Ben was estranged from the family, from the sounds of things. I didn't have time for much more."

"That's okay. Thanks for the start."

She was surprised the detective was satisfied. He wasn't usually the kind to accept the minimum.

She looked inside the living room where the man was lying on the floor. There was a pool of blood around his head, drawing her attention to the hole in the side of his temple. There was a Glock21 in his right hand, his finger still trapped in the trigger guard. "Is there something I can help you with in your investigation?"

Bullock knelt down beside the body on the floor and stared at the man's hand holding the gun. There was something about the angle of the victim's fingers that drew her attention. His pointer finger was stiffening in a curl, but the finger was well over the trigger—almost so far that it would have made it challenging for him to have pulled effectively.

"What do you notice about this man?" Bullock asked, motioning to the decedent's remains.

Ben Trapper's face was longer than his brother's, but they both had the same chiseled jawline. Ben had a thick wad of hair on his chin in an ill-kempt attempt at a goatee. She usually liked facial hair on a man, but if the man had been alive, it would have done nothing to enhance his looks.

Cameron was definitely the better looking of the siblings. Beyond him identifying the remains as his brother's, he hadn't told her much about the man on the floor before them. She glanced toward the front of the house where Cameron was standing with Deputy Vetter, one of the younger guys in their office.

Bullock cleared his throat, pulling her back to the question at hand.

"I would say he has been down at least four hours as rigor mortis has begun to set in, based upon the state of his hands and facial features."

"Good," Bullock said, nodding approvingly. "What else do you notice?"

She wasn't sure what he wanted her to take note of, exactly, and she tried to follow his gaze. The man was wearing a dirty pair of jeans; mud was caked around the ankles. The mud looked like the kind that came from tromping around in the pasture on a wet day, yet the morning had been relatively dry. He was wearing a highlighter-yellow, road-worker-type work shirt that had faded oil stains throughout.

There was a long scar down the man's right arm and along it was a black jaguar tattoo, which made the cat appear as though it was prowling on the edge of some fleshy cliff if viewed from just the right angle.

"Do you see it?" Bullock asked.

"See what, Detective?"

He sent her a sly smile. "First," he led, "do you think this man is a victim of murder or suicide?"

From his toothy smile and the flicker of light in Bullock's eye, she felt as though she was walking into some kind of trap. "When I first entered, I would have said suicide. However, based on the position of his finger on the Glock's trigger, I'm thinking it's possible his hand was staged on the weapon."

Bullock's smile grew more wicked. "Is that right?"

"So, you think it was murder?"

"I'm not sure, but I would say that his death deserves further investigation."

Bullock put his hand on her shoulder. "Good job. That's a helluva an answer."

She had never thought of the detective as being on her side before, and certainly not as her friend. His warmth with her was throwing her for a loop, but it wasn't unwelcome. It was nice to have him willing to stand in her corner when it came to learning the craft of investigation—it was a skill set that could only be honed through hours of practice and hundreds of calls. Without officers like him—those who were willing to share their accrued knowledge—valuable experience and lessons were lost and it was the victims and their families who most felt the loss and pain of poorly trained and executed investigations.

"From what I figure," he continued, "based on our guy's temp, he's been down for at least four hours, but possibly more—like you said. Which means that these deaths likely occurred just before dawn."

"Rancher's hours. Makes sense."

Bullock nodded. "Whoever was behind these deaths knew the pattern of life on the ranch. Means that they were somehow connected. This wasn't just some stranger off the highway who popped in and randomly started attacking."

Truth be told, she hadn't even thought about something like that as a possibility. That, right there, was why he was the detective and, if she ever wanted to become one, it would take a heck of a lot of time.

"In cases like these, it is a safe bet to focus on the most obvious suspect—they are usually the one who is guilty of the crime. To me, I gotta say I think it's pretty cut and dry."

She was far from seeing these deaths as cut and dry. Two minutes ago, she had thought it likely it was a simple murder-suicide. "What do you think happened?"

He nudged his chin in the direction of the front door. "I think your boy out there, Cameron, is quite possibly behind this. He is the one with the means and the motivation to do something like this."

Emily stepped back, pressing her back against the wall, though she was fully aware that she shouldn't have been touching anything in the room. "What makes you think it's cut and dry?" She just couldn't follow the detective's line of thinking, it felt like such a leap.

She followed his gaze to the mantel over the fireplace at the heart of the room. On it sat a collection of family photos. They were all in matching oak frames. From right to left, there were pictures of Leonard and his wife, then with a baby, and a picture with another, another and another, until their images were showing flecks of gray hair at their temples and they had four grown children. Then the wife disappeared and Leonard looked noticeably wizened, deep crow's feet etching the corners of his eyes.

There were also pictures of each of the kids in their high school graduation gowns and of the girls graduating from the University of Montana. After that, the pictures ended—and it was as if the family had come to an end.

Her gaze drifted down to Ben's dead body.

If the family had been scattered to the wind before, the loss of the patriarch and the second brother would definitely do it no favors.

"From what I can make of things—" Bullock nudged his chin toward the photos "—Cameron and his sisters are going to be the ones who stand to inherit the ranch now that Leonard and the other brother are out of the way."

"Do you really think that's enough of a reason for him to commit murder? I wouldn't share a hairbrush with my sister let alone a ranch. Two sisters forced to share with him would only make it worse."

"True," Bullock agreed. "However, has anyone reached out to them? We also haven't seen the will. It wouldn't surprise me if the guy who owned this place was a little bit on the misogynistic side and wasn't the kind to leave land to a female child."

His statement struck a nerve, making her grit her teeth until her jaw ached. She hated that the problem was so widespread that Bullock had a fair point.

"From the looks of you and Cameron together, I would say you've built a pretty good rapport. Yes?" Bullock stepped toward her and gently pulled her away from the wall as though he had noticed her faux pas but instead of condemning her was happy to merely silently correct.

How could he be so kind and yet irritate her about misogyny and Cameron so much all at the same time?

"We do seem to get along," she admitted, though she wasn't sure she wanted to as she wasn't exactly sure where Bullock was leading her.

"Good. That's good." He gave her a smile that made it clear she was about to be voluntold a task. "I need you to run him downtown. Take him into our interview room. I want you to get him on camera. Get as much information as you can. If you get enough to charge him, I want you to place him under arrest."

Chapter Five

Emily sauntered toward them as Cameron sat with Deputy Vetter in front of the barn, watching. He felt like such a fool just sitting there, waiting for his fate to be sealed. There was nothing he could do, nothing he could say or not say, that could deliver him from this chaos.

He needed to call the ranch's attorney's and set everything in motion with the family's trust and getting all the bank accounts transferred over to just his name so no one could misallocate funds. He couldn't afford anything else going sideways.

He'd heard so many horror stories about family ranches going to rubble in the aftermath of its owner's demise. In one instance, a ranch a few miles down the road had had a million-dollar lien placed against it the day the owner died, for work that had supposedly taken place. There was no record of the work having been done, but there had been so much happening on the ranch and it had gone to probate for so long, that no one could prove otherwise. As it had stood, there were receipts from the company who'd placed the lien and the courts had sided with the company even though it was known on the street that the lien had been a money-grabbing scam by an out-of-stater who had seen an opportunity to falsely make a claim and win, and they had seized it.

The Trappers shouldn't be going to probate for anything, but there was always something when death came knocking—and that was natural deaths, not even considering deaths like those Cameron was dealing with. He had to make sure everything was legally taken care of so no one had time to do anything reckless.

Wait, it would look horrible if I did that before my father's body is even off the ranch.

Yet, just like any big circus—the show had to go on—bills had to be paid, the mortgage was due on the first of the month, which was just a few days away. Then there were all the other bills he was sure the ranch had hanging over its head, farriers, grain, gas, and they'd had just taken in one of their trucks for a new transmission.

Normally, his father had taken care of finances. He'd never let Cameron do the books, but now that would fall on his shoulders and he feared what he would be walking into.

What scared him most, if he had to admit it, wasn't what he was facing and what he knew had to be done—it was all the unknowns.

He couldn't wrap his head around it. Sure, they hadn't been the tightest family, but there wasn't the kind of animosity that would lead to something like this happening out of the blue. That was, unless his father hadn't been telling him everything. And that, that right there, was something that was entirely possible.

Leonard was the type of guy who'd loved to keep things close to the chest. It was a tale as old as time in the ranching community; they were tough as nails and he and those like him could handle anything that life threw their way with a level of quiet indifference and stoicism that rivaled the granite batholiths embedded in the belly of the Rockies.

There had been one year when he was growing up that a forest fire had swept through the back of the ranch and destroyed the summer range, killing hundreds of their livestock. At the time, their grandfather, Leo Sr., had still been alive and, together, the fathers had barely spoken a single word about the tragic disaster. Looking back, without his grandfather in control, Cameron was sure that the ranch and the family wouldn't have survived the storm.

It hit him: now he was at the helm of the ship. He was the only man in the family left standing. What was more, his ship was empty. Only he, two sisters in the wind and the ranch still remained.

Was this the future his grandfather had wanted? Had he hoped for something more for his family? Or was the ranch all that had mattered?

Just as his grandfather's voice came to his mind, Emily's feet came into view in the dirt in front of him. "Heya, Cam," she said like she was trying to sound friendly, but there was a tiredness to her tone that made him glance up to see if that same weariness could be found in her eyes. It was. "I know you wanted to get the other half of your cattle moved today, but unfortunately, I'm going to need to get more folks onto the ranch to continue our investigation. To do so, I'm going to need to run you downtown. You game?"

That sounded like a whole lot of words for her telling him that she needed to interrogate him.

His body tensed. "I didn't have anything to do with what I found."

She put her hand on his shoulder as though that would in some way make what she was saying better and less like a slap in the face. He pulled back and out of her touch. A flicker of rejection splashed over her features but was quickly masked by indifference. "I know you don't. We just need to talk. Come along with me." She motioned for him to stand up and she turned to have him follow.

He couldn't help but notice that her question had now turned into a command.

The younger deputy nodded in acknowledgment as he stood up. "Good luck, man. I'm sure I'll be seeing you later."

"Yep." He swallowed down the nerves creeping up from his stomach.

His boots crunched in the gravel as he made his way after Emily and he pulled down his cowboy hat just a little bit snugger on his forehead than he liked. Something about the pressure of it made him feel a touch more secure. He could handle this, her, the situation, all of it. If his grandfather could face a mass die-off and decimated property, he could handle answering questions about a situation in which he knew he was innocent.

At least there was some hope. She hadn't seemed upset with him, or like he was seriously a suspect. She just wanted to talk to him. Everything would be fine. All he had to do was go along with her.

His attempt to mollify himself was working right up to the point until they reached her patrol car and she opened the back door. He stared at the Plexiglas divider, which ran between the front seat and the hard plastic back seat where she motioned for him to sit.

He didn't know why he was surprised. Of course, he wouldn't be riding to the police station in the front seat. This wasn't a social visit. She was beautiful and he couldn't deny that he felt some strange desire for her, but that didn't make them friends. It didn't make them anything. In fact, on the surface, and from a logical point of view, he reminded himself that they were really enemies.

Climbing into the confinement of the back seat of the car, he was reminded of the last time he'd ridden in one. He'd been a senior in high school and Deputy Sutherland had picked him up for an MIP—minor in possession—at a kegger up the logging road near Lewis Trail. If he hadn't been drunk and passed out in the back of his best friend's pick-up, the guy would have never caught him.

However, as it was, it had probably been a good thing that the deputy had picked him up and taken him home, as he likely would have frozen to death otherwise. In the end, the judge had dropped the charges and he had gotten off with a slap on the wrist and fencing duties for a month from his father. Fencing had been far worse a sentence than anything the judge would have passed down. He still bore the scars from that summer's barbed wire on his hands.

Emily got in the car and they bumped down the rutted driveway and out toward the highway. They passed the pasture, where Bessie and Ginger were happily grazing on the green grass. Bessie gave a haughty swish of the tail as they passed by and it made him chuckle—at least one thing hadn't changed today.

"Do you need some air back there? I know it can get a little stuffy." Emily caught his gaze in the rearview mirror.

"Sure." She didn't need to keep up this fake friendship thing. No matter how she treated him, his statement wasn't going to change.

The air clicked on and a cool breeze passed over his skin. With it came the scent of dirt and grass pollen that had been caught in the air ducts of the car. It fluttered down and scattered over his blue jeans like ashes.

Emily sneezed in the front seat. "Bless you," he said instinctively.

She dabbed at her nose. "Thanks." She looked back at him. "Just so you know, you have the right to remain silent. You can also call your attorney at any time."

His heart clenched. "Are you placing me under arrest?"

She couldn't possibly... He hadn't given her any reason. He had just been at the wrong place at the wrong time. He had no reason to kill his brother or his father.

"No. I'm just making you aware of your rights. You are free to go at any time."

Free to go? Is she kidding? It wasn't like he could just jump out of her moving vehicle.

She had to know he was trapped.

"I thought you just wanted me out of the way. Why don't you just tell me the truth?" he asked, finally unable to play her game any longer.

"I am." She turned around as she came to a stop at the highway. "I'm just taking you to our offices for our convenience. It's the easiest place to question you about everything. I can get another person in the room with me this way as well."

He relaxed slightly as he looked at her worried expression. She had legitimately seemed concerned with him reacting as strongly as he had. Maybe she didn't think he was behind something nefarious after all.

She smiled at him and the strange attraction he felt toward her returned. Maybe he had overreacted in thinking she couldn't be his friend. Maybe she was trying to be his ally and help him make sense of everything. Maybe it was best that he left his father's death scene. It certainly hadn't seemed right sitting there, yards away from his body.

Emily hadn't said it, but she was doing him a favor.

His mind was just all over the place, and it was justifiable.

"I get it," he said, relaxing into the hard plastic seat. It pressed into the backs of his knees and made his jeans pinch his skin, but he didn't move and let the pain simply wash over him as the sensation was a welcome reprieve from the emotional waves he had been riding.

"I'm sorry that everything has to be this way," she said. She tapped on the steering wheel like she was playing some invisible drum.

Her candor surprised him. "I know that you're just doing your job. And I hope *you* know that I really didn't have anything to do with my father's or my brother's deaths. I don't hate my dad. And I wished neither of them harm. My dad and I actually got along pretty well. Sure, we had our fights, like I told you, but by and large we were friends. We had each other's backs, and we could rely on one another like no one else could. After my mother died, we were all that was left."

She let out a long exhale. "I know what it's like to experience that level of loss. It tends to reconfigure your life in a way that you just had no idea about or could expect."

"Yeah. We were moving forward well though. It has been quite a few years since my father had lost my mom and I thought he had moved past it. We were getting back on our feet, and the ranch was doing great. That was until the last couple of years, and he was saying he had gotten us in a little bit of debt, but something like that is not that uncommon for ranches. It's just part of the cycle."

"So, you'd say that there was some level of financial instability on the ranch?"

He paused, thinking about the note his father had taken out and the piles of bills sitting on the desk in the main office. "Sure."

"Do you think that this debt could have had anything to do with what happened this morning?" She glanced at him in the mirror.

"My father wasn't great with money, but the only debt I know anything about for sure was that which he held with the banks. I don't see them coming out to kill him. It seems counterproductive to kill a man if they want to get their money back."

"You're right, but I'm sure I don't have to explain to you that, when it comes to money, damned near anything is possible." She tapped her finger on the wheel. "Did your father have any mental health issues that I need to know about?"

The question caught him off guard. Mental health wasn't something that was talked about in his family, no matter how much it probably should have been. Especially after the death of his mother and the resulting depression that his father had faced after her passing.

"He wasn't diagnosed with anything, but he had his ups and downs like everyone else. Lately, he had seemed like he had been more stressed, but when I talked to him about his shift in behavior, he hadn't wanted to open up."

"What do you mean by his *shift in behavior*?" she pressed, pulling down the main street, which led to the courthouse and the sheriff's office.

"He was antsy. Lots of phone calls and busier than usual. I'd been doing a lot of the day-to-day running of the ranch while he'd been doing more of the business side of things."

Emily made a tsking sound as she sucked on her teeth, and it made him tense. "Have you taken out any loans in your name on behalf of the ranch?"

His stomach sank as he realized how bad his owing the ranch and his father money could possibly look at this moment. "Yes. I had drawn money from the ranch account to pay off my ex-wife, April. We settled out of court, and I owed her seventy thousand dollars. My father floated me the money."

"Oh." Her sound was guttural and almost pained.

He hated it.

"I planned on paying him and the ranch back. I was working on it. I just needed to get back on my feet. It was why I was forced to stay here, to keep working the ranch."

"So, you didn't want to stay here?" Her voice suddenly had a harder edge, more coplike. "Your dad forced your hand with the money?"

The truth was that he had, but that wasn't the only reason Cameron had stayed. He loved the ranch. He had just grown up wanting something more than being a rancher whose life was dictated by the weather, politics and the fickle nature of beef prices. He wanted to tell her everything. He wanted to open up to the beautiful woman who smiled at him and whose eyes sparkled when she looked at him, but he couldn't talk to the cop who was now glaring back at him in the rearview mirror. Just like that, he had a feeling he had gone from being a possible suspect to one utterance away from wearing a set of glittering handcuffs.

He looked out at the redbrick building and the looming domed courthouse. He'd never really noticed it before, but all the windows on the main floor were covered with thick black steel bars, making it look eerily like a prison. Maybe he had never noticed them before as he had never been a suspect in a murder—he had never had to worry that once he walked in, he may not walk out a free man.

Chapter Six

Emily stared at the red Ford F-150 that was parked near the front doors of the sheriff's office. Todd knew she was working, and he was aware that he wasn't to see her unless it was previously arranged or on their assigned parenting schedule. Yet, there was that damned pickup truck with the Rocky Mountain Elk Foundation specialty license plate and the cracked front windshield from the drive they took four years ago to Seattle.

He had been so angry that day. She had been running a little late with Stacy. Getting her ready had taken longer than expected as Stacy hadn't wanted to get dressed and had thrown a full-blown, body-flailing-on-the-floor, temper tantrum when Emily had tried to get her to put her clothes on. That had led to a spitting-food breakfast, which had led to a kitchen floor cleanup and a quick cry in the bathroom, none of which Todd had seen. When he'd walked in from packing the truck, he'd been on her and she had snapped at him, which had only made things worse.

Looking back, it was a good metaphor for their relationship—each had been blind to the needs and realities of the other and both had been angry and lashing out on the other. She hadn't been perfect, but Todd had been more than unkind—especially when he'd turned to Autumn Jessop to talk about what a bad wife and mother Emily was and would forever be. It hadn't taken long for them to fall into bed together and for her to find out.

As they neared the pickup and she pulled into her parking spot, she saw Todd sitting in the driver's seat. In the back, in her car seat, Stacy was thankfully fast asleep and didn't see the police car.

Why were they here?

Today wasn't Emily's day with her, and as badly as she wanted to scoop up her daughter and take her home, it wasn't convenient. Todd could see she was busy and had someone in her unit. He couldn't have possibly thought this was a good time to stop by, and yet there he sat.

As she came to a stop, she turned around to face Cameron in the back seat. "I'll need you to hang tight for a second. I need to deal with something really quick, and then we'll head inside." She jumped out of the car, not giving him time to respond or ask questions.

Todd was getting out of his pickup as she approached.

Even though it had only been a couple of weeks since the last time she had seen him out of his truck and without his hat, it seemed as though his hairline had receded even farther. Now, his dark chestnut hair was almost back to his ears. It wouldn't be long before he would be completely bald. His impending hair loss had always been a source of embarrassment to him. He'd tried every hair product to reduce hair loss known to man.

In fact, it was along those lines that she had found out about Autumn. One day, she had come home to find a pamphlet on the table for a hair transplant procedure out of Turkey. As desperate as he had been to keep his hair, he had told her he would never go that far. Apparently, that had changed when other women had entered the picture.

It brought her a little bit of joy to see that he was losing the battle. It was petty, she was aware, but after all she had been through with him, all the battles and war she had lost in the divorce, it was the little things—or hairs this time—that brought her a glimmer of joy.

"What are you doing here, Todd?" Annoyance filled her voice. "I'm working. You're not supposed to be here unannounced."

He rolled his eyes like a petulant teenager, as if she were the one who was acting out of line. "Look, I don't wanna be here and around you any more than you wanna be around me. However, something came up and I don't have anybody to watch Stacy. Even your stupid neighbor lady wasn't home. Penny or whatever her stupid name is."

If it had been the first time he had done this to her, she would have been slightly more patient with him, and yet this was the third time in the last six months that he had shown up in her life and had "an emergency" and couldn't take their daughter. Before, it hadn't been a problem, but the other times she hadn't been at work.

"Todd, I can't take her. I'm in the middle of a homicide investigation." She motioned toward her car where Cameron sat.

He was watching and as she looked his way he quickly glanced away. She couldn't begrudge him for watching her personal drama unfolding. It was completely unprofessional and out of line. Warmth rose in her cheeks even though she tried to control her embarrassment.

Todd looked over at Cameron and seemed unsurprised. "You must like having him in your back seat. You always had a thing for cowboys."

Her embarrassment was instantly replaced by rage.

She started to form her rebuttal but she checked herself.

It didn't do her any good to fight with Todd. He was just trying to get under her skin. In fact, making her angry and hurting her feelings might have been his favorite hobby—it sure had been when they had been together. She doubted some things ever changed.

When he seemed to realize he wasn't going to get a rise out of her, his shoulders slumped slightly and he turned to his back door and their daughter. She had fallen asleep. Her Mickey and Minnie Mouse ponytail holders were askew and most of her hair was stuck to the chocolate that was smeared all over her face.

"I told you I can't take her. I meant it, Todd." She moved to stop him from opening the door and waking up their child. She didn't want to upset Stacy by having her daughter wake up and see her and then think that—even for a second—Mommy didn't want her.

"You have to," he said, pushing past her and opening the door.

"Todd!"

"Kiddo, you gotta wake up. You're going with your mom."

She clenched her teeth so hard that they squeaked under the pressure. He was such an inconsiderate, manipulative jerk. It was always about Todd and what he needed—regardless of anyone else. This time, he was not only putting Emily's job on the line, but he was also quite possibly putting her daughter in danger.

Emily wanted to think that Cameron was a good man, everything in her heart told her he was, but she had fallen for Todd—clearly, when it came to men, she couldn't always be trusted.

Her first priority and her first concern had to be about the welfare and safety of her daughter.

"Where are you going that is so important, Todd?"

He said something that she couldn't hear as he pulled Stacy out of her car seat and sat her down on the ground. He grabbed her princess backpack and pushed it into Emily's hands. "Here, just take it." The pack was sticky and there was a glob of what looked like gum stuck to the front, it was complete with patches of dog hair and lint stuck in its pink gooey surface.

Stacy rubbed her fist in her eye and she smiled up at her with her sweet little toothy grin as she spotted her. "Hi, Mommy," she said in her cherubic, five-year-old, high-pitched voice.

"Hi, ladybug," she said, slipping her hand into her daughter's sticky hand. From this morning to now, there was no chance that her daughter had washed or brushed any part of her body and, based on her face, the only thing she had probably eaten was candy.

It had already been slated to be a long day, but having a sugared-up, potentially grumpy kiddo on her hands was a recipe for disaster. Looking at Stacy, though, there was no way she would let her go back with her dad. Emily didn't really like it when Stacy was with him for the few days he had custody of her and seeing her disheveled and unwanted reaffirmed her need to take her—no matter the consequences.

For now, her daughter could sit in the sergeant's office until she was done talking to Cameron or something.

She slung the backpack over her shoulder and then picked Stacy up and put her on her hip. As she turned to speak to Todd, he was already getting back in his pickup. He slammed the door in her face. He didn't even look back in their direction as he started the engine and tore off down the road, kicking up gravel as he hit the gas.

He knew her well enough that he had known she wouldn't say no to him leaving Stacy with her like this. When it came to her little ladybug, there was nothing she wouldn't sacrifice for her—and there wasn't anything stopping Todd from taking advantage, regardless of the parameters set forth by their mediated and agreed-upon parenting plan. It was on days like this that she was glad they were going back and renegotiating the damned thing.

Stacy snuggled into her, pressing her sweaty and sticky face into the crook of her neck. Her daughter smelled like stale cigarette smoke. She would need a bath tonight.

Emily turned toward the front doors of the office, where Cameron was sitting in her cruiser. He waved at Stacy and she could feel her daughter smile against her chest. She stuck up her hand in a grabby hand wave.

It tore at her that she would have to take her inside the office and hand her off to go into a full-blown interview, all while the office would be in a tither about her bringing in her daughter to work and expecting them to babysit. Of course, they would all be sweet and accommodating to her face, but behind her back, it would be an entirely different story.

Katie, the woman who worked at the front desk, loved to stir the pot. If there wasn't something going on in the office, she would find some kind of drama to start. This would be just the sort of thing she loved to sink her teeth into and use against someone in perpetuity.

Though Emily couldn't prove it, she was almost positive Katie wrote down everyone's secrets and flaws so if she needed ammunition to blackmail or start something, she could go to her little black book—most in the office called her the Crypt Keeper for that very reason.

Katie wore big, black-rimmed glasses that made her look

a little bit like Edna Mode on *The Incredibles*, and the thought of walking in and having Katie gaze at her over the top of those stupid glasses while judging away made her stomach churn. Between that look, the gossip and the judgment, she realized the last place she wanted to be was inside that building. She could question Cameron anywhere. If anything, maybe she could get him to open up more if she treated him like a friend instead of a suspect.

Besides, he had just lost his brother and his father. From the time she had spent with him, he didn't seem like the type who would have committed this crime as Bullock had assumed. In fact, based on his body language and the way he spoke about the event, she was convinced he was innocent. And if what she assumed was correct, and he had nothing to do with their deaths, he needed to have a safe place to turn.

Emily stopped beside Cameron's door. She opened the door and Cameron stepped out, slicked down his hair and put on his dirty white cowboy hat.

"Hiya, cutie," he said, leaning down slightly so he could be at Stacy's level where she was snuggling.

His greeting made her instantly like him a bit more. Most men she knew were standoffish or in a rush to hand off kids—Todd as example number one.

Stacy squirmed and pushed off her, moving to be put down. Emily was surprised, but she put her daughter on her feet and took her by the hand. Normally, Stacy was shy when it came to new people, and especially men. When she had met Todd's brother, it had taken her two weeks before she would even look at him when he talked to her.

"I'm Stassy," she said, holding her *s*, thanks to her wiggling front tooth, and extending her chubby hand like a mini-adult but squeezing Emily's extra hard for reassurance.

"Very nice to meet you, Ms. Stacy. I'm Cam," Cameron said, taking her hand and giving it a gentle shake. He got down on one knee and bowed before her. He took off his cowboy hat before pressing his forehead to the top of her hand like a knight paying homage to a princess.

She giggled and the sound brought a smile to Emily's lips. The man knew his way to all the ladies' hearts.

He stood up.

"Did you eat yet, ladybug?" she asked.

She shook her head. "I'm hungry."

Looking at how much chocolate she had on her, it was no wonder. The sugar rush had probably worn off and left a pit in her stomach. She'd need to feed her daughter before she got grumpy or there would be all hell to pay. "Do you mind if we grab some lunch?" she asked Cameron.

It felt strange, breaking so far from what they were supposed to be doing, but she had to make the best of a bad situation and she had to be the queen of the pivot.

He smiled. "Anything is better than that back seat."

Her daughter couldn't take her eyes off the brunette cowboy as he slipped his hat back over his curly locks. Emily didn't want to admit it, but she could completely understand Stacy's desire to stare at the man. He was undeniably handsome with those sky-blue eyes that seemed even brighter than they had this morning thanks to the sun. His face was tan and when he smiled, it made the little lines around his eyes collect at the corners and lead like road maps to the center of his soul.

"Are you coming with us, Cam?" her daughter asked, tilting her head ever so slightly.

Cameron glanced over at Emily and she gave him a nod. "Is it okay with you if I tag along with you and your beautiful mama?"

"You better. You need to eat. You're a growing boy." Stacy put her hands on her hips and frowned up at him.

He laughed. "Well then, it sounds like I have my marching orders."

He reached his hand out for Stacy's and she slipped her little hand into his tanned fingers. She let go of her mother and skipped forward as she and Cameron started to walk toward the heart of town where all the diners and cafés could be found.

Beautiful? She stood watching the duo walking ahead of her as she tried to make sense of his compliment.

He had to have just been being nice for the benefit of making friends with her daughter. It was definitely in his best interest to want to get in good with her and Stacy. It would make his life immeasurably easier—in fact, it already had. It had saved him from being sucked into the belly of the courthouse.

Or, what if he'd meant it? What if he really did think she was beautiful?

The thought made her blush.

Emily had never really thought much about her looks after high school. She had her routines, and she took care of herself, making sure she did her hair and makeup every day, but beyond that—it was just habit.

As she moved to follow behind them, she caught a glimpse of her reflection in the windshield. She straightened her shirt and fixed a hair that had fallen loose of her hair tie and was flagging in the light breeze.

Surely, he was just being nice, but it was flattering. It had been a long time since anyone had treated her as anything but a coworker or a pain in their rear end. It was nice to be reminded that she was still seen as something more than just a mom or a cop—he saw her as a woman.

Cam looked back over his shoulder at her and sent her a wilting smile as her daughter started to skip. For a moment, Emily nearly forgot where she was and what she had been sent there to do. Instead, all she could think about was what it would be like to have a world like this with a cowboy like him, and a beautiful and loving family.

It was just too bad her dreams never seemed to become reality.

Chapter Seven

Cameron had always had a way with children, but things had come even more naturally with Stacy. He couldn't explain why, but the two of them had taken an instant liking to each other and all the way through lunch the little girl hadn't stopped talking to him. Emily had seemed a touch standoffish at the beginning of the meal, or perhaps it was that she had other things on her mind—he would have, if he had been in her shoes, given the little performance her ex had put on there in the road outside the cop shop.

He felt bad for her. That guy had put her in one hell of a position.

Cam didn't blame Emily for not wanting to drag him and her little girl into the office. He could only imagine how it would have been received. It was cute when a dad brought a little kid into the office, but not so much if they dropped them off for a whole day of babysitting.

He sipped on his last bit of coffee in the heavy brown coffee cup, reminiscent of former days, as the girls made their way to the restroom to wash hands after their chicken strips. He stared down at the place mat with his and Stacy's red crayon drawing of a stick-figure pirate with a parrot on his shoulder and his sword drawn. The silly picture made him smile.

He'd never given much thought about being a father.

His ex-wife hadn't wanted children and been adamant about their not getting pregnant; he hadn't pressed the issue at the time.

Thank goodness, they hadn't had children. It would have made his decision to divorce so much harder. It had been hard enough as it was. Even with her infidelity, he'd still loved April. He could have forgiven her, but he couldn't have forgotten. She had broken his heart and when he had found out, he'd known he would never be able to trust a woman again.

He stared down at the pirate.

Emily wasn't like most women; she was a law enforcement officer. Their entire lives were built on trust and honor. Their word was their bond. Without integrity, they were nothing.

He picked up the red crayon and started to color in the blade of the sword as he thought about Emily's strikingly blue eyes. They were almost the same shade of blue as his, but there was a hint of brown around their centers. Wasn't that called hazel?

As he colored the knife, his mind wandered to her standing by his father's body and the knife protruding out of his father's chest. The Ruana.

He pulled his phone out of his pocket and opened his gallery. Tapping on his photos, he pulled up the picture he had taken of his father's body resting against the back tire of the pickup truck. He zoomed in on his dad. It was macabre, but he realized he hadn't really looked closely at the knife.

It was probably nothing, but it seemed strange to him that it was his father's knife that had been used to kill him. His father had loved that knife, and it had been one of his most prized possessions. If someone had wanted to really put it to him, that was the weapon they would have wanted to use to do the job.

Or, if it wasn't a premeditated thing, it would have just been convenient. Maybe the killer had run into his father outside and gotten into a fight. His father had probably drawn it, and the guy had fought it out his father's hands. Maybe.

What about Ben though? If Ben had been behind his father's death, why would he have taken his own life? Why wouldn't he have just committed suicide by his father? And why wouldn't he have just shot his father if he'd wanted him dead?

So many things about what had happened, and the order of events, confused him. Nothing seemed to line up.

As he gazed at the picture, he looked down at his father's belt. The knife sheath was empty.

He swiped to the picture he had taken of Ben through the window. In the photo, Emily was crouching down beside his brother's body. There was an orb of light thanks to the reflection of his flash in the window and it obscured the area around his brother's feet, but he could make out the gun and his brother's hand.

He didn't recognize the gun as one of his or his father's, so it must have been one Ben had purchased after he had left the place; or maybe it wasn't his at all.

He just couldn't make sense of why his brother would have brought a gun to the ranch in the first place. His father and his brother hadn't been fighting, at least that Cam had known about. His dad normally let him in on big things, and he hadn't even mentioned Ben as of late. Everything they had been dealing with was the day-to-day running of the place and the ever-evolving debt that his father had often complained about.

Stacy came running up and slid belly-down into the seat next to him then wiggled back up into a sitting position. She picked up her fork and started eating more of the french fries that she had left on her plate.

"You all set?" Emily asked. "We still need to talk, but I need to get her home and start her bedtime routine. She's normally asleep by 7:30."

Was she asking him back to her place?

He tried to check his look of surprise. "Let's hit it." He leaned toward Stacy. "You ready, kiddo?"

Stacy popped another fry into her mouth and she nodded, sliding out from the bench seat.

She slipped her hand into his; it was still damp from the bathroom, but he didn't mind. He liked the feeling of her little starfish fingers in the center of his palm. He liked knowing she was safe with him and, unlike the guy—who Emily had told him was a dude named Todd, her ex-husband and Stacy's dad—who had just dropped her and run earlier in the day, he wouldn't just leave her without warning.

Todd had seemed like a real piece of work. He couldn't understand what Emily had ever seen in the dude. Even from a distance, he'd looked like a loser. And what guy would just drop his kid off at a police station when he could clearly see that Cameron was in the back of her patrol car—even if *he* was not really a problem?

The dude was a peach.

He had to remind himself that his opinion of her ex-husband and her life didn't really matter. He wasn't her boyfriend. Heck, they weren't even really friends. This was just some strange life-required pause in her interrogation of him.

The only good news was that if she really thought he was behind any the deaths, he doubted she would have allowed for their wavering from protocol. His butt would have been in some holding cell by now or something; he didn't really know how the whole cop and questioning thing worked. All he knew was what he had seen on shows, and even when it came to that, he didn't watch a whole lot of television.

They walked out of the restaurant, but instead of heading toward her patrol car, they turned in the other direction and walked down the dirt alley behind the Coffee Cup. Their footfalls crunched in the dirt and broken glass that littered the alley, but the girls didn't seem to notice.

Stacy's hand started to sweat in his in the summer heat and he slowed down his pace in an effort to keep in step with her. Emily took her other hand and looked over at him. Stacy looked up at them and smiled, but under her eyes were dark circles.

She really was a cute kid.

Emily stopped at a gate in a chain-link fence around a white farmhouse-style, two-story house. It was decorated with black shutters and at its peak there were black Victorian pediments with incredibly elaborate scrollwork. The house was antiquated but well kept and the yard was beautifully maintained.

"Is this your house?" he asked, unable to hide the surprise in his voice.

He wasn't sure why he was surprised. Of course, she would have a place as beautiful and put together as her. Yet, if he had envisioned her home, it would have been something modern. Minimalist but classy and high-end. She would have the best of things but understated. A little bit of everything.

She couldn't have been all those things. As he thought about it as they walked to the front door and she unlocked it, he realized how much his characterization didn't make sense. But then it did: she was just a collection of contrasts.

He tried not to stare at her ass as she bent down to pick up Stacy and place her on her hip. Her utility belt cut into her waist and the grip of her gun dug into her side thanks to the weight of the little girl on the other side. But Emily didn't seem to notice. She must have been the primary caregiver.

The woman worked her tail off. He appreciated that in another person.

He followed the girls inside and Emily led him to her living room. At its center was a large leather sofa, the kind that came from specialty furniture stores where even the lamps were hundreds of dollars and only the wealthy and interior designers shopped.

The entire room was in style with the sofa. Warm and welcoming, beckoning to be noticed. It was all as classy as she was.

Emily took Stacy upstairs and, after a quick bath—complete with giggles—put her daughter to bed. While he waited, he clicked through the pictures from this morning on his phone.

The stairs creaked as Emily made her way downstairs and back to him. "Sorry about that. She just does best when I keep her on her bedtime routine."

He clicked off his screen and put his phone down. "It's all good. We all do best with our routines, I get it."

Emily walked by him and sat down in the leather recliner, which seemed to fit her body like it had been sculpted for her. She must have spent many nights rocking Stacy to sleep in the thing. It made him feel things he hadn't felt in a long time, not since he had been married. Being around her so much made him miss that feeling of not just comradery and partnership, but of a deep sense of home and belonging—and what he missed most, love.

Not that he loved her. It was just that he missed the sensation and connection that came with being loved and loving another.

Until now, he hadn't really considered getting into another relationship again—and certainly not getting married.

"I know it's unconventional, all of this," she said, motioning around her house.

"You mean bringing a suspect in a potential murder-suicide investigation back to your house?" He laughed, relaxing back into the seat on the couch.

Or a double homicide, the jury is still out, he thought.

"If I was worried that you actually had something to do with your father's and brother's deaths, I would have never even considered bringing you here, or having you around my daughter."

He thought about the look she had given him when Todd had handed off Stacy and she had walked over and let him out of the car. It had been in that moment when she had made her decision. She had a hell of a lot more faith in humans than he did, but he was thankful that, in this case, her faith was well-placed in him.

"I'm honored." He dipped his head in sincerity.

"That being said, Detective Bullock needs to pin this on someone, and he wanted me to place you under arrest if you gave me any indication that you were behind this. When it comes to the public, when there are homicides, the next thing we field is mass fear that it will happen to them. People fear the boogeyman in the night."

"I am the one who should be afraid. For all I know, someone out there who may want the men in my family dead," he said, not even thinking about what he was saying until it had already escaped his mouth. Yet, as soon as he had said it, he realized how right he was.

She stared at him, her eyes wide as though she, too, hadn't thought about the legitimacy of his statement before now, either. "Do you have any idea who could be behind this?"

He shook his head. "I've wracked my brain. The only thing I've come up with is my ex-wife, the bank my dad borrowed money from and whomever my brother was tied up with. None of it really makes sense to me though. My ex and I don't really have anything to do with each other and I bought her out. We haven't talked since."

"Do you have access to all the ranch's financial records?" she asked, but there was a strange expression on her face—bordering on mischievous.

She was sexier than ever.

"I'm sure I can pull them up, but my dad was the one in control of everything." He stared at her hazel eyes, not so long as to make things weird but he couldn't look away from her playful expression.

"I can't look at those records without getting a search warrant and going through Detective Bullock."

He didn't mind saving her work. In fact, if there was anything he could do to speed up their investigation and figure out who was behind the deaths, the better. It made him feel exposed, knowing that there was someone out there who wanted his family, and possibly him, dead. But did they really want him dead? It was a strange feeling not to know for sure.

If they wanted him dead, they could have just stayed a little bit longer and waited for him to arrive, and they could have killed him just as easily as they had killed Ben and his father. That was if they knew that he was set to arrive. Maybe they'd been interrupted, maybe somebody had shown up on the ranch or they had gotten scared.

There were so many things running through his mind. He also wanted to know about her relationship with Detective Bullock. They had appeared to get along, which seemed strange. Being a woman in a small-town sheriff's office couldn't have been easy. It hadn't looked as though they'd had a relationship beyond friendship, but he had no idea.

"I know this is coming out of nowhere, but I just have to ask, is anybody going to walk through that door tonight and be upset that I am here?" He motioned toward the front door.

The mischievous look on her face disappeared. "No, the last man I had in my life—and I hate to admit this—was Todd. And you can see how well that went between us."

He bit the inside of his cheek to stop his smile. He didn't want her to misread it.

"I didn't want to talk to you about him in front of Stacy too much, but he has a tendency to take advantage of me when it comes to her. He isn't a nice man. And if he wasn't her father, I probably would have never stayed here."

That was the only reason he could be grateful for the guy's existence. "I'm glad you stayed. As for marrying him, we all make mistakes in our lives." He paused. "I like to think of first marriages like a pancake, it never comes out quite right. Most end up in the trash."

She laughed, and it made his heart lighten. He didn't know how much he had needed that until now.

He wanted to know what Todd had done to hurt her, but at the same time in this single moment he could tell that she needed to relax and take comfort in levity as badly as he did. They both hated Todd, only the fervor with which Cameron couldn't stand the guy would change with more information. And even that was debatable as, right now, he couldn't care less if the guy lived or died. Stacy and Emily both deserved better in their lives.

Emily's phone pinged with a message. She opened it up and her face darkened as she read whatever was on the screen.

"Is everything okay?" he asked.

She didn't seem to hear him as she typed away in response to the message. After a few more pings, she finally looked up. "Did you say something?"

"You okay?" he repeated.

She nodded. "That was the detective. They're holding the bodies until morning, and I will need to come back and write up my reports. He's leaving the scene for tonight, but they have an officer holding it." She stared at her phone, but he could tell that she really wasn't looking at it and was just zoning out.

"Did he find anything of interest?"

She looked at him, a haunted expression upon her face. She said nothing for a long moment. Whatever was bothering her, she didn't want to tell him.

"Just tell me. Whatever it is, it's okay."

She blinked then pinched her lips together before taking a long breath. "Your father..."

"Yes?"

She reached over to him and put her hand on his knee. Under most circumstances, her warm touch would have been a comfort but now he found it disconcerting. "His fingerprints were all over the gun found in your brother's hand. Bullock thinks it's possible he was the one to pull the trigger."

Chapter Eight

It was strange how quickly someone could move from being a stranger to being a friend. Emily couldn't have pinpointed the exact moment when she'd gone from looking at Cameron like a major suspect to the man she now was attempting to comfort, but here they were.

She stared at her fingers on his thigh and felt the warmth radiating up through his jeans. It tore at her that she had to tell him about the possibility that his father could have played a role in his brother's death. Yet, it still didn't make heads or tails of how his father had come to be stabbed outside by the truck—or why his father would have staged the gun in his brother's hand.

It was just a lead, but it made things a whole lot more complicated.

Cameron reached down with his left hand and put it on top of hers. He didn't look at her and instead reached over to the phone beside him on the couch with his free hand and started tapping away on the screen. She tried not to move her fingers beneath his.

The motion of his putting his hand on hers had seemed to come so naturally to him, like they had been dating forever and it was just a typical Tuesday night—and yet, she was in the power role. However, was she really? She had given up any professionalism the moment her daughter had arrived, and she had driven the nail in the coffin when she had told him about Todd and her relationship status.

He didn't seem to be aware of the feelings amassing within her, but she was glad.

He looked up from his phone's screen. "According to Stockman's Bank, we were running lean. Which he had told me." He moved closer to the side of the couch to be closer to her and so she could see his phone.

As he moved, her hand fell away from his leg. Where his hand had been on hers started to chill and she wanted to reach out and put his hand back, but it was best to leave things as professional as possible. She had already crossed enough lines; there was no point in going past anymore. If they had a relationship now, it could be disastrous at several levels—starting with the investigation and moving all the way to how it would affect Stacy.

She looked down at the bank account records. There were payments to what appeared to be the mortgage company, electric, the ranch supply store, gas stations and the grocery store. She motioned to touch his phone and he answered with a simple nod. She scrolled up. Near the middle of the month, on the fifteenth, was a seventeen-thousand-dollar charge. "Do you know what this is for?"

He shook his head. "No idea. This is my dad's account."

There was a series of large cash deposits, one every week and sometimes twice. "Didn't you say you guys were struggling for funds?" She did some quick math. "According to what I'm seeing here, just in cash deposits, your father was depositing more than forty-thousand dollars a month. Then you have what looks like your cattle sales and your regular business profits that go through your corporate name."

"Forty thousand? There is no way." He jerked back his

phone and clicked through each month like she couldn't have possibly been right. Yet, as he slowed down, she could see it click that what she had said was accurate. "It... This doesn't make sense. We had to take out loans for our new equipment. We were scraping by."

"Yes, it looks like your father was spending almost that same amount each month. It seems like *huge* amounts of money were going to odd number-based points of sales—probably websites or something web-based. Do you know what your father could have been spending that much money on each month?"

He looked completely at a loss. "I told you everything I know about. We have a huge debt on a new machine we got last year. If we had this kind of money, where my dad could just piss it away like this on the internet, I can't believe he wouldn't have first paid off that machine. It's at eight percent interest. It's insane."

"But you admit your father is terrible with money?"

"Definitely." He exhaled, hard. He dropped his phone on the couch and then dropped his head into his hands, rubbing his temples. "None of this is making any sense—my brother being here, my father making and spending that kind of money, and why they ended up dead."

"We will figure it out." She stood up and walked over to him, sitting down next to him on the couch. She put her hand on his shoulder and leaned closer until their legs touched. It was a simple touch, but warmth radiated between them like shared breath. "But your dad wasn't selling drugs or anything, was he?" she teased with a laugh to lighten the mood.

"The closest thing my dad ever got to drugs was chewing tobacco and drinking beer—he did like his Banquets." He smiled at what must have been the memory. "In fact, it's fair to say most of the charges at the gas stations were probably for a tank of gas, Copenhagen and a case of beer." He reached up and put his hand on hers.

"Then he was a true Montana rancher." She smiled at him as he stroked the back of her hand with his thumb.

He caught her gaze and she couldn't look away. Those eyes. Those incredible eyes. If she looked into them long enough, she was sure she would fall in. Like they were the depths of an ancient lake and the way to survive drowning was to swim straight to the island that was his heart. She had to hope that it wasn't completely made of stone.

"I wanted to say thank you." He took her hand in his and moved it toward his mouth. She could feel the warmth of his words on her fingertips, making parts of her awaken that had long been dormant.

"Thank me for what?" she asked, her sound airy thanks to the sensations coursing through her body and threatening to take over whatever control she had on her thoughts and abilities to speak.

"For believing in me. You didn't know me. You took a chance in believing in me. I will do everything I can to prove to you that you made a good choice—that I'm a man worth your faith." The way he spoke made her feel like he wasn't just talking about her case anymore.

He leaned forward and his lips brushed against the skin of her fingers.

"I... I believe you. I want to help you." She watched his lips connect with her hand and she grew impossibly wet as the heat of his mouth brushed over her skin. "We should go upstairs."

He looked up from his kiss and smiled at her, a sexy half smile that spoke of all the things she imagined him doing to her. She wanted to move in close and kiss those lips. They were so plump and she could imagine how they would feel on her tongue. He probably tasted like peppermint gum with a touch of salty man—and the flavor that made him *him*. If she had to bet, he probably tasted just as good as he smelled.

She moved slightly nearer, half afraid that she was reading this all wrong and he would jerk back and call her out for making a move. She drew in a long breath, pulling his manly scent deep into her lungs. He smelled like the ranch—fresh air mixed with hay and sweat. His scent was mixed with the aromas of the day and it made a heady concoction. She could actually feel her pupils dilate as her desire for him raced through her body.

Like he could feel how much she wanted him, he started to move toward her until she could almost feel his lips press against her. He was so close. Their eyes locked and she smiled at him.

He reached up and freed her hair from her ponytail, letting it cascade down her shoulders. He loosened her hair gently before moving his fingers up the back of her scalp. She leaned her head into his palm, letting him control her. It felt so good.

He moved her close, and he took her mouth with his.

The kiss. It was everything.

His thumbs moved up her face by her ears as he took control of her completely with both hands. His fingers moved through her hair. It was so sensual as his tongue flicked against hers and their flavors mixed.

She had been right—he tasted just as she had imagined, but if anything, it was better than she had expected. He tasted like ambrosia and the nectar of the gods that she had read about in her college English classes. She felt goddess-like now, springing to life in his hands like a flower that had been waiting for the sun's rays to come to full bloom.

Her hands found his chest and she moved back from his lips just slightly to look him in the eyes, to see if he was feeling what she was feeling. His eyes were heavy with lust and wanting.

There was a creak of the floorboards and she paused. After a few seconds, there was the sound of footfalls and the squeak of the third step.

Emily pulled away, out of Cameron's touch. She instantly hated it, but as she settled back into the couch, Stacy's ruffle-haired head appeared around the corner of the bottom of the stairs.

"Mommy?" she said, her voice sounding tired.

"Yes, ladybug?"

"Can Cam read me a story?" she asked, looking at Cameron who was smoothing down his hair.

He smiled at her and then slapped his knees as he stood up. "You got it, kiddo. What do you want? *Peter Rabbit* or *The Wizard of Oz*?"

There was no way her daughter had heard either of either of those classics, but Stacy smiled widely. "You pick."

As he walked off and took Stacy by the hand, Emily's disappointment disappeared and was replaced by a renewed sense of hope for her and her daughter's future.

Chapter Nine

He was a kid addict. Though he had never thought it would happen, he had fallen head over heels in love with Stacy. That kid was the cutest thing he had ever seen and, if given the chance, he would do anything to keep her safe—and that was to say nothing about her mother.

Now when it came to Emily, he couldn't say it was love, but that kiss… He couldn't think of a kiss that had ever been hotter—not even in the movies.

She was so far out of his league that he didn't even understand why she had kissed him in the first place. Or had he kissed her?

Last night and yesterday had been such a blur of activities and emotions that it didn't even feel like it could have all been real. Why was it that life could sometimes seem like it would go by so slowly and then suddenly everything would happen all at once?

Emily was over at her neighbor's, who had agreed to watch Stacy for the day while she went to work. The neighbor, an older retired woman named Penny, was apparently Stacy's normal caregiver and hated Todd just as much as he did—at least from what little he had overheard from her and Emily's phone call that morning. He'd listened while Stacy was eating her pancakes—complete with blueberries, which had left little seeds stuck up in her gums until her mom had made her brush her teeth.

While he waited, he went back to his phone and pulled up the bank records. As he went deeper into them, he noticed there were several to the big-rig company—Goemer's Diesel—that the WGC used for their truck parts. They kept two eighteen-wheelers on-site to haul cattle around the ranch and to sales when they needed. The rigs were old and had a habit of breaking down whenever they were actually needed. Cam had been planning on using one yesterday to move the cows up to the summer pasture.

When he'd gone to start the damned thing, Old Red, he'd called it, he'd found the alternator had gone out. He'd called the shop and ordered another one. It was probably ready to be picked up by now.

He ran his hand over his face as he thought about the cattle. They still needed to be moved. He also needed to get back to the ranch to feed the horses and make sure everything was taken care of for the morning. By now, the animals were probably getting antsy.

Bessie, the sassy horse, was definitely going to give him an earful when he got there.

Emily came strolling in the house. "You certainly know the way to a girl's heart, don't you?"

He put his phone away. He wanted to ask her if he knew his way to hers, but he bit his tongue. They had stopped at a good place last night, before things had gone too far and there was no going back. As much as he was attracted to her and he wanted things to progress, they couldn't be together. She was the cop investigating his father's and brother's murders. Until things were cleared and he was no longer a suspect at all, it felt wrong that they would be romantically involved.

He didn't want to compromise Emily, her investigation or her career.

"Your daughter is a sweetheart. You've done a really good job with her. You should be proud."

"I'm a long way from the home stretch, especially when it comes to things with her dad. However, thank you. I appreciate it. I don't hear that very often."

"I bet you don't." He felt awkward about saying that, and wished he hadn't, but he didn't know exactly why.

She cleared her throat, like she was feeling just as awkward as he was. "So, I need to look into all the leads today." She looked at the couch where he had piled up the blankets and stacked the pillows neatly from where he'd ended up last night. "Did you think of anything else while you were trying to sleep?"

"I just need to get back to the ranch, would that be okay? I know that the scene is still off limits, I don't wanna be around my father or brother. I just need to get in and take care of the animals."

Her smile disappeared. She nodded. "That shouldn't be a problem. Detective Bullock is already on his way there. Vetter has been there for an hour, and he relieved the deputy who was holding the scene for us last night. Just so you know, we are hoping to get the bodies out of there today. Do you have a funeral home that you would like to work with?"

Just like that, he came crashing back to reality and all the endorphins and happiness he had been feeling dissipated. There was so much to do. So many choices to make. So much chaos to deal with.

"Just use Gardiner Brothers. Cremation is fine. And I'm sure that we'll have to do autopsies, that's fine." He nodded, absentmindedly, trying not to think of their bodies being cut open on some cold stainless-steel table in a morgue somewhere.

She walked over to him. For a moment, he thought she was going to put her hand on him to comfort him, but she stopped short. It was as if she knew that what had happened last night was as far as they should take things as well. "Let's go."

She led the way to the door and waited for him to go outside before locking the door behind them. For a minute, he looked for their car outside and then remembered that they had parked by the diner. They walked in silence through the alley and around the block to her car. The town was already humming with tourists who were window-shopping along the little downtown area.

There was a rock and mineral shop and the door opened with the jingle of a bell; from inside he could hear kids laughing and talking. Farther down was an ice cream and espresso shop that had a line for morning coffees. Most of the people in line were plain women with huge purses and oversize hats, holding cell phones and tapping away instead of looking at the beautiful mountains surrounding them.

He let Emily walk in front of him and he watched the swish of her hips as she moved in her uniform pants. From under her shirt, around her middle, there was a thick band where yesterday he'd noticed she was carrying another gun in front. He wanted to know why she carried two guns, but then again, it made sense that she did.

If he was a law enforcement officer, he would have wanted to double carry as well. In their line of work, there was no room for gun malfunctions. If something happened and they lost use of their weapon, it would be terrifying. The old adage *Don't bring a knife to a gunfight* came to mind.

On the other hand, he hadn't heard of anyone in the area being part of an officer-involved shooting at any time in the recent past. Hopefully, she had never been in a situation where she had been forced to use her weapon on a civilian.

Instead of leading him to the back door of her patrol unit, as she had yesterday, she opened the passenger's-side door and smiled at him. He climbed in, and she didn't even close the door behind him. Instead, she let him close the door himself. He took it as a sign of major progress.

They made small talk about Stacy and her preschool as they headed for the ranch. According to Emily, Stacy was looking forward to starting kindergarten in the fall, and she had been reading for a year. She hadn't needed to tell him the last part. When he'd read to her last night, she had taken over for him on several occasions when he hadn't given Winnie the Pooh enough inflections in his voice.

The thought brought a smile to his face just as they pulled up to the yellow caution tape the sheriff's office had strung up around the crime scene that was his family's ranch.

He let out a long exhale as he got out of the car. Emily smiled over at him. It was a conciliatory smile, the kind that promised that things would get better, but they both knew it was something she couldn't guarantee.

The detective was already on scene and he made his way over to them. "How's it going?" He looked directly at Cam, like he was trying to decide whether or not Emily's faith in him was well-deserved.

"Good," Emily said, taking the helm. "We made some progress on the financial records. I'm going to look into that a little bit today, if that's okay with you?"

The detective looked him up and down before turning his attention to his deputy. "Yes, that would be fine." He nodded approvingly. "I got the judge to sign off on the warrant and the bank is working on getting us the official records. In the meantime, I have reached out to the FBI regarding the online charges and both men's cell phone records. When the warrant comes through, we will get them everything they need. You can take point on that. Good?"

Emily nodded.

Seeing her in action was a turn-on and it actually took Cameron off guard. He thought she was sexy before, but seeing a woman in a powerful alpha role was hot. It also made him wonder if they could get along if they dated. They were both type A personalities in a lot of ways. They were bound to butt heads.

Then again, he was putting the cart in front of the horse. Just because they'd kissed didn't mean they were going to be on the relationship wagon.

Cameron walked over toward the barn. He tried not to look at his dad's pickup, where he knew his father was still resting. He couldn't help but wonder how long his father could sit out there before he would start to really decay. By now, the flies must have started to come to the body. With cows, flies showed up almost as soon as the animal died. It was almost impressive how fast.

He went into the barn, grabbing hay and dropping it into the horses' stalls one by one until they were all taken care of. For the most part, this time of year, the horses were fine grazing, but he still liked to give them a little bit of hay, especially since today he wouldn't be able to turn them out like he normally would.

Next, he set about getting the pellets and grain mixtures together with the mineral powders and oils for each horse. Each animal took something a bit different, based on their nutritional needs thanks to their age, weight and breed.

Bessie, of course, was the most finicky and wouldn't eat anything with too much alfalfa.

She really was a pain. Yet, she was the one who had first alerted him to his father's passing.

What was he going to do with her now that his father was gone? She was wholeheartedly his horse. Cameron sighed as she walked up and put her head over the door of the stall and watched as he mixed her grain bucket. "Hey, pretty lady." He swirled the mix, poured it into her black feeder bucket and walked to her. She blew out as he neared, clearly impatient that he had taken so long to get her breakfast today.

"I know, I know. I got it though." He smiled, running his hand over her forehead. "You are just about as patient as Dad."

Or as Dad was, he silently corrected himself.

He slid the bucket into the stall and Bessie tore into the food like she hadn't been fed in a month. She was so dramatic sometimes. He looked her over while she ate. Luckily she didn't appear to have any ill-effects or rub marks from where the saddle had sat askew on her yesterday while she had run amok on the ranch.

He followed suit with the rest of the horses, finishing with Ginger, his bay. She was gentle and sweet and rested her head on his shoulder as he bent over to put her grain under the slat in her door. He caressed her, holding her head against him, and petted her with his eyes closed for a long minute. Sometimes, especially in moments like this, he wondered if animals could sense things beyond just happy and sad.

Of course, they could pick up on emotions; that was documented. But in this case, when he was so overwhelmed, could she sense how confused he was? From the way she nuzzled him, it seemed like she knew and wanted to help with it all.

He loved the animal.

There had been other horses he had been close to in the past. In many ways, they were like dogs, but larger and smarter. He'd had Ginger since she'd been born on the ranch fifteen years ago. He'd been there the night she'd arrived, and he'd nursed her through colic when he'd thought they'd lose her for sure. When she'd gotten healthy, he'd worked to break her and train her for driving cattle and trail riding in the fall.

She was his horse through and through. And more, he could have ridden her without a saddle and without a harness or reins. He could have just sat upon her bare back and she would move with him like they were of one mind, thanks to the touch of his thighs and the subtle movements of his body—many of which he wasn't sure he was aware of.

That girl had to know him better than he knew himself.

As he opened his eyes and let go of Ginger so she could eat, he looked down on the floor of the barn. In the dirty hay outside the door of Bessie's stall was a red hair tie. He walked over and picked it up off the floor. There was a bunch of brown hair stuck around it.

He couldn't think of the last time they'd had a woman in the barn—except Emily yesterday when she had brought the horses back. Even then, he couldn't remember if she had been in the barn. Plus, she didn't seem like the red scrunchie type of girl. In fact, he'd remembered exactly the kind of black hair band he'd pulled out of her hair last night before he'd kissed her. It was the same kind she had in her hair this morning.

He dropped the hair tie back onto the ground, wishing

he hadn't picked it up. He'd made a mistake moving it from where he'd first noticed it.

It was probably nothing, he told himself as he made his way outside toward Emily and the deputy and detective who were still standing around and talking.

"Emily?" he asked, feeling strange interrupting the group.

They all went silent.

He realized his misstep as he'd called her by her first name. "I mean *Deputy Monahan*. I think I found something in the barn that might be of interest. Something that doesn't make sense." He motioned for them to follow. "It's small, but…"

They followed him inside the barn.

"I know I shouldn't have, but I picked it up to see what it was. There is brunette hair on it. I think it's a woman's hair tie. We don't have any women working on the ranch and we haven't had any women guests that I've known about in the last few weeks—at least not after the last barn cleanup. That was just last week. We had Trevor do a full muck-out."

"And you know for sure that there are no girls on his crew?" Detective Bullock asked.

He nodded.

Bullock waved over at a woman who was carrying a camera and, until now, Cameron hadn't noticed. The woman started to make her way over. "This is our evidence tech, Adrianna Walken. I'm going to have her go over the barn. We'd walked through but hadn't found anything in here that we considered to be a part of the active crime scene. Now, that is going to change. That means you will have to leave."

"I can't leave the horses uncared for." He shook his head adamantly.

Bullock crossed his arms over his chest and looked down

at the floor as though he was thinking. He paused for a long moment. "I can respect that. This is a working ranch. I won't keep you out, but please don't disturb anything else before we have a chance to document everything. Fair?"

Cameron nodded. "I need to water them then I can be done for the day."

"That's not a problem."

Emily cleared her throat, getting his attention. "Didn't you need to move the cattle?"

He looked back at Ginger, who had stuck her head over the door of her stall and was looking out at them with curiosity. "I do. They need to get on fresh grass soon." He thought for a moment. "I need to get in touch with Trevor and see if he can run them without me."

"Perfect. In the meantime, we are going to get the bodies off to the medical examiner. I'm going to push to have the autopsies done quickly." Bullock looked like he wanted to add something but he remained silent. "As soon as you're done watering the horses, I'd appreciate you waiting outside the barn. Deputy Monahan will be your contact person."

Cameron nodded. Based on the look on the detective's face, he had a feeling that the man knew something less than professional had happened between him and Emily last night. Thankfully, he was discreet enough not to make a big deal about it. He could understand why Emily liked the man. Perhaps when and if they got to the bottom of this investigation, he would like the man as well.

EMILY PLACED THE black bag on the ground next to Leonard's body. The rigor had taken full effect and his corpse was totally stiff and impossible to move. She wished she could have moved him yesterday but, given the mysterious circumstances of his death and the need to fully investigate the scene, she could understand why Bullock hadn't wanted to release the bodies.

Adrianna got in close, taking pictures of the hilt of the knife. There was a bloody handprint on the elk-antler handle. It looked as though Adrianna had already gotten prints off the handle, thanks to some powder left in the creases of the horn. It was a beautiful knife.

Ruanas had a reputation of being well crafted and each one was handmade and one of a kind. They had been around for multiple generations and when she had looked this morning, some of the older knives were selling online for tens of thousands of dollars. Even the new ones weren't cheap and carried a price tag of several hundred dollars.

From what Bullock had said when he'd looked over the body—though he hadn't removed any clothing items and had done just a basic inspection—it had appeared as though Leonard had been stabbed at least ten times. Several times in the abdomen, as well as many defensive injuries to the backs of his arms.

Leaning down, she peeked at the arms of his jean jacket and looked at the bloodied edges of his sleeves. The man had definitely put up a good fight. She had to guess he was a lot like Cameron. She would think he would do just the same—except she couldn't imagine, or maybe it was *bear*, the thought of Cameron losing the battle for his life.

After making sure Adrianna had taken all the pictures she had needed of the front of the body, Emily placed a tube over the knife in the man's chest and carefully secured it in place to make sure it wouldn't be disturbed during their transit or move to the medical examiner's office.

She pulled the bag under Leonard's leg. "You ready to lift him?"

"Let's turn him to the side so I can get pictures under

him and behind him on the truck," Adrianna said, pushing back the sleeves on her black office-issued jacket with big yellow letters on the front that read "Tech."

Emily stood up and checked to make sure that Cameron was out of sight.

He was sitting on the buckboard bench in front of the barn. His fingers were tented between his knees like he was deep in thought. She couldn't believe how cool, calm and collected he was in the face of his family's storm.

It struck her as odd that he could be so emotionally reserved. He was either the kind who came out of the womb with extreme serenity, or he had been a product of life beating him down to the point of emotional numbness. She hoped that he was just calm by nature.

In her work, she had come across both kinds in men and women. It seemed like the beaten-by-life types came with a look in their eyes that was unmistakable: a cloud of darkness that couldn't be lifted no matter how much laughter or joy seeped in around the edges of their agony. It was like it was a permanent storm in the center of their soul, like the storm on Saturn that would never abate and instead threatened to swallow up or destroy whatever got in its way.

She thought about the look he had given her last night; the want. He had needed her last night, but until now she thought it had been because of some ethereal connection between them. However, standing by his father's body, she wondered if perhaps it was that he'd needed to be comforted and she had simply been the closest person.

The thought tore at her in ways she couldn't deal with at the moment and she turned back to Leonard.

She motioned for Deputy Vetter to help her with the man's body. Vetter looked over at Cameron and smirked. She wanted to slap the look right off his face.

"Why don't you take the upper body?" she said, motioning toward his shoulder. "Let's tip him to the right and take some pictures and we will move the bag under. We need to make sure we get good images of everything we can before we get him out of here."

Vetter nodded. "You got it, boss."

He was pushing it. Until now, they had been getting along. She didn't know why he'd called her "boss." It wasn't like him to call her names or put her down. She had been giving him more instructions than normal though. Maybe he was just having a bad morning or something.

They walked over to the remains and Vetter pulled the body to the right. He moaned; the sound low and guttural as the corpse expelled pent-up gases. The sound made the hair on her arms rise even though she had heard it many times before.

There was no give in any of Leonard's limbs and his body was heavy with death. He lay oddly on the ground, off-center, with his head rigid and unmoving on his shoulders.

Behind the man, on the truck's fender, was a smeared bloody handprint. "Holy…" Vetter said.

"Detective!" she called to Bullock, who was talking on his phone just inside the open doors of the barn. "You need to get over here."

He rushed over, slipping the phone into his pocket. Adrianna was clicking away with her camera and she placed an evidence tag, which included a ruler, next to the print, carefully documenting it.

From the way the handprint sat, it looked as though Leonard had grabbed the truck as he had started to fall. However, it was also possible that the handprint they were looking at wasn't his but the person's who had killed him—if they had put his body in that position.

Based on the position of Ben's body inside the house and the staging of the gun, she had to think that Leonard's body had been staged, too. It was a strange position, to make him look like he was sleeping outside against his pickup. It was almost as if the person who had killed him had wanted whoever came upon the scene not to recognize the man was dead for a while. In fact, that was exactly what had happened.

But why would someone need to do something like that? Why would they need more time?

Or maybe the person hadn't meant to kill Leonard. They had placed him in a manner that could have indicated respect. There had been a pretty significant fight. That had to mean they were likely looking for a man—someone who Leonard would have gone to in a fight. It would have had to have been someone stronger than the older rancher. But that was saying a lot.

Bullock didn't say anything, but he was taking notes in his phone. Whenever he did that, she knew to leave him alone; it meant he was in the zone. Maybe he was making more headway in the case.

According to what he'd told them when she'd arrived at the ranch, they had a positive on the smear on the hallway that it was human blood and they had managed to pull a series of fingerprints. He'd planned on having the fingerprints run through the database today. Unfortunately, the prints on the knife had come back as completely unusable thanks to the texture of the elk antler on the grip.

Maybe they could get lucky with this print. They wouldn't know if they got what they needed to identify who had been on this ranch besides the Trapper men until they were back at the office.

The sooner, the better—that way, Cameron's name could be cleared.

A thought struck her... *What if the handprint is Cameron's?*

She pushed away the intrusive thought. There was no way. "Is it okay if we continue to move him, Detective?"

Bullock looked up at her and stared for a long moment, like he needed to come back to reality before he could answer. "Sure. Let's get both bodies out of here. I think we have most of what we need. This...this might also help." He nudged his chin in the direction of the fender.

It didn't take long for her and Vetter to get the bag around the stiff body. Leonard's seated remains, complete with the knife tube sticking out of his chest, looked strange in the body bag on the gurney.

Deputy Vetter stood at the end of the gurney as they wheeled it toward the coroner's van Vetter had brought from the office on the detective's orders. Maybe that had been part of his annoyance with her, as she was the acting coroner and he had been tasked with running the bodies around in her stead since she had been asked to help with questioning Cameron.

"Can you believe this?" Vetter whispered, looking toward Cameron to make sure he couldn't hear him.

"Believe what?" she asked.

"Cameron had to have done this. He's guilty," he said, taking her by surprise. "He stands to inherit the whole place with his dad and brother out of the way. Plus, he did one hell of a chop job pressing his dad's fingerprints on the gun before staging it in his brother's hand. That whole scene was just *bad*."

"He didn't—"

"Dollars to donuts, that handprint on the truck is Cameron's." He motioned toward the truck as they neared the black coroner's van that was parked near the eighteen-wheeler set up for moving cattle. He stared at Cameron for a long moment, as though he was weighing and measuring him with his gaze before looking back at her. "Detective Bullock's good. He's going to love to string him up by his ankles."

"Bullock won't stop until he gets blood on his teeth, that is for sure, but Cameron didn't do this. He isn't the type and there are two other sisters he would have to share his inheritance with. That doesn't quite add up." She checked her annoyance with the deputy as she opened the back doors of the van. As it opened, it smelled like stale air and death. "Ready to put him in?"

Vetter nodded.

Thankfully, even though they had an office with a limited budget, they had a lift for their gurneys, so no one ever had to haul bodies in and out of the vehicles. It had saved many people from getting hurt. After getting the body up and clicking him into place, she stepped out and closed the doors. When she turned, Cameron was staring directly at her and she caught his gaze.

"I'm going to ask him a few questions," she said to Vetter, motioning toward Cameron with her chin.

"You need backup?"

She waved off the newbie deputy who couldn't read the get-lost vibe she was really trying to put off. "Why don't you go ahead and get started with the next body? Grab Adrianna and get the pictures done with Ben. Let me know if you need my help in there."

Though she didn't really need anything from Cameron,

and she should have probably just gone inside to help with moving Ben, she couldn't stand being so close to Vetter. She could understand his line of thinking. In fact, she had thought many of the same things he had, but for some reason his assertions rubbed her all the wrong ways.

Cameron's gaze didn't waver as she sauntered over to him, swaying her hips slightly more than was necessary and, though she realized she was doing it, she didn't stop herself. It didn't make sense to her that she would allow herself to put on this little display, especially given the circumstances, but a little hint of sex couldn't make things worse for him. At least, she hoped not.

He scooted down on the bench and patted the spot beside him as she approached. "Take a seat, if you'd like." He sounded a little awkward, as though he wasn't sure he should be asking after what had happened last night and what was happening now—she didn't blame him.

She sat down beside him, spreading her legs slightly so their knees brushed against each other. He leaned in slightly instead of pulling away as she had expected. She was relieved. "How are you doing?"

"Are you actually worried about me or are you trying to just start a conversation so you can ask me more questions?" he asked, quirking an eyebrow. "If you are worried, you don't need to be and, as for interrogating me—you can just jump right to it. I have nothing to hide, and you know it."

"I know you don't. And I hope you know that I'm not looking in your direction," she countered, trying to not find his devilish charm more enticing than she should.

"Is that right?" He gave her a rakish smile that made whatever reticence she had in falling for this man slip away.

She couldn't help herself; he was the sexiest cowboy she had ever seen and, dammit, if he didn't know.

"Did you talk to your ranch hand?" she asked.

"Trevor?"

She nodded.

"I've been texting him, letting him know what has been happening on the ranch. He hasn't said much, which isn't outside the norm. This morning, he hasn't been responding at all. Which also isn't unlike him. When he gets like this, I just GPS his ass. Today, I tracked his location to The Mint Bar downtown. I'll have to run down there to talk to him. You game?"

She nodded. "For now, we are at a standstill while Bullock is going through the barn. The bodies need to get to the ME, and we are waiting on results from the fingerprints. Since he lives on the ranch, we do need to get a statement from him."

"I can't promise he is sober."

"Was he on the ranch in the last two days?"

Cam shook his head. "I don't think so. He was supposed to be with his kid."

That was one dead-end lead, but she'd still need Trevor's statement.

She couldn't stop staring at Cam and a smile flickered over her lips. It took her by surprise, given the circumstances, but she couldn't help herself.

With him looking at her like that, she wished things could have continued last night. There were storm clouds within his eyes, but when he looked at her, the storm seemed to calm, and the tempest within her did the same.

She took in a breath as she recalled the way his hand had moved up the back of her neck and through her hair. It was so intense, the way he had touched her. He had taken her like he had owned her. There was no being timid or questions—only possession.

Chapter Ten

It took longer than expected to leave the ranch. Emily ended up having to help the young-looking deputy load up Ben's body into the back of the black coroner's van.

It was strange sitting there watching his family disappear into the vehicle. It didn't escape him that it was quite possibly the last time he would see them.

His family wasn't the kind to do a big wake or viewing, but after the cremations, perhaps he would have Reverend Daniels come over to the ranch and do a little service for family friends. He'd have to order a headstone for the family plot. He wasn't even sure if there was a place in the graveyard for his brother. He only knew there was one for his father because when his mother had died, they had both put their names on the headstone together. All he had to do was add the date.

It was also strange, and so surreal. It wasn't that he hadn't thought about his father's potential demise, it was just that he had never expected it to come so soon or unexpectedly. Like most of the men in his family, he thought his father would live into his mideighties and go out strong. Though, from what Emily had said, he had gone out as a fighter.

It felt strange being back in the passenger seat of the squad car again, and perhaps that was adding to his feelings. In some ways it all felt unavoidable—like death and taxes. He chuckled, the sound under his breath.

At least he was in the front of the car and his wrists weren't in cuffs. His mom would never have believed such a thing when he was younger. He and Ben had been wild children growing up—throwing bottle rockets down the culverts and whipping snowballs at passing cars on the highways. More than once, they'd had the police show up on their doorstep.

The Mint Bar was at the opposite end of West Glacier from Emily's place, but not too far from the ranch. It harkened back to days when the ranch hands would get off work and pile into pickups and head down to the watering hole and then stagger back to the ranch at the end of the night. Based on the aesthetic of the place, not much had changed from those days, either.

It was a dive by anyone's standards. The flickering neon lights in the windows and the faded band posters kept most of the nonlocals at bay as most tourists who came to West Glacier were looking for the glitz and glam of the Montana experience that they saw on television, not the true state that was built on cow patties and wheat hulls.

Where there was that type of required labor, there was also a different culture that came with it that few talked about—the low-rent bordellos and brothels that had once been scattered up and down the streets of every town in the West. That wasn't to say those kinds of services weren't still available. From what he'd heard from Ben and the boys around the ranch, they certainly were, but they were no longer nearly as obvious or as advertised.

As he walked with Emily up to the front door of The Mint, he looked up to the second floor of the Old West–style brick-and-white-stucco building. There were six small windows and they were set closely together. The rooms upstairs must have been small—the kind that were used for the specialty services offered by the soiled doves.

The bells on the door jingled as they made their way inside the bar. It smelled like stale beer, fryer grease, and decades of cigarettes even though smoking was no longer allowed in public buildings. The floor was sticky as they made their way up to the bar where there were five men already seated and drinking mugs of pilsners. It reminded him of growing up as he had spent more nights in here playing darts and drinking beer with Ben and his friends than he could even remember.

The thought of those nights made a piercing pain stab through his chest. He was going to miss his brother. They had been best friends for the better parts of their lives.

Sure, they had gone their separate ways in the recent past. But there had been a part of him that had held out a hope that one day his brother would come home and they would go back to the old days—when they'd been tight. Things would never have been the same, but they could have learned to like each other again.

He would never forget the time his brother had found a deceased skunk and had been told to move it away from the house. Instead of carefully moving it without touching the animal, the kid had pushed it onto a shovel with his cowboy boot. Later that night, he'd worn his boots into the house and put them in front of the air intake for the entire house.

Their mother had been furious.

He'd spent hours scrubbing those boots—and making it up to their mom.

It had taken weeks for the smell to completely disappear from the house.

Emily paused and looked over at him. She'd pulled her

hair loose, letting it fall over her shoulders. He loved that look on her, it made her appear less rigid and more approachable, and perhaps that was why she had chosen to do it. "Which one is your hand?" she whispered, glancing in the direction of the bar.

She looked so beautiful in her uniform with her hair down that he felt a niggle of covetousness within him. He wanted to tell all the men in the bar that she was his. He'd never felt that way in his life, but everything about her and what was happening between them was different than anything that he'd felt before.

Besides, she wasn't his and he wasn't hers. They had kissed, nothing more.

When had he become a guy who took a kiss so seriously? He had been going through so much. Maybe she had just taken pity on him and wanted to make him feel better. Though the detective she worked with hadn't said anything about him calling her by her first name, he could tell that she was probably going to hear about that later. And he didn't want to be the reason she got in trouble at work. He wasn't worth the risk. He was just a dumb ranch kid with more trouble on his plate than reward he could offer.

"He's the one at the end there," he said, pointing in Trevor's direction. "Give me a minute and I will talk to him. He may not respond well to a deputy rolling up on him if he has been drinking."

Trevor had been known to have a temper on bad days—at least when he'd been young and dumb. Cameron would like to assume he'd outgrown his temper, but when it came to Emily, he wasn't about to take any chances.

Trevor was talking to the guy next to him and didn't seem to have noticed them. Cam made his way over and as he neared, Trevor finally looked up and saw him. His eyes were red from a long night—or days—of drinking and little to no sleep. To say he looked rough was an understatement. In fact, he wasn't sure that he had ever seen Trevor look this bad.

"How you doing, man?" he asked, moving to the bar next to the ranch hand.

Trevor was wearing a hat that had once been light brown but now was nearly black thanks to sweat, dirt and time. He was wearing a loose-fitting, button-down Ariat shirt that had worn out around the corners of the breast pockets to the point you could see the once-white tank top he wore beneath. He smelled like piss and Copenhagen. He was in a rough way and if Cam had to guess, it had been more than just a couple of days since he'd taken a shower.

Trevor grunted, looking down at the beer in his hand. "I've had better damned days, but I got no right complainin' to you." He lifted the beer and took a long, drawn-out slug. He slammed the glass down on the bar after draining the rest of the liquid and motioned for the bartender to get him another.

She gave Cameron a questioning look and he shook his head, letting her know he wasn't interested in drinking this early.

The bartender wiped her hands on the rag at her waist before making her way over and grabbing Trevor's mug to pour him another. They sat in silence watching her work until she returned with a foamy beer. "You sure you don't want anything?" She looked over at Emily. "Whatever she and you want...it's on the house."

"Thanks, but she's on the clock and it's a little early for me."

"This is the guy I was telling you about," Trevor said to the bartender.

She looked at him and her eyes widened. "Oh, man, I'm so sorry to hear about your dad and your brother." She wiped her hands on the towel again, like it was a safety blanket. "I met your brother just the other night. He was a decent guy. Tipped me well."

"What?" he asked, taken aback. "You met Ben?"

The bartender nodded, but another couple had walked in and she was called away to the other end of the bar where they had sat down and were ready to order drinks. Cameron motioned for Emily to come over. "Trev, I want you to meet the deputy that is helping investigate our case. This is Deputy Monahan. She's doing one heck of a job."

Trevor stood up and moved to make room for her to take his spot at the bar. "Nice to meet you, Deputy," he said, giving her an acknowledging tip of the head. "I appreciate all you're doin' to help out the ranch. It's gonna be real tough on all of us. Hell, it already is."

"I'm sorry for your losses, Trevor." Emily put her hand on his shoulder and Trevor twitched slightly as he leaned into the bar.

He sloppily moved out of her touch and sat on a barstool farther down the bar. "Let me get you guys some lunch," he said, motioning for them both to sit. "They do actually have pretty good burgers here, and I could probably use a bite. That is, if they are serving food. We may have to ask, it's a little early." His words came slow, like he was forcing them through the hazy fog of alcohol.

The fact that he could be so coherent given how he smelled and looked was impressive. That, or he hadn't been drinking as long or as hard as Cameron had assumed.

Emily sent him a glance that told him she could use some food and conversation. He was glad she was up to being a good sport around a bad drunk.

Cameron sat down beside Trevor. "Did you know that the bartender—"

"Heidi." Trevor pointed a finger at the blonde pouring two drafts.

"Yes, Heidi," Cameron said, continuing. "Did you know she had seen Ben?"

He shrugged. "She mentioned it, but we didn't talk about it much. Didn't seem real important. Everyone stops by the bar on their way into town, you know how it is. It's the best way to get in touch with your friends. You know everyone's here."

He wasn't wrong, at least not when it came to the group of friends Ben ran with. The same couldn't be said of Cameron's, at least not anymore. Though he couldn't say he had very many friends beyond the feed store people, the diner staff and other ranchers.

A man a few barstools down from them stood up. He was wearing a green vest over a blue-flannel shirt. His hair was long, and he wore it pulled back into a ponytail that spilled down his back. Cameron didn't know why, but the guy seemed out of place in the bar and, as he looked at him, he quickly threw money on the bar and hightailed it outside. Strange.

"You know that guy?" he asked Trevor, motioning after the dude who'd just left.

Trevor shook his head. "He's been sitting there for a bit. Didn't say much. Just that he's from North Dakota. Traveling through."

"North Dakota?" Emily asked, leaning over the bar so she could look directly at Trevor.

"Yeah, why?" He gave a one-shoulder shrug.

"That's where Ben was coming from, right?" she asked.

"Yeah," Cam said, nodding.

It was a long haul from North Dakota to West Glacier and there wasn't a direct route. For someone to want to get from one place to the other, they had to connect from a variety of highways and onto and off Interstate 90. They'd have to *want* to get to West Glacier—it was just a dot on a map if someone wasn't headed to Glacier National Park. No one was just *traveling through* from North Dakota. His statement didn't pass the sniff test.

Cameron gave Emily an appraising glance and she shot him a rise of the brows. She must have been thinking along the same lines.

Heidi came sauntering back over, towel in hand. "Did I hear you guys say you wanted to order some food?"

"Get 'em a couple of cheeseburgers, fries and all the fixin's," Trevor ordered, not waiting for a menu or for them to make any decisions.

It didn't matter to Cam, but he wasn't sure about Emily. He checked, but instead of seeming annoyed or put out, Emily just nodded at the bartender. "After you let the cook know our order, would you mind coming back though? I need to ask you a few more questions about Ben."

Heidi glanced down the bar and, making sure everyone had full beers, she nodded. "I'll be right back."

Trevor took another long drink of his beer. "I saw you called. I'm sorry I didn't answer, Cam."

Cameron tipped his head. "It's okay. I get it. I'm having a hard time with everything as well. However, you know that we have to get back to work. Things are still needing to get done back at the WGC."

Trevor didn't say anything, and his head just dropped low over his beer as he nodded. "I know we gotta finish moving the cattle up to the mountain—that's overdue. I just… Your dad is normally the one who heads that up."

He and Cam's father were extremely close, as Trevor had nearly grown up on the ranch. He'd worked there since he was eighteen years old and had lived down in the bunkhouse near the stock pond after he had come to the ranch when his parents had kicked him out. He hadn't graduated from high school and his prospects in life hadn't been great, but he'd always had an incredibly strong work ethic. In fact, the ranch was the one thing he cared about above anything else.

The only problems they'd ever had with him were a few trips to the drunk tank and a fistfight that had ended in a broken beer bottle to the side of his head, which had nearly taken off his ear. They had ended up taking him into the emergency room and sitting with him while he'd gotten nearly one hundred stitches. The doc had told him he needed to go to a plastic surgeon but, of course, the cowboy had told him he didn't need to look pretty—he just needed to have an ear attached to his head.

"I know you loved my dad. We all did…at least most of the time," Cameron said with a laugh as he thought about all the times he had lost his patience with his dad. He'd even been angry with Leonard yesterday when he'd arrived on the ranch about the financial state of the place.

What a confusing mess that was turning out to be, thanks to the banking records they had gone through last night.

Cam wouldn't be surprised if it took months for the detective to get to the bottom of what had happened with his father and brother—that was, if he was ever able to make sense of the mess things had become. He was certainly at a loss.

"Your dad did more for me than any other person on this planet. I wouldn't have had a home if it hadn't been for him." Trevor's voice cracked as he spoke, and it made Cameron pause.

He hadn't realized until now why Trevor would have been so upset. Of course, he not only would have been saddened by the family's loss, but he would also be afraid that he was no longer going to be a part of the ranch.

"Trevor, just so you know, as long as I'm on the ranch, you will be, too." Cameron put his hand on the guy's shoulder. "Now that Ben's gone, you are the closest person I have left to a brother. I'm going to need your help more than ever."

Trevor perked up. He lifted his head and some of the heaviness that had been in his eyes seemed to dissipate. "You don't have to say that just to make me feel better. I don't need pity."

"You know I don't do pity."

Trevor looked at Emily.

"Not even to get a lady," Cameron added, smirking at Trevor.

"You read my damned mind." Trevor finally smiled.

Heidi walked over. "Did you say something about a lady?"

Cameron winked at Trevor. "I can't say the same thing about you when it comes to getting ladies," he leaned in and whispered.

Trevor smirked.

Emily smiled at Heidi. "We were talking about you," she fibbed. "You said you had seen Ben in here. When was that, exactly?"

"He was in here twice actually. But the first night it was just really quick with some woman." Heidi looked up and to the left, like she was trying to recall a memory. "She was dark-haired, thin and looked worse for the wear, if you know what I mean."

Emily nodded. "Did you know this woman?"

Heidi shook her head. "I hadn't seen her around here before. Ben didn't introduce her, and though they had come in together, they left separately. I didn't see who she left with though. All I know is that she was gone when he decided to go."

"And you didn't see her come in with him the following night?" Emily asked.

Heidi shook her head. "The next night he was in here and he was chatting with the guy who just left." She took a couple steps down the bar and picked up the cash the guy had left and tapped it on the wood before turning and closing out his bill. She stuffed the couple of ones left over in the silver canister next to the till. "He was just as cheap with his tips as he was the other night, too."

"Do you know him? Is he a regular?"

Again, Heidi shook her head. "He has only been coming in this last week or so. Doesn't really talk much. Gotta say, it's kind of nice, but it's unusual for someone who takes a seat at the bar. Usually when someone sits up here, it means they are looking to talk to me—either to share a sob story or to chat me up. He didn't seem interested in either."

Cam'd never thought about the sociology of a bar before and why people picked where they sat, but the bartender was probably right. When he didn't want to talk to people, he sat away from the bar at a table and pretended to watch sports on the big screen. He would walk up to the bar to get a drink when he wanted one, or he would wait for the server to wait on him. And, if he really didn't want to talk, he wouldn't have been in the bar in the first place.

It made him wonder why the man had come there.

When he had heard who they were, and the conversations they were having, he hadn't even taken the time to get his check or finish his beer. He had been in one hell of a hurry to leave.

"Do you know where we could possibly find that guy?" he asked.

Heidi shrugged. "Like I said, he didn't really talk to me."

Trevor shot him a sideways glance as Emily said something he couldn't quite hear to the bartender. He watched as she slipped the girl her business card.

Trevor knew something and, for the first time since he'd realized his father was dead, Cam finally felt like he was getting close to finding answers.

Chapter Eleven

It was clear Trevor was in no shape to take the cattle up on the mountain or give a statement that was usable in court. Cameron and Emily ate their lunch, paid the tab and made their way out of the bar.

The burgers had been just as good as Trevor had promised. Her stomach was full, and they had spent the last hour talking about Trevor and Cameron growing up on the ranch.

She'd had no idea that they had spent so much time together. They'd seemed just as close as Cameron and Ben in many ways. In fact, maybe closer. It was no wonder that Trevor had found his way to the bar while everything was happening at the ranch. If she had had a choice to stay or leave in a situation like theirs, she would have gone to the bar as well.

She sent a quick text message to her neighbor to check on Stacy. Penny messaged a second later and said she was doing great.

Emily got in the cruiser and tapped her fingers on the steering wheel, humming away.

Her phone pinged with messages from Bullock. He'd been busy all morning. They hadn't found much in the barn, but there had been some footprints that seemed consistent with women's cowboy boots. He was going to look into it a little further, along with Adrianna and Vetter.

According to Bullock, the bodies had been delivered to the crime lab in Missoula and they would try to get the results back to them as quickly as possible. Depending on the backlog of cases, that could mean anywhere from half a day to two weeks.

Going to the bar had been far more helpful than she could have ever expected or anticipated—even without getting an official statement from Trevor. It was funny how things worked out sometimes.

This wasn't the first time in her career where she had just gotten lucky and been in the right place at the right time. That was actually how she had become a cop in the first place.

She hadn't grown up dreaming about being a police officer. No, far from it.

Emily had always thought she would go into something with animals. She had always had an affinity for stray cats, adopting them off the streets then bringing them home, cleaning them up, feeding them and nursing them back to health. Most of the times, they would disappear the next day—probably to go back to their real house—but she had always felt like she was saving the world one kitty at a time.

Her life would have been so different if she'd become a vet. She looked over at Cameron. He was texting away on his phone and he seemed to be deep in thought.

Since they had left the bar, he had been acting a little bit strange. From the atmosphere between Trevor and Cameron, it was like there had been a conversation bonding them that she wasn't privy to, and she didn't like it. She wanted to ask what was going on or what had happened, but she decided to just wait to see if Cameron would open up to her.

"Did you find anything out from the bartender about the guy?" Cameron asked.

"Just what you heard. I gave her my card and made sure she knew that she could call me if he returned to the bar. He definitely seemed in a hurry to get out of there when he saw us. Had you ever seen that guy before?"

Cameron shook his head. "I wonder if we looked up my brother's phone records if we could see if he was calling somebody else here in town. That might link us up with this guy."

She texted detective Bullock about the records. "Done. Good idea. We'll see if we can come up with anything, but sometimes getting those records takes a little bit."

"You know, I thought this detective thing worked a whole lot faster." Cameron turned slightly in his seat as he looked at her.

She laughed. "Dude, real police work isn't anything like TV. Even the initial investigation takes forever. At least, it feels like it. Sometimes it can take a couple of weeks before we even release the initial crime scene. Though, I think we'll be done with the one at the ranch within the next day or so."

He seemed surprised. "I seriously thought it would take like a day and we could get right back in. In fact, I thought I'd be sleeping in my own bed tonight. You're saying I won't be?"

She shook her head. "I highly doubt it. I'm sorry to tell you that."

As soon as she said that, she was tempted to invite him to come back to her place and spend the night once again. On the other hand, she was worried about Stacy and what she would think. It was strange enough for Emily to have a man spend the night once, but what would her daughter think of him spending twice in a row? She didn't want Stacy to get too emotionally connected to this guy when he was nothing more than a part of a case—even if he had kissed her.

To mask her confusion, she put the car in gear and pulled out of the bar parking lot. She didn't know where she was going. The next logical step would have been to track down the man who had last been seen with Ben, but she had no idea where to start looking.

She started to head aimlessly toward Main Street, but turned left so she wouldn't have to drive past the diner and the alley that led to her house. She didn't want either of them getting any ideas.

If she really thought about it, the person she was most worried about getting attached to Cameron was herself. She couldn't have him spend another night if she was going to keep him at arm's length. If he kissed her again like he did before, she would never be able to remain objective with him. As it was, there was no forgetting how he had felt against her skin.

Just the thought of him kissing her made her want to drive him straight back to her place. She shifted in her seat at the thought.

As though he could read her mind, Cameron reached over and took her hand with his. He did it with authority and ownership, but it was also considerate and gentle—as if she had a choice to retract her hand but he already knew she wouldn't.

He squeezed her hand tightly when she didn't pull away.

She smiled over at him. "I don't know what we're doing,"

she said, "and I don't want to analyze it. Are you okay if this is all it is, at least for now?"

"I don't want to put you in a compromising position with your job or your investigation. I get that this," he said, motioning to each of them with his free hand, "is probably because you feel sorry for me and you're trying to comfort me, or something. But whatever it is, I'm grateful. I'm glad to have you in my corner. I'm glad to have your hand in mine." He lifted her hand up and kissed the back of it softly. "And yes, I'm totally fine with this being all we are."

"Thank you."

"And for tonight," he continued, "why don't you take me to the Arrow Lodge at the edge of town and just drop me off? They take cash and they are cheap. It's all I need for one night."

She nodded.

She couldn't believe how self-aware this cowboy was. Most cowboys she'd met couldn't put sentences together that were more than four words. He constantly impressed her. Yet she kept pushing him away. She wanted to tell him that she wanted more and that she wanted him to come home with her and that she wanted a relationship. She wanted somebody to help her raise Stacy. However, she also didn't want to force that role onto any man.

She wanted to have a relationship that worked first, not a dad for Stacy and then a relationship. Far too many of her recently divorced friends with young kids had made that exact mistake. They had fallen for men who had befriended their child or children simply because their children liked the guy. They'd forgotten about the fact that first they had to have aligning values and attractions to the actual man.

While Emily knew there was no question that she was incredibly attracted to Cameron—the instant she had seen him on the ranch she had thought he was quite possibly the sexiest man she had ever seen, complete with the cowboy hat—she couldn't say she knew everything about him. The bar had proven that.

It had also demonstrated that there was so much more to him that she enjoyed. Just now, he'd proven to her that he knew who he was and that he was in touch with what he wanted and that he could vocalize his needs. That in and of itself was strange for any man. At least, any man she had ever dated in the past. Maybe he was just too good for her.

What if he was out of her league?

"You know, you're worried that I'm just being nice to you because I'm trying to make you feel better. However, how do I know that you're not doing the same thing with me?" She turned the squad car toward the highway. "Maybe you felt bad for me after you watched me be humiliated by my ex-husband."

"You guys were something," Cam said, whistling through his teeth.

"We did put on quite a show, but that was nothing. He's done so much worse to me, I almost hate to admit it to you." She ran her hand over her face as she groaned. "I just need to shut up. I shouldn't be telling you."

"Stop. You don't need to worry. I told you. I know how exes can be. I have an ex-wife, too, April. We went through some pretty tough days."

"You didn't tell me why you guys broke up. What happened?" she asked.

Now he was the one who appeared to be shifting uncomfortably in his seat, but it seemed to be for entirely different reasons. "I was away from the ranch a lot. At least, the ranch house. It was my job at the time to go to a lot of the sales. I also did a lot of work in Helena to lobby for agricultural stipends and learn how we could best manage our finances according to state law."

Now his self-awareness and articulation made more sense. He wasn't just a cowboy; he was also a statesman and a politician. Though, who wasn't to say a cowboy couldn't be self-aware, even if she hadn't met one.

"I hope you know you're getting sexier by the minute." She smiled at him. "But continue your story."

He chuckled, but there was a tiredness in his voice that told her there was a lot of pain behind what had happened with his ex-wife. "While I was gone, it was a known fact that my wife wasn't happy. I knew it as well."

She had a sinking feeling that she knew where this story was headed, and as much as she didn't want him to have to continue, she needed to know for sure.

"If I had been older and wiser, I would have come home and taken her right into my arms and had her travel all over the state with me. I would have made us go into marriage counseling or whatever needed to be done. However, I was stupid. I thought things could be handled over the phone and through texting. When I called, she said she was fine. I believed her. I mean we didn't fight."

She felt for him. "How did you guys meet?"

"She and I went to high school together. It was stupid. We were the yearbook couple, if you know what I mean. Homecoming queen and king. Voted the couple that was most likely to get married. It was funny, though, because in reality we weren't having sex and we weren't doing the things that people assumed we were. In high school, we were mostly just really good friends, and we watched movies together and just hung out like buddies."

She nodded. "I had really great friends that were of the

opposite sex as well. Nobody gets it. Everyone always assumes that there is some romantic element."

He pinched his lips together as he nodded. "Yeah. And we tried to navigate that," he said, moving his hand like it was a raft navigating a turbulent river. "However we ended up just giving in to what everybody assumed. And we were stuck in this relationship and stuck into marriage because it was the logical next step. And we loved each other enough. I thought that we made each other happy."

Reminded of her thoughts on true love from just yesterday. "Do you believe in true love?"

He made a strange, strangling noise. "Can you define that for me?" he asked after a long pause.

Once again, she was taken aback by how much they had in common. However, this time she wasn't sure that she entirely liked it. Part of her wished that he knew the answer and he would sweep her away with some grand rejoinder about love. Maybe she was totally warped by romantic movies just like he was about cop shows. They both had assumed some things and gotten them completely wrong.

The hotel he wanted her to take him to wasn't far down the road. It was a little bit too early for check-in, but in a place like this, normally they would sign him in no matter what time. However, she didn't want to have him leave her just yet, so she slowed way down. Cars started passing them on the highway, even though she was in her police unit. Normally, it would have annoyed her, but today she didn't even give it a second thought. Instead, all she could think about was love.

"If I could define true love for you, I don't think I'd be divorced. In fact, I don't think I would have been married in the first place. That being said, I don't have any regrets. Like every parent before me that's gone through divorce and has a child, I'm really grateful that I have my daughter. I wouldn't be the same without her—she's the reason I'm alive."

He quirked his eyebrow. "See, I'm glad I didn't have kids because I don't think I could have left. Even with the circumstances being what they were."

"You didn't tell me what happened…"

He sighed, the sound filled the space between them and, even though it was quiet in that moment, it sounded louder than the highway noise under their tires. "When I came home from my last trip to Helena, I walked into the bunkhouse where she and I lived, and she was in there with Ben."

She thought that his sigh had been loud, but her gasp was ten times louder.

Of all the things she thought he was going to tell her, that had been near the bottom of the list. However, his reaction to his father's and brother's deaths did make a hell of a lot more sense now. It was no wonder that he hadn't cried. He had to have been experiencing so many emotions; emotions that she hadn't even started to understand yesterday.

Even now, knowing what she did, she couldn't understand how this man was functioning.

They drove in silence all the way to the hotel. She had no idea what to say.

She wanted to thank him for being honest and telling her what had to be his most embarrassing and raw secret. It had to be humiliating to admit that his brother had done him so wrong. He had spoken about Ben being his best friend and his comrade growing up. For his brother to have done something so brutal with a woman he'd also grown up with had to be so painful.

She wanted to just take him in her arms and hold him and

make everything right. But how could a man like him, who had been through so much betrayal, ever trust anyone, let alone a virtual stranger like her. People he had known for years had lied to him. Who was to say that she wouldn't?

How had he even been strong enough to want to kiss her? He'd had to make himself so vulnerable to want to do something like that with her.

It had meant so much last night for him to take that step, but now that single kiss meant even more.

She hated it.

They had promised each other that their holding hands would be as far as this would go today. For this horribly broken man, she now realized that promises were something that couldn't be broken.

Chapter Twelve

Cameron looked at the seedy '70s era hotel and settled deeper into the front seat of Emily's car. She hadn't argued when he'd asked her to bring him here, but he'd wished she would have. Sure, it was logical that he wouldn't go back to her place and there was no way in hell he was going to spend a night in that bunkhouse on the ranch, but sitting here, he would have taken just about anywhere else.

"You know...that guy from the bar, he must be staying somewhere. Did you see what kind of vehicle he drove away in when he left The Mint?" he asked, stalling.

"I was thinking about that earlier," she said after a long pause.

Ever since he had opened up to her about his ex, she had been *off*. She had said that she shouldn't have told him so much about Todd, but looking at their conversation and how it turned out, he was the one who had taken things way too far.

They didn't know each other well enough for him to unleash his past onto her like he had—even if she was investigating his brother's death. What Ben had done to him several years ago had no relevance on his brother's demise.

"If you want, we can sit here for a few minutes. Do a little stakeout," he offered.

She smirked. "A stakeout?" She giggled. "Who are we, Starsky and Hutch?"

He laughed, acting put out. "Well, when you say it like that, we sound ridiculous. All I mean is that if we sit here, maybe we can catch sight of the guy."

"I like your thinking, but this isn't the 1970s and we probably aren't going to get as lucky as we did by running into him at the bar. That was just good fortune. Now he knows we might be looking for him. He will probably be laying low. Which means he isn't going to be walking out in front of black-and-whites." She motioned to her car.

"Oh," he said, feeling rejected and silly. "I'm sure you have other cases to work on. I'll let you get back to your job." He put his hand on the door handle.

He couldn't believe how selfish and wrapped up he'd gotten in his own world. Of course she had other calls and other people in the community to help. He had been so focused on his family and his past, he hadn't even stopped to consider that there might be other families out there in West Glacier who were going through their own emergencies and needed her.

"Stop." She took his hand and moved it over toward her chest and as she did, he brushed against the gun in her bellyband. "I didn't mean it like that. And I don't want you to go into this hotel, either. In fact, if we are being honest, I don't really know what I want other than for you not to go in there and I don't want to go back to working alone."

"Are you saying you don't want to be without me?" he teased.

She smiled, letting his hand fall from her chest. "Well, now I wouldn't mind quite as much."

"Ha!" He laughed. "You know you love every second." As he said it, a warmth rose in his cheeks. He hadn't meant *love*, but there was no pulling in the word after it had left his lips.

Her hand stiffened and there was a long awkward pause between them. He stared out the windshield as a woman in a pair of cut-off jeans and a hot-pink tank top walked out of one of the rooms at the far end and lit a cigarette. She leaned against the wall and perched her black boot against the rock wall behind her.

A minute later, an older man—who was probably in his late forties—came out. He was buttoning the top button of his gray short-sleeved shirt. He was wearing black Dockers and he looked like he held a white-collar job. If Cameron had to guess, he was probably a real-estate agent or something along those lines.

The guy was out of place. He was also taking a room at the hotel—though, he had a feeling he was getting the room for a different reason.

The woman took a long drag on her cigarette, tilting her head back until her blond hair that was flipped up into a claw clip actually brushed the wall behind her. She let out a cloud of smoke above her and then looked down and smiled at the man. She said something and blew the man a kiss before he turned and walked toward his newer-model Porsche that was parked a few down from them.

He stopped and his eyes widened as he spotted their car. Then he dropped his head and stared at the ground before nearly running to his car. He got in and squealed his tires as he sped away.

"Boy, that guy was in one heck of a hurry," he said.

"What he was up to can be charged as a felony in Montana. He was smart to be in a hurry—though he would have been smarter to not pay for adult pleasures in the first place."

"Is that really what you think he was doing?" he asked, actually a little surprised. Sure, he had assumed that might have been what was happening based on the location and everything, but it was one thing for him to assume and another for a cop to actually confirm his suspicions.

"It's hard to prove. The women who are involved in that type of work aren't going to admit it and they aren't going to testify. If they get arrested and they say anything, they are only charged with misdemeanors. When they get out—if they have said anything, they are beaten by their pimps...or worse."

He stared at the woman who was still smoking against the wall. She looked tired and thin. There was a large black tattoo of a phoenix on her thigh, but instead of rising from the ashes it looked as though it was rising up from the crook of her knee and going straight back into the shadows cast by her shorts.

"How do you slow this problem down?" he asked.

She gave a dry laugh. "There's no slowing down the world's oldest profession. The state has done a lot of different things to try to control it. However, there is no stopping it. From time to time, we work with the FBI and create task forces in which we run sting operations where we try to capture predators who are preying on young girls. However, beyond that, the best we can do is arrest the men who are known to buy the services."

"So, you only arrest the johns?"

"Pretty much," she said, nodding. "And we try to stop human trafficking—but mostly when it comes to young girls. Women who have been at it very long are normally enlisted by pimps. Very few are on their own for a variety of reasons. But regardless of who they work for...like I said, they aren't going to testify against anyone who is working on the streets. It goes against their codes."

It felt a little weird to him that in their line of work, there was a code. Yet, who was he to judge.

Where he could safely make a judgment call without feeling too bad, however, was in the fact that he was not about to spend the night at that location. "On that note, I don't think I'm going to check in. I'll just go ahead and camp out tonight. It's warm enough out, the stars can be my blanket."

She let go of his hand and turned to her computer installed on the mount between them. She tapped away on the keyboard. "I put a BOLO out on a man matching the description of the guy we saw at the bar. Perhaps we can get the name. In the meantime, I'm gonna give Heidi a call and see if I can obtain video surveillance from the bar to see if I can pull his face. Maybe we can get a positive identification on him. One way or another, we need to get his name."

"You know, while you were busy with the bartender, Trevor and I got to talking," Cameron said. "Apparently, he overheard the guy we've been looking for talking a little bit. I don't know if it can help, but he said that it didn't sound like the guy knew his way around town very well."

Emily frowned. "That's not that odd if a guy said he was just passing through."

"I know, but from the way Trevor was talking about it, it kind of sounded like the guy wasn't driving. He didn't know for sure, but he thought maybe Ben had brought him here and now the guy was stranded."

Her eyebrows popped up. "And you are just now telling me this?"

"Trevor wasn't sure. And hell, we don't even know who

the guy is. It's all a guessing game. I didn't want to make things even more of a crapshoot. You know?"

She sighed. "I can appreciate the sentiment. You have to understand, though, a lot of what we do is follow dead-end leads. Sometimes we have to play Telephone, where we hear things third-hand and have to track down the truth from a variety of sources. It can be a huge undertaking."

"I figured as much. I didn't want to make things worse." And right now, as hard as they were trying, it felt like they had taken two steps forward in the investigation and then three steps back. He was even more at a loss than before. At least before, he had thought it was maybe just a murder-suicide.

Now, he knew it wasn't and he knew there were more people involved—quite possibly the man at the bar. Yet, even that was not certain.

"If the guy's stranded and he isn't driving around, then he is going to have to come back to the bar, or somewhere close to there to eat dinner. He hasn't gone too far," Emily said like she was thinking out loud rather than really talking to him. "I think we should head back into town. Maybe your stakeout idea wasn't too bad after all."

The woman leaning on the wall finally seemed to notice them. She stared over in their direction. She was squinting hard even though it wasn't that sunny. Her dark makeup was smeared down her face in places. He hadn't noticed that before, but then again, she hadn't really been looking at them. There was something in her face and the way she moved that made him wonder if she was high.

As she pushed herself off the wall with her foot, she struggled to find her balance before turning away from them. She looked over her bony shoulder at the patrol car one last time before disappearing back into the hotel room. The door slammed shut behind her.

"Is there some way we can help her?" he asked, motioning toward the closed door.

She flipped down her visor and pulled out a business card from a cardholder stacked with a variety of cards in a variety of colors. She handed him one that said, "National Human Trafficking Hotline." There was an 800 number and a tagline that read, "We'll Listen. We'll Help."

"I have found that usually working girls don't want help, or they are so abused and groomed that they don't think they deserve it. Many are ashamed and don't think their families will take them back. However, this hotline can help get them out of this lifestyle." She handed him the card.

He took it and stared down at the embossed number. He wondered how many women had stared at the number like he was now.

"You can slip it under her door—I'll keep my distance because I'm in uniform and she might freak out if she sees me approach."

He nodded as he opened the car door and stepped out into the parking lot. He moved fast, flipping the card between his fingers and making a thrumming sound as he hurried to the room. He slipped the card under the door and knocked.

He didn't wait for the woman to answer and instead jogged back to Emily.

Jumping into the squad car, he slammed the door and clicked his seat belt into place just as the woman opened the hotel room door. She looked around outside, almost as if she were expecting to see someone, and was annoyed that no one was there. Then she noticed the card on the floor.

She bent over to pick it up.

After staring at it for a long minute, she looked over at them and, in one smooth and well-practiced motion, tore the business card in two. She threw it outside and flipped them the bird before disappearing inside her room.

Emily had been right. Sometimes it was impossible to save those who weren't ready to be saved. Grooming could build a nearly impenetrable cage.

Chapter Thirteen

Emily's phone rang as they were headed back to the center of West Glacier. It was the owner of The Mint Bar, Tim Porter. She had talked with him over the years for a variety of a cases, as it wasn't uncommon for her regulars to show up or frequent local bars.

The good news was that she had a pretty good working relationship with the man. "Hey, Tim, how's it going?" she answered.

"Heya, Deputy Monahan, I heard you needed access to our camera files."

She was waiting for him to drop the bomb that she was going to need a search warrant.

While she and Tim got along, he was also the kind of bar owner who stood up for his customers. He had to walk a very fine line when it came to the small local community. He couldn't be seen by the rebels and outliers as someone who buddied up with law enforcement, but he also didn't want to screw things up with cops in case things went sideways at night and he needed to call them to help.

"I don't need everything. I was just hoping to get a good still of the bar when we were in there. If you've got one of the man who left, and of him getting into a vehicle, that would be great as well."

Tim chuckled. "Heidi already gave me a heads-up. I pulled a picture of you guys at the bar. I'll send it right over. I have watched the cameras outside. Doesn't look like the guy got into a vehicle. He walked south on Main Street, toward St. Paul's Church and the post office. You might be able to get more footage from them if you need it."

Tim was all over it. This guy definitely wasn't a regular and it was working in her favor.

"That would be great. I appreciate all your help with this, Tim. Please let me know if there's anything you need in return," she said more out of habit than anything else.

Tim cleared his throat. "Actually, you know those two other guys that were sitting at the bar with you? Larry and Jake?"

She barely remembered their faces, but she recalled that they were both wearing highlighter-yellow shirts worn by road crew workers. "Yeah, I think so. What about them?" she asked.

"They are brothers. The last name is Henderson. I think they are renting the apartment just above the Cussler Bakery. You know where I'm talking about?" he asked.

She thought about the cupcake and pastry shop that pretty much made all the specialty cakes for every event in the town. It was about two blocks down from where she lived and a block off Main Street. "Yeah, I know the place. What about the brothers?"

"They have a six-hundred-and-fifty-dollar tab open at the bar. I told Heidi not to serve them anymore, but they got aggressive. It was a choice between her safety and beer—she decided to give them the beers and I don't blame her."

"What were you hoping I would do to help you?" Emily asked, wondering how wrapped up in trouble Tim wanted these guys to be.

"I was thinking you could bring them in on misdemeanor theft. Nothing major, just a slap on the wrist. If they pay their bill, don't bring them in and I won't press charges. Plus, you and I'll be square."

It annoyed her slightly that Tim thought he could so blatantly use her for his own gains, but she had found in the past that the people causing him problems were generally the same people causing her issues as well. Dollars to donuts, if she ran these Henderson brothers through her system, at least one of them probably had an open warrant.

"Just go ahead and send me the footage I need, and I'll take care of the brothers for you. Hopefully, the tab will be paid by the end of the day. If not, I'll let you know that they have been arrested and we will be waiting for word from you as to whether you want to press charges."

She could hear the clicking of computer keys in the background. "There you go. I just sent that e-mail off. I appreciate your help. Talk to you later."

Emily opened up her e-mail as soon as Tim hung up the phone. She was met with an image of the guy in the green-flannel shirt with his long ponytail and an unkempt beard. As before, she didn't recognize the man, and he didn't look like anyone she knew from within the town.

She zoomed in on the man's face and made sure it was not blurry before inserting it into her computer system and doing an image search. A variety of similar-looking men in mug shots popped up on her screen, but none of them looked identical to the man in the image from the bar.

She blew out a huff.

"Everything okay?" Cameron asked.

"Yeah. We are going to have to run an errand really quick though. That okay?"

Cameron nodded. "I'm not in a big rush to camp out." He chuckled.

She had tried to warn him about the reality of some situations, but there was nothing like being faced with someone who didn't want to help themselves. "Sex workers don't stay in that lifestyle forever—especially the ones who are doing it willingly. Most do get out of it, safely. There's not a lot of studies on it. Few want to talk about their pasts, but I would say that at least ninety percent of the women that go into that kind of lifestyle do come out alive. Thankfully, for those who are trafficked or are traumatized by what they experienced, there are a lot of nonprofit organizations out there trying to help."

He nodded, but she could tell that he was really bothered by what he had seen. She was, too, but over time she had become numbed to the problem and the shadow epidemic of human trafficking in the country.

That wasn't to say that it always hadn't been a problem, but it definitely increased thanks to the internet and cell phones.

"What's the errand we need to do?" he asked, pulling her from her melee of thoughts.

"Tim hooked me up with the image we needed for our BOLO, so I made the update." She clicked a few buttons on her computer and sent the image out statewide. She turned the computer so he could see what she had done. "Hopefully, this will help us to identify the guy we're looking for, and maybe another agency will pick him up. These actually tend to work pretty well. While we wait for the results on that, though, I told Tim we'd go pick up a couple of guys who ran out on their bar bill."

"That's what I thought I heard you say. I just thought I

got it wrong. It seems under your pay grade or something." He chuckled.

"Not everything we do is glitzy. A lot of the time, we are just gophers or therapists. Though, in your case we are actually doing something. You wouldn't believe some of the calls we get though. I'm not even kidding. One time we had a mom call about her son because he wouldn't eat his dinner."

He looked at her like she had lost her mind. "That is ridiculous."

She nodded. "It was definitely ridiculous, and the woman got off with a warning from Dispatch and we didn't respond, but that kind of thing happens. We show up to a lot of places where it's just two adults yelling at each other over something stupid. Usually something involving money or cars. Things that seem really big in the moment, but once people are calm, it's not so important." She turned on her blinker and it clicked as she turned left and they made their way toward the bakery.

The bakery was closed for the day and they climbed up the rickety white open stairs on the side of the building to the second-floor apartment's front door. Emily knocked on the door beside the four-panel glass windows covered with a curtain yellowed with age but she was sure had once been white maybe thirty years ago.

There was a grumble from inside the apartment, but she couldn't quite make out what the person inside had been saying.

"Flathead County Sheriff's Office! Open the door!" she ordered, using a tone that clearly meant business but was one decibel from yelling. If the guys didn't want to play ball, that would be what would come next.

A man came to the door. He was wearing the same highlighter-yellow shirt that he had been wearing at The Mint and his face was still dirty. As the door swung open, she could see that he was holding a gold Coors Banquet beer can in his hand. "Something I can help you with?" he asked, looking surprised to see a sheriff's deputy standing on the other side of the door.

"Jake?" she asked.

"Larry." He lifted the can in his hand slightly. "Jake's in the shower. What did he do? He leave something at the bar?"

"No, actually I was hoping to ask you a few questions. You have a minute?"

The man gave her an appraising look, like he was trying to do a quick run-through of his life and think of every misdeed and decide if there was anything in his list of questionable actions that would get him arrested.

"As long as you work with me, you shouldn't have too much to worry about. I'd rather not drag you and your brother to jail tonight."

Larry gave her a little nod. "What do you need to know?" He stepped out of the door and onto the tiny porch with them. It was cramped with all three of them, but he closed the door behind him.

It made her wonder what he was hiding inside of his apartment, but without a search warrant or probable cause, there wasn't much she could do. "Do you recall the man from the bar, when we ran into you? He was seated a couple barstools down from you. Left in a hurry."

Larry nodded. "He was there when we got there after work. Didn't say much. Really nursed his beer. In fact, I think he only drank maybe one or two the whole time we were there."

"How long were you guys there?" she asked.

"Probably an hour and a half."

"Did he say anything to you?" She was half tempted to cross her fingers.

Larry leaned against the railing and crossed his arms over his chest in thought. "He said he was pissed off about something. Sounded like he was having problems with his girlfriend maybe."

"How do you know?"

"Some woman called him while we were sitting there. She sounded really upset. He was trying to calm her down. I don't really know what they were talking about, but he said he was gonna meet up with her later." He shrugged.

She tried to hide her excitement, but she shot Cameron a quick glance. He smiled at her like he, too, understood the significance of what the man had just told them. Perhaps the woman the man had been talking to was the same one who had left the hair tie in the barn. Maybe those two were responsible for killing Leonard and Ben. If she could get her hands on these two suspects, maybe she could get the answers Cameron so desperately needed and they could put this mystery to rest, and perhaps they could actually see if they could have a relationship.

There was a lot that rested on her ability to find answers.

"Did you catch either of their names?" she asked.

"I think he called her an odd woman's name. Something I hadn't heard before, but I couldn't tell you what it was. It was just really unique. I'd know it if I heard it again, though, you know?" Larry's face pinched slightly, like he felt bad that he couldn't be more help.

"No, that's good. Super helpful. Thank you for that," Emily said. "If you see the guy again, or if you remember the woman's name, I'd appreciate you giving me a call." She reached into her chest pocket and pulled out one of her business cards and handed it to the man. "My name and my office number and extension are right there if you need to get in touch."

He took it and shoved it in his back pocket.

She turned to go and then remembered why they had come in the first place. "Oh, wait," she said, stopping. "I need you to run down to The Mint and pay your tab. If you don't, I'm going to come back here and arrest you and your brother. You got it?"

Larry's face paled. "Yes, ma'am... I mean, Officer."

"It's Deputy Monahan." She sent him a half smile, attempting to take some of the chill off her words. "And keep ahead of your bar tab. He's trying to make a living. He doesn't need to be chasing down bills all the time. Got it?"

Larry nodded. "Yes, Deputy Monahan."

"I'll be checking, so get it done soon. Like, within the hour." She motioned for Cameron to start heading down the stairs. "You guys have a good night. And don't forget to not drink and drive, you might want to get to walking so you can make it there on time."

She made her way downstairs as she heard the door to the apartment close behind her. All things considered, that unexpected stop had gone surprisingly well. As Cameron walked in front of her, she also got the added benefit of seeing his trademark Copenhagen can mark in the back pocket of his Wranglers. Not that she was just looking at that circular mark.

He really was a sexy man.

It would be incredible to be able to wake up with him every day.

Even though they had discussed boundaries before they had even gotten to the hotel, she couldn't help herself now that she was walking with him. She couldn't stand the thought of him not having a safe place to go for the night. She waited until they were both safely tucked inside her car before she said anything. "So, what do you think about spending another night at my house?"

"Are you worried that Larry's going to come for you in the night?" he teased. "I have to say I don't think he was really that upset. If anything, the most upset I think he was about anything was that he was going to have to pay his tab."

She laughed. "I'm just confused how anybody could get that big of a bar tab? That's impressive when all he drinks is beer. And not even expensive beer."

"I don't think it's about the type of beer, I think it's about the quantity and the number of times he hit that bar." He made a pinched expression. "I know that when I was going through my divorce there were a couple of weeks that I put up some impressive tab numbers, too. Thankfully, I can safely say those days are behind me."

She didn't want to ask if they truly were, or if the reality of his new life hadn't set in. She had a feeling that when grief struck, he would have a harder time of it than he anticipated. However, if she was lucky and she was allowed to follow her heart, perhaps she could be the one to stand by his side and support him through this turmoil.

Chapter Fourteen

It had been a long day and though it was only dinnertime, Cameron was ready to get out of the police cruiser. Those seats were not made to sit in all day, at least not the passenger side. He hadn't wanted to complain to Emily, who had seemed content driving around and doing what had to be done for her job, but he was relieved when she asked if he wanted to call it a day and go pick up Stacy.

They pulled up in front of the garage and she turned off the engine. "Usually, I like to leave my car outside or down the street. It tends to keep any problems to a minimum."

He could understand the thinking, but he was also a touch surprised that it didn't elicit more vandalism by teenagers who didn't understand the ramifications of their behaviors and were on a mission to impress their friends through acts of rebellion. He and Ben hadn't done anything quite so dumb when they had been teens, but they had come darned close.

Emily stepped out and closed the door and he followed. "Speaking of neighbors, here comes Penny," Emily said, and he looked in the direction she was indicating.

There, walking toward them, was an older woman who was wearing a T-shirt with Whiskey Helps emblazoned across the front and a flag on the sleeve. Her gray hair was cut short into a pixie, and she was wearing a pair of men's Levi's. Surprisingly, the matronly woman didn't have the little girl in tow.

"Is Stacy taking a nap?" Emily asked, glancing instinctively down at her watch and scowling.

"No," Penny grumbled. "Didn't you get my text message?"

"No," Emily said, pulling out her phone. "What happened? Is Stacy okay?"

"Yeah, she is fine. But your jerk of an ex was just here. He took her. Said it was his night to keep her. I tried to stall him, but you know how well he and I get along." She made a *pfft* sound and rolled her eyes. "You didn't say anything about him picking her up, and I didn't want to let her go, but he was being a real tool."

"That, I can believe." Emily closed her eyes as she exhaled. She tilted her head back and rolled her neck like she was trying to stave off a headache. "Tonight isn't Todd's night and he knows it. I appreciate you trying to stall him. I'm sure he was in a hurry since he knew I was probably getting off work any minute."

Cameron was surprised. Todd hadn't seemed like the type of guy, at least from what Emily had told him and from what he had first seen, to want to fight for time with his kid—or to spontaneously want extra overnight stays. However, this wasn't the time to bring it up as it would probably only make Penny feel even worse about letting the girl slip out of her fingers.

Emily was texting on her phone. From where he stood, he could see she was texting Todd, though he couldn't see exactly what she was saying. However, from the speed of her fingers, she was furious, and Todd was getting a screenful.

Penny stood there awkwardly staring at Emily. Cameron

stepped up and offered her his hand in introduction. "By the way, Penny, my name is Cameron Trapper. Emily is working with me on a case. I've heard good things about you."

"The double homicide out at the cattle ranch?" Penny asked. She squinted her eyes and gave him a good once-over before she settled on his face. Her features relaxed as his gaze met hers.

"Yes, that's it." He would have asked how she knew, but it was a small town and his last name had been large at one time.

"Todd seemed to know that you spent the night here. He started to ask me to give him a call if you stayed again, but he stopped when he remembered who he was talking to," Penny said, puffing up her wide chest. "That man knows I wouldn't turn my steering wheel to save him if he was standing out in traffic."

Emily jerked her head up from her phone. "He said *what now*?"

Penny nodded. "You heard me right. I'm sure your daughter won't know not to say anything. Your goose is cooked if you wanted to keep that a secret."

Emily groaned. "Todd is going to have a field day with this one. I can't believe he already knew. What, does he have cameras planted around the house or something? *Gah*..." She went back to frantically texting.

He hoped she hadn't meant what she said, and she didn't really think Todd was the type of guy who would spy on her like that—or, more accurately, *stalk* her.

As for her texting, he couldn't tell whether Todd was replying, but it didn't seem to matter with the diatribe that Emily was sending.

He put his hand on her lower back. "Thanks for letting us know about Stacy. None of what happened was your fault.

We will get it all handled, Penny." It felt strange handling the situation with the neighbor in Emily's stead, given the fact that Penny had far more time with the little girl than he had, but in this case, he had to help Emily even if it meant his own discomfort.

Penny gave him an appreciative nod as if she understood what he was attempting to do and didn't take his dismissal as a slight. "If you need anything, even in the middle of the night, I'm around. Again, I'm sorry I let her go. I know you said it's not my fault, but I wish I coulda done more to help."

Emily looked up from her phone. "Seriously, not your fault. Todd is just...well, *Todd*." She said his name with a look of distaste.

Clearly, the women had spent many hours talking about the man and had developed a strong bond. He was glad that Emily had such a great neighbor and friend in her corner.

Penny turned to leave and head back to the blue two-story house next door that was similar in style but maybe a few years older than Emily's. As she reached the gate to her yard, she turned back. "And hey, don't forget, I have a gun if you need an extra shooter." She winked, but he could tell from the tone of her voice that she was only kind of kidding.

It made him like her even more.

Emily relaxed under his hand as Penny waved goodbye and walked into her house.

"I can't believe Todd did this. He couldn't give two—"

"Has he done this type of thing before?"

"Taken Stacy without letting me know?" She shook her head. "Never."

That was concerning. "Have you brought guys home after your divorce?"

She looked down at her phone, clicked off the screen

and shoved it in her back pocket. "Who I have over here, or don't have over here, is none of Todd's business."

"That's not what I asked."

She looked away from him and then started to walk toward the door. "I haven't. Plus, Todd and I were supposed to meet with the mediator this week. We were modifying the parenting plan. He has been fighting for more hours. I think he is just playing games."

"And yet he just dropped her off to you during your workday?"

She shrugged. "He may have done that because he knew I wouldn't be able to watch her. That I'd have to give her to Penny. He could show the mediator that I don't actually care about my child—or something. Sometimes the things he does...well, they don't even make sense to me. He can be really manipulative and twisted."

"It sounds like you made the right decision in getting a divorce."

She nodded, but she didn't look back at him until she was inside. She waited for him to follow her in before she closed the door behind him and slipped the chain lock in place. "I've never had a regret when it comes to that. My only regret is that I have to put Stacy through this. He is using her like a pawn—clearly."

"You think he is just trying to mess with you by using her? Or do you think he really is trying to get more time with Stacy?"

She walked into the kitchen, poured herself a glass of water and downed it in one long drink. "I don't know what he is thinking, really. He isn't making anything easy. I thought all of this was behind me when the divorce was finalized. I didn't really think we would have to be back in lawyer's offices so soon after things were done and the decree was finalized. However, I think that he likes to control me this way."

Cameron had gone through so many emotions in the last day, but none was as strong as the anger he was feeling right now. He couldn't change or affect what had happened at the ranch, but he could still make a difference when it came to Emily and her daughter. Maybe he could still help them.

If he saw Todd again, he would be hard-pressed not to teach the guy one heck of a lesson.

"Has he texted you back?"

She shook her head.

"Do you know where he is living, or where he would have taken her?"

She sighed. "I already texted his mom. That is where he has been living. She hasn't seen him today, but she said she would let me know if they showed up. She is a bit of a drive away and, if they just left here, they may go and get dinner and then head out that way. He is probably ignoring me on purpose. It may be a couple hours until we hear anything."

"I know you probably don't want to go down this road, but if in a situation like this—without you guys agreeing on his taking Stacy with you—couldn't that constitute kidnapping?"

"We share custody, and it would get into a *he-said, she-said* battle because we are currently trying to renegotiate the parenting plan. It wouldn't go well, and it would end up looking bad for both of us if we ended up in court over it. It's best if we just get along—or, in this case, I just let him have his way." She ran her hand over the back of her neck as she looked up at the ceiling for a moment.

He felt bad for her.

"I'm sorry, Emily."

"Why are you sorry?" She frowned at him as she sat her glass back down on the counter.

"I'm sorry that I might be part of the reason he is messing with you and putting you and your daughter in danger. I didn't mean to make trouble in your private life. If you need, I can just head out. I can get a taxi to a different, more *upscale* hotel." He smiled, but even to him the action felt tired.

"You didn't cause this. Plus, I think Stacy is safe. I don't think Todd would do anything to hurt Stacy. He says he loves her."

"Are you sure that he wouldn't hurt her?" he asked, not wanting to scare her but concerned after everything that she had told him.

From the look on her face, she was thinking about all the ways Todd could hurt her when it came to her daughter. As a law enforcement officer, she had to know only too well what humans were capable of.

She chewed on her lip. "I know we just got here, but would you be okay if we swung over by Todd's place?"

As badly as he wanted to stay put and have a night alone with Emily, he nodded. "I thought you might want to do that." He opened the door and stepped outside. "I hope you know I'm worried about Stacy, too."

Since Todd hadn't left Penny's that long before they had arrived, it was possible that if they hurried, they could catch up with him on the highway.

She walked outside and they jogged to the car. They drove in stony silence for a few minutes until Emily finally cleared her throat. "Todd's mom's name is Alice. She's very nice, but Todd's dad was a lot like him."

"Do you mean cruel?" He couldn't believe that they had

started out with him being interrogated by her and now he was the one asking the tough questions.

"I think that he was raised by a narcissistic father and some of those characteristics were passed down." She pulled onto the highway. "Alice wasn't overly heartbroken when her husband died of a heart attack a few years ago. She didn't even end up having a memorial service for him."

He could understand the woman's feelings for a variety of reasons. His thoughts went back to his father and his brother, and it suddenly felt like he had taken a fist straight to the gut.

For a moment, he had found reprieve from his own life, but the hit had come out of nowhere.

He'd heard that happened with grief—that it was a blow that would just randomly land. Whomever had told him that in the past had been right. He was just lucky he was sitting down, in an uncomfortable seat or not.

Emily reached over and put her hand out palm up, expectantly. "Things will get easier. At least, that's what Alice told me."

He had no idea how she knew what he was thinking about and what he was feeling, but as he took her hand and gripped her fingers protectively, he was glad that she could read him so well. "I appreciate hearing that."

"If you don't want to have a service for your brother, and you just want to do kind of what Alice did… I'll be there by your side if you want. Or, if you want to have a party…like an Irish send-off or a party for you, whatever you need. I've got you."

He laughed and some of the ache in his chest receded. She really was one hell of a woman.

"I'm thinking Jameson whiskey at The Mint. I bet Tim will throw us a deal if Larry actually pays his tab." He smiled.

"Heidi thought you were pretty cute," she teased.

He quirked his brow. "Oh, yeah?"

"You want me to get her number for you?"

He leaned back, surprised that she would offer such a thing when her hand was in his. "Are you kidding me right now? Why would you say something like that?"

She giggled. "What? Are you saying that you aren't interested in Heidi?" She gave him an appraising glance.

"Oh," he said, realizing what she was getting at. "I'm not interested in Heidi… There is a woman I am interested in, and I'm looking forward to getting to know her a lot better if and when she gives me a chance."

Emily smiled. "I think you have a pretty good shot with an answer like that."

He kissed her fingers and as he did, he was reminded of how much he appreciated being around her. She could turn his sorrow around with simply a smile and as long as he'd been dating, he couldn't remember a woman who'd ever had that type of effect on him. It had to mean something.

Her face went serious for a moment and she looked as though she wanted to say something, but instead, she sucked in a breath and squeezed his hand.

"You know, you can tell me anything. You can trust me," he said. "I'd hope by now I've proven myself."

She looked at him. "I know." Her phone buzzed and she let go of his hand as she pulled it out of her pocket. As she did, he spotted the name Bullock.

"Hello?" she answered.

There was a grumble of a man's voice. Bullock spoke for a long time as Emily drove down the highway. She nodded a few times as she gave "yes, sirs" and "no, sirs" as if the detective could see her through the phone.

She told him about Stacy being taken. Bullock's tone

grew deeper, and though he couldn't hear the man's words, Cameron could tell her colleague was angry.

As Emily pulled down a dirt road, she said her farewells and hung up with the detective. She stared out the window for a long minute as she drove. He wanted to ask her what he'd had to say, but it wasn't his place.

She pulled to a stop in front of an old ranch-style house. There was a '90s era Buick parked in front. Its front end was rusted and the rear bumper was crushed where it must have been in an accident sometime in the past.

"Is this Alice's place?" he asked.

Emily nodded, but she didn't speak as she got out of the car.

She was so quiet and so *off* that a lump formed in his stomach. Before Bullock had called, they had been talking about a relationship. Now she wasn't even speaking to him. He was confused. What had the detective found that could have upset her so much? Was it something at the scene that she didn't want to tell him?

He wasn't sure if she wanted him to stay in the car or follow her to the front door, so he stayed in place. Given the situation with Todd, he didn't want to make things worse or give the man more fodder for manipulation. If anything, he should have waited at the end of the road or something so, if Todd was here, he wouldn't have seen him in the car.

Then again, they had nothing to hide. Todd could take his judgment and anger and shove it. Emily was a grown and divorced woman who was free to date any man she wanted. Well, she was free to date any man she wasn't investigating.

Maybe *that* was what was bothering her. Perhaps Bullock had reminded her about the implications of their relationship if this case went to court and they were put on the stand and forced to answer questions presented by a defense attorney.

He'd already compromised her enough with Todd and her daughter, but dammit if he didn't want to still take her in his arms and make everything bad that was happening in their lives disappear.

Chapter Fifteen

Emily stood on Alice's front porch for a long moment. She hesitated to knock on the door. She knew Alice had undoubtedly heard them drive up, may even have watched them through a crack in the window coverings.

Yet she wasn't ready to face her former mother-in-law.

It wasn't that she didn't like Alice—in fact, she was the only person in Todd's family she could still have a somewhat amiable conversation with. Rather, it was the fact that she had to be here at all that was rubbing her the wrong way. There were a ton of other things she could have been doing and yet Alice's son had insisted on creating problems where there shouldn't have been any.

Emily thought about the conversation she'd had with Cameron. She might have been wrong in telling him the truth about Todd and his manipulative behaviors. It was too much, too soon. She wasn't a girl who needed rescuing, or pity. At the same time, she didn't want Cameron thinking that she was a bad mom or that this was some strange game Todd was playing in an attempt to win her back.

She looked at the car one more time and Cameron smiled up at her. He was a good man. If she was in a better place in her life, he would have been the perfect guy. Her mind flashed to their kiss. That kiss had been the most perfect moment in her life, aside from moments with her daughter, in years.

She couldn't think about that now. She had to focus on the safety of her daughter. And she had to get things under control with Todd. Obviously, he wanted to create problems. Whether it was because of Cameron or because of something else that he had drummed up in his mind, it appeared as though he was making it his mission to punish her.

Todd's truck wasn't outside, but that didn't mean Stacy wasn't there. Knowing him, he'd grabbed her and then just handed her off to his mother after he'd put on a big show to make himself look better. For all she knew, maybe he had a new woman in his life and that was what this was all about. Or it could have been for the judge, or a combination of both. Who knew with Todd.

She knocked on the door, violently hoping that Stacy would come running to answer. She was met with the sound of heavy footfalls from the other side of the closed door. The locks clicked and as the door creaked open, Alice came into view. She was wearing a hot-pink body suit that clung to her like Saran wrap. For being in her late sixties, she looked great.

Alice looked surprised to see her. "Emily, what's happening?"

"I know you said you'd give us a call if Todd showed up, but I'm really worried about Stacy. Have you heard from or seen them at all?"

Alice put her hand on her hip as she stared out at Cameron. She furrowed her brow and, for a moment, she looked a lot like her son.

"Honey," she said, taking her by the arm and leading her inside as she shut the door behind them—but not before throwing one more look of disgust out at Cameron.

Alice motioned for her to follow her into the kitchen. The house was modular, the kind that had been produced in the late '90s and sold in mass quantities. While it was nice, it had already started to show signs of breaking down faster than a traditionally built home. Alice had needed to replace the roof and some of the trusses, which, she'd explained to Emily, had cost her nearly as much as the house had originally cost to purchase.

In the corner of the living room, there was a plastic Playskool toy box overflowing with toys, most of which Emily recognized as hand-me-downs from when Todd had been a child and were now Stacy's. On top was a Hulk fist that was faded and stitched where Todd had once punched it through a bathroom mirror.

Looking back, she had made some horrible decisions in her life. It wasn't like there hadn't been plenty of red flags when it came to Todd, she had just been too blind and too young to see them.

Alice's kitchen was barely stocked, as per usual. But she had her trademark bottle of Tito's and club soda in the refrigerator, which she grabbed out and started to pour without asking. She handed a glass of vodka and soda to Emily before pouring herself one as well.

"I know you like lime in yours, but I'm fresh out. Sorry." She didn't sound like she really cared. If anything, she sounded like she was glad that Emily had provided her with an excuse to pour a drink.

If Todd was her son, she'd want to drink, too. She wondered if Alice was embarrassed about her son's behavior, and that was where her reaction was stemming from.

"Thanks for the drink," Emily said, raising the glass but not taking a sip as she was still in uniform even though she was off the clock. "You didn't answer my question though. Have you heard from your son?"

Alice didn't seem to be able to meet her eyes. It didn't help quell the fear Emily was feeling. "If you know something, Alice, please tell me. You must understand how I'm feeling. My child is missing."

Alice pinched the bridge of her nose and let out a long sigh. She closed her eyes and leaned against the counter, letting it support her weight. "He called right before you got here. I talked to him about what was going on. He didn't want me to tell you, but he is running up to Canada."

Emily's hand holding the drink started to shake with rage and the liquid sloshed over her fingers, forcing her to put the glass down on the counter. Now it was Emily who was forced to put both hands on the surface to hold herself in place. She was going to kill him.

How could her ex-husband kidnap their child and abscond to Canada? What if he never came back? She'd heard horror stories about mothers and fathers being torn from children's lives forever just like this. Once a child left the country, it was incredibly difficult and very expensive to get them back. Todd knew it, too.

He had stolen her child.

"Where did he go?" she asked, trying not to let her fear and anger turn to tears.

"He wanted to take her fishing in Fernie," Alice said.

"Fishing? Seriously?" Emily couldn't think of more than a handful of times Todd had ever gone fishing. And he had certainly never taken Stacy fishing before. She didn't even have a rod. It made all her warning bells go off.

"Do you know where he's staying there?" Emily asked, trying to stay calm. She would need as much information as she could get to give to the Royal Canadian Mounted Police in order to get her daughter back.

Alice put her hand on top of Emily's. "I don't know if this is going to make you feel better or not, but Todd is seeing a new woman. She lives up in Fernie. I think that is why he's really going up there."

Emily let out a long exhale. Strangely enough, the fact that her ex-husband was dating someone new was actually a relief. It didn't feel quite so much like he was trying to steal her daughter. They weren't out of the woods; he still had to come back with her. But she was less afraid that they would be gone forever. Todd was still Todd.

"So, you don't think he's really fishing?" She looked over at Alice and finally decided to take a long drink from the proffered vodka. One drink wouldn't hurt.

"I think the only thing he's really fishing for is his new girlfriend's approval. Though he may or may not actually go fishing to impress her. You know how these things work." She gave half-hearted shrug and a wave of the hand.

If he was trying to impress a new woman, he wouldn't want Stacy to get hurt and she found comfort in the thought. At least that was one fear that she could take off her plate.

"Do you know when he was planning on coming back?" she asked. "When does he have to work?"

"I think he works in a couple days, but I'm just taking a guess." Alice looked over at the calendar hanging on the wall like it would hold the answer, but it showed nothing. "Here's the deal, honey. You and I both know that Todd loves your daughter—regardless of the mess you two have going. He screwed up here. He shouldn't have taken her without talking to you first, but he isn't great at dealing with things sometimes."

"He can't just take my daughter."

"She's his daughter, too."

Rage roiled within her. Alice wasn't wrong, and she wasn't going to argue with her over that point. However, there were rules about healthy parenting and co-parenting and until he learned to follow them, she would have to take the steps necessary to make sure he would never be able to pull something like this again.

If Emily could prove that Stacy had gone with him unwillingly, she could wrap him up with possible kidnapping charges. Then she could have an Amber Alert placed for Stacy. And then, hopefully, her daughter could be back in her arms by the end of the night. She would also probably never have to worry about sharing custody with Todd—and he would likely be heading for prison.

The other options she had were to have him charged with parental interference when he got back. Or, have nothing happen at all through the courts and legal system, and they could simply talk and go over what he could and couldn't do in the future.

She pulled out her phone and texted him again, begging him to respond and to let her know where he was with Stacy and when they would be back. Her response would be based on his—the ball was in his court.

With her anger what it was, she wanted to string him up. However, between the two of them, she had to be the responsible and levelheaded parent. And she had to keep in mind what was truly best for Stacy. She wasn't totally convinced that included time with her father at this present second, but maybe Emily would change when her daughter was safely tucked back in her arms.

Todd just didn't think sometimes, or ever, depending on who a person asked.

She sighed and put her phone back in her pocket.

Alice emptied her glass and poured herself another.

"Wait," Emily said, pushing her nearly full glass over. "You can have mine. I'm not going to finish it. I need to go. We just both need to hope that Todd makes the right choice and Stacy is returned safe."

Chapter Sixteen

Emily walked into her house, stripped off her utility belt and laid it down on the table next to the front door. It felt good to feel the weight leave her hips and lower back. She leaned forward, shifting her weight until she heard popping sounds.

It had been one hell of a long day.

"It will all be okay. I'm sure he'll be back tomorrow. He has to know that his ass is on the line. Did you tell him you are going to get law enforcement involved if he doesn't respond?" Cameron asked, walking in behind her and closing her front door.

She watched his tanned hands work as he slid the gold chain into place, securing the front door. It was silly to put so much faith in such a silly little chain to keep her safe. A chain wasn't about to stop someone who was hell-bent on coming into her house if they wanted. Yet it helped her sleep better at night. It was funny how a person told themselves trivial lies in order to comfort themselves, even when they knew better.

It was so much like what she was telling herself about Todd right now.

"Yes, he'll be back. He knows what he's doing is wrong." She smiled, wishing she had her own bottle of Tito's here to quell all her nerves. There would be no sleep in her world tonight. Stacy was safe, but it killed Emily that she didn't know where exactly she was.

Cameron took her by the hand. He walked her into the living room and stood her by the couch. He put his hands down on her hips. "I promise you, I'm not going to do anything you don't ask for or want. I am only going to try to be here for you. Okay?"

Every part of her sparked. Energy coursed through her body and she clenched with lust. Yet she held back. She didn't need more chaos, but she could let him supplicate her tonight and help her relax.

He reached toward her. "Is it okay if I unbutton your shirt?" he asked, smiling.

She sucked her bottom lip into her mouth and she stepped back until she touched the top of the couch, where she rested her weight. She nodded.

He started at the top button. He slowly moved the smooth little plastic piece through the threaded hole with his thick, callused fingers before moving to the next and the next. She watched his hands work. There was something so sexy about his hands. They were dark and tanned; the color of treated leather.

His fingernails were thick and kept short, but round and clean. The tips of his fingers were rough from years of hard work and they made a scraping sound as he worked against the polyester fabric of her shirt. The soft sound made her body contract and ache as she thought of those textured fingers working her in more forbidden places.

She made a soft, moaning groan as she reached up and threaded her fingers through his hair and lifted his cowboy hat. With her left hand, she pulled it off and flung it over to the recliner. He could get that later.

He pulled her shirt loose from her pants forcibly, tugging and making her panties pull against her. She giggled at the sweet and welcome sensation.

"I should have guessed that you liked it just a touch hard." He smirked, the look on his face so sexy that she wanted to rip his clothes off and finish him, but she stopped herself.

He was only there to help her relax. That didn't mean they were taking things to the bedroom—unless she decided.

She was in control.

Cameron reached up and slid the shirt free of her shoulders and down off her arms. It tickled her skin, making her flesh prickle as he pulled it free. He folded it delicately as he sat it on the top of the couch beside her, taking his time, as if he was enjoying making her wait.

He smiled at her. "May I remove your gun?" he asked, pointing at her Glock in the bellyband at her waist.

She nodded.

He waggled his finger, motioning for her to turn slightly so he could reach behind her to loosen the Velcro. It made a ripping sound as he pulled it loose and removed the thick elastic band. He lifted the gun free of her and the cool evening air flowed against her sweaty skin. It always felt so strange taking that gun off. She felt at her most vulnerable—even being without clothing was less uncomfortable than being without a weapon.

She wanted to reach for it for a brief second, and her fingers instinctively moved. However, she stopped herself as she watched him carefully wrap the gun in the bellyband and place it gently on top of her shirt, the barrel facing away from them.

Reaching up, she ran her hand over her skin feeling the

sweaty spot where the gun had sat. It was strange how something so foreign could become part of a person. It was like a limb and, even though it was not there, she could still feel its phantom weight.

He knelt in front of her and untied her boots. She put her hands on his shoulders to steady herself and she could feel his well-defined muscles working. The sensation did nothing for her resolve to keep him from her bed.

Pulling her boots free, he walked them over to the front door and, bending over, he sat them straight and aligned on the mat. She stared at his round ass, the mark on his jeans more noticeable than ever. The funny thing was, she had never seen him chew. Did they make jeans with the mark on them now?

He readjusted the boots, making the toes touch. It seemed a little overdone, and it made her wonder if he knew she was watching him and he was showing off for her. It made her like him more. It wasn't as though he needed to try for that to happen; she liked him so much already it was becoming painful.

He stood up and turned to face her, sending her his trademark smirk. "What happens next is completely up to you. I can rub your feet, or I can rub your back. That is, if you'd like me to."

He knew damn well she wasn't going to pass an offer like that up. If he was like most guys, this massage would last about two minutes and then it would turn into something else entirely. However, feeling the way she was, it may not have been Cameron leading things in that direction. In fact, he was the one who wasn't pushing things that way.

She wasn't used to having this kind of control over men. She could get used to it.

"Let's take a shower. Then my room," she said, pointing down the hall.

"Whoa." He actually looked surprised at her being so forward. "Are you sure that's where you wanna go?"

"I didn't say let's get naked. I just wanna relax and feel the water on my skin. If you're going to rub my back, it seems like the best place." She sent him a coy smile that she hoped was at least half as sexy as the one he was giving her.

Two could play his teasing game.

She took him by the hand, lacing their fingers together and walked in front of him. She turned around and walked backward down the hall, playfully smiling at him as she pulled her hair free of her ponytail and brushed it loose with her fingers so it fell freely over her shoulders.

It felt good to have it brush against her skin.

He stared at her as she moved her hips and they neared the bathroom. "Do you have any freaking clue how beautiful you are? Has anyone ever told you?"

She shook her head.

"You are," he said, sounding a little breathless. "You are the most beautiful woman I have ever seen. You are stunning."

She tried not to blush, but the way he was looking at her together with his words made the heat rise in her cheeks. There was no doubt he meant what he was saying, and it made her swoon.

This man was perfect. He was everything she wanted.

Well, except maybe one thing.

Truth be told, as much as she appreciated a man who respected her boundaries and didn't want to take things any further than she felt comfortable, she also wanted a man who knew what he wanted and wasn't afraid to take it—and that also meant *her*.

Confused by all her feelings, wants and desires, she turned away from him and walked into her bathroom and turned on the shower. It was just as she had left it this morning, her makeup lined up according to usage and everything in its exact place.

She pulled out an extra fluffy white towel and laid it on the counter for him.

If she was about to take the next step with Cameron, she wanted to make sure she was giving it the right amount of thought and making a good decision.

Then again, who was she kidding? She had made the decision that she would to take things to the next level with him the minute she'd let him start undressing her. However, she wasn't going to be the one to make the first move. If he didn't take what he wanted, she wasn't going to ask. She wasn't the type of woman who wanted to be dominant, at least not usually.

She turned her back to him as she looked in the mirror and pushed a wayward hair behind her ear. He started to massage her back over her sweaty tank top, but the ridges of her shirt pressed into her skin.

She wanted to take it off, but the idea went against her resolve.

He kept rubbing, moving down to her hips, then down her to her lower back. His touch felt so good, and she felt her body relaxing against the counter in front of her. This was what she needed.

She became so relaxed she closed her eyes, she wasn't sure how she was still standing, but she didn't care.

He moved up to her back, starting on her shoulders again. "If you're comfortable, you can take off some of your extra clothes. I could do a better job in the shower—with a little lather." He sent her a sexy smile in the mirror.

"So, you want to see me naked?" She was done playing. *In or out?*

He chuckled. "I don't just want to see you naked. I want to be buried between your thighs."

Game on.

She moved away from his touch and turned around to face him. In one fluid motion, she pulled her tank top over her head, exposing her black bra. Reaching down to her pants, she unbuttoned the top.

"Stop right there," he ordered.

She looked up with wide eyes. Had he changed his mind when he'd seen her take off her top?

He folded her into his arms, taking his lips with hers and devouring her. She forgot everything but his touch and the way his warm body felt against her exposed skin.

His tongue flicked against hers, making her mind race to all the places his tongue could travel on her body...and all the things he could make her feel.

She wanted it all—all of him.

"I undress you, if you are giving me the honor of you."

His words were so proper and so perfect, and she loved his perspective. She had lost the reality that giving her body to another person was just that—an honor. In return, his giving his to her was the same. Their choosing to do this would mean something; it wouldn't be like most relationships of this generation—it wouldn't be a one-night stand, it wouldn't be meaningless sex or a situationship.

She leaned in and their kiss met in the middle.

She unbuttoned his shirt and pushed it off his shoulders and let it hit the floor behind him, then she unzipped his pants. She pushed them down, exposing his blue boxers, which were working hard to hold his body in check. He was blessed with more than any man she had ever seen, so much that it made her heart race. Hopefully, their bodies would fit in the ways they both needed.

He looked to her for approval.

"Yes," she said, smiling wide. "Oh...*yes*."

He beamed. "I'm glad you like what you see."

She couldn't wait to feel him.

He reached for her and unbound her pants and let them fall atop his. Her panties were almost the same color as his boxers, and it seemed like a good sign. He pulled off his boxers.

Cameron ran his finger along the top of her panties and pulled her closer, making her gasp. He kissed her as he pushed his fingers down until he found her. He ran his fingers over her, rubbing her and making her moan in his mouth.

He pulled his hand out of her panties. He moved and pulled her panties down her legs.

They stepped inside the shower and let the warm water wash over their bodies as they found each other.

He worked her like she was a joystick, rolling and rubbing in just the right ways. She pressed into his hand, making him move harder against her and his hand filled with water and intensified the sensation. "More," she begged.

Her head swam with endorphins. He smiled at her as pressed her body against the wall and he dropped to his knees in front of her and then put her left leg over his shoulder.

His mouth found her.

She pressed her head back against the wall, floating on the sensation of his tasting her. Just when she thought it couldn't get better, he stood up and found her with his body. He pressed inside her, making her gasp.

He moved slowly at first, letting her get used to him.

She moved together with him, wrapping her legs around him, pulling him deeper and reveling in the sweet pain that came with him filling every space within her.

He felt so good, and he grew harder inside her, making her wonder if he was close. Just as she wondered if he was going to finish, he paused and—without pulling out—he moved to the floor of the shower until she was atop and the water was pouring down her back.

She was riding her cowboy like he was her bronc, and she loved every single second of it. But as she rolled her hips, she knew she wouldn't last long. He fit her perfectly, as if he was made just for her.

Every cell of her body begged for release as the pressure intensified. She started to slow, but instead of letting her wait, Cameron took hold of her hips and moved her body for her, driving her with him. With his hands strong on her hips, he worked her body until they finished, their bodies shaking together.

Chapter Seventeen

Last night was hands down the best of his life—and not just because of the sex, but that had been the best, too. Cameron was busy doing their breakfast dishes as Emily came down the hallway still drying her hair with a towel after this morning's shower—which had only reminded her of all the positions he'd had her in only hours before.

"Thanks for doing that. You didn't need to clean up." She walked over and kissed him on the cheek like this was just their normal morning.

They were the picture of domestic bliss and he loved it. This was definitely something he could get used to.

"Did you talk to Bullock?" he asked.

She wrapped the towel around her head. Even without a single drop of makeup and without her hair done, she was just as beautiful as the first moment he had seen her. She would always be.

"Yeah, I talked to him for a few before your shower. They found the guy from the bar, his name is Eli Schuster."

"Did they arrest him?"

"Yes, but not for the murders. They found him at the Arrow Lodge. He was one of the *guests*. The woman at the bar was the one we had seen before at the hotel." She sighed. "They are going to question him about everything, but as of now, it doesn't sound like he knows anything."

"What happened to the woman?"

She shrugged. "On another note, Bullock has decided to open your ranch back up so you can get back in for your animals." There was a touch of sadness in her voice.

He understood; the sadness was echoed in his soul. He nodded as if it was all he could do.

"He also said more of the fingerprints came back. It was actually kind of weird." She grabbed a rag and started to wipe down the countertop.

"What do you mean *weird*?"

She shrugged. "Well, it's not a huge surprise, but a lot of the fingerprints came back both as yours and as Trevor's."

He nodded. "Yeah. I'm in the house quite a bit. Though, I hadn't been in there that morning."

"I recalled you saying that." She wiped down the stove and walked over to rinse the rag before hanging it over the faucet. "When was the last time you know Trevor was in the house?"

He shrugged. "Trevor had his kid that day. He may have gone in there that morning, but I don't know. Did Bullock question him? If he hasn't, I'm sure I can get Trevor to come in and talk to him."

"Yeah, let's set that up. I am sure once we do, we can make sense of why he had so many prints in the house."

"So, none of that is really weird…" he continued, pressing her.

"Well, there is another set of prints that aren't coming up as linked to anyone in our database. They searched all night."

"That's good, isn't it?" he asked, pushing the dishwasher

closed and wiping off his hands. The news brought him a renewed sense of excitement.

"It is, but it isn't. We know that it is very possible there is someone else that may be involved with their deaths, and you may be cleared. However, it means that we have nowhere to start in identifying them. To get them, we will just have to get lucky."

"Is there a way you can figure out if a fingerprint is a man or a woman's, you know…based on size or something?" He felt stupid for asking, but he honestly didn't know.

"No, because sizes vary by person—even age. There are a tremendous number of variables."

He nodded. It made complete sense.

"But, on another positive note, if we bring someone in and they match, we are in the money." She smiled widely and it brought thoughts of her on top of him flash in his mind.

She was a beautiful woman.

"If I've learned anything in the last twelve hours, it's that I'm a very lucky man." He walked behind her and put his hand on her hip, kissing her neck.

She put her hand on the side of his face and leaned into his kiss as she smiled. "I'm the lucky one." She kissed him. "I do need to get to work though. Plus, I need to try to get in touch with Todd again. He hasn't texted, but he's been posting pictures of Stacy on social media."

It was something. At least they could find some comfort in the fact that her daughter was safe, even though her ex was a total jerk. He was impressed with how levelheaded she was in handling the situation. He didn't know how he would have been, as he didn't have a child himself and he certainly wasn't in a position that he could pass judgment. However, he was furious for Emily and Stacy wasn't even his daughter.

He considered that for a moment.

What would it be like to have a child? And what about a child that wasn't biologically his?

He wouldn't care who the baby belonged to by genes. He would love them the same—especially Stacy. He already loved her. And as for her mom...

He looked over at Emily and smiled.

She smiled at him. "I'm going to go finish my hair, then we can hit the road. You ready?"

He nodded, but the truth was that he never wanted to leave this stolen moment of bliss. He didn't want to go back to the ranch. If it wasn't for his family's honor, their legacy and the need to find justice, he would have been happy to live here, waiting for Stacy to be returned, forever.

He watched her as she made her way to the bedroom.

While he waited, he called Trevor.

He answered on the second ring even though it was early in the morning. "How's it going, man?"

"Good. You running the cattle up today?" he asked.

"I was planning on it. Did you want to join me?"

Cameron stared down the hallway. He had never missed a chance to move the cattle. It was one of the most fun experiences of the year. It was a lot of work and Trevor would need the extra hands, but he also didn't want to leave Emily—especially when she still hadn't heard from Todd about her daughter.

"I'll let you know."

"Where are you?" Trevor asked.

He looked at Stacy's newborn announcement that was framed and hanging in the hallway. "I'm working on the murders."

"So, you're with *her*." Trevor chuckled. "It's okay. She's hot. I get it."

"Whatever, man. You just worry about the cows. They need to get up to the mountains."

"They aren't the only ones thinking about mountains right now," Trevor said, laughing. "Enjoy those peaks. You know where to find me." He hung up the phone.

It didn't take long for Emily to get ready and when she came out, her hair was pulled tight against her head. She walked to the front door and put on her boots, then came over to the couch and picked up her bellyband and strapped it around her waist and followed it with her utility belt and her uniform shirt.

"Who were you talking to?" she asked.

"Trevor." He smiled. "He is going to move the cows for me."

She nodded. "I bet you're relieved. I know you've been worried about them."

"Every day we wait is a day that we may end up having to possibly hay them in the winter. It's lost revenues. My dad already cost us a ton of money—or at least I thought he had." His thoughts went to the strange money exchanges in his father's bank account. So many things just didn't make sense. "Did Bullock look into my father's financial records?"

"I bet. I haven't asked him, but that is always one of the first things they pull. That, and cell phone records. Don't worry, he is pretty thorough. He's good at his job."

"I have no doubt. He seems like he is patient with you, like he is trying to bring you up the ranks."

"He is a good teacher. I don't know about wanting to bring me up, but I do think he wants to make sure I'm good at my job and an asset to the team. My being proficient is good for everyone and good for families."

"Would you want to be a detective?" he asked.

She thought for a moment. "It would be a lot of extra work and responsibility, and I'm not sure how it would affect my time with Stacy, but if I could do it without interfering with my parenting, yes. I enjoy the work."

"You are great at it," he said.

Smiling at him, she clicked her belt and adjusted everything into place. "And you are a fantastic man."

As they made their way outside, Emily's phone rang. She stopped midstride. "Todd! Where the hell are you?" she exclaimed, answering the phone.

As badly as Cameron wanted to listen in on the phone call, it wasn't his business. He kept walking and leaned against her cruiser, waiting for her. From the expression on her face as she spoke to her ex-husband, she was furious. She had every right.

He wanted to reach through the phone for her.

At least the man was calling. For once, he was doing something right.

Emily looked over at him and put her finger up, indicating that she would just be a second. He waved her off. She could take just as much time as she needed. That man needed a tongue-lashing that only she could adequately provide.

He kept catching expletives, and it made him smile. The man deserved to be called every name in the book. After a few minutes, some of her anger seemed to abate and from what he could hear, it sounded as though Todd was on his way back over the border. Fernie was only a three-hour drive from where they were, so it wouldn't take long for Stacy to be back home and safe.

He still couldn't believe that the man had taken the little girl over an international border without clear permission from her mother. Until now, he hadn't even thought to ask her about a passport, but Todd must have had one for Stacy. In the end, it didn't matter. All that mattered was he had done what he had done. Now Stacy just needed to remain safe. Until she was back, though, he couldn't relax. Clearly, Todd wasn't the type of person Cam could assume would make the right decisions.

He couldn't take anything for granted with this guy, and neither could Emily.

She hung up the phone. Before putting it away, she made a quick call to Penny. He tried not to listen in, but he could hear her letting her neighbor know to keep an eye out for Todd in case he decided to swing by her house and drop Stacy off without warning. Penny said something and she sounded relieved in the background as they said goodbye.

Emily shoved the phone back into her back pocket. She lifted her chin up toward the sky, closing her eyes. She let out a long breath and it sounded almost like a growl. She needed a moment, and he respected that.

After she collected herself, she made her way over to him and they both got into the car in relative silence. "Well, at least Alice was right. Todd was just trying to impress some chick. I'm sure I'm not done having it out with him. But he should have Stacy home soon."

"I'm glad to hear it."

"He also knew that you would spend the night, again. Apparently, he has his spies working overtime." She put the car into gear and got the show on the road.

He didn't know what to say about their being watched. However, it made him deeply uncomfortable. It was a small town, and it wasn't like his truck was outside. So, whomever was feeding Todd information had to have seen him walk into her house or else they had been looking in a window. Either way, people were paying close attention.

"I'm sorry, Emily. I shouldn't have stayed here last night, but I'm not sorry about what happened between us. I won't apologize for that. Ever." He reached his hand over and she slipped hers in his.

"And you don't have to. That was incredible. I didn't know I could feel like that. You awaken parts of me…" The car accelerated slightly. "As for spies, I don't care. He's going to do whatever he's going to do anyways. I still have the upper hand. And it's not like he's not dating someone, too."

Cameron grinned. He loved that she said they were dating. He wasn't sure that he wanted to call it to her attention though. "Exactly. Screw him."

She tapped her fingers on the steering wheel.

When they arrived at the ranch, theirs was the only police vehicle. Though he had known that it had been cleared, and it was no longer considered a crime scene, it still felt like one. He half expected Detective Bullock to come walking out of the barn as they stopped.

Trevor's pickup was parked beside the barn, where he must have been inside getting ready to take the cattle out.

"I was hoping to do a walk-through in the house, do you mind?" Emily asked. "I've gone through the pictures a ton of times, but I feel like I'm missing something."

He nodded. "Help yourself. In fact, I'll go in with you. I haven't been in the house since before everything happened. I've been wondering what everything looks like and what I was going to have to deal with when I got back inside."

"I should warn you," she said, "we don't clean up crime scenes. So, your house is probably going to be a mess. I know there was some blood where your brother went down. You need to be prepared for what you might walk into."

She put her hand on his and gave it a squeeze before letting it fall away.

"I just appreciate you being here. This would be a hell of a thing having to face it alone."

She nodded and, as she moved, a tendril of hair fell into her face, the effect making her look less like a deputy and more like the woman he had come to know so well last night.

"Before we run in there, though, let's check on Trevor." He pointed at the barn. "Maybe, if you're not too busy, we can help him move the cattle. It's a lot easier with more hands, but I know you have to work and there's a lot of things you need to do. So don't feel pressured. I'd much rather you find the people that killed my family." His words came out in a hurry.

She sent him a gentle, understanding smile, like she understood the mix of feelings he was experiencing. "Sure, and if you want, we can also go into the house when we get back. If you're not ready to deal with this and see what's waiting… I understand. It's a lot."

Until she had said that, he hadn't realized that his wanting to go see Trevor was his way of avoiding the inevitable. Yet she was right. He wasn't sure he was ready to walk into that living room—he could still envision his brother's lifeless eyes staring at him. They would haunt him for years.

He could only imagine what was going to happen to him when he got in the house that now had sat with the scent of death for a few days and the blood smear near the doorway leading to the bedrooms. He had no idea how he would react when he had to wipe the bloody handprints off the walls.

The thought made his stomach churn.

As they made their way into the barn, Trevor was nowhere in sight. None of the horses or tack was missing. Cam glanced out into the parking area and noticed, for the first time, that one of the big ranch trucks with the horse trailer was gone.

It made sense; Trevor may have had to grab another hand from a neighboring ranch to help him on the drive since he thought he may have been working alone. Cameron would have done the same thing.

It was only a couple of miles' ride to where they had to move the cattle, but Trevor had probably taken the trailer and dropped it up there to help transport them back after the drive and was having the other hand give him a ride back to where they'd get the horses together.

He shrugged it off. Trevor knew exactly what he was doing. Cam trusted him implicitly.

And yet his thoughts went back to the bloody handprint.

"Didn't you say that some of the fingerprints on the scene came back as Trevor's?" he asked.

Emily walked up beside him. "Yes, why?"

"Where were his fingerprints found?" he asked.

She took out her phone and pulled up some information. "According to Bullock, it was around the living room, door handles... Normal locations one would expect for a guy that was coming and going from the house. It was mostly in the same areas where we found yours."

"Hmm." That was good; it made him feel more at ease. "Did they get any prints from the bloody handprint on the wall? Can you all do that from blood?"

She nodded. "Of course. Yeah, we got some. One set of bloody handprints was your brother's. Another handprint we located was belonging to that unknown source."

"But it wasn't Trevor's?" he asked directly.

She frowned, looking concerned. "You haven't mentioned that he would have been capable of this before. Are you seriously concerned that he may have done this? Or that he may have played a role in their deaths?"

He ran his hands over his face in exasperation. "I don't know what to think. My mind's all over the place."

She looked at him for a long moment, assessing him. "Yeah, let's just go for a ride today. The house can wait. Bullock has everything in motion for your case. And Stacy's on her way home. We have cell phone service the whole ride, right?"

"I think so, but I don't always use my phone while we're doing these kinds of things."

"I'm only worried that if someone reaches out about that BOLO, I need to be able to be in contact with the outside world."

Cell service was a legitimate concern in the mountains of Montana. "If we are out of service, we won't be for very long. Is that okay? If not, we can just work on cleaning up the house." Even as he said the words, his entire body tightened with anxiety.

She shook her head. "Babe, last night you rescued me from my fear and anger. Today it's my turn to rescue you."

Chapter Eighteen

Emily hadn't ridden a horse in years, and she shifted in the saddle in an attempt to keep it from rubbing uncomfortably against her tailbone. If they were going to go too far, she would have to change some things or she would have one heck of a saddle sore. The leather creaked as she moved and the horse flicked its ears back at her, not liking her movement.

She was riding Cameron's horse, Ginger, who was ironically a bay mare. She was a sweetheart. When Emily had come up to her, the bay had remembered her and gently nuzzled her face. She'd never considered herself a horse person, but this horse was one that could get her to change her mind. She ran her hand down the mare's neck and gave her a soft pat.

The horse blew out a relaxed breath as she walked forward, her gait smooth and even.

She was a dream to ride, or at least she would be if it weren't for the ill-fitting saddle.

If she was ever really going to consider getting more involved with Cameron, and if it became something more permanent—she blushed at the thought—she would need to start her transition to rancher's girlfriend with the purchase of a new saddle.

Cameron looked over his shoulder at her. "You're doing okay back there?"

"Just trying to find my sea legs." She smiled.

He slowed his mare down so their horses were side by side. "You just want to make sure that you engage your core. You want to focus on sitting up straight and keeping the weight off your back pockets. The only part that should be moving on you is your hip joints and it should be moving with the horse. Put your heels down, knee out in the stirrup. And we lead with our pelvis and thighs more than we do with the bit. Horses have really sensitive mouths, so you don't have to move the reins much to make them listen."

At least now she understood why the horse was having such a problem with her shifting haphazardly in the saddle. It made her feel worse about her discomfort. Without being free to shift when necessary to alleviate rubbing, she wasn't sure what she was going to do. It looked like it was about to be a very long day.

Emily focused on her posture and engaged her core. As she did, she found she wiggled less in the saddle and she sat up straighter. There was less rubbing.

Had he noticed that she was rubbing? Or had he just known she was going to have problems?

Regardless, she appreciated he was there to help before things took a turn for the worse and she wasn't able to walk when she got down.

With his simple suggestions, the pain Emily had been experiencing abated. It wasn't gone completely, but it was a lot better. Even her knees were feeling better. She definitely had a lot to learn.

They made their way deep into the pasture and through a series of gates, closing all of them behind themselves. When they reached the last pasture, they came upon a large herd of Black Angus cattle. At least, she assumed they were Black Angus; they were large and black and, as far as she knew, that was what they were called.

"How many head do you have here?" she asked, lifting her chin in the direction of the cows.

"This is just part of the herd. We have moved some of them up to spring range already. However, this is the second half and there's about five hundred head. We've been pushing them into this pasture now for the last couple weeks and they've eaten it down pretty far."

She looked around and, sure enough, the grass had been munched down to nubs and there were distinct mud trails all around the edges of the pasture that she could see.

Emily didn't know much about how open range worked, but she knew that in the State of Montana it was legal for ranchers to put their cattle on public lands during the summer months. It was part of agreements made during pioneering days, and it was still in effect. The law helped families keep large herds of cattle, and the animals' grazing helped decrease fire danger in national forests.

Not everyone liked it, but it had been a mutually beneficial relationship for the state and cattle growers for decades. It also helped keep public lands out of the hands of private buyers.

For those reasons, she would always be a fan.

"We need to find the lead heifer and get her moving. After we do, most of the others will follow her." He pointed in the direction of the mountains. "We're going to run them east and up that drainage there." He motioned toward a ravine that gradually moved up between the two mountains nearest them.

"Are all these heifers?" She didn't know anything about cows other than brown cows did not, in fact, produce chocolate milk, like her ranching grandfather had once tried to convince her. She chuckled at the memory.

"No, we have some steers that we cut this spring in the group. They'll go to sale in the fall, but we need to fatten them up first period. That's another reason that the range is so important."

"Where is Trevor? Do you have any idea?" She looked at the ravine in the mountains where they were riding up to, searching for roads, but men were obvious.

"There's a good chance we'll catch him on the dirt road that runs along the base of the mountain there—you can't really see it because of the timber. It's an old logging road, and it's pretty beat up. Locals use it for summer recreation, us ranchers use it for the cattle and then hunters use it in the fall, but that's about it." He paused. "Actually, that's not entirely true. Now that there's all these new mapping apps, which show all the roads, we've had a lot more traffic. It's not a secret anymore."

She nodded, not sure what to say. Technology was a double-edged sword.

They rode in silence for a bit as she thought about how much Stacy would have loved to have been along. She'd always loved horses. She had a collection of them in her bedroom. Maybe one of these days Emily could bring her out to the ranch and introduce her to Ginger or one of the other gentle horses that they had in the stables.

She thought about Stacy pretending there were cowboys with her little horses and how there had been cattle rustlers stealing away her best black stallion while she played. It had been up to the cowboys to bring back the stallion, it had been a whole *thing*.

"Does anyone ever bother your cattle when they're on the range?"

"We always lose one or two. A lot of times it's to grizzly bears or wolves. We're pretty close to Glacier Park, and as a result there's lots of predation. As for people, you know as well as I do it's hard to predict what they will do. So far, we've been lucky, but we have found strange things up here over the years. One year we even found a deserted truck that someone had stolen and abandoned in the woods."

"This would be a good place for something like that," she said, brushing her hair out of her face.

"What's that?" he asked.

"Making something disappear, or someone."

He studied her for a minute with an impish grin on his face. "Do I have to worry about you making *me* disappear? That sounded a little evil." He laughed.

"That's not how I meant it at all, and you know that."

He shrugged playfully. "You know anybody could be the killer. Who's to say you weren't dating my brother and you ran afoul of him or something? *Duh duh duh...*" he hummed, like the thrumming of a murder mystery game show hook.

She was glad he could joke around about his loss; it showed he was starting to heal. She pointed to his cowboy hat. "Just like you white-hat wearers, I'm one of the good guys."

They weaved their horses through the cattle until he seemed to spot what appeared to be the lead cow and he picked his way over toward her. "Was it the hat that gave me away? That's how you decided that I was a good guy?" He chuckled. "If it's that simple to convince the cops, I'm surprised all criminals don't just adopt white hats." He tipped the brim in her direction.

"Well, now I don't know what to think, if you're acting

all cute with me like that. Maybe you're trying too hard." She sent him a wide, playful smile.

He slapped her gently with the extra length of reins in his hand. "I don't have to be so nice," he said, a sultry edge in his voice that made her think of last night's activities.

Emily couldn't wait for another chance to be in his arms. With Stacy coming home, they may not get another opportunity. It pulled at her heart. They would have to take things slow from here, one day at a time. It would all depend on how things went when Stacy got back.

She knew her role as a mother was the crux of her identity. She couldn't help it, it was who she was—and would always be. Her daughter was the most important thing in her life and would continue to be, even when she grew up and moved away. Any man in her life would have to understand that and be on board—and in support of them both. That was something she hadn't really talked about with Cameron.

He slipped a leather strap loose on his saddle and took hold of his rope, or lariat, as he had called it when they had been getting the horses saddled up to go out. "That's our girl, right there," he said, pointing at the one he had seemed to take notice of as the lead cow. "I'm going to rope her and then get her moving with me. Sometimes that's a little easier, as long as she doesn't throw a fit. If she does, we may have a bit of a rodeo on our hands."

She nibbled on her lip, envisioning herself on the back of a bucking bronco. "If things do go sideways, what do you want me to do?"

"Ginger is a good girl, just lead her away. You're in control."

Emily tried to calm her racing heart by taking a slow, deep breath but it wasn't as effective as she had hoped. Ginger tilted her ear back like she was a schoolteacher pointing at her in reprimand. She sat up straighter in the saddle and steeled her resolve. She had to trust Ginger.

Cameron swirled the lariat over his head, extending the rope as it revolved and then he loosed it. It arched over the cow's head and he pulled it back and wrapped it around the saddle's horn. The heifer jerked with surprise but didn't fight the lead. Instead, she looked lazily back at Cameron, the whites of her eyes showing as she chewed her cud.

Cameron huffed a laugh.

"Are you kidding me?" Emily asked, almost disappointed by the lack of excitement and the cow's response. "I thought there were going to be fireworks. You just wanted to show off your rope work, didn't you?"

He sent her that sexy smile. "You didn't think I was really gonna put you in danger, did you?"

She tried to slap him with the loose ends of her reins this time, but she missed him by a mile. He laughed at her.

"You have a long way to go before you're gonna be a full-on cowgirl, but I'll get you there."

"Is that right?" she teased. "Do you think I'm gonna be sticking around long enough for you to train me?" She tried to stop the excitement and giddiness she felt from entering her voice. All she wanted to do was become his cowgirl.

"If you're not interested…"

She shrugged. "I don't know if I'm interested in dating a showoff." She motioned to the lariat in his hand.

He rode up to the black cow and slipped the loop off her neck and scratched behind her ear. The yellow number tag on her ear read 82. "Eighty-two here has been around for a long time, at least for cow standards. She's been the lead for the last couple drives. She's my buddy." He tapped her on the haunches and she started plodding forward. "She'll pretty much follow us wherever we go. Then the other ones will line up. You just have to ride next to me."

"If it's this easy, do we even need Trevor and the other hands at all?" She glanced up at the mountain draw in front of them. It wasn't that far, maybe another half mile and they'd be to the mouth of the ravine.

"First, they're animals. Everything can change in a split second. Cows are not known for their intelligence, either. A single bee can throw this all off."

She nodded. She had seen enough movies to understand a stampede.

"Plus, normally it's the calves that you have to watch for. They tend to get split up from their mothers and start bawling. Then the mothers straggle behind trying to get to their little ones and it causes problems. So, you need a couple guys behind to pick up the loose head."

"If you want, I can ride in the back of the herd and help there until they arrive."

His face scrunched like he was seriously considering her offer but was torn. She was glad to see him look like that because she didn't want to leave him. "Let's just keep you up here for now. I don't want you getting hurt. If something happened back there, I wouldn't know, and I couldn't help you quickly enough."

Just when she thought she couldn't like him more. There he went, making her fall for him again. He was such a gentleman.

"When we get on the other side of this fence, though, and we get into the open range, I might have to change things up if Trevor's not up there. When the cows start breaking loose and wandering, I may need you to work that back end a little bit more and push them forward. I don't want them trying to get back in the pasture."

It made sense, but she silently begged that Trevor would be there.

"We also can't let them start going up or down that logging road. They just have to go straight across and up the drainage. Sometimes that's where they get a little confused. I like to set a cowboy on each side of the herd to push them up there, so they don't get any stupid ideas."

"Well, here's hoping Trevor and your other hands are there." The last thing she wanted was to have to chase down stray cows. She doubted the rest of them would be as amenable to her roping them or leading them as 82 was with Cameron.

She glanced behind them and 82 was still plodding along, its hoofs clomping in the dirt and kicking up mud as she moved directly in line behind his horse. The rest of the cattle had started to do exactly what Cameron had told her they would, and they were lining up behind the lead cow in single file.

She wondered what they thought. Either they thought they were going to be fed, they were incredibly trusting, or, as Cameron had said, kind of lacking intelligence.

Then again, lining up was not a sign of stupidity, it was just a sign of conformity. And one could argue that it could be used as a way to escape predation. However, she had a feeling that she was giving them way too much credit.

As they neared the edge of the pasture leading to the logging road and the mouth of the draw, Emily had to readjust her bellyband slightly. The end of the mag and the grip on the Glock had started to rub against her chest and take off a thin layer of skin.

This was the first time she'd had that problem, but it was the bellyband or the saddle sore on her behind. In this case, it was a lot easier to adjust the band and loosen her gun. She dropped it down, letting the gun sit just over her belt buckle with the band barely folded.

She'd have to remember to readjust it before getting down or it would flop off if she wasn't careful.

"I think I see the ranch truck," Cameron said, pointing ahead.

She was relieved. They'd have this handled in no time. Then they could go back to trying to get answers for Bullock. She checked her phone one more time, hoping to see an e-mail pop up with information about their unknown suspect, but there was nothing on the subject. The only e-mails she'd received were the standards in office garbage and one from the medical examiner's office that Bullock had forwarded.

She clicked on that e-mail and opened the attachment, which included the autopsy report for Ben. She scanned the findings; most were what they had expected. Cameron's brother had died from a gunshot wound, consistent with that of a 9mm handgun. They had found part of the bullet lodged within his skull.

From the bullet and the gun that was recovered on scene, they were able to say conclusively that the round that killed him had come from the gun found in his hand. However, due to the angle of entry and exit, it could not have been Ben who had fired the weapon.

Again, it didn't come as a surprise.

According to the examiner, they were placing the time of death at approximately 5:00 a.m.

She closed the report and clicked on the second attachment, which was for Leonard. Again, there weren't many surprises. He had suffered from a series of ante-mortem stab wounds, consistent with that inflicted by a 7-inch blade at or near the time of death. However, the wound that had likely killed him was a stab wound to the aorta. That wound had caused the man to bleed out almost instantly.

According to the examiner, they had put his time of death at approximately 4:00 a.m.

She stared at her phone. This meant conclusively that Leonard could not have killed Ben. There was no way. And whoever had killed Leonard, had likely murdered Ben as well.

With the e-mails was a simple note that read, *Thought you might find this interesting.*

That was an understatement.

As they rode up to the edge of the pasture, they approached a ranch pickup that looked similar to the one where she had found Leonard's body. Seeing that pickup, she had a sinking feeling that once again she was going to have to deal with a whole lot more than she'd bargained for—and this time, she may well be walking into a killer's trap.

Chapter Nineteen

Cameron didn't see Trevor or one of the hands he'd brought along anywhere. In fact, there weren't even horses tied to the trailer, as he would have expected. He stopped, trying to listen for the sounds of footfalls within the metal trailer. By now, if the horses were inside, they would be getting antsy, especially with the noise of the cows so close by. However, he heard nothing.

"Why don't you wait here for a second? I'm gonna go check on things. I'll be right back. Keep an eye on 82." He motioned toward the lead.

Emily nodded.

He knew she had no clue what to do if that old cow wandered off, but he could get things back under control if she failed. He just needed to give Emily a task to keep her mind occupied, so she didn't worry. She was able to read his face and know what he was thinking, and it didn't always work out to his advantage.

For some reason, things with Trevor weren't feeling quite right lately, and he didn't know why. He trusted Trevor and he always had. It was unlike him to not be around when Cam needed him the most.

Yet, his absence could have meant many things—the most glaring being that he was somehow complicit. That was something that didn't sit well with Cameron as, in most ways, Leonard was as much the ranch hand's dad as he was Cameron's. For Trevor to kill him would have been tantamount to patricide.

The only conceivable way he could think of Trevor doing something to hurt his dad would be if he'd done it accidentally or drunkenly, but he couldn't imagine that Trevor wouldn't turn himself in. He loved this family. At the bare minimum, he would have told Cam then run off or something.

There's no way Trevor could have been behind the murders. He was just off center right now.

Then again, he was even off the mark with the cattle, which was unheard of. He was never this disorganized when moving herds, and Cameron didn't like it.

He opened the gate, and he and Bessie slipped through and he closed it behind him, making sure the cow didn't follow. He rode up to the horse trailer and peeked inside, but it was empty. It didn't even appear as if there had been horses inside it all.

That was strange. Trevor had to have brought the horses here somehow. There hadn't been any sign of them on the ride up from the barn.

He tried not to panic.

Trevor wouldn't drive a truck up here with a trailer without horses in it. He knew the work that needed to be done. He wouldn't waste the gas. This made no sense.

He reached down and patted his pocket. All he was carrying with him was his standard pocketknife and a black bandanna. He glanced over at Emily. From where he was sitting, he could tell she was carrying a gun.

It had been stupid of him not to bring a handgun on their little drive, but he normally didn't—in the many years they had been moving their cattle up the mountain, he'd never needed one. His dad was always the one who brought a pistol. It was just their system. Rarely had they ever needed one. In fact, he believed in bear spray when it came to predators on their cows, which had never been a problem during a drive.

Most of the time, carrying a gun on the hip was more uncomfortable than it was worth, and it was why he didn't do it. But he definitely regretted the decision today.

He tried to tell himself that he was making something out of nothing.

Maybe Trevor had just parked the empty trailer here and was riding in from somewhere else. Or maybe the other ranch hand had driven the trailer here and walked or gotten a ride back. There were a lot of scenarios that Cam could be missing. He took his phone out and sent a quick message to Trevor.

He waited a long moment, but in true Trevor fashion, the message remained unread.

If everything proved to be in his head, Cameron and his pseudo brother were going to have a serious conversation as soon as they got back to the ranch house. This not answering the phone thing was driving him crazy. It was like having a kid around.

He thought of Stacy—a five-year-old had to be easier to deal with. In her case, at least Emily didn't expect her to answer the phone.

Hopefully, Stacy was safe and would be home soon.

As much as Cam wanted to pummel Todd, he would have to be careful about which battles he could fight. Emily had a lot to lose when it came to her daughter, and he couldn't make things worse by acting a fool.

If they were going to become a major part of his life,

as he hoped, Todd wasn't the only man who needed to respect boundaries.

He looked around the truck, but there weren't any prints he could see, and everything seemed in order. He tried to tell himself that the knot in his gut was just an overreaction and he was being hypervigilant for no reason.

Trevor had probably just parked the truck there, empty for later, and jumped in another rig to go get the horses and then leave from the barn. They were probably behind them and looking for the cattle. No big deal.

If Trevor and no other hands were there, he and Emily were just going to have to do this themselves. He didn't want to wait all day and risk having the cows mill around again in the pasture for no reason.

Tag 82 had been pretty amenable. All they had to do was get her up the draw another half mile. It wouldn't be a problem. Emily had been doing great on the horse.

He waved his fingers at Emily, getting her attention. "Why don't you go ahead and open the gate and lead that cow through? Let's just start moving them up. If they're pushing the cows from behind, we don't want them bunching up. That will create problems and we don't want them getting into the barbed wire."

She nodded. "You got it."

"First," he said, putting his finger up, "I'm going to move the ranch truck sideways on the road, it can act as a barrier for the cows. That will keep them moving forward. Then we only have to worry about the one side."

She gave him the thumbs-up, turned the horse around and moved some of the cows back from the fence. Though she had said she didn't know much about horses, it was clear that her time on her grandparent's ranch had stuck with her. It was funny how sometimes the work done as a kid had a way of imprinting on a person and almost becoming muscle memory.

He rode over to a big pine on the far side of the road and tied up Bessie, who gave him the stink eye as he climbed down.

"Don't worry, I'm not leaving you here."

It might have been in his head, but he could have sworn that the normally sassy horse was not herself since his father's passing. She hadn't even tried to buck him or ignore his lead today. That was totally unlike the paint. He felt for her. Before he walked away, he gave her a good scratch and she closed her eyes in gratitude.

When he was done, he walked over to the truck and opened the unlocked door. Like all the ranch trucks, he flipped down the visor and the keys fell into his hand. The system was one that saved everyone steps and headaches as it wasn't uncommon for a person to have to move vehicles around or run a truck from one place to another in a hurry. No one needed to ask to use one; as far as they were concerned, it was just another tool.

Thrown in the passenger seat was a white sweatshirt with an embroidered red Canadian maple leaf on the front. From the tag, it was a woman's size small. There was what looked like blood on the wrists and up the arms. He stared at it for a long moment.

There wasn't a woman working on the ranch.

Trevor didn't have a girlfriend.

As of right now, Trevor *was missing*.

How would a woman have known to bring the truck out here and why would she have?

He moved to back up and close the driver's-side door. As he backed up, he felt a cold steel barrel press against the base of his skull. "Don't move, or I will put a bullet in you just like I did your brother," a man said.

He didn't recognize the voice.

He looked up through the front glass of the pickup to see if Emily was watching, but she had her back to him and was working with the cows behind the fence in the pasture. She had no idea anything was happening.

He thought about calling out to her, but even if she heard him, it wouldn't do any good and it would only put them in further danger.

Where had the man come from?

"What do you want?" he asked, trying his best to remain calm. He wanted to turn around and face the man, but he was afraid to move. This dude, whoever he was, wasn't afraid to kill—he'd already proven that.

If Cameron was to survive and keep Emily from getting hurt, he was going to have to play along. First things first, he needed to make sure Emily didn't find herself in the line of fire.

"I want you to know, none of this had to happen." The man sounded torn, almost apologetic.

Cam took it as a good sign. At least the guy holding the gun to his head wasn't just some psychotic killer who would just kill anyone without reason and without feeling some sense of remorse. That was something he could perhaps work with to keep things under control—and this man's sense of remorse could perhaps even keep Cam alive.

"Why is that, man?" he asked, trying to sound empathetic.

The gun shook violently, like the man's hand was getting tired, or else he was starting to lose his nerve.

"Because…your brother shouldn't have been such an idiot. I told him not to come here. I told him."

Cameron turned around. Standing there with that self-righteous smirk he'd seen once before, was Todd. However, standing not ten feet behind him and looking beaten down, was Trevor.

"Todd? Trevor?" He was so confused. He didn't have a clue these guys even knew each other. "Todd, I thought you were in Canada?"

"I needed an alibi in case I had to murder you." He shrugged.

His stomach clenched. "How did you know my brother?"

Todd lowered the gun, but kept it pressed into Cam's stomach, not letting him forget that it was there if he tried something stupid.

"Your brother and I had a good thing going with your father and the ranch." He nudged his chin in the direction of Emily and the pasture. "If you don't do anything stupid, maybe we can keep that good thing going."

Cam had no idea what Todd was talking about, but whatever his father, Ben and Trevor had found themselves a part of…clearly, he didn't want to be involved, even if Todd hadn't been the ringleader. Having Todd at the helm only made it that much easier to tell him to pound sand.

However, Cam had to wait.

"I'm listening," he said, the gun digging into his shirt.

"First," Todd said, looking over at Emily, "you need to get that witch Emily over here and put her in the trailer. She needs to be out of our way."

He wasn't going for that idea. He wasn't locking her anywhere. "No."

"If you don't put her in the trailer, cool, calm and collected like—without setting off the alarms—then I will just go ahead and shoot her. If I did, it would solve a hell of a lot of problems for me." Todd sucked his teeth. "The only reason I ain't already is that my daughter loves her mama."

So, the guy did have some kind of heart—even if it was fetid and black.

Trevor finally walked over. "I'm sorry, Cam. I didn't want none of this to happen. I told your dad just to go with everything your brother wanted, but he didn't want things your brother's way. He said he wanted out. They got into a fight."

"He wanted out of *what*?"

Trevor looked at his boots. "They were running girls out of Canada—Fernie—through here sometimes and then into North Dakota and into the rough-necking camps. Your dad was laundering the money for your brother."

"What in the—" His father had done a lot of things to make ends meet at the ranch, but making money like that was something he'd never thought Leonard'd stoop to.

"He didn't know what Ben was doin'," Trevor continued. "He was just taking his cut. Yet when your brother stopped by this time, he had one of the girls with him. Your dad figured it out. He blew a rod and Ben had to take him out."

Cameron hated what his father had done in laundering the money. Who knows what would happen with the ranch if Detective Bullock found out, but at least he'd put his foot down with the rest. His father had tried to do the right thing in the end; it had cost him his life.

And his son had been the one to kill him. The truth slashed at Cam like grizzly claws.

"Your brother was doing a lot of drugs," Todd said. "He had become a liability. I'm sure you will see that in the paperwork you get back eventually. It's why I had my girl kill him. She knew it was either him or her who had to die to appease me. They weren't supposed to kill Leonard. They screwed everything up."

Trevor motioned toward Emily. "I'll go get her. She knows me."

Todd nodded. "Be quick about it."

"Don't hurt her and don't you dare put her in that trailer," Cam said to Trevor.

Trevor nodded.

He trusted Trevor a whole lot more than he trusted Todd, but it was his blind trust of Trevor that had led him to this moment. Trevor had known all along who had been involved in the murders and he had lied.

"Trevor, why *did* you lie to me about this? If you knew what had happened at the ranch, why didn't you at least give me a heads-up, so I didn't think someone also wanted me dead?"

"Who said I don't?" Todd asked.

"If you did, I would already be piled up on the ground." He pointed at the dirt beside the pickup.

"I was going to, but you haven't been without that woman. I was gonna tell you at the bar, but all you were doing was making eyes at her. I figured you'd just go and tell her what we'd done and I'd have my ass in jail." Trevor sighed. "I just needed a chance to get you to understand."

"After all my father and I have done for you, why would you go against him?"

Trevor shook his head adamantly. "I wasn't, I swear. I was trying to make him see that he needed to keep doing business with Todd and Ben. They were keeping the ranch afloat. I was on the ranch's side."

Todd pointed at Trevor like his statement was a testimonial.

"Maybe you can listen to me better than your father,"

Trevor continued. "All I want, is to run sixty thousand dollars more a month."

He thought back to the banking records. "So, you want one-hundred-thousand dollars a month through us? That will draw some red flags. And how can we make that look legitimate in the ranching industry? We don't work with that kind of cash."

"No, but marijuana is legal in the State of Montana, and it is a cash-based industry," Todd said. "Put up some greenhouses. I don't care if you don't grow anything. Just do the paperwork."

"Where will I get the money for all this *paperwork*?" he asked, playing along.

"I'll give you one-hundred-thousand dollars in cash this week to start. All you have to do is say yes. From then on, you will take care of our money. You can take ten percent. Same as your father."

"Twenty and I have conditions."

"Fifteen and what are these conditions?" Todd countered.

"First, return Stacy, leave Emily out of this and give her full custody—no more renegotiation or mediation. Second, I want the girl who killed my brother. She needs to pay. There has to be justice."

Todd stared at him for a solid minute and there was a smirk on his lips. "You don't know what you are asking."

Oh, but he did. He was putting a price on Todd's child and forcing this man to stop using his daughter as a pawn. Stacy deserved better.

He pushed Todd off him. "Bring me the woman and bring Emily the signed parenting agreement tomorrow. If you do, I'll do as you want. Okay?"

Todd sent him a devilish, fanged grin. "You have a deal."

Chapter Twenty

Cameron came riding up beside her on Bessie, his face was ashen and gaunt like he had been sick.

"Are you okay?" Emily asked, wanting to reach over and check his temperature with her hand, but he was too far away.

He nodded, but he didn't say anything. "Let's go." He motioned back toward the ranch.

"What?" she asked, confused. "Don't we need to move the cows into the summer range?"

He was riding ahead of her back in the direction in which they had come. The cows they'd led up and that she'd been trying to keep from wandering off were now starting to scatter every which way. It didn't make sense. None of it.

They'd been having fun, they'd been going to drive the cows across the road, he'd gone to the truck and now this.

He must be sick.

She tried not to be worried.

Even sick, she would have thought he would have made sure the cows had been moved up that draw. They were so close to getting it done. All they had to do was move them another half mile. The majority of the work had already been done.

Plus, he'd just left the truck sitting there—abandoned. Why? What had been inside?

Nothing made sense.

Her cop alarm bells were going off like mad.

"Cam?" she called after him, but he didn't even look back at her and he kept riding. "Cameron?" she called again. Again, he didn't slow down.

She nudged her horse into a trot as they broke through the tail end of the herd of cows.

Ginger's hooves thumped on the dirt and she moved faster, but as she did, so did Bessie and Cameron in front of them.

He didn't want her to catch him.

What in the...

The wind whistled by her ears as they picked up speed and she stood in the stirrups. She leaned forward slightly and let her knees take the impact of the horse's footfalls. Her hair broke free of her hair tie with the jarring force of the wind and the gallop and she couldn't help the laugh that tore from her lips. The sound was half crazed and free, but it felt as good as the wind on her face and the whirring speed of the horse beneath her. In this wild moment, she was the predator in a chase and damn if it didn't feel great.

The bay struggled, but she finally reached the paint. Emily had a feeling that Cameron had pulled up and allowed them to catch up as Ginger had more speed than most horses she had seen that weren't thoroughbreds. It was as if that horse had come straight off the wild herds of the plains from generations past. She was a thing of beauty.

The ranch house was in sight as they slowed down. It was amazing how fast the trip back was compared to their slow plod with the cows up had been.

"Are you going to tell me what's wrong or are you going

to make me actually take you into the interview room at the station this time?" she teased, hoping that it would make him laugh and open up.

Instead, the smile that had formed on his lips from the ride vanished and his eyes widened. Some of the color in his cheeks disappeared. "Everything is fine. I think that it's best if you head back to your place though. You need to get things handled with your daughter."

Your daughter? The way he'd said that was so cold and clinical. It was as if he was a stranger.

Emily and Stacy hadn't known Cameron that long. Yet so much had happened. So much had changed and developed in such a short amount of time that it felt like the world had flipped and he was now at the center of hers.

She didn't know how to respond or what to think.

She was just *hurt*.

"Just head back to the barn and tie Ginger up at the post there." He motioned to the hitching post out front. "I'll unsaddle her. You just go."

Just like that, she was dismissed.

CAMERON WALKED INTO the barn and started unsaddling Ginger. He slipped off the reins and put on her halter and tied her to the loop in the barn so he could take care of her while Bessie waited outside.

He was a disaster. He didn't know what to do and now he could tell that he had hurt the one person he loved. In fact, she was the only person he had left in this world whom he cared about—well, except her daughter, but they were really a package deal.

He smiled at the thought.

If nothing else, if he just went along with the stupid deal like he'd promised, he could check a lot of boxes. He could save the ranch, save Emily and her daughter, and never have to worry about the financial future of the place again. Plus, he'd solved the murder and there would be some sort of justice for his brother's death.

Or, at least there could be—but what would he do with the woman once Todd brought her to him?

He wasn't a judge.

Just because Todd told him that the murder had happened that way didn't mean it had. People lied all the time and Todd was definitely not above it—even if the bloody sweatshirt and the handprints seemed to back up his account.

He pulled the saddle off Ginger's back along with the blanket. It was wet with sweat, and he carried it over to the tack room and hung it on the rack. He grabbed a currycomb and headed back to the waiting horse. She leaned into him as he started to rub her down.

If he just turned this all over to Bullock, then the detective could be the one to start the wheels of justice. Yet, if Cameron told Bullock, he put the future of the ranch at risk and would put the legacy of his family in jeopardy.

He couldn't be the one to lose everything…even if it was his father's choices that had gotten them to this point, Cam was the one who was risking his future.

There had to be a way to get ahead of this and handle it in a manner that he could get everything he wanted, but he didn't live in some fantasy world. This was his reality and reality didn't work that way. He couldn't get everything he wanted, no one ever did.

It felt like it came down to a singular, heartbreaking choice—love or legacy.

He'd only known Emily and her daughter for a few days, but it was all it had taken to know they were what he wanted in his ideal world. Yet the ranch had been his entire life up to this point, and it had consumed the lives of multiple generations before him.

If he became a criminal, he could save it all and maybe even get the girl—that was, if she would want to be with a morally gray man.

There was no way.

He loved Emily and he respected the sacrifices of his family, but he would never allow himself to follow the path his brother had taken and condone human trafficking. It sickened him.

He'd loved his brother as a child, but he hated the man he'd become after he'd left the ranch. That was to say nothing of the effects he had upon Cam when he'd had the affair with April.

He just couldn't understand how his brother had so dramatically lost his way.

Todd had said he'd been using drugs. It fell in line with his devolving behavior and morals, but it also made Cam feel as if he had failed his brother by not seeing the signs and getting him help earlier.

He had failed in so many ways, but none of that mattered now. All that mattered was that he made the right choices moving forward.

He had twenty-four hours before meeting Todd and Trevor to figure out exactly what those right choices were and what they meant for his future.

Chapter Twenty-One

Emily had been a cop long enough to trust her gut. When something, or someone, felt *off*, she acted, and she didn't question herself. It was one of the things in this job that gave her a leg up on the rest of the world. And, man oh man, was Cameron *off*.

As soon as she'd arrived at the ranch, she'd gotten into her car and, instead of heading home or back to town, had turned down the road that veered off the ranch road and headed back up toward where the ranch truck and trailer had been parked.

The logging road wyed and she took the right fork, but even though it was the logically correct direction, it wasn't how logging roads always worked. Sometimes they doublebacked, went straight up or came to an abrupt dead end. So, instead of driving aimlessly in hopes she was going the right way, she pulled over to check the maps to make sure she was on the right road.

Of course, her service was cutting out and the internet was painfully slow. Sometimes it was just the car that caused the problem.

Getting out, she walked back a little bit toward the wye to get better service. As she did, she heard the distinct sound of a truck coming toward her. Not wanting to be noticed, she stepped into the timber and brush that lined the roadside. She hunkered down, concealing herself as best she could while holding on to an azalea bush that provided ground cover beside her.

Unless someone was really paying attention, she was sure she wouldn't be seen.

Coming around the corner and kicking up dust was the red Ford she knew only too well. Todd was in the driver's seat and Trevor was riding next to him. It was hard to tell from where she sat, but it looked like there were other people in the back seat of the pickup as well.

She gasped as she gripped the bush harder, letting the little branches pierce the soft flesh of her palm.

Why were Todd and Trevor together?

It dawned on her.

They had to have been working together. That meant only one thing—Todd was somehow connected to what was happening on the ranch.

She didn't understand how or why, but she wasn't surprised. That was why Todd had dumped Stacy on her in the middle of her investigation. He'd done that on purpose to make things more complicated. He had wanted to slow them down, or at least keep her out of it.

Of course, she was the one who could most easily recognize him if given the opportunity.

No wonder Cam had been acting so strange.

He had told her to go home, to wait for Stacy.

Had he made some kind of bargain?

He would.

There was no doubt in her mind that he would do anything to keep Stacy, and her, safe. That also meant putting himself in danger.

She couldn't let him risk himself for them.

The Ford went racing by. In the back was a woman she didn't recognize and, beside her, with her thumb in her mouth, was Stacy.

Her heart plummeted.

She needed her daughter back.

She needed Stacy tucked safely in her arms and away from that man.

As soon as they were out of view, she raced to her car. Before getting in, she called Detective Bullock. He answered on the first ring. "I think I have our killers," she said, sounding breathless. "They are in a red Ford F-150 driven by Todd Monahan."

"Your ex-husband?" Bullock asked, shock rattling his voice.

"Yes."

"I know. Your friend Cameron already called and told me what happened."

She paused, surprised that Cam had decided to call Bullock but not her—he must have had his reasons. She didn't know everything that had happened, but she could find out Cameron's reasons for everything later. Right now, she needed to worry about her daughter. "Stacy is in that pickup along with two other occupants, Trevor and an unknown woman. They are headed in the direction of the WGC Ranch."

"I have everyone headed in that direction. Don't do anything until you have backup," Bullock ordered. "I need you to become the next detective in my unit, and I don't need you getting hurt."

If he'd said that in any other moment, she would have smiled and been excited, but right now she barely heard him. "Thanks, boss. I'll try to hold."

"Don't try. Do."

She hung up the phone and climbed into her patrol car.

She needed to get to Stacy.

Until now, she had hated Todd and thought he was a nuisance, but she'd never thought he was a real threat to her daughter's safety. She should have known better. A man who could basically kidnap his child and take her across international borders without consent didn't have compassion for others, or many moral boundaries.

She'd had a child with a monster.

Her monster had become Cameron's monster, too.

Emily sucked in a choking cry. She didn't have time to feel right now. There was only time for action and to set things right. There was only time to save her daughter and seek justice.

No matter what Bullock said, she couldn't wait to get her daughter back. She needed to know she was safe.

She started her engine and hit the gas. She drove as fast as she could, fishtailing in the light car on the corners. She didn't care as she hit the accelerator coming out of the curves.

Todd must have been going fifty and he'd had one heck of a head start.

It wasn't until she was on the straightaway and out of the timbered area that she spotted Todd's pickup. He was almost to the driveway of the ranch.

She flipped on her lights and sirens and pushed the car to the max, coming up fast on him.

As she neared, she saw Stacy's little head pop up in the back window. She smiled and waved, but the brunette woman beside her grabbed her and pushed her down.

Anger pulsed through Emily. She didn't know who the woman was, but she had no right to touch her daughter.

The woman would pay.

Instead of slowing down and pulling over, Todd sped up.

She couldn't believe it. There was no way her ex was going to put her daughter in even further danger by getting in a high-speed chase with her.

Emily turned on the loudspeaker. "Todd Monahan, pull over. I repeat, pull the vehicle over!"

She let Dispatch know she was in pursuit. Bullock was going to be furious, but it was too late to stop now.

As the truck neared the entrance of the ranch, a black Ford pickup pulled out in front of him, blocking the road. There was a barbed-wire fence on both sides of the road. There was no going around. Todd only had one option—stop or T-bone the truck.

He skidded to a stop, but she knew it wasn't to keep their daughter safe—he just loved that truck too much to allow it to be damaged.

Cameron stepped out of his pickup and, raising a rifle to his shoulder, took aim squarely at Todd.

She went back to the loudspeaker. "Cameron, don't!" she screamed. She pressed the gas as hard as she could.

She drove as fast as she could, careening down the road and skidding to a sideways stop behind Todd's pickup and boxing him in.

"No one shoot!" she yelled over the loudspeaker.

If anyone fired a weapon, Stacy would be caught in the crossfire.

She threw her gear into Park and drew the Glock from her bellyband as she got out of the car. She pointed it straight at the driver's-side door.

"Todd, put your hands out of the window!" she ordered.

Todd opened the door of his pickup, not following instructions.

"Don't take another step or I will be forced to shoot!" she yelled.

Todd stepped out of the truck and turned to face her. His right hand was on the door of the pickup, but his other was still inside the truck. She couldn't tell what he was holding.

She didn't want to shoot.

If he was holding a gun, it could take him less than a second to draw and shoot. He could kill her in a second.

Her daughter could be a witness to her murder.

Or Stacy could be a witness to her shooting her father in self-defense.

She didn't want her to see any of this.

Her gaze flickered to the back window. Stacy's little face was staring out at her.

As she glanced back at Todd, his hand had moved. It was behind his back.

"Get on the ground, Todd!" She felt almost manic.

Everything she had learned at the academy told her to shoot. She was well within her rights, but if there was nothing in his hand or if it was just a cell phone or something, she would come out of this event looking like an overzealous cop—or worse, a vengeful ex-wife. Every part of this investigation would be analyzed after the fact. She was going to be heavily scrutinized. She had to be so careful.

Yet her life and her daughter's welfare were on the line.

Cameron stepped around the front of Todd's truck to the right. "Trevor, April, get out!" he yelled, motioning toward them with his rifle.

April? The woman in the truck—the one who'd had the nerve to touch her daughter—was his ex-wife?

Oh, she was so going to jail.

Trevor opened the door and climbed out. He dropped to the ground and laid down with his hands on the back of his head. At least he had a brain.

The woman followed suit.

Todd, however, kept walking toward her.

"Put your hands above your head, Todd. If you don't, I will be forced to shoot!" she ordered.

Todd moved his hands slowly to where she could see them. In the hand, which had been behind his back, was a cell phone.

She rushed toward him and shoulder-checked him, throwing him to the ground. As she moved, he reached for her gun. He caught her off guard and, in his fight, took hold of her gun. She tried to twist it free of his hand, but he was so strong.

She wrestled for it, trying to get it back. With her right hand, she reached down and unholstered her other weapon. Pushing it up into his ribs, she pulled the trigger. She would never forget the sound or the feel of the gases exploding from the end of the barrel between their wrestling bodies.

Todd made a gurgling sound and his body went limp. She'd never wanted to be drawn into in an officer-involved shooting—but Todd had made the choice. He had never respected her, and in this case, he'd forgotten who she was at her core—a warrior.

Chapter Twenty-Two

Stacy was sitting on Cam's shoulders as they walked out into the center of the pasture. She was giggling as Cameron pretended to be a pony, trotting around and making her bounce.

The sight made Emily smile.

They had been through so much in the last couple of months that it was a relief to just relax and enjoy the last lazy days of summer.

Stacy had recovered remarkably well after learning about her father's death. Thankfully, she hadn't been able to see the fight or the shooting.

April was in jail awaiting sentencing after being found guilty of first-degree murder in the death of Benjamin Trapper. During the court testimonies, it had come out that she had continued her relationship with Ben and they had been working together to set up the trafficking ring. She was working as what they called a "bottom" or "right hand" and grooming women to feel safe to work under Ben and the guys running them in various areas of the country.

All in all, they had ended up identifying more than fifty women who'd been working for Ben and April, including the woman they had seen at the Arrow Lodge who had ripped the business card in two. She hadn't been happy to see them and, after the trial, she had disappeared once again.

They'd connected many of the women up with the resources, health care and counseling services they'd needed. Because of his help, Cameron and the ranch's corporation were given immunity for his father's roles in money laundering.

Todd's truck was sitting in the impound yard and would be going to the salvage yard to be recycled.

Emily couldn't be happier to know that his prized possession would soon be crushed.

"Mama, you coming?" Stacy asked, looking back at her. "Ginger is waiting!"

Emily hurried up, moving to their side. Cam reached down and took her hand with his.

Ginger, hearing her name from across the field, started to trot toward them. She was saddled up, which struck Emily as highly unusual.

They hadn't talked about taking Stacy riding today, but now Stacy's excitement made more sense.

Her daughter had fallen in love with Ginger the second she had set eyes on her, and the feeling had been mutual. What had once been Cameron's horse had instantly become Stacy's. He didn't have a hope of the bay mare ever being his again—and it was so much so, the horse's loyalties had even become a joke.

Ginger trotted to a gentle stop beside her girl. She lifted her head, waiting for the little girl's fingers to touch her nose. As she did, Ginger flipped her mane with excitement.

It was the sweetest thing.

"Let's get you up there in the saddle," Cam said, lifting Stacy off his shoulders and moving her into the saddle.

She giggled wildly, putting her hands over her mouth as she wiggled into the saddle. "Are you going to do it yet?"

He laughed. "*Shh…* Don't give it away."

She shook her head, clamping her hands over her mouth even harder and looking over at her mother and then back to Cam.

"What are you two up to?" Emily asked.

Stacy wiggled with excitement again, making Ginger look back at her with what amounted to a mare's smile.

"Do you want to get it out for her?" Cam asked.

Stacy reached into the panier behind the saddle and took out a little red-velvet box. "Can I show her?"

"Yes, ladybug," he said, using their now-shared nickname.

Emily's heart raced as she stared at the velvet box. That couldn't be what she hoped it was. She wiggled on her toes with excitement, like her daughter had in the saddle. She put her hands over her mouth as she giggled. "You aren't… You didn't!" she exclaimed, looking to Cam.

He smiled wildly. "I don't have to, if you are going to say no."

Stacy opened the box with far too much force and the ring inside jerked wildly. She and Cameron jumped to catch it just in case the ring inside went flying, and they bumped hard into one another.

"Oh…" Emily exclaimed. "That was close."

"To you saying no?" Cam teased.

"You haven't even asked." She smiled.

"True. May I have the ring?"

Stacy nodded.

Cameron took the box from Stacy and dropped to his knee as Stacy giggled. "Ms. Emily, I have loved you and Stacy from the first moment I met you. There is nothing I wouldn't do for you ladies." He smiled up at Emily. "Would you do me the honor of being my wife?"

Stacy squealed. "Mama, say yes!"

Emily laughed. "Should I?"

Stacy nodded wildly.

"Well, I got my marching orders." She smiled. "Yes, Cameron Trapper. I would love to be your wife."

Until she had met Cameron, Emily hadn't been a believer in true love. Yet, when she kissed him, she knew exactly what it meant—true love was knowing that through thick and thin, sickness and health, and peace and war, two people would stand with one another forever.

* * * * *

COLTON REUNION

ADDISON FOX

For Beth, Lois, Sam, Rob and Jess.

Thank you for the lovely invitation to join you all at sea. I was writing this book while we sailed and knew I wanted to dedicate it to you all in memory of the fun we had.

Of course, Neil already knows…

Chapter One

Paige Barnes fought the trembling in her fingers as she packed up her camera equipment in her well-worn leather shoulder bag.

It's just nerves.

She'd steadily whispered that admonition to herself, over and over, as she spent the night tossing and turning in bed.

Sadly, she was no closer to believing it now than she'd been at four that morning.

She was, however, going to be late for the helipad if she didn't get a move on.

The helipad.

The destination had confused her when she first read the travel documents her assistant had pulled together; she'd puzzled over any reason on earth she'd need to get into a helicopter. Even during her years in modeling, she'd had minimal opportunities to travel in such a luxurious—and horribly unsustainable—way. But she'd do it now.

For her client.

And for her own peace of mind.

Because the destination that sat at the other end of the short helicopter flight was Mariposa, one of the most exclusive properties in the West.

The Colton family had owned Mariposa for years, but

the current generation had taken a property that had been known for its luxurious privacy and created something indulgently exclusive.

Celebrities stayed at Mariposa. So did heads of state and the uber wealthy.

And it all sat under the managerial control of Adam Colton.

A small shiver skittered down her spine as an image of the man filled her thoughts. Tall. Handsome. And the scion of a family that had become synonymous the world over with the idea of exclusive luxury.

Paige tried to shake all of it off as she checked the small pocket where she kept her extra drives for her camera.

You can do this.

And she *could* do this. It had been well over a decade since she'd last seen Adam. She'd do this job with the professionalism that was her hallmark and move on.

When it came to that man, she was good at moving on. She'd done it before, and there was no way it could be more difficult this time around.

Her heart had already healed, after all. Her close friends might even have said *hardened*. But she could no longer call herself innocent or naive.

What Adam Colton hadn't managed to kill, modeling had finished off.

So she'd made herself strong. Practical. And she'd crafted a solid career out of hard work and an understanding that everyone had to depend on themselves to make the life they wanted.

There were no fairy tales.

And there certainly weren't any happy-ever-afters.

A person had to work for what they wanted. Rely on themselves and, with focus and discipline, reach for their dreams.

Depending on another person as the path to happiness was an inherently flawed strategy.

Since she also considered herself a fundamentally positive person, despite her inwardly directed beliefs, Paige had learned to channel that wide-eyed practicality into her work.

She might not believe in some magical world where all aspects of life fell into place, but she did channel a dreamy focus with her photography that hinted at one.

Was it false?

Paige hoisted the bag over her shoulder and headed for the door of her hotel room.

She didn't want to think of it that way. Instead, she preferred to put her work firmly in the bucket of visual fantasy.

People were smart, and they knew how life worked. If her photography gave them a pretty canvas to project a few happy moments on? Well, she could live with that.

Quite well, as a matter of fact.

The pilot holding the sign was right where her assistant had promised, a sign held high with her name on it. Paige greeted the man with a polite nod and confirmation of who she was and, in moments, was ensconced in the helicopter with the words *Mariposa Resort* written discreetly on the side of the jet-black body. The butter-soft leather seats were the height of luxury, and Paige let herself relax as they gently rose up into the air.

The sparse landscape spread out before her as she took in the view through her window, the red rocks of the state park an impressive backdrop to the short flight to Mariposa.

She could use this vista, Paige realized as she considered all the photos she wanted to capture for the shoot. She'd been so focused up to now on seeing Adam again, she'd admittedly spent less time than she normally did planning her shot list. The resort would take center stage, per the contract, but the area surrounding it would add a layer of natural beauty that she simply had to photograph.

No sooner had they reached flying altitude did she feel the subtle dip in height and then the resort came into view.

You're the reason he left me.

The thought popped into her mind, so completely unbidden that it was shocking how deeply she felt it. How hard it was to face that reality, that the man she'd loved had, in the end, chosen a beautiful pile of bricks over her.

But oh, was it beautiful.

The helicopter gave her a unique vantage point of the resort, the way it spread out over the base of the canyon, those gorgeous limestone spears of red rocks providing a backdrop to the property. Several buildings made up the facilities, with rich green grass intermittently filling the spaces between seating areas. Even from up here, she could see firepits with cozy chairs around them to support after-spa chats or quiet conversations during cocktail hour.

And a bit farther, nestled behind the buildings, was an impressive Olympic-size pool replete with a lush waterfall at one end and a separate hot tub at the other.

"Mr. Colton sends his deepest apologies in advance," the voice of her pilot came on through her headset. "He's been called into a meeting to deal with an urgent matter and will be along as soon as he can get it all wrapped up. He's asked me to take you straightaway to the restaurant and a meeting with Ms. Colton."

Was that an actual shot of disappointment she felt?

"Yes, it'll be fine to meet with Ms. Colton."

She assumed he meant Adam's sister, Laura, the co-owner of Mariposa. Though they hadn't met when she and

Adam dated years ago, he'd spoken of his sister often. Even then, they'd had a strong bond, and Paige had an image in her mind of a determined young woman who lived and breathed the family business just like her brother.

As they set down on a helipad on the back side of the resort, Paige knew that the meeting with Laura was only going to put off the inevitable.

She'd taken a job with the Coltons for the next week.

Adam Colton—the first and only man she'd ever loved—was a part of it.

Ten years might have blunted her feelings, but way down deep, she knew the truth.

She might be a woman who didn't believe in happy-ever-afters, but it was only because she'd never gotten hers.

ONE DAY WITHOUT a crisis.

Adam Colton imagined that precious state—a whole day in the life of running his business—and recognized it for what it was.

Wishful thinking.

Sort of like his memories of Paige Barnes.

When he'd set up this publicity shoot for the family resort, he'd believed himself well able to handle seeing his college girlfriend again. He hadn't chosen her himself, but when the magazine editor who was featuring Mariposa identified Paige as the perfect photographer for the piece, he'd readily agreed.

Was it a bad idea?

Adam hadn't thought so up to now, but the nerves humming beneath his skin suggested otherwise.

Would they both feel that ready tug of attraction that had characterized their relationship from the very beginning?

Or had he managed to kill anything good when he'd let her know that their relationship couldn't continue after graduation?

Of course, he well knew, he hadn't just ruined something good between them.

He'd well and truly ended what had been *us*. The moniker that had denoted them as a couple from the very first days after meeting each other. The only truly complete *us* he'd ever had in his life.

Adam shoved his phone into the breast pocket of his suit before standing from the conference room table. Although it had been pressing, his meeting with Marketing had wrapped and he was satisfied they'd dealt with the PR flare-up that could have turned ugly if his marketing team wasn't so on top of their game.

There was no room to go back to that dark place they'd been in these past few months. Wasn't that why he was even doing this shoot in the first place?

Why he'd, once again, put the betterment of Mariposa in front of his own personal needs?

And why he'd recognized the value of letting Paige Barnes back into his life?

He'd followed her career through the years.

The modeling work she'd done after college had put her in demand for a while, but it was the transition she'd made into photography that had catapulted her into the highest echelon of professional circles. She was one of the most celebrated portrait photographers in the market, and her work was increasingly getting recognition on a global scale.

Why wouldn't he want her photographing Mariposa?

Especially after all the scandals they'd sustained these past several months.

The murdered woman in the cabanas. His father and

stepmother's efforts to take over Mariposa. Even the strange stalkings they'd had to deal with had been deeply unsettling.

All of it had combined to put him in a position where the daily crises of running an exclusive resort looked like child's play beside the swirling crime that had plagued his family and his business.

But it was time to make a new start. That was the message Marketing was taking back to squelch this morning's PR situation. It was also what this photo shoot was about. A high-profile article that would restore Mariposa in people's minds as *the* resort to put on their wish list.

And if it meant he had to work with Paige Barnes for a few days?

Of course he could handle it, just as he managed everything else for the resort that meant the world to him.

How hard could it be, after all?

They'd parted on civil terms, even if he could still remember the hurt in her deep green eyes when he'd told her he needed to focus on his family business after graduation.

At the time, he'd believed himself unable to split his focus. Especially because Paige often made him forget the challenges of his family and the Colton legacy back in Arizona.

How often had he thought about those carefree months they'd spent together in the years since?

It wasn't a set of memories he often allowed himself, but there were moments…the quiet ones, at the end of a long day, when he admitted to himself that his life was far lonelier than he'd ever thought it would—or could—be. A feeling that had grown of late as he watched his siblings couple up these past months.

He was happy for all of them and would never begrudge

them this time in their lives. Even if he had come to realize just how much he'd given up to keep the family business and the Colton reputation intact.

Time to get to it, Colton.

The walk from the business area of the resort to where his sister had set them up for a working lunch was a short trek down the hallway, and Adam resolutely shook off those nerves.

This was business.

He'd made the choice once to walk away from her. He certainly wasn't going to question that choice a decade later.

Life had moved on.

For both of them.

A grand thought, Adam realized as he stepped into the conference room set up for their meeting. It was even a thought he managed to hang on to through a polite hello.

It was only when those vivid green eyes met his, her hand encased in his for a congenial shake, that Adam recognized just how misguided he'd been.

Because it might have been ten years since they'd seen each other, but every moment of every one of those years faded away as their fingers met.

As awareness tingled its way up his arm, delivering a shock straight to his heart.

And as that bright green seemed to stare straight through him, never once warming in all the ways he remembered.

With laughter.

With gentleness.

Or with the sweetest heat that could flare between them with minimal provocation.

He'd made his choice so many years ago, Adam acknowledged to himself. And there was no going back.

PAIGE FOUGHT THE urge to wiggle her arm, not quite realizing just how sensitive a handshake could be. A valid attempt at keeping her cool, she admitted as she stared at the man she hadn't seen in ten years, but false all the same.

Especially because *this* touch reminded her of that other one, so long ago. Another day, when she was still innocent and carefree, when Adam's electric touch had sparked a sort of fervent hope deep inside her.

That first day they'd met, so many years ago.

"I'm Adam Colton." A tilted grin lit up handsome features in a face that hadn't fully settled into its adult form as the guy extended his hand across the library table.

Paige took him in, the impish grin doing nothing to mask the defined planes of his face. Hard slashes of cheekbones would deepen the slight hollows beneath them, and the straight jaw would grow more defined, especially if the trim physique was any indication of how he cared for himself.

She recognized these things about people.

Her own image was constantly scrutinized since she'd signed up for a few modeling gigs to help pay for school and her camera equipment.

Paige had tried to get used to it, especially since her face was getting more and more well-known around campus as the months passed and the opportunities piled up. While the attention was kind and most of her classmates were cool about it all, she struggled to give it meaning. Her face and body were the means to an end—namely avoiding college debt—and she'd use them to her advantage.

Modeling paid the bills, nothing more.

But what she saw through a lens—how light, shadow and life played over a face—was far more interesting to her.

And the man standing before her was fascinating.

Paige extended her hand. "Paige Barnes."

"Do you mind if I join you?"

His words faded as the sheer electricity of her hand in his blindsided her. She was a deeply practical person—her upbringing had required it—but something about Adam Colton woke up places she'd never realized were asleep.

The memory faded as Paige keyed back in to the small but elegant conference room and Adam's expectant blue gaze.

She allowed her own to linger on him a few beats more, satisfied to realize she'd imagined his fully adult form well. Those cheekbones had hardened into interesting slashes, and his shoulders had rounded out, broadening with the promise she'd seen a decade ago.

He was still lanky, but she sensed a strength in him that others would likely overlook at first. He wore *pampered rich guy* well, but she knew he was so much more.

Was shocked to realize just how vividly she remembered how much *more* he really was.

The human form was her business, and Paige had struggled from the very first to resist this one.

Which was the exact reason she'd fought the endless waves of nerves all morning.

Since she hated feeling vulnerable to anything, she gave herself one final moment to compose herself and put her client-facing smile firmly in place.

"Adam, it's nice to see you again."

"Welcome to Mariposa."

If she sensed a subtle dissatisfaction with her cordial response, wasn't that to be expected?

She might not have an endless string of notches on her lipstick case, but the two of them did have a relationship. A fiery, expansive one, at that. They'd dated for more than six months, and, at least from her side, it had been the most serious relationship of her life.

He'd obviously not felt the same since he'd put coming home to Arizona above their relationship, and it was that knowledge Paige securely wrapped around herself.

She'd obviously come in a distant second to running the family business.

"The property is beautiful. And the helicopter ride in is quite an experience."

Adam's sister, Laura, had already come around the table to refresh her coffee at the small sideboard along the wall. The pretty woman was nearly as tall as Paige, with blue eyes that matched her brother's but hair a lighter shade of blond that swung just above her shoulders in a sleek bob.

"It's an extravagance, but a bit necessary based on where we're situated here at the base of Red Rocks, considering the privacy and exclusivity many of our clients require. We do work to offset the emissions with several sustainability efforts here at the resort."

"That's a part of your business plan?" Paige heard the surprise in her own voice and notched it down a few beats. "I think it's wonderful you've built that into your working model."

Adam took a sip of his own coffee. "It's one of several sustainability efforts my sister and I have insisted on since taking over the running of the resort."

"Have you spoken with Isabella about working that into the magazine piece? I think that would do quite well with the audience you're targeting with the press."

Laura smiled before laying a hand on Paige's arm. "I'll leave you two to that discussion. My brother's the PR wiz. I prefer to keep my focus on the clients, and we have a rather wealthy one landing in—" She broke off as she glanced down at her watch. "Twenty minutes. I'd like to check on her room before heading down to the lobby. I'll look forward to giving you a full tour of the resort later this afternoon."

They made arrangements to meet in the lobby after the exclusive guest was settled in, and all too soon Paige was left alone with Adam.

"My sister's always on the move. And that's even with just coming back from her honeymoon."

Paige had gotten a bit of a gossip session before heading here and knew that Laura had only recently married. Something odd tugged at her. Not quite jealousy, but that subtle sense she could never quite shake that married and happy-ever-after were for others, never for her.

Shaking it off—there was no place for maudlin thoughts on a job—she easily parried back. "Since you had to deal with a crisis before heading in here, it sounds like you're a matched set."

The smile—the one she'd always associated with him, a tempting cross between impish and boyish—flashed. "We are that. I believe some of the staff accuses us of sharing one brain, as a matter of fact."

"It's good you have each other to depend on." Paige glanced around, aiming for professional yet casual. They might not have seen each other in over a decade, but they knew each other. Had made love to each other.

Acting too cold would only suggest more interest on her part than she wanted to express.

She might be willing to admit to herself that she'd carried a blazing torch for Adam Colton for ten years, but she'd be damned if she wanted him to see that.

Gesturing toward the conference table that filled the room, Paige took a seat, settling her coffee on the table before setting down the small leather folder case she'd carried in. "I'd like to discuss several of the shots I'm interested in capturing while I'm here. The resort is going to photograph beautifully, but I have some ideas for some less traditional shots as well."

Obviously intrigued, Adam moved toward the table. "Do you think Isabella will put them in the article?"

"I'll give her a choice, and I suspect she'll use the more traditional images for the luxury piece she's planning to publish. I actually have ulterior motives."

"Oh?" His mouth settled in a hard line, apparently bracing himself.

"'Oh' is right. I'm quite confident when you see some of my less traditional shots, you're going to be paying my fees to put each and every one up on your website and in your promotional materials."

"That's quite a statement." Adam's mouth relaxed a bit, a small smile hovering around the corners. "Especially since I'm rather fond of the sales materials we updated less than six months ago."

"They're nice."

"Nice?" His brows shot up at that.

"They work. Pretty pictures of a pretty place."

"I'm not sure I've ever been insulted with such *pretty* words," he said, tone dry as unbuttered toast.

"No insult intended," Paige said, even as she admitted to herself there was a slight insult absolutely intended.

Even as she knew it was more than that.

If she had to accept that she'd been tossed aside from the best relationship of her life for a freaking hotel, she damn well expected it to look good to others. Pedestrian photos of the golf course and spa and well-appointed hotel rooms just felt like...well, like an affront.

"Look, image is my business. I know you're doing this piece because of the bad press that has hit here these past few months. You can use that to your benefit."

"Murder is a benefit?"

That dry tone was back, along with a subtle, simmering anger she hadn't quite banked on.

"I'm not saying that. What I am saying is, you were dealt a bad hand that you're trying to overcome. You wouldn't have looked to book this PR piece if you didn't need to make up some lost ground."

"This is my business, Paige. We don't lose ground or pander to the masses."

"Then what do you do, Adam?"

She couldn't resist tossing the emphasis on his name back at him.

"What's that supposed to mean?"

"You've got a grand, exclusive resort that you've made your life. Someone tried to destroy that and all you've worked for. Why not go for broke? Really make something of the bad press and turn it on its ear."

"I don't need to turn anything. I need a few pretty pictures and a nice article that suggests Mariposa is still a place to relax and refresh for those who demand elite, luxury experiences."

Paige had no idea why she was pressing this—only now that she'd gotten a good head of steam, she couldn't quite stop.

He had made this resort his life and had left her in the process. Wasn't she entitled to an opinion on the matter?

Or maybe, more to the point, a few jabs she'd earned as the scorned party?

Which was why she shrugged, masking her features in that bland, careless look she'd perfected as a model.

"Your choice. All I'll say is that people love a mystery, even the ones who can afford elite, luxury experiences. They might love it even more. And you have the ability to serve that up to them on a sexy, sultry platter."

"I appreciate the feedback, but I've invited you here to take some photos. That's all."

Paige stood at that. "Then I best be on my way. I have a resort to explore. I'll make sure I find the exact right spots to set up my tripod and get you a few glamour shots."

She was up and out of her chair, portfolio in hand, when a hard, firm palm came down on her forearm, stilling her movement.

The grip was light—she could have shaken it off easily—but it packed a punch all the same.

Adam Colton had his hand on her.

And damn it if she wasn't curious enough to stay and see what came next.

Chapter Two

Adam wasn't sure how it had happened.

One moment he was the wealthy hotelier, completely in control of himself and his environment, and the next he felt himself spiraling at her words.

At her heartbreaking face.

And at the truth.

Damn it, that was the hardest part to swallow.

She was 100 percent right.

They'd taken a hit these past months. From his stepmother, Glenna's, shocking interference in the resort to his father's troubles with the family business, Colton Textiles, to the horror of a murder on the grounds, the pressure had been enormous.

Although the perpetrator had been caught, it still gnawed at him that one of their own—yoga instructor Allison Brewer—had been murdered by an out-of-control talent manager. A man who'd refused to leave her alone.

Adam and his siblings had been forced to reconsider some of their policies at Mariposa. The deliberate choice to avoid closed-circuit cameras, as well as many discreet amenities that catered to privacy, had made it all too easy for someone to do significant harm.

Had they been wrong all this time in prioritizing privacy over safety?

Or did they simply need to rethink how they managed security?

He knew Laura still carried considerable guilt over Allison's death. Along with Laura's new husband, Noah Steele, a former detective and foster brother of the murdered Allison, they were working on ways to keep the privacy their clients demanded while ensuring something like that couldn't happen again.

Yet it had.

Just a few months after they'd begun to heal over Allison's death, the problems started again.

Because he'd believed things were getting better, he'd invited his college roommate Max Powell to take refuge at the resort. A celebrity chef with a popular TV show, Max had been facing challenges of his own back in New York. Adam had suggested to Max that he could use the space as a way to relax and recharge his batteries out of the way of prying eyes and the increasing intrusions of his fan base back home.

Only Arizona had proven to be as dangerous as New York—nearly more so—when a guardrail on one of the more difficult hiking trails broke, nearly killing Alexis, Mariposa's best concierge. He'd assigned Alexis to Max specifically because she was so valued by the resort, and he knew she'd care for his friend and maintain his privacy in every way.

It was only when Max's troubles followed him from New York that the depths of the problems he'd been facing had become clear. Max's assistant on his TV show had followed him to Arizona, stalking him with the intention of killing him in the errant belief Max had been in love with her.

The woman had nearly killed Alexis. Max had chased after her, saving Alexis even as Noah was on his way with the local police to capture the angry stalker.

Adam had apologized to Max repeatedly, but Max had shrugged it all off since the experience had drawn him and Alexis close, the two starting a relationship in the midst of the danger.

Even more problems had followed on the heels of both incidents, and Adam wasn't sure of anything any longer.

And now Paige thought they could gloss over it with some photographs?

It was simplistic and...

And even as it frustrated him, he couldn't deny her point.

People were intrigued by what had happened. Despite the repeated danger, their bookings were up again after a brief downturn. And for as terrible as it all was, he, Laura and their brother, Josh, had used what had happened to reevaluate areas that weren't right and were working to make them better.

Noah had even retired from the force and shifted his skills to managing all security for Mariposa.

Adam hated that people had been hurt in the process, but he refused to accept that their suffering had happened in vain.

Glancing down, he realized his hand was still on Paige's forearm, and he pulled it back. "I'm sorry. These experiences are still raw. People got hurt."

The fire that had flared in her eyes, carrying her through the various arguments she was making for her potential shot list, faded a bit.

"I realize that, and I'm sorry for it." She reached out, laying her hand over the one he'd so recently dropped to his side. "Truly sorry. My comments aren't about making light of that or what has happened here. But you *are* still planning to stay open, right?"

"Of course." He couldn't remember ever feeling *more* determined. Even those months after college, when he'd made the difficult choice to leave her to her modeling career in New York, he hadn't been this fervent in his focus.

Mariposa was his life, and while that might not say much about him, he was determined to ensure his laser focus on the family resort hadn't been for nothing.

Or what else had every decision he'd made in his adult life been for?

"Then use that, Adam. Find a way to make all that's happened mean something."

"You're rather convincing."

She smiled at that. "Image is my business. You hired me for a reason. Let me do my job."

"You've made quite a career for yourself. I'm just surprised you gave up the modeling. When we were in college, you had a good thing going there."

The fire in her eyes had faded fully, replaced with something that dulled that vivid green.

Something he couldn't put his finger on but was there all the same.

"Modeling never meant all that much to me beyond the money. It paid for school. For my camera equipment. And it gave me access to some of the best photographers in the world."

"They gave away their trade secrets?"

Although he'd asked the question with a slight veneer of amusement, he was surprised to see how quickly that light in her gaze flared back to life.

"You'd be amazed what people will share. Everyone wants to talk about their work. About what they love. I learned so much in those years modeling. From light and shadow to the mechanics of the camera itself, each gig was a new course in learning from a master. It was amazing." She shook her head, the long fall of auburn hair draping around her shoulders in a way he remembered with aching clarity.

He remembered even more wrapping his hands in those soft strands, the subtle red tones burnished gold streaming over his fingers.

Ten minutes in her company, Adam thought. If he were honest, the memories of his time with Paige had never fully left him, but they had grown worse as he'd anticipated her arrival at Mariposa.

Since there was nothing to be done about the choices he'd made long ago and could never take back, he pushed them aside.

He had to push them aside.

"How about if I start on that tour Laura promised? I can give you a sense of the property and then give you some time to explore." He stopped, nearly reconsidered his words before pushing on. "I know you declined the offer when the job details were finalized, but you can stay here on property."

"I appreciate it, but I'm good in town."

"If you change your mind—"

"I won't. But I do appreciate it, Adam."

She picked up her items from where she'd settled them on the conference table, the conversation about where she was staying obviously at an end.

It was only when she turned back to face him that he pasted on his at-your-service smile and gestured toward the door.

"Let's go, then."

And as he followed her out of the room, he had to admit that the memories of her he'd carried for ten years hadn't done her justice. Neither had the myriad photos he'd seen of her through the years.

Nothing could quite capture that vitality and sheer romantic beauty unless you were actually looking at Paige Barnes.

Too bad he'd given up any right to feelings for her—save regret—long ago.

Round one, over.

Paige couldn't quite get the clang of a ringing bell out of her mind as she walked with Adam around the resort.

She'd made it through their first meeting.

That was what she had to keep in mind and stay focused on.

She'd poked a bit—okay, more than a bit—but she'd been cordial and professional, too. Which she'd take as a win since the memory of Adam Colton had loomed large for way too long in her mind.

And she was right.

Simple glamour shots weren't what he needed right now. The resort needed a bold look that hinted at the allure of the place.

And wow, it was quite a place.

She'd always counted herself lucky that her modeling career had taken her to many places around the world at a young age. The twin education—of learning about other parts of the globe and what she'd always thought of as her photography apprenticeship—had set her up in ways college never had.

Not that she wasn't grateful for that time, but aside from

Adam, in many ways it felt like she'd simply marked time for those four years.

Waiting.

For her life to begin and her dreams to come true.

How's that any different from now?

That sly voice whispered through her thoughts, wafting and weaving a truth she seldom dwelled on.

Her life was nomadic, and her roots were so shallow as to be nonexistent. And beyond those glorious six months she'd spent with Adam, she had very little ties to anyone or anything.

"Max is here."

Paige keyed back in to Adam's comments as they came to the main common area of the resort. "Max Powell?"

"Yep. He's a big celebrity chef now. He came here a few months ago to get away from the pressure in New York but has found his way to staying and making Arizona his home base."

Paige caught something. It hovered lightly—barely there, like a soft breeze—but she caught it all the same.

Subtle hints of envy, even though she wasn't quite sure why.

"I saw him about five years ago, right after he opened a location in New York. I've followed his career and am so happy for him and all his success." She smiled. "And wow, can that man cook. I had a salmon-in-bourbon-reduction dish I'd consider giving my eyeteeth to taste again."

"Maybe we can arrange something."

"I'd like to see him again."

And she would, even if the intimacy in Adam's gaze hit somewhere in the bottom of her stomach, setting off a swarm of butterflies with manic wings.

She had to get this back onto solid ground.

Thoughts of easy dinners with old friends wasn't why she was here. In fact, nothing about the past needed to be part of this.

Wasn't that what she'd told herself for the past few weeks since taking the assignment?

She'd nearly missed out on it because of a different job in Hawaii she had expected to run until the end of the month. But the celebrity she was photographing had needed to make an unplanned trip for some reshoots on his upcoming film, and she was sent home, ready and available when Isabella called her with the opportunity.

At a more fanciful time in her life, she'd have called it fate. Back when she'd believed in all that. Fate. Destiny. Divining your future from a series of signs.

Thankfully, she was long past that.

Wishing on stars and looking for signs were the pathways to heartache, nothing more.

The universe simply didn't send signs. If it did, she'd never have gotten involved with Adam Colton in the first place.

She'd still have parents who loved her instead of abandoning her to a life on her own.

And she'd have found her way to a more normal lifestyle, one devoid of last-minute trips and life out of a suitcase.

It smacked of *poor little rich girl* thinking, which was why she avoided thinking about Adam at all. Or her nomadic life.

Most days she liked it.

And on the rare days when she wished for something else?

Well, she pulled out her camera, took a long walk and sought to bring her life right back into focus.

SHE WAS SAD.

The realization hit hard and fast, and Adam wondered how he'd never seen it before. Because now that he looked at Paige—really looked at her, past that heartbreaking beauty and competent professionalism that poured off her—he realized what was underneath.

A well of sadness that nearly took his breath away.

Paige Barnes was a beautiful woman. It was so easy to be distracted by that fact, and he had to admit to himself that he absolutely had been stymied by it.

He certainly had been when they'd first met.

Even after six months of knowing her and living with her, he'd still ultimately convinced himself that things wouldn't go the distance between them if he were far away in Arizona and she were traveling the world modeling.

And now. This morning.

All he'd seen was that blazing beauty, a mix of soft skin and sharply angled cheekbones and a long, leggy body that drew the eye.

The woman could wear a shower curtain and look good.

Which made the fact that she paid little to no attention to her own features a funny sort of joke on the universe.

Yet for all that smooth skin and those elegant features, there was a woman underneath. A real person with feelings and emotions and thoughts.

He'd been enamored to discover all that when they'd dated, yet he'd still given in to his own insecurities and his deep, almost feral need to live out his Colton legacy.

What did that say about him?

Since it wasn't anything good, Adam could only hope the ensuing years had been better to her.

"How have you been, Paige? Since college."

The question seemed to catch her off guard, and she

nearly tripped as they crossed the main hotel lobby toward a water feature he wanted to show her outside. The Red Rocks of Arizona speared up behind the resort and made a stunning backdrop to one of the many private areas they'd created for their visitors.

Conversation spots. Lounging areas. Relaxing chairs. All shrouded by the beauty of the rocks that ringed the resort.

With ease, he steadied her with a light grip on her elbow and kept them moving forward.

"I've been fine. Always busy, always hustling." She shifted slightly away from him and his touch. "All the usual things people do as they work to build a career."

"I'm surprised you haven't married."

She stilled at that, her gaze narrowing as she turned the full wattage of her green glare on him. "You make personal observations like that to every professional who comes to your resort?"

"Since I haven't had anyone else here who I dated, slept with and practically lived with, I figured it wouldn't be appropriate."

"Way to make it even less appropriate."

He shrugged, ignoring the shot of vulnerability that had pushed him to ask her the question in the first place. "It's a simple observation between friends."

"Former friends." She stopped, as if weighing her words, before continuing. "You know, I nearly passed on this opportunity. Nearly traded off work because I knew you'd be here. But I came anyway. Swallowed my pride and told myself I needed to see the bigger picture."

"What picture is that?"

"Life moves on, Adam. It did for you, and after a lot of soul searching, it finally did for me, too. I'm not going back to that place."

"What place?"

"The one where you have any influence over my life. The one where I harbor a single minute of sadness or upset at being thrown over by a guy for a hotel. The one where I give you another damn tear."

With that, she turned on one wickedly pointed high heel and headed back the way they'd come.

An avenging goddess leaving him crushed in her wake.

He deserved it.

More, he'd pressed and pushed because it had never sat comfortably how they'd ended things.

Nope, Colton, you don't get off that easy.

Because it had all been about how *he'd* ended things.

It had all been him.

His need to make a mark with his family legacy. His need to get away from that gnawing beast that kept telling him she'd never stay with him for the long haul. And that subtle but unyielding message that his family unit was never quite as secure as it should have been and he couldn't possibly live too far away.

So he watched her walk away and vowed to apologize later. After he managed to get his own thoughts in order and firmly out of jerk territory.

"You look like you saw a ghost."

Adam turned to find his brother, Josh, standing there, clad in pressed shorts and a well-fit white T-shirt with *Mariposa* outlined in embroidery over his left pectoral.

"I think I did."

"The hot photographer who flew over a few hours ago from Sedona?"

Something dark swirled in his gut at the all-too accurate description of Paige.

"You say that about all our guests?"

"Hey," Josh slapped a hand over his chest, his fingers nearly covering the Mariposa logo. "I'm a happily involved man. There's no one else for me besides Kelli, but I'm not dead, either. Pair of legs like that walks into the resort, a man notices."

"Smooth, little brother. Real smooth."

"For a long time, I was." His blue eyes grew thoughtful. "Thankfully, Kelli saved me from that horrible existence."

It wasn't just Josh who'd needed saving. Kelli had gotten into unexpected trouble at Mariposa after being mistaken for the previous female bartender at L Bar.

A local gang set on robbing the region's banks had come after her, thinking the former bartender's boyfriend had hidden some of their stash.

They'd ultimately worked it out—and pulled an effective sting to catch the robbers—but it wasn't without even more upheaval and risk to the resort.

Would it ever calm down?

"So, about that ghost…" Josh pressed, pulling Adam from the litany of problems they'd faced these past months.

"Her name's Paige Barnes. She was my girlfriend in college, right before I came back to Arizona."

Josh nodded in understanding, even though Adam had always kept his relationship with Paige close to the vest. "The one who got away."

"The one I left."

"And now she's back and hotter than you remembered."

"I've always remembered pretty well." The comment was as dry as the red dust that often blew down from the mountains. "And she's still amazing."

"Now she's back. You've seen the way we've been coupling up around here. Laura and Noah. Me and Kelli. Max and Alexis. Even our baby sister has gotten in on the act with despicable Glenna's decidedly-not-despicable nephew. If Dani and Matt can make it work with all the family baggage on both sides, there's hope for everyone."

It warmed Adam's heart to hear how Josh referred to their half sister, Dani. Especially because he'd come to think of her as his sister, too. Nothing halfway about it.

Dani had found love and, to Josh's point, in the most unlikely of circumstances, with their stepmother's nephew.

Although they'd all been distrustful of Matt at the start, everyone had come around when it was obvious how much he cared for Dani and how little time he had for his aunt's antics.

And it had given them one more reminder that their stepmother wasn't to be trusted.

Ever.

"Seriously." Josh slapped him on the shoulder. "Maybe it's your time."

"I don't think Paige would agree with you."

His brother's gaze was speculative. "Maybe you can just start by being the great guy I know you to be instead of the master-of-the-universe routine you pull around here. Let her see a different side of you."

It wasn't the first time either of his siblings had accused him of being heavy-handed. Or overly involved with Mariposa.

But hadn't the past few months proven him right yet again?

It wasn't just the danger and suspicious things that had happened here, either.

His father's inability to manage his life with any sense of decorum or restraint had flared up once more, and he'd put the family business in jeopardy with his behavior.

Problems that now extended to the resort.

Despite the fact that his late mother had kept Mariposa distinctly separate from her husband's family business of fine-fabric importing, his father had always wanted to get his hands on the resort. Now that Colton Textiles was circling the drain from bad business practices and overall laziness on the part of his father, Clive had set his sights on Mariposa.

It was unfathomable.

And all too real.

Especially since the land beneath the resort was held in trust by Colton Textiles.

It could all come crashing down if they didn't get the damned timing right.

His lawyers were trying to be optimistic, but Adam had discussed it at length with Laura, Josh and Dani, and they had fair cause to worry.

Add on all the issues they'd had these past months, and they weren't sitting in the best position. Bookings might be up out of some sort of macabre interest, but they'd had to invest quite a bit to upgrade security.

It was a lot. And as oldest, it all rested on his shoulders.

And now he had the only woman he'd ever truly had feelings for back in his life.

Could things get worse?

He'd learned a long time ago not to ask that question. Especially because the answer was inevitably yes.

Chapter Three

Paige didn't believe in second chances, so sitting in Laura Colton's—now Laura Colton Steele's—office felt like a waste of time.

But emotions aside, could she really walk out on this job?

She'd never done it before, but there was always a first time.

Only, if she walked off the job now, it would feel like cowardice instead of an actual professional disagreement, and that was the part that didn't settle well in her gut.

"Can I get you anything?" Laura smiled from where she stood at a sideboard in her office, pouring a fresh cup of coffee from a carafe.

"I wouldn't turn down some more coffee."

As she stood up, Laura waved her to sit back down at the small meeting table on the windowed side of her office that overlooked the property. "I'll get it. Then I'd love to talk to you about something."

"Of course."

Although Laura's tone held an easy quality, Paige was well aware there was more.

There *had* to be more, especially since it was Laura who'd intercepted her storming back into the main lobby.

The woman returned with two mugs, setting one down in front of Paige before taking her seat.

"What do you think of Mariposa?"

"It's magnificent. It's easy to see on the ground how impeccable everything is, but I had the extra benefit of flying in over it, and it's exquisite."

"Like a jewel, my mother always said." Laura took a sip of her coffee before setting it down. "She'd be horrified if she knew all that had happened here over the past six months."

Paige knew their mother had died many years before. When Adam was fourteen, she remembered. Although it briefly crossed her mind to keep the thought to herself, Paige went with instinct.

And the genuine warmth she recognized in Laura's face.

"I knew Adam in college, so I know your mother's been gone a long time. This place meant quite a lot to her?"

"It meant everything. She's the reason we even own the resort. When her father died, she used his inheritance to purchase the property."

For all she thought she knew, that was definitely new information, and Paige was intrigued, in spite of that still-simmering desire to walk away.

"My mother preferred to stay here while my father remained in Los Angeles running the Colton family business." Laura's blue gaze—so like her brother's—drifted toward the windows before returning to Paige. "Some of my happiest memories are those years growing up here with her."

"It didn't bother you that your father was so far away?"

Laura sighed at that before a grim smile tilted her lips. "It's unfortunate to say, but life's usually better when my father's far away."

"Family can be…" Paige paused, offering a small smile of her own. "Difficult. I'm sorry."

And she was. Although she'd have given anything to have a different relationship with her own parents, Paige had long ago accepted what she had gotten. A gambler with an addiction problem for a father and a disillusioned mother who never understood why, on the rare occasions he came back into their lives, Dusty Barnes refused to stay for long.

It was a difficult reality, that idea that the people who were supposed to love you most in the world were too caught up in their own problems and lives to be there.

To be present.

But it happened every day in families all over the world.

"Unfortunately, my father's been a bit too close for comfort lately."

"Causing problems?"

"Quite a few, on top of the incidents we've had here."

Laura glanced down at her coffee before looking back up, seemingly resolved. "It's not public knowledge, but it's not exactly a secret, either. And I figure if you're here, entering various places over the grounds, I have to believe your extra-observant eyes might come in handy."

Paige was intrigued beyond her earlier upset. "What is actually going on? I did some research before coming and know about a few of the incidents, but it sounds like there's quite a bit more."

"My father's run the family business into the ground, so he's decided Mariposa is ripe for the plucking to give him the cash infusion he needs."

"I'm no real estate maven, but is that even possible?"

Laura nodded. "In this case, yes. My mother might have owned the resort, but Colton Textiles owns the land. A neat maneuver we discovered my father managed while my mother was in the throes of her cancer battle."

If she'd been asked even ten minutes ago if she had a shred of compassion left in her body for Adam Colton, Paige would have said no, never.

But this?

"What are you all going to do?"

"It's been a lot of keeping our fingers in the dam and searching for out clauses."

"Let me guess—there aren't many."

Laura's slight head shake was proof enough. "Not a one."

The situation sounded dire, and on top of the terrible events that had taken place at Mariposa, it was an unfathomable problem. How could their father treat their lives so carelessly?

Even as the thought registered, the last time she'd seen her father drifted through her mind.

"Come on, Paigey. Just a few thousand'll get me through."

"I don't have that sort of money."

"'Course you do." His deep green eyes, which might have matched the ones she looked at each day in the mirror, had gone worn and bloodshot, the folds of skin around them flappy with wrinkles. *"You're a big shot. I know you've got the money for dear old Dad."*

"Having it and being willing to give it to you are two different things."

He'd actually slammed his coffee cup down on the tabletop at that, making her glad she'd selected a diner near his apartment and far away from her home in Newport Beach.

"You're a cold-ass bitch, you know that?"

Paige had simply sat there, taking it. Knowing that she was a target and nothing more. One whom he'd come to because he'd run out of other options, not because he actually cared about her.

So she'd sat there and listened to it all, allowing him to say terrible, awful things to her.

And when it was over, she'd stood and stared down at him as she tossed money for the breakfast on the counter.

"Don't call me ever again."

Those words still haunted her, but she'd worked hard to blot them out so that they only wormed their way in at the worst moments. The ones where she was tired or sad and had already given in to the exhaustion that could ride a person into the abyss of memories.

Adam often occupied a spot on that greatest-hits reel, too.

Memories of how things had just ended, without warning.

In the end, that had been the anger she'd held on to. The one that still burned like a hot coal held tight in the palm.

But she had to admit, Laura's candidness went a long way toward painting a picture of Adam she'd never really known.

Whether it was because he'd held it back or their relationship had never reached that point or even just the carelessness of youth, she'd not known much past the death of his mother.

But if he equated Mariposa with her? And had shared beloved times here as a child?

It made his attachment to the resort a bit easier to understand.

If only he'd given her that context.

"May I ask you a question in return?" Laura asked, breaking through those swirling what ifs.

"Of course."

"You said you knew my brother in college. Were you the woman he dated at the end of his time in New York?" Laura waved a hand before rushing on. "In transparency, I'm asking out of my own curiosity. Adam never said much about that time, but he's spoken of you through the years. I've always heard a solid thread of wistfulness there."

Wistfulness?

Although it didn't change what had happened—or the fact that she'd ultimately lost to Adam's unwillingness to share his life or why he needed to come back to Arizona—Paige couldn't deny it was another chink in the armor she'd wrapped firmly around herself for this job.

"We did date. For about six months before graduation."

"I'm sorry things didn't work out."

It was Paige's turn to ask the questions. "Why is that?"

"I am so lucky in the relationship I have with my brother. With both my brothers, actually. Which is probably why I shouldn't say anything. But I will," Laura said, a genuine twinkle in her eyes. "Outside of childhood, I've never known a time in his life when Adam was happier."

"Oh, well, that's nice to hear."

"It's true, Paige. I don't expect you to forgive him or move past whatever happened then, but I do think it's important that you know that. Or that you know what the rest of us saw when we looked at or talked to Adam during that time."

Paige wasn't sure what the right response was. Ten years was a long time to carry a torch, but it was an equally long time to hold a grudge.

Was it time to maybe just accept they'd both moved on? Gone on to the lives they were supposed to have?

"Thank you, then. It's a lovely compliment."

"Good. Now that we have that settled, let me walk you through some details on the property."

Laura reached for a thick binder that she'd set on the edge of the conference table before they sat down, opening to a page that held a fold-out map of Mariposa and its grounds.

Although Paige listened to Laura and about each area she pointed out on the map, she'd own to herself that she actually heard very little.

All she could think about were Laura's comments about Adam and his happiness during the time the two of them were together.

She could relate because it had been the happiest time of her life, too.

It didn't fix all that had come before, but it still meant something. In fact, she thought as she leaned in closer to review a few photos Laura had pulled from the binder, in some ways it felt like it meant everything.

ADAM FOUND THEM THERE, heads bent together, an hour later. His pep talk from his brother still filled his mind, but even a stroll around the grounds hadn't settled his roiling thoughts.

Which made little sense because there were very few problems he couldn't think through with a hearty walk around the property.

None of those prior walks came after seeing your former lover.

Since his inward restlessness held a stark layer of truth, Adam had finally given up and gone in search of Laura in hopes the two of them could smooth things over with Paige.

He couldn't afford to have her walk off this job, the history between the two of them be damned. That much was absolute.

"Laura, I—" He stilled his knock on the door when he realized Paige sat at his sister's conference table.

"Adam. Come on in. I was just giving Paige an overview of the property as well as pointing out a few areas she may want to consider for her shot list."

There was something oddly knowing in his sister's gaze, and he wondered what the two of them had possibly discussed before he'd arrived. The question did battle with Paige's departing words an hour before, suggesting she'd shed tears over him.

Of all the things he'd expected as part of their reentry into one another's lives, that thought hadn't registered very high on his list.

Unbidden, a memory of one of their earliest dates came back to his mind.

The two of them at a packed nightclub near campus, dancing late into the night. She'd laughed and smiled at him, her gaze on no one but him, as they'd entwined themselves around each other through song after song.

It had been heady, that night and every night after. Her attention was solely for him. Even when others were around, her gaze would meet his or her fingers would lightly graze along his body. Simple touches that said she was aware of him.

That she wanted to be with him.

Through all these years, had he really lulled himself into believing his leaving had left her pain free?

Worse, was he wrong in his assumption that their breakup wouldn't be that devastating because she would inevitably move on quickly once he was gone?

Vowing to do something about it with private words to Paige, Adam stepped through the door, his sister's gaze expectant as she waited for him to join them.

"I'd love to see what areas you're suggesting."

He spent a minute or two getting himself coffee from Laura's sideboard, but even he knew it was nothing more than a ploy to buy himself a few steadying breaths.

Especially because the increasing press of memories had him reconsidering everything he'd thought for the past decade.

And he didn't come off like a very good guy in the mental retelling of their breakup.

He took the open seat next to Paige and noticed the hastily scribbled notes she'd written on a small notepad. A few things were circled, but the one that caught his attention was the reference to setting up a shot against the red rocks of the mountainside.

Adam tapped the notepad. "You'd like to take a photo on the rocks?"

"I'd like to explore what's possible. Either putting myself up above and shooting down or putting the models above so I can capture images up." She shrugged. "Maybe both. But there's something haunting about the color of the rocks, and with or without the models, I'd love to give a few things a try there."

"Josh has some rappelling equipment we can probably use for safety," Laura said, excitement bubbling beneath her words. "In fact, I'd like to get his thoughts. We might be able to do a few shots for the resort, outside of the magazine piece, that support some of his more advanced outside activities. I'm going to go get him." Laura was already up and out of her chair before she stilled on a hearty laugh. "We will, of course, pay you for all the work. But I can see the vibrancy you're talking about, and I'd love for you to capture that."

With the typical quick movements his sister was known

for, Laura was gone barely a minute after Adam had sat down.

Paige turned to smile at him, no hints of their earlier quarrel evident. "She seems excited."

"I think we all are. Which is only one of the many reasons I owe you an apology for earlier. You deserved better than my childish attitude and attempts to ask you about your personal life, and I am sorry. I hope you'll stay on and keep this assignment with us."

Paige considered him for a moment, her gaze unyielding, before seeming to come to some sort of decision. "I was nervous earlier. Seeing you again. I wasn't my best self, and I'm sorry for that."

"I—" He stopped, her words fully registering. "You were nervous?"

"Yeah, Adam. Of course I was. I haven't seen you in ten years, and the last time I did was you breaking things off between us. I am human."

And she was.

Human.

In that moment, the vulnerability highlighting her cheeks in a subtle pink, Adam realized she was exactly that.

"I'm sorry. For all of it. I don't think I ever gave you that credit."

"What does that mean?"

Although the question was pointed, he didn't hear anger. Gentle curiosity, maybe, but that was all.

"You have to know that you're a stunningly beautiful woman. I always believed I saw beyond that to the person inside, but if I'm being honest, I realize I assumed that beauty protected you from some of life's harsher realities."

"Like breakups?"

"Breakups. Relationships. Pain of any kind, to be honest.

I guess—" He shook his head, staring down at his coffee and wishing there was wisdom to be found in the depths of that cup.

But there was only him and what he hoped was an apology that could begin to make a few things right.

With that, he lifted his head, unwilling to give her anything less than a direct answer.

"I'm fumbling this horribly. What I'm trying to say is that I think I elevated you so much that I didn't give you proper credit for being human, too. I'm more sorry than I can say about that."

Myriad emotions crossed her face, that compelling bone structure a canvas for her thoughts.

But it was the quick light of acceptance that struck Adam as not only forgiving but also far more kind than he deserved.

"I'm not sure I'd like to be judged forever on who I was at twenty-one."

"I don't know about that. The woman I remember was someone pretty great. Hardworking. Kind. Determined."

That clear acceptance vanished, her face settling into stark lines. "If you thought that, why did you leave?"

"I needed to come back here."

Adam was surprised to realize how present that time still was in his mind. Even a decade's worth of hard work and a diligent focus on putting distance between Mariposa and his father's interests couldn't quell what he'd felt then.

And, sadly, still faced now.

That bone-numbing fear his father would do something to ruin Mariposa. That his mother's legacy would be destroyed if he didn't ensure the resort had a future.

Part of him recognized how empty that was, putting

a business over love. And yet, Mariposa was more than a business.

It was the only part of his mother he had left.

"You've made something pretty amazing here," Paige finally said. "I'm glad it's worked out for you."

As he considered all that had happened these past few months—including his father's latest fight to sell off the property in order to keep Colton Textiles solvent—Adam couldn't help but feel it had all been for nothing.

He'd lost the woman he loved.

He was facing the loss of his home.

And he had to come to grips with the fact that he'd failed his dead mother as surely as he'd failed everyone else.

"That's kind of you to say," Adam finally said.

Paige wasn't sure if it was kindness so much as a bland platitude she'd managed to dig up to keep the conversation from veering back to that unpleasant place they'd been earlier.

What else was there to say?

Time had done its work on both of them, two adults living separate lives.

And if she were honest, even if given the choice to go back, she couldn't say that she would.

For all its challenges and her sadness in her quiet moments, she liked the life she'd built these past ten years. She loved her photography career, and even her modeling work had given her a life beyond her imaginings.

"Mariposa is an amazing place. I'm looking forward to photographing it."

"So you will stay on and take the assignment?"

"I'll stay."

Quiet descended once more between them, and Paige

was about to let him know that she was leaving for the day when he laid a hand over hers on the top of the small table.

"I never meant to hurt you. I realize now just how badly I behaved and that I did hurt you anyway."

Paige stared down at where their hands were joined, an ocean of need welling up inside her.

Had she ever stopped wanting this man?

She'd dated plenty since their breakup, both by choice and by her own personal determination, refusing to sit and dwell on what she could no longer have.

There'd been some wonderful men who'd been part of her life.

But none of them had been Adam.

Still, she continued to search. She'd refused to believe that the best romance of her life had already come and gone.

Even if no one she'd met so far had managed to give off the sort of sparks and heat that she'd shared with Adam.

A determined woman kept looking.

And she'd keep searching after this strange interlude, too.

Glancing back up to Adam, she smiled. "Thank you. I appreciate the apology. And I'm sort of glad we got all this out of the way here at first."

"Out of the way?"

A layer of surprise lay beneath his words, and Paige realized this was her chance.

A way to keep the distance she so desperately needed between them.

"Well, sure. We had some history, and now we've had a chance to air it out. Give it a bit of breathing room so we can put it behind us."

"Right." He nodded, removing his hand from where it still lay overtop hers. "That's for the best."

Was the man actually so clueless that he thought they'd pick up where they'd left off?

Because pushing that button would lead them nowhere but back to a fight, Paige ignored it. After gathering her things together, she stood, careful to keep her tone breezy and carefree. "Yes, it's for the best."

Later, she'd worry about how much that effort cost her. But right now, it was a source of pride that she refused to let him see how much it all hurt to be back in each other's orbit again.

"I can plan to be back here tomorrow morning. In the meantime, I want to review my notes and start putting together a proposed shot list and schedule for the next several days."

"That sounds good. We can reconvene for lunch tomorrow and go over it all."

Paige nodded before a genuine thought hit her. "How am I going to get back to my hotel? And then back here tomorrow? There have to be more ways to travel than a helicopter."

His grin—a tad boyish and altogether rueful—flashed. "We can absolutely transport you back and forth that way, but we do have a small service road in and out of the resort as well. I'll see that a car's set up to take you back today."

"And tomorrow?"

"Why don't I come into Sedona instead and take you to lunch? There's a wonderful seafood restaurant a few blocks down from your hotel. We'll take the car back here after, and you can work on your shot list through the afternoon."

The thought briefly flashed through her mind that meals with Adam weren't a great idea, but it was standard protocol to share meals with clients.

And that's all he was now.

Her client.

Or rather, Isabella was the client and Adam was the high flyer who'd managed to get a spot on her PR radar.

Regardless, they were back to business, and that's where they needed to stay.

"That sounds great. I'll meet you at the restaurant at noon."

Adam stood, and in short order they were back in the exquisite lobby, a quiet sort of efficiency filling the space. Adam called for a driver, ready and waiting in the lobby, and then he was walking her toward the exit.

"I am glad you're here, Paige."

Before she could react, he'd leaned forward, his lips lingering a heartbeat too long against her cheek before he pulled away.

"I'll see you tomorrow for lunch."

"I'll see you then."

She headed for the car, refusing to look back to see if Adam was still standing there.

But she was forced to feel the heat of his lips, like a brand against her cheek, the entire ride back to her hotel.

Chapter Four

Noah Steele wasn't used to a life of privilege or even the slightest measure of pampering, but he'd certainly gotten used to life with his wife.

His *wife*.

That lone word floated over and over in his mind, every implication of what it meant that he was now a married man filling his thoughts.

A lifetime commitment.

Shared spaces.

And most of all, every day with Laura Colton, the woman he loved.

He glanced up when she came into the smallest bedroom of her rather spacious bungalow, which he'd turned into an office, her eyes bright with excitement before she leaned down and pressed a long, lingering kiss to his lips.

"What did I do to earn that?" He couldn't hold back the smile as he glanced up at her.

She smiled back, a witchy come-hither look in her eyes that never failed to make him lose a few brain cells as she dropped into his lap before wrapping her arms around his neck. "Just being you is enough."

"While I appreciate that in every way, I can't help but think there's a *but* in there."

One lone eyebrow popped up over her right eye. "You caught that?"

"I'm becoming quite an expert in reading Laura Colton Steele."

"Are you, now?"

"I figure it's a lifelong puzzle I'll never fully get right, but I'm going to give it my best shot."

She pressed another kiss to his lips, murmuring, "See that you do."

But it was the small sigh as she lifted her head that had him adding a check to the "score one for the new husband" box in his mind.

Every rookie needed some reinforcement, after all, that they were doing a good job.

"There is a *but*. And I know it's going to feel like a huge newlywed trap closing over your ankle, but I need your honest opinion on this one."

Noah envisioned erasing that hard-earned check as he stared at his wife. "Oh no."

"No, it's not bad, per se. But I would like a male opinion."

"About?"

"Adam's old girlfriend is here. Or back, I should say, in his life. She's the photographer who's handling the PR we negotiated for that high-end luxury magazine."

"The one with unlimited access?" Noah asked the question even as he recognized the tension that lined the words.

He wasn't a fan of unlimited anything when it came to security, and he'd shared as much with his wife. Operations details he managed in the role of new security expert for Mariposa, supporting and expanding on all the good work already in place from Roland, their head of security.

Not as her husband.

"Yes, All-Seeing Danger Ranger. That one. She's also

capturing lush photography and a peek behind the curtain, so to speak. And she's Adam's ex."

"And this is our business because—" He deliberately left his question hanging there even if his lips had twitched a bit at the "Danger Ranger" moniker.

"He's my brother and I want him to be happy."

"Of course you do."

"And so much of the weird and the horrible happening around here has fallen on his shoulders."

He brushed a small lock of hair off her cheek. "I'd say you've all borne that burden equally."

"Yes, but I've had you. He's been dealing with this all alone, and I worry about him."

"So playing matchmaker is going to make it all better?"

Noah kept his voice gentle, but he knew his wife was a woman full of determination and no small measure of get-it-done-ness, which he admired the hell out of.

He also recognized it was a trait that made her ever-so-slightly scary to anyone who got in her way.

Not that he was scared, of course…

But he'd learned from their very first meeting that Laura was a determined woman with a never-say-die attitude. It was why Mariposa was such an impressive place.

It was also why she'd managed to rise above her mother's death at a young age, as well as the destructive streak her father seemed determined to operate with when it came to his children.

And, Noah thought with an inward sigh, it was why she was so determined to help the ones she loved.

"I'm not playing matchmaker. I'm just—" She broke off as her gaze grew thoughtful. "I just don't want them to let the past get in the way of their future."

"I'm not sure it's up to you."

"I know. Really, I do. Relationships are hard enough without the emotional baggage of what came before. But I also know my brother, and he was never the same after he arrived here after college."

Although his experience with the Colton family had only begun at the start of the year, when he came to Mariposa to uncover what had happened to his foster sister, Allison, after she was murdered on the property, Noah had recognized the collective ambition and solidarity of Laura and her siblings from the start.

They worked hard, and they had a bone-deep belief in the importance of their work, the privacy they cultivated, and the haven they'd built in and among the red rocks of Arizona.

What he'd also recognized from the start was how much each of the siblings kept a tight rein on their emotions. He'd been lucky to find his way forward with Laura, love forging a path even through the thornier areas of both their personalities.

He'd also found a way forward with Josh and Dani. Whether it was the fact that both were younger or just different in the way they approached their responsibilities, he wasn't sure, but there was an openness there he'd managed to cultivate with both of them.

But his brother-in-law, Adam, had been the most reserved. He was a good man—Noah had never doubted that—but he'd developed a few impressions of Adam that had only grown stronger the more time he spent with the eldest Colton.

Making Mariposa an unbridled success was of paramount importance.

Overcoming the challenges they all faced with their father was a daily battle.

And something—or perhaps it was someone—had left Adam Colton with a deep well of sadness somewhere in his past.

Noah had always chalked it up to the siblings losing their mother so young, but with Laura's matchmaking efforts and the news that an old flame had returned, he now had to wonder if that sadness he'd always sensed in his brother-in-law came from a very specific source.

Things had finally calmed a bit around the resort, even if they were still dealing with his father-in-law's attempts to take over the property. Yet even with solving his foster sister's murder and removing some of the less savory characters who'd attempted to harm some of the celebrities who came to the resort for its privacy, Noah vowed to himself to keep watch.

He wasn't fully convinced they were out of the woods yet, and he'd told Laura and her siblings as much. Their father remained a concern, and his second wife, Glenna, had a seeming determination to do menace that managed to show through beneath the elegant facade she put on.

Adam was known for his legendary focus and commitment to the resort and to his family, but a past love—especially one he'd never gotten over—could be a distraction.

Worse, it could give Clive and Glenna just the path they needed to sneak in under Adam's defenses if they were already down.

So he'd keep an eye out, Noah vowed once more as he pulled his wife close for a kiss. And as he lingered over her lips, he knew it was more than simply keeping watch.

The Coltons were his family now.

And there was nothing he wouldn't do to keep them safe.

Adam hit the end of his five-mile run and reduced the treadmill to a walking pace as he reached for his water bottle. Although he usually got his workout in early, wrapping up by five thirty in the morning was relatively ridiculous, even for him.

A fact that was evident by the barely light-streaked morning sky outside the gym windows and the nearly empty room that only had two other occupants in the far corner, spotting each other with the weight equipment.

He avoided the resort fitness facilities, never knowing when guests would choose to use the well-equipped space, and instead favored the employee gym they kept in one of the out-of-the-way places on the property. Like everything else about his professional life, his focus was the exclusivity of Mariposa and ensuring guests never felt the actual workings of a hotel around them.

Instead, he wanted them to feel they operated in a world of privacy—a secure space that not only fulfilled their needs but also recognized them before they did.

It would have been silly if it weren't such a calling. For all of them.

Yet, even more important, it was a tribute to his mother, Annabeth. For the solace she'd found here in her personal corner of paradise. She'd built a home for him, Laura and Josh. It was a home they'd extended to Dani as well.

And it was his life's work to honor that and to craft an experience that gave others that well of peace she'd always found here.

It was a good goal, Adam thought as he threw his workout towel into the laundry basket he passed on his way out, but one he was having a hard time finding himself.

Peace.

Because if his sleepless night was any indication, he'd have none of it as long as Paige Barnes was in Arizona.

I'm sort of glad we got all this out of the way here at first...

Her words still echoed in his mind, running on a loop since their meeting the day before. Was that what they'd done? Gotten it all *out of the way*? Did he even want that?

Did he have a choice?

It wasn't like he'd had a hell of a lot of peace for the past decade. Sure, he'd managed his life to a strict standard of control. But faced with the rush of memories that had dragged him down the day before, the uncomfortable thought it had all been for nothing had settled, burrowing deep.

He was a man who lived and acted with purpose, so it was beyond humbling to realize his decision to leave Paige and New York and come back to Arizona had done emotional damage.

Damage they now had *out of the way*.

Was he more like his father than he thought?

For all his devotion to his mother's vision and the memories of a loving environment she'd created for him and his siblings, his father had been the exact opposite. So opposite that it was often hard to understand what his mother had found in her marriage in the first place.

He'd long recognized—and owned—that had been part of his reticence all those years ago.

Yes, Mariposa had been his priority. So much so he'd ended his relationship and headed straight back to Arizona. But he'd also recognized that single-minded focus made him as unsuitable a mate as the example his father had set.

Adam preferred to believe he lived a life far more altruistic than his father's, but the end result was still the same.

Adam Colton didn't do relationships.

Casual, private affairs that he could control from start to finish? Yes.

A commitment to another that would consume his life? Absolutely not.

It was an uncomfortable realization about himself he'd managed to live with for the past decade. So why had Paige's arrival back into his life upended that as easily as kicking over a sandcastle?

He returned to his private bungalow to shower and change, and was still thinking about it as he walked into his office shortly after six. The offices were quiet other than the manager who was always on through the night. Adam snagged himself a cup of coffee from the ever-present and always-on pot before settling down at his desk.

How was he back in this place?

Yes, it had been hard to walk away from Paige all those years ago, but it was a decision he'd lived with. More than that, he'd had every confidence she'd move on quite well without him.

Which made the fact that he couldn't get her comments out of his mind—or find anything good in them—his problem to manage.

We had some history, and now we've had a chance to air it out... Give it a bit of breathing room so we can put it behind us.

Breathing room.

It all sounded so professional and grown-up. And so opposite of the vibrant woman he'd known and loved.

He'd never said the words at the time, but he *had* loved Paige.

Only now, they had their past *out of the way* and had *breathing room* to work together on this PR piece for Mariposa.

Hell.

He tossed his pen, nearly knocking over his coffee mug in the process. The notes he'd intended to put together for their lunch meeting faded from his mind as he recalled the day before and those first moments in her presence again.

She was amazing.

Beautiful, yes. Even more so than when they'd been younger, the ensuing years adding character to her face, which had only made it more interesting.

More stunning, really.

And evidence of all the time they'd missed together.

Adam stood, recognizing he wasn't going to get any paperwork done this morning. He crossed around his desk and retrieved his pen before walking back out to the lobby. His lunch with Paige was going to focus on the various shots he wanted around the property, so he'd use his phone to take a few snaps that he could share with her.

It wasn't much, but it gave him some sense of purpose as he walked the property, which was coming to life with its morning routine.

"Keep frowning like that and you're going to scare the guests away."

Adam turned from where he held his phone up to grab a photo of the large art installation in the west corner of the lobby to find Alexis Reed smiling at him. She was arm in arm with her boyfriend, Max Powell.

Both of them grinned at him even as Max's eyes narrowed while he stood there, taking him in with the knowing gaze of a close friend. "You look like hell, man."

"Just a busy week." Adam forced a smile, willing himself to relax. "And too much to do."

"Speaking of busy..."

Alexis lifted up on tiptoe to press a kiss to Max's lips before turning back to Adam. A sense of joy filled her hazel eyes as she stepped away from the tall man. She was dressed conservatively for the day as their head concierge, but even the severe bun she kept her hair in only showcased the pretty flush that shadowed her cheekbones.

Max watched her go, his smile nothing short of besotted.

Before Adam could say anything, his friend was already turning to face him. "She's incredible."

"I'm happy for you. Both."

And he was.

Max's career as a celebrity chef with his own TV show was a dream come true, but his ambition had also taken a lot from him. So it mattered that, despite their mutual prickliness when they first met, things had turned quickly to love for Max and Alexis.

"It's also my incredible life partner who let me in on the news that Paige Barnes was here yesterday."

"Alexis doesn't miss a trick."

It was a skill Adam prized in her role as Mariposa's head concierge, but one he'd have preferred didn't extend to his personal life.

"She's here capturing photos for an upcoming PR piece."

Dark eyebrows rose in question over Max's deep brown eyes. "And you're okay with it?"

"Of course."

Max nodded, and Adam believed himself to be out of the proverbial woods on an uncomfortable conversation.

He should have known better, especially when it came to the only other person who knew him as well as his siblings.

"Sure you are. She was only your sun, moon and stars in college."

"That was a long time ago."

Max seemed to weigh those words before simply nodding. "Let her know I'd love to see her while she's here."

"We're meeting for lunch today, but I'll be sure to bring her to the kitchen next time she's here at the resort."

They'd already announced the news that Max would be doing the next season of his show at Mariposa, and he regularly haunted the resort kitchens. Their in-house chef had been gracious with the space, and the two had become fast friends.

"I'll do you one better. Get that woman back here and I'll make you two a special dinner."

The thought was tempting, but Adam only shook his head, unwilling to give that thought room to roost. "I ruined my shot at a second chance a long time ago. Paige's presence at Mariposa is strictly professional."

Max eyed him, and Adam got the distinct sense his friend—the one who rarely kept his mouth shut about *anything*—was going to remain silent.

"What?" he finally asked.

"Nothing."

"Yeah. Right."

"No, actually. I like Paige. And despite my better judgment, you're my best friend." Max shot him an insolent smile. "You two made a great couple, but I get it. Life and all its changes did its work…on all of us."

Adam stepped in before Max could further reinforce the reality that had kept him tossing and turning all night.

"And it was a long time ago, and it's over."

"What are you doing?"

Paige had asked herself that question roughly every five minutes for the past three hours.

Not only was she no closer to an answer as she gave one last glance at herself in the mirror before gathering up her purse, but she couldn't seem to stop the endless cycle of nerves that roiled through her stomach.

It's just a job.

No matter how much history she had with Adam Colton, she had to keep the work as her North Star.

Hadn't work seen her through the past ten years? Why stop now?

Besides, she'd already survived the hardest part. They'd seen each other again, and she hadn't disintegrated on the spot or made a total fool out of herself.

She could have been a bit less prickly, but hey, a woman was entitled to a bit of lingering pique.

Especially while visiting the hotel she'd been dumped for.

Only now that she'd seen Mariposa in person—and more important, seen Adam there—she understood why the place mattered so much.

Her conversation the day before with Laura about Annabeth had shed a surprising amount of light on Adam's decision a decade ago.

She's the reason we even own the resort. When her father died, she used his inheritance to purchase the property...

My mother preferred to stay here while my father remained in Los Angeles, running the Colton family business...

Some of my happiest memories are those years growing up here with her...

Happy memories.

Laura's words had stuck with Paige, and a decade's worth of feelings of abandonment faded, the sting pulled out of them with such a simple truth. For all her feelings for Adam, she hadn't been immune to the subtle veil of sadness that had been a hallmark of his personality.

And now she knew why.

A place was far more than just bricks and mortar when it was home. That went double when you associated it with the memory of someone you loved so much.

Although most of her work was now with models, she'd done a lot of family photography to pay the bills in her early days. The shoots that still lingered in her memory were the ones where the home was as much a part of the shoot as the family. Her favorite had been a session in an old farmhouse in upstate New York she'd done just before her move out to California.

The pair celebrating their sixtieth anniversary had wanted their children, grandchildren and two great-grandchildren in the photo, and even now she remembered the continuous laughter and happiness that had filled the afternoon.

With the new understanding of Adam's need to come back to Arizona, Laura's words had given her additional concern when she considered what was barely veiled contempt for their father.

Had she missed just how challenging Adam's home life was all those years ago?

Or had he been adept at hiding it?

Paige pulled her hotel-room door behind her, feeling the door click into place, and headed for the restaurant. The five-minute walk would do her good, giving a bit more time to calm those churning thoughts that filled her mind.

The past ten years had been all about dissecting her own

feelings and reactions toward the end of her and Adam's relationship. While she wouldn't take ownership for information she hadn't known at the time, the continued proof that there was more driving his decision than simply walking away was…well, not exactly hopeful, but a new piece of information she hadn't had before.

"Ms. Barnes?"

She glanced over at the concierge, who waved her down from his post just outside the front door. "Yes?"

"Ms. Barnes, I'm Patrick. I'm sorry to trouble you as you're on the way out, but I wanted to make sure the car service to the heliport was to your satisfaction yesterday. I know we were a bit late in getting the car set up, and I wanted to offer my apologies."

Paige waved a hand, not even remembering the extra ten minutes she'd spent in the lush lobby before his reminder. "Please don't give it another thought. I haven't."

He smiled, a look of relief coming over his features. He didn't look much past twenty-five, and the drive to both impress and work his way up was obvious.

This one had ambition.

It was funny when that thought lodged tight in her chest, images of Adam from ten years before filling her mind's eye.

He'd been equally serious, his focus on the future evident even then. She hadn't believed it would be a future that didn't include her, and she carried a fair amount of regret she hadn't understood that at the time.

But…

Shaking it off, Paige admonished herself in light of the past day. It was time to move on and move forward. She'd believed she'd done just that, but her endlessly maudlin thoughts suggested otherwise.

It was time to put the past firmly where it belonged.

Actually *in* the past.

Obviously oblivious to her personal mental victory, Patrick offered, "Please let me get you a car to wherever it is you're going."

"It's a short walk. I'm only going about three blocks from the hotel."

He looked pained by the admission, but he had enough training to respect her wishes. "If you're sure."

"Absolutely." Paige took a step off the hotel sidewalk and onto the cobbled pavers that made up the driveway beneath the portico. She belatedly realized making the move backward wasn't ideal, her heel sticking in the crevice between two pavers.

"Oh, Ms. Barnes!" Patrick leaped forward to help her as she windmilled to keep her balance.

Her focus was on keeping herself upright, her heavy shoulder bag adding to the tug of a possible fall.

It was the only reason she didn't hear the squeal of tires as a large black SUV came barreling through the portico, straight for her.

Chapter Five

Adam followed the restaurant hostess to his table—one with a view of the activity on the sidewalk outside—and was surprised to feel a momentary shot of satisfaction that he'd arrived first.

Own the situation. Maintain the upper hand. Stand your ground...

He stopped himself as the thoughts racing through his mind caught up with his feelings. Was that what this was about?

It was wholly a business mindset, one he'd honed of late in the tense and fraught corporate chess match with his father.

But had it become indicative of who he really was?

One more question that sat uncomfortably on his mind now that Paige had appeared back in his life.

He'd accepted long ago that Mariposa wasn't just a job for him and knew his siblings felt the same. He'd understood that about himself but had always counterbalanced it with a belief that he acted fairly and knew how to find joy in his life.

It was only with the reminder of just how happy he'd been in those months with Paige so long ago—and how little of that same happiness he'd felt since—that he was forced to reconsider.

And in the reconsidering, acknowledge that, on some level, he'd deliberately blunted his feelings of that time together.

"Mr. Colton?" He glanced up to find his server smiling broadly, distinct notes of invitation in her eyes. "May I get you still or sparkling water for the table?"

A small memory of Paige's ever-present bottle of seltzer from so many years ago filled his mind. "Sparkling, please."

"Of course."

The server gave him one final smile, the small light of attraction dimming at his simple response before she headed off to fulfill his request.

A large black town car pulled up outside, his position near the window giving him a prime view. Paige stepped out, dressed in a sleek pantsuit, her hair framing her face. Adam greedily took the brief moment, her unawareness of him sitting there giving him a chance to look a bit closer than he could once she sat down.

It was only as he took in the tense lines of her face that he immediately realized something was wrong.

Before he could even check the impulse, he was on his feet and had crossed the restaurant so fast he met her at the door.

"Paige? What's the matter? What happened?"

"Adam!" She stared at him as she stepped through the restaurant doorway. "What are—" She shook her head. "You got here first. I'm sorry I'm late."

"Paige." He reached for her hands, holding her still and waiting until she looked at him. "What happened?"

"I just—" She glanced down at where their hands were

joined before her gaze met his again. "I was nearly run over at the hotel. This big SUV just came out of nowhere."

Although he'd never had any reason to stay there, he'd had drinks any number of times at her hotel and could picture the layout. "How could that happen? The hotel has a sidewalk out front."

"It was in the portico. I was just getting ready to walk over here, and someone came barreling through the entrance. I was so shaken the parking attendant insisted on driving me over."

"He should have caught the jerk who nearly ran you down."

"He tried. He took off after him, but the driver must have been embarrassed and peeled out of the parking lot." Paige shook her head and dislodged her hands from his. "I'm fine. Really, I am. I kept telling Patrick that as well, but he drove me the few blocks over here all the same."

"As he should have."

She glanced around, her eyes widening as she realized they'd become the center of attention at the front of the restaurant, the lunch crowd growing as people showed up for their midday meetings. "Adam, can we please just sit down?"

He escorted her through the restaurant, unable to stop touching her. When she didn't shake off the gentle hand he laid on her lower back, Adam took that as a good sign they'd moved past whatever tension had driven their meeting the day before.

He was just so happy she was all right, even as the persistent image of a three-ton vehicle bearing down on her had settled in his mind's eye, turning his insides liquid.

After settling Paige in her chair, he took the seat opposite, pleased to see some color had come back into her cheeks. "You're sure you're okay?"

"Yes, of course."

The answer was more than fair—she was unharmed—but he caught something odd in the crisp reply. "What is it?"

"It's just—" She stopped and let out a low sigh. "I know everyone's in a hurry everywhere, but this is the second near miss I've had since I got to Arizona."

Whatever calm he'd found on their walk through the restaurant came back harder and darker. "What do you mean?"

"It's silly of me to connect them, but I had a similar experience when I landed at the airport. Some jerk nearly drove onto the curb, they were so close to me. I jumped back just in time, and they ended up driving off."

"No one helped you? There are always cops hanging around the parking area."

"The two on duty were farther down the pickup area, and by the time I got down to make a complaint, the car was long gone." She took a sip of her sparkling water. "I chalked it up to the way people get so frazzled picking up and dropping off travelers, but it is strange."

It was more than strange, and even without all that had happened at Mariposa the past several months, Adam would have been concerned with the two near misses.

But *with* all that had happened at the resort?

It didn't settle easily at all.

"It's unfortunate some people don't know how to drive in crowded places, but what are you going to do?" Paige lifted her menu. "It didn't help that I got my heel stuck. But now that it's past me, I have to say, I'm starving. What's good here?"

Adam got the clear sense she was switching topics on

purpose, but he played along. He'd talk to Noah later about his concerns and see what his brother-in-law thought about the exceedingly strange coincidence.

"Their short rib soft tacos are amazing. And the Nicoise salad is also great."

"You had me at ribs." She laid her menu down and took another sip of her water.

"We'll make that two."

As he laid down his own menu, Adam gave himself a few beats of silence to relax and regroup. Between the sleepless night, the continued dissection of his own behavior and the fact that Paige had nearly been hurt, his thoughts were all over the place.

But even a few minutes in her presence did something to him.

He felt himself calming, simply enjoying the novelty of having Paige Barnes sitting across from him.

It was emotionally dangerous territory, Adam well knew. But as his gaze met her vivid green one across the table, he couldn't find it inside himself to hold back.

PAIGE TOOK A bite of her soft taco and nearly moaned at the delicious mix of flavors. The meat was cooked perfectly, and the spice of the sauce, coupled with the coolness of the sour cream, had made for a practically perfect lunch.

It's your dining companion that's made it all the way perfect, a small voice taunted her as she dabbed her lips with her napkin.

Once they'd gotten past the adrenaline rush of her near miss at the hotel, their conversation had flowed through any number of topics. She got the distinct sense Adam would have liked to dissect the situation with the SUV driver—

and figured he'd get back around to it—but he'd been nothing but engaging.

It tugged at her, if she were honest. A gentle reminder of why she'd missed him so much.

Yes, she'd always been bothered by her inability to fully move on from their relationship, but this lunch had only managed to reinforce the mental arguments she always made to herself when one of her relationships met its inevitable end.

No man since their relationship in college had made her feel like Adam. Which had the unfortunate outcome that her adult life had been a continuous hunt to find that relationship high once again.

But she refused to stop looking.

Her conviction on that point was absolute.

A point that would have felt a bit more solid if she weren't sitting here thinking about how good Adam looked and how much she was enjoying herself.

Adam smiled, pulling her out of her thoughts. "Did the tacos live up to their promise?"

"They're fantastic. This was an excellent suggestion for lunch."

"I'm glad you enjoyed it." Adam settled his napkin beside his plate and leaned back in his chair. "I figured this would be a good place to catch up before heading back to Mariposa. I wanted to have a spot that was a bit more neutral to share some of what's been plaguing us."

"I know you've had a few problems. You may be able to maintain a level of exclusivity at the property, but news about celebrities and high society finds a way out."

"There has been that. But I think you should know what's going on with my family, too."

"Laura did mention some things yesterday." Although

his sister had shared quite a bit the day before, it was interesting that Adam felt the need to share the same.

What had the Colton siblings really been dealing with? Especially if they felt compelled to share the problems they were having, both with the resort and, even more intimately, with their father.

For whatever connection she and Adam had once shared, she wasn't entitled to pry into his family life.

"What did Laura say?"

"She talked about your parents' marriage and how you all spent so much time here while your father remained in California. She also shared his attempts to come after the resort in order to save his business."

Adam's smile was grim as he nodded through her recollection of the conversation with Laura. "You've got the high points, then."

Paige considered how to play this and ultimately decided she could ask. It was up to him if he answered. "Is that all?"

"As to the business, yes. Did Laura mention my father's second wife, Glenna?"

"No, I can't say that she did."

"He remarried after a respectable time of mourning, but he could have spared us all the public show of grief. My mother never mattered to him beyond a means to an end. That's been abundantly clear over the past several months."

"Laura said he tricked her into getting the land Mariposa sits on."

"I think that was the final proof that he just didn't care. The affairs and the distance? We were all happier when he wasn't around." Adam reached for his glass and took a sip, seeming to gather his thoughts. "But he found a way to undermine the one place she loved. More, the place that truly belonged to her. It's diabolical."

"I am sorry, Adam."

The shadows that hazed his eyes, making his focus distant, cleared as he looked at her. "*I'm* sorry. There are days when it feels overwhelming and then others when I feel as if it's nothing more than a wealthy man's problem and I'm as much a champion of Mariposa as a victim to it."

It was an interesting perspective and one she'd never have imagined. She'd spent the past decade convinced a pile of bricks in Arizona had taken away a vital part of her life.

And now?

Now she felt a driving urge to help Adam save it.

It was a very weird one-eighty, but it was true all the same.

"I hope my photos go some of the way toward helping you."

"I hope they do, too."

His gaze was speculative as he looked at her across the table. Their waitress had been by a couple of times, once to bring a fresh bottle of sparkling water and another to check on them, even if *them* had clearly meant only Adam. In both cases, Adam had been polite but had barely given the woman much beyond a glance, despite the slightly obvious hope by their waitress that he would notice her.

It had left Paige feeling…seen. And maybe a little bit pleased that while they might not be doing anything more than having a business lunch, he was respectful and courteous.

But now?

With that attention on her, so intense and magnetic?

Well, it left her with decidedly less-than-professional thoughts.

Seeking to keep them on level ground—or as level as it got when it came to family dynamics—Paige realized he'd mentioned his stepmother but hadn't elaborated any further. "Has Glenna been involved in the takeover along with your father?"

Whatever subtle awareness had flared between them flattened at the mention of his stepmother. "She's in league with him but has also operated with her own miserable intentions. I don't know my father is smart enough or original enough to manage some of the things Glenna's executed over the past five months."

"Executed?"

"My father might have figured out how to steal Mariposa, but he's not a clever man. I've always observed that he's a big talker who believes his own words absolutely. He married a woman who feeds that and then goes off on her own to execute her plans."

The sentiments were harsh in the extreme, and Paige wondered how she'd never understood or known this about Adam's life. His mother had passed when he was a teenager, and there'd still been a number of years between her death and Adam's time in college.

All of it spent with an exceptionally poor relationship with his father.

Yet Adam had never said anything.

It stung, she admitted to herself, even as she was forced to acknowledge she hadn't been quick to share the details of her own family situation. But even with that stark truth, she couldn't quite dismiss the fact that it smarted, not knowing any of this about Adam.

Never knowing anything at all.

ADAM SENSED THE shift in their conversation but couldn't quite figure out why.

Yes, his comments about his father were harsh, but they

were honest. And if Laura had already given Paige an overview of what had been happening with his father's attempts to take over Mariposa, then she couldn't be all that surprised by his family revelations.

So why was she upset?

The easy conversation that had sparked throughout lunch vanished, and by the time their server came to collect their plates, the mood between them was stilted and tense. He quickly picked up the check, waving away her protests to handle it, and before he could really process just how south things had gone, they were back out in front of the restaurant.

"I drove into town and can take you back with me. We can continue our review of the resort and the possible shot list."

"No helicopter?" A light breeze picked up a few loose tendrils of her hair, the pretty shade of red gold in the afternoon sun.

The question may have been asked as a joke, but he heard the spikes beneath all the same.

"It's a bit longer by car, but it's a pretty drive taking the various roads through the red rocks. I'd like to show it to you. It's a different perspective from the ground than up in the air."

"Sure."

"Paige, I—" He stopped, not sure what to say. *Are you mad at me?* felt equal parts juvenile as well as borderline groveling since he had no idea what he might have said to upset her.

It was that truth that finally had him giving in and going with his gut. "I can't help but feel I misstepped during lunch and upset you. I'm sorry for it, but I'd like to know what I said."

She brushed away those tantalizing tendrils and gestured toward a small bench a short distance from the restaurant entrance. "Why don't we sit down?"

Although he wanted to know what he'd said or done to upset her, as they took a seat, Adam couldn't deny just how disappointed he was that they were back to this place at all. While he didn't expect absolution for breaking them up a decade ago, he had come to lunch today believing they were on a path forward to working together.

Maybe their easy and free-flowing conversation throughout lunch had given him the wrong impression.

Maybe they would never get back to common ground based on their history.

Did he even want that?

Especially when *common ground* sounded so ordinary. So professional. So...unlike what they'd had before.

What was uncommon.

Uncommon enough that you tossed it away.

Out of fear? Ignorance? A commitment to family that blunted out everything else?

The list was endless, Adam realized as he took a seat beside her.

"I'm the one who owes you an apology," Paige began. "I don't normally lack an ability to regulate my emotions, but something about seeing you again, Adam—" She stopped, gathering her words. "It's shaken me."

"I'm not unaffected, either."

And he wasn't.

The turmoil he'd felt since she set foot in Mariposa the day before was proof of that. Although it was at odds with his thoughts before lunch—about maintaining the upper hand in their exchange—Adam found he liked this version of himself far better.

"While I may not be unaffected, I also don't know what I said. Please talk to me. Tell me."

"It's not what you said, it's what was implied. About us."

He suspected his confusion was stamped all over his face as Paige rushed on.

"What you shared about your family? Your poor relationship with your father and his lack of respect for your mother? Those are difficult experiences. Hurtful ones, too. Yet before today, I didn't know these details about your life or your relationship with your dad."

"He's not someone I enjoy talking about."

"I get that, but..." Her focus drifted toward the street and the traffic passing through downtown. It was only when that sharp green gaze returned to his that he saw the hurt clearly stamped there.

"I thought I was a part of your life. So to realize that I never even rated a discussion about your family or your life back here or losing your mother—" It was in the small sigh that crested, halting her words, that Adam finally understood. "All I can tell you is that it struck a nerve I didn't even recognize was exposed."

"I see."

And in seeing, he realized just how closed off his behavior really was.

They'd had a connection from the start, but even with that—with finding someone he felt so comfortable with—he'd still held back.

With her, certainly. But it was only with her willingness to address it that he had to admit that he'd lied to himself, too. Because in holding back these details of his life, he'd also told himself the lie that none of it mattered.

That he was above it.

Where's that gotten you, Colton?

Sadly, the answer was clear. Alone and in a heap of business trouble with the one person who should know better. The one person on the planet who should support him and believe in him no matter what.

The embarrassment he carried over his father's behavior and near abandonment of his children had cut Adam deeply as a young man. Even now, with more than thirty years of being Clive Colton's son—one who was well aware of his father's failings—he was still ashamed by how dysfunctional his family relationships were.

"My relationship with my father has never been a good one. My mother deliberately moved me and my siblings here to Arizona to keep much-needed distance. After she died things didn't get much better, even though we had to move back to California to live with him."

"He wasn't there for you?"

"No." He registered just how bleak that answer was, and quickly added, "We didn't suddenly have a big father-son reunion."

"I'm sorry for that."

"I want to be, but I've never quite gotten there. He made his choices and continues to make them. His latest stunt is just further evidence of that."

"Do you think he'll be successful?"

"Right now, it's a matter of how long I can stall him. Dani holds two percent of Colton Textiles. Added to what my siblings and I have, it's enough to give us the controlling majority."

"That should be enough, then?"

"It would be, but Dani only found out recently that she had the shares. Her late mother had willed them to her brother, Dani's uncle, but he's been disinherited for trying to extort us and hurt Dani. Now she needs a few weeks to get everything ironed out and work through the inheritance red tape."

"Do you think it will come through in time?"

"It has to."

It was the only thing he had left in this whole mess with his father to hang on to.

"Look, Paige, I can't go back and change what happened before. I was young and determined to keep my feelings about my family at a distance. I can see now how that crept into our relationship, too, since I never talked about it."

"I appreciate you telling me now. And—" A few of those loose tendrils still caught the breeze and wisped around her face as she seemed to weigh her words. "I know a lot of time has passed, but I'm here for you if you need a friend. Someone with a fresh set of eyes who hasn't been in the thick of this with you."

He reached out and laid a hand over hers, barely even conscious of the gesture until he'd done it.

The moment he touched her, the soft skin on the back of her hand under his, a flood of memories washed over him.

They'd been a physical couple when they were together, sharing easy touches and soft caresses from the earliest days of being together. A soft touch on her back or holding hands as they walked through campus or even the simplicity of sitting close enough that their legs touched.

Just like the easy conversation, it was amazing to realize just how quickly it came back.

More, how effortless it all was.

If that were true, he realized with head-slamming clarity, why hadn't he put in more effort when he'd had the chance?

"Paige, I am sorry."

Her smile was gentle and, if he was reading it right, tinged with sadness, too.

God, how had he ruined things so badly? And far worse, how could he have been so oblivious to the pain his choices had caused?

"I think you've apologized enough."

"I'm not sure I have. I messed up before. What was between us and what we could have had. I can't change it, and if I'm being honest, knowing all that's come in the past ten years, I can't lie to you and say I would. But I can apologize for hurting you. You didn't deserve that."

"Thank you." Paige smiled, her eyes shiny even though no tears fell.

On a nod, she stood, seeming to come to some decision. Her voice quavered slightly, but her smile was resolute. "Why don't we head to Mariposa now? I've got some shots I want to frame up, and I'd like to confirm schedules so we can be as unobtrusive as possible once we begin shooting."

"That works."

He stood, that lingering emptiness he couldn't quite manage at having his past come back and slap him in the face still hovering around his shoulders, but Adam vowed to shake it off.

Paige was clearly prepared to move forward. He needed to do the same.

It was his last thought as she stepped off the curb, just as tires squealed and a black SUV came out of nowhere, heading straight for her.

Chapter Six

"Paige!"

The scream ripped from Adam's throat as he ran for her, the short distance seeming endless as he raced to close the gap between them.

A rush of air that was much too close swept over both of them as he pulled Paige into his arms. The SUV swerved away before continuing down the street, honking horns echoing in its wake.

A harsh ringing filled his ears along with the steady thought that he needed to get information on the SUV, like make, model and license plate, but it was all he could do to gather Paige close and hold her tightly to his chest.

"Are you okay?"

"Oh, Adam!" She pulled back, her green eyes wide with terror. "What's going on?"

"I wish I knew."

"Do you think it's the same car as at the hotel? It's like I'm cursed or something."

He wasn't sure what to think even as it crossed his mind she might have been targeted.

But why?

No one beyond him and his siblings and a few select staff

members at Mariposa knew she was even here. And what would be the point of targeting her, anyway?

The idea of a curse was silly, even if it did offer up one more reminder from when they were together in college. Paige had always been a big believer in fate and destiny, and they, along with Max, had spent more than a few late nights arguing about free will and predestination over one of Max's creations and a bottle of wine.

Since a few of those conversations had nearly led to a fight, he opted for more diplomacy than he had at twenty-one and avoided the curse remark altogether.

"Did it look like the same car?"

"I'm not sure. I didn't get a look when I was at the hotel, and I wasn't looking this time, either, since my back was to the street."

It was an interesting point, and if she was being targeted in some way, it would give a distinct advantage if she had no chance of seeing the driver.

But it also brought him back to the bigger question of why she'd be targeted at all.

"Let's get out of here, and I'll have my brother-in-law, Noah, contact the restaurant *and* the hotel to get the security footage. We'll look at it and see if we can get a read on the driver or the license plate."

"Is that Laura's husband?"

"Yes, and he also happens to be a homicide detective. Since meeting Laura and getting married, he's shifted his professional focus and is supporting security at Mariposa, with his captain's blessing."

"Homicide?"

"On semi-leave," Adam quickly rushed to reassure her. And with the obvious fear underneath her question, he realized he'd be better off running his theories past Noah first before saying much more.

"Tell you what. Why don't we skip Mariposa today and we can pick up tomorrow?"

"No." She shook her head. "That's silly. I'm fine, and I'm not going to go hide in my hotel room because of something that is actually nothing."

"You sure?"

"Positive. Besides—" she smiled "—I saw your grimace when I mentioned a curse. I'm not going to miss an entire car ride trying to convince you that I'm right."

NEVER SEND A man to do a woman's job.

Glenna Bennett Colton had practiced that credo for more than four decades, and she'd sadly never been wrong.

She disconnected the call with the driver she'd contracted, then slammed her phone down on the gold-inlay credenza she used in her office.

Damn it, what a mess.

The bumbling idiot she'd hired to run down Paige Barnes hadn't simply missed once, but twice, today. And he'd taken his shot in places that carried an incredibly high risk of discovery.

Just like at the airport, when all he was supposed to do was confirm she'd arrived. He'd later claimed he just *took his shot* at the woman since it was so easy, but it was a rogue move that offered far more risk than reward.

Even if he did swear up and down that he'd masked the license plate with mud and shielded himself from view.

Likely story, Glenna thought, unless he'd figured out a way to drive without needing to see through the windshield. Since that was unlikely, she needed to move on with a new approach.

It didn't help it was a hastily put-together plan, but she'd needed to act quickly once her spy at Mariposa let her know there was someone new in the picture.

Someone who—as the rumors flew around the Mariposa staff—Adam had known and dated before. Her mole at Mariposa, Sasha Hightower, had overheard the details as Max talked to Alexis about his and Adam's mutual friend from college.

Or, as Sasha had relayed, a woman who wasn't only Max's friend but also Adam's ex-girlfriend.

And now she was here in Arizona.

It could be a coincidence, Glenna considered as she took a seat at her desk and pulled up a search browser on her computer. She wasn't at all close to her stepson, but Sasha had been a font of information, and she was well-placed as a front desk clerk to know the comings and goings of Clive's children.

A woman from Adam's past could be dangerous. Especially if it tapped into a softer side of her stepson she'd never been quite sure existed.

Of course…

She ran a finger around the stem of her wineglass, the richly hued gold color of her favorite chardonnay glistening through the crystal.

It all came down to a matter of choice. Should she gamble that Adam's long-ago romance could sprout feelings again she could use against him, or would a distraction of someone he was no longer with only make him more determined in his quest to save Mariposa?

Although she'd never considered herself a romantic, it would make sense to try to leverage the first. And with Sasha in place, she'd have an eagle-eyed view of how things were progressing.

Yes, Glenna thought as she took a sip of her wine, this could work. Distract him with the woman from his past and then use her as one more weapon to hurt him.

It could work.

Even better, it *would* work.

She'd make sure of it, she vowed to herself as she picked up her phone once more to make another phone call.

One to someone who wasn't going to fail this time.

PAIGE TOOK IN the drive to Mariposa with a blend of awe and still-lingering fear that she couldn't quite shake.

Two near hit-and-runs in the span of a few hours had a way of doing that, she reasoned with herself when she caught her pulse racing at the remembered incidents.

She was trying to put on a brave face for Adam, but what were the chances of something like that happening? And while she didn't want to put too much stock in the idea of a curse, was there something to that general idea? Bad vibes, maybe?

Or worse, had she messed with fate in some way by taking this job?

She and Adam hadn't been in each other's lives for a decade. Yet now they were thrown back together, in the midst of serious unrest in his family *and* in his business. Worse, it was a turmoil that stemmed from the fact that the two were so intimately linked.

Did she need to take these near accidents as signs she should just leave?

There were plenty of good photographers who could capture the beauty of the resort. She could pull up at least five or six right now in her phone and see who was available.

"I can hear those very serious thoughts from all the way

over here." Adam's voice held the light notes of a tease, but tension pulsed beneath it.

"You know what I'm thinking?"

"Let me guess. It goes something along the lines of how you need to leave and find someone new for this gig. You're also thinking that your presence is some sort of intrusion on my life. And, oh, wait—" He stopped and turned to smile at her as he slowed to make a turn into the road that led to the resort. "You keep going over and over that idea of a curse as some sort of sign from that ever-knowing entity called fate."

It was humbling to be read so easily. Even more so by someone she wanted to keep up a solid shield of indifference toward.

"That's so not fair."

"The question is if I'm right."

Although Mariposa wasn't yet visible, the ridge of red rocks that rimmed the property rose up beside the car window, and Paige focused on them now. Sedona and the surrounding red landscape—a special sort of magic from nature that was the result of the iron minerals that made up the rocks—had always carried an air of the mystical. Whether someone believed all the way in psychic energy and spiritual enlightenment, there was something special about the place.

At minimum, nature's absolute majesty was on full display.

But for someone who did believe in the ability to channel one's inner voice and power? Well, it was humbling to realize just how emotionally naked that made her here in the midst of all this natural beauty and wonder.

Especially when so much of her inner vulnerability right now was tied to her history with Adam.

She finally turned away from the car window to face him again. "You're partially right."

"What did I miss?"

"First, how about if we remove the word *curse* and instead substitute the words *bad vibes* and stones that should have been left unturned?"

"I haven't seen any stones?" Even though his gaze was firmly forward, Paige didn't miss the small grin that tilted the corner of his lips.

"We're the stones, Adam. You and me and all that came before. Even the fact that Max is here is a little odd, don't you think? It's like ten years haven't even passed."

Only they had.

Ten long years where they'd gone on about their lives, focused on becoming whomever they were each supposed to be.

Yet now here they were, tugged back into some strange world where other than being older and wiser, they were together again.

She'd never really allowed herself to fantasize about Adam Colton coming back into her life. She'd understood early on that no matter how she felt about him or where she'd believed their relationship had been headed, when he broke things off it was for good. There might have been copious tears about that fact, but Paige had never given herself the room to fantasize that things would be different.

They weren't and never would be.

Adam was gone.

Which made this reentrance into each other's lives so difficult to process.

The door she'd believed not just closed but also locked and sealed over had now opened again.

And walking through it felt far too easy.

"You're also not an intrusion, Paige."

He said it softly as he drove through the electric gate at the back of the property, rolling past the slow-moving entrance, but he could have screamed it for all the power those words held.

"I think you're wrong there."

More majesty—this time in the form of the exquisite resort that sat like a jewel in the midst of nature—enveloped them as they drove deeper into the property.

Even here, in the area clearly marked for employees, she could see the extra care and touches that made Mariposa special. It might not have the same flash and panache of the main guest areas, but for as far as she could see, there were obvious signs of luxury.

The well-appointed bungalows that made up a portion of the employee property. The low office buildings that were impeccably maintained, with flower beds that could have greeted a queen. And the sparkling white golf carts that buzzed around with purpose, some carrying casual yet well-dressed staff, others with maintenance crew that carted everything from soil and mulch to more flats filled with blooming flowers.

Mariposa was magnificent. A dream, really.

And while she was coming to appreciate it, the place had occupied a place in her mind that was close to a nightmare.

"I don't belong here. And maybe those accidents were the unmistakable proof I need to leave."

"Come on, Paige. You don't really believe that, do you?"

"What else can I think?"

Something flashed in his gaze—it was gone so fast she could almost believe it had never been, but it caught her up all the same.

"You think something darker is at play?"

"I think we've had a lot of problems here over the past few months, and I want Noah to rule it out. That's all." He pulled into a parking space with his name on it and put the car in Park before turning to face her. "I don't think this is fate or a curse, and I'm hard-pressed to believe it's even something nefarious. But I'll feel better once my brother-in-law looks into it and chalks it up to nothing more than some speed-loving jerk who doesn't know how to drive."

They both got out of the car, and while Paige couldn't quite say she was reassured, she did believe Adam's earnestness. Especially when he met her at the back of the car and gestured toward the business offices across the way. "Why don't we both feel better and go talk to Noah now?"

She nodded, already feeling a bit calmer at the prospect of talking to someone with the experience to figure out what was going on. "I'd like that."

Adam extended his elbow, offering her a place to settle her hand. It was the old-school gesture of a gentleman, and she nearly shook it off before thinking better of it.

Who was she to pass up a strong arm to hold?

And if it meant taking comfort from Adam Colton—something she'd sworn she'd never do again—well, she'd just have to chalk it up to the work of a moment.

And ignore how warm and strong and firm his biceps felt pressed against hers.

ADAM DIDN'T CONSIDER himself a prude, but the image of his sister and her new husband—locked tight in each other's arms as he pushed his way into Noah's office—caught him off guard.

Way off guard.

It also had heat creeping up his neck as Paige almost walked into his back because he'd come to such an abrupt stop.

"Don't you know how to knock?" Noah growled, lifting his lips from Laura's but not actually stepping away from his new wife.

"Don't you know how to close office doors?"

Laura slipped from her husband's embrace and put on a small smile, seemingly nonchalant with being caught in such an intimate moment. He'd give his sister credit—she nearly pulled it off, too. She might have actually managed it if half of her hair wasn't coming out of its updo and she didn't have a large smear of lipstick at the corner of her mouth.

"Adam. Paige." Laura nodded before quickly crossing to the sideboard and small fridge in the corner of Noah's office. "Let me get you both waters."

She lingered a few minutes, pulling the clip out of her hair and fluffing it in front of a decorative mirror over the sideboard. Adam knew the exact moment Laura saw the lipstick smudge when a small squeal floated across the room and she frantically reached for a napkin near the fridge.

"We haven't met yet." Noah extended a hand to Paige. "Noah Steele."

"Paige Barnes."

Noah gestured them to the sitting area of the office, made up of an L-shaped sectional couch set off by a long glass-topped coffee table.

"The photographer?" Noah asked as he took his seat, more evidence that he might not have been part of the Mariposa family—or the Colton family, for that matter—for very long, but he was absolutely clued into everything happening.

At Mariposa *and* with the family.

"Yes, I'm here to shoot the property for the next issue of *Exquisite Living Magazine*."

"This is the big feature Adam and I were able to place." Laura handed over the waters before sliding in smoothly next to her husband on the sofa. "It's going to go a long way toward restoring faith in the property by the luxury clientele we seek."

"Oh, I don't know." Noah's gaze drifted lovingly over his wife before coming to rest first on Paige and then directly on Adam. "They'll never say it, but I think our celebrity clientele enjoy the air of danger just a wee bit, don't you think?"

Noah was driving to a point—of that, Adam had no doubt—but he also couldn't discount his brother-in-law's words. While there had been a definite uptick in questions around security protocols, they weren't exactly down on bookings as a result of the events of the past few months.

People thought they were being discreet—and many of their celebrity clients passed questions through a handler rather than asking directly—but there was a definite buzz when guests checked in with their entourages. The front desk had been trained on just what to say. A mix of comments that delivered confidence yet didn't dismiss the air of mystery surrounding the proceedings.

And in the background, Noah and the security team had amped up surveillance and screening all around the property. It was invisible to their guests, but it was there all the same.

"Enjoying the perceived risk and actually being *in* danger are two different things," Laura cut in smoothly.

Noah looked over at Laura, his gaze what could only be called adoring. "Which I suspect is part of why your brother has interrupted a private moment, my love."

It was easy, Adam thought, to dismiss Noah on first glance. He was a formidable-looking man, with his thick, well-muscled torso covered in tattoos and his growly personality.

But there was a sharp sense of his surroundings, as well as a BS detector that operated at all times.

His sister had a matched sense of radar, which had put them at odds at first and then quickly in cahoots, but it was also one of the reasons they so clearly fit together.

Complemented each other, really.

And it was why he'd brought Paige here now.

He glanced over at her. She'd been mostly quiet, taking in the moment. He remembered that about her from when they dated, too. Because her looks were so arresting, people often assumed that she had a forward personality that matched the fact that *they'd* noticed her.

Instead, she always seemed more than ready to give others the spotlight and was often more at ease after she'd had time to adjust to a new situation versus diving right in.

"Paige had a few incidents this morning. I'd like to rule them as accidents, but I think we need to keep with our current theme and take extra precautions."

"What sort of incidents?" Laura asked in a rush, leaning forward. "Here at Mariposa?"

"No, no." Paige was equally quick to reassure her. "At my hotel, and then as Adam and I were leaving our lunch meeting."

It struck him that she'd called their lunch a *meeting* instead of a date. He had no right to be startled about that fact—it fully *was* a business lunch—but it stung all the same.

Which was one more reason they needed to be here. With

someone who had both the professional experience as well as the objectivity needed to assess Paige's near accidents.

He certainly didn't, if he was inwardly mooning about what to call a meal with the woman.

Not a date.

Obviously.

Noah went straight into question mode, and Paige shared all that had happened at her hotel and then after their lunch.

"Did you recognize anything about the car?" Noah asked.

"No." Paige set down her water without taking a sip. "My back was turned both times, and it all happened so fast. I was startled, so I guess I didn't catch a lot of specifics. But both times it was a big SUV. I don't know if it was the same one, but it could have been."

"We'll get the video tapes from the hotel and the restaurant. I'll also talk to my co-workers with the police." Noah added a wolfish grin. "They like to think they're rid of me with the work I'm doing here, so I enjoy keeping them on their toes."

"Do you think it was on purpose? I don't see any reason why anyone would want to target me."

"Could anyone have followed you here? A problem from home, maybe?"

Adam understood where Laura was going. Although a lot of their problems over the past few months had stemmed from Glenna's interference at Mariposa, there had been outliers as well. Dani's uncle had followed her here to get his hands on her inheritance. And Max had dealt with problems from his TV show that had followed him from New York.

"I can't think of anything," Paige said. "I travel a lot for my job, and when I'm home I'm actually something of a homebody. Nothing even slightly upsetting has happened."

Noah nodded at that. "Now that we've discussed it, do think about it. It can be something simple that you initially dismissed, but—" He stopped, his gaze pointed first to Laura and then to Adam.

"But what?"

"I think what Noah's trying to say is that we've had our fair share of problems here," Laura smoothly picked up for her husband. "I think we have to be honest about that and with you."

Adam caught his sister's gaze and knew her intentions without her even saying a word.

He hated what he had to say but knew that he owed it to Paige to be honest.

"If you want to pass on this job, Paige, we will of course understand."

Paige turned toward him. "You want me to leave?"

"I want you to feel you can make whatever decision is right for you."

PAIGE WASN'T SURE if she was insulted or hurt.

Quit this gig?

Sure, she'd been on the verge of doing just that the day before, but it was over dealing with Adam and their shared past.

But they'd worked through it.

With honesty and the clear admission of what had ended their relationship a decade before and that it was time to move on.

Photographing Mariposa was moving on.

Hell, being *here* was moving on.

And now he wanted her to go?

"I took this job on, and I'm going to see it through."

"That was before those two incidents earlier."

"Incidents Noah is going to look into. Incidents," she quickly added, "that are likely just unpleasant accidents."

"That's quite a turnaround from curses and taunting fate."

Paige had never considered herself a loud or confrontational person, but she was hardly a doormat.

"Don't toss that back at me. Heat-of-the-moment impressions and confusion over nearly being run down by more than a few tons of SUV is a far cry from thinking there's something criminal going on that I'd run away from with my tail between my legs."

"Why don't we give you a few minutes?" Laura said, her smooth efficiency already obvious as she stood, grabbing her husband's hand to do the same. "Noah can make those calls from my office."

Paige waited until they'd left, Laura closing the door softly behind them, before she stood and whirled on Adam. "What is with you? I don't need you to play my protector. I'm a professional, and I'm here to do my job."

"Giving you an out because there are issues at my resort is hardly calling you unprofessional."

"I don't see you leaving and closing up shop. Or your sister. Or any of the numerous staff you have here. You haven't given them an out or asked them to leave despite the risks."

"This is different."

"How?"

"Because it is. You're not employed by us. And damn it, Paige! Someone tried to run you down today."

"I hardly think—"

She was working up a solid argument—or so she'd tell herself later—when Adam just moved into her space and pulled her close, crushing her against him as his lips found hers.

The move was so unexpected it was all she could do to fist her hands in his shirt and hang on.

And oh…what a ride.

Long, aching moments spun out between them as Adam's lips devoured hers.

Urgent.

Needy.

And wholly familiar yet foreign all at once.

She remembered this man. Had spent years remembering what it was like to kiss him and be in his arms and to make love with him.

But the reality of not having any of those experiences for the past ten years had faded just how intense and overwhelming he was in the moment.

His body was harder than she remembered. Still long and lean, but with the additional filling out that came with age. The Adam she'd been with ten years ago still had the lines of youth. The man holding her now was fit and firm, his body in its prime.

Somewhere down deep, Paige recognized she should step away. If for no other reason than simple pride. But the events of the day and the overwhelming emotions of being near him again and…well, hell, the fact that she *wanted* to kiss him had all eroded the better angles of her nature.

Right now, all she wanted was to take comfort in his arms and *feel* again.

None of it, however, could erase the irritation and ire she had at his suggestion she leave Mariposa and just walk away from her work and her commitments.

It was that truth that had her finally stepping back.

Only to find the need to move back into him was nearly overwhelming.

So much so that she actually took a few steps backward, pleased she managed to remain steady on her four-inch heels.

"Paige, I—" Adam broke off, his blue eyes wide with desire and something that smacked of regret.

It was that reality that kept her ire fully fueled.

"I'm not a woman who believes in violence in any form, but if you apologize to me, I may actually punch you."

With the sudden and desperate need to clear the air, Paige glanced around the office. It was sparse—a match for what she perceived in Noah Steele—with only a few pieces of black-and-white artwork on the walls. Other than a framed photo of him and Laura on his desk, that was the only personal touch she'd seen.

"There's some vibe going on in this room. First your sister and brother-in-law. Now you and me. Do you all pipe something through the vents here?"

"What?"

Happy that she'd finally caught him as off guard as he'd done to her with that damn kiss, Paige felt the carefree burst of laughter bubble up in her chest.

"The room has sex vibes, that's all. Newlyweds have a way of throwing those off effortlessly in their wake. That's all this was."

"No, it wasn't."

Paige held his gaze, refusing to let go. "Yes, Adam. That's all it was. So we're going to forget about this, and I'm going to go work on my shot list and you're not going to talk to me any longer about quitting this gig or going back home to California."

"There's no such thing as 'sex vibes.'"

"As someone who looks at people for a living, I can one hundred percent tell you there are. But we won't argue the point."

As if to punctuate it, she moved back over to Adam and laid a hand over his cheek, patting it lightly.

It would have been better if her hand hadn't shaken slightly as she touched his skin once more, but when she stepped back, she was satisfied she had managed to make her point.

"I'm going to go do my work, and I'll have someone at your front desk manage a car to take me back to the hotel when I'm done. Then I'll meet you here tomorrow morning with my final list of suggestions for your and Laura's approval so we can get this project going."

"I... Fine," He acquiesced. "That's fine. I'll make sure we have a driver ready when you are. But I'm picking you up tomorrow morning."

Whatever feelings she had of having the upper hand faded as Adam went straight back into take-charge mode.

"You don't need to do that."

"Yes, I do. And I will. I'd drive you back today, but I have an afternoon meeting with the lawyers that is expected to go late into the evening. I can't move it."

"If it's about your father, you shouldn't."

Figuring a hasty retreat was in order since she was in imminent risk of staring at his lips again, Paige turned and left.

But no matter how hard she focused the rest of the afternoon or how many nooks and crannies she investigated around the property in search of the perfect spot, she couldn't quite find one nearly as interesting or enticing as the middle of that sparse office with the sex vibes.

PAIGE AWOKE FROM heated dreams to find herself wrapped up tight in tangled sheets. Early-morning summer sun speared through the blinds she hadn't bothered to pull last night after she'd gotten into her hotel room, and a low, steady throb filled her belly as the heat of the dream still thrummed through her.

What was she thinking?

The question was as weak as her will had been the day before, kissing Adam, but it was valid all the same.

What was she possibly thinking, to not just accept Adam Colton's advances but to lean into them with barely veiled need?

She had to keep the upper hand in all this. Wasn't that what that pat to his cheek had been all about before she left Noah's office? A silly bid to retain some semblance of control over the situation?

It had felt necessary.

And wasn't that just the problem?

Paige sat up with a start as the reality of the past two days became clear. Whatever history they might have, she'd been treating this time with Adam like an emotional chess match.

And that had to stop.

She was here for a job, one that would be over in a matter of days. She'd head back to the resort today, map out some of her lighting and by tomorrow morning when the talent arrived, she'd know exactly where she wanted to position them.

The entire process was slated for three days, and that was only to manage around the ever-so-slight possibility of bad weather. Otherwise, by the end of the week she'd be on her way back to California and Adam would once again become a memory.

One that could rest considerably easier now that they'd seen each other again.

It was a good theory, Paige thought as she got out of bed

and padded to the bathroom. And maybe kissing Adam was inevitable because of all that history. Now any lingering curiosity of what lived in both their memories had been sated.

"Again, lovely theory, Barnes," she muttered to herself in the mirror as she put toothpaste on her toothbrush and started the first task to get ready for the day.

Because even with an exhaustive list of shots filling her mind, she couldn't stop thinking about the way it felt to kiss Adam again.

The feel of his arms as they wrapped around her.

The press of his hard chest against her breasts.

Why was it so easy to summon it all back into the forefront of her mind?

Even all these hours later, she could still conjure the feel of his lips pressed against hers. She could also have sworn that she'd caught the distinctly masculine scent of him several times since leaving his company.

She'd turn only to find air, but the sensation was there all the same.

Disgusted with her errant thoughts, she paced back into the bedroom and flipped on morning TV. She'd been so exhausted the night before she had skipped dinner, falling asleep with her tablet on her lap as she built her shot list. It briefly crossed her mind now to order room service, but Adam would be here soon to pick her up, and she could grab something at Mariposa.

After snagging a bottle of water off the dresser unit, she unscrewed the cap, surprised when it came off so easily she spilled water over the carpet and nearly onto herself.

"Easy girl." She took several long, deep sips, willing the rush of nervous energy to fade. The water was oddly flat, and she held it up, wondering if bottled water had an expiration date.

It was only as light refracted against the small reservoir left in the bottom of the plastic that she felt the room spin.

Hard.

Her hand shook as she lowered it, an immediate wave of nausea flooding her system.

What was wrong?

It was her last thought as a sharp metallic taste filled her mouth and the room went black.

Chapter Seven

Adam paced the lobby of Paige's hotel, irritated to have been kept waiting so long.

He hadn't noticed her tardiness at first, so preoccupied with seeing her again after their shared kiss yesterday that it was a full five minutes before he even realized he was pacing the lobby.

He hadn't gotten the kiss—or her—out of his thoughts for longer than a few minutes at a stretch, and *damn it*, he didn't need this distraction. A point that was only reinforced by spending the next ten minutes on an urgent call with his lawyer—a frustrating punctuation point to an endlessly long meeting the day before.

But that had ended more than five minutes ago, and there was still no sign of her.

She hadn't responded to his two texts, either.

He didn't know her room number and had worked in hospitality long enough to know that the front desk wouldn't give it to him, so he went straight to the manager's office. He didn't know Yvette Sanders well, but he was acquainted with most people in the Sedona hospitality community, and he hoped he could prevail upon her good sense to take him up to Paige's room.

None of this sat well with him.

Whatever strained moments had passed between him and Paige over the past forty-eight hours, this level of unprofessional behavior wasn't anything he'd have expected. Add on her upset at the suggestion she should walk off the job, and it made even less sense.

With that realization, something niggled beneath the irritation. It was a small kernel that bloomed quickly, and he picked up the pace to Yvette's office. By the time he reached her, the fast-evolving discomfort had grown nearly manic.

She must have seen it in his face, because the pretty, welcoming smile that creased her dark skin quickly faded. "Adam. What's wrong?"

"I'm supposed to meet someone who hasn't come down. I'm—" He took a hard breath. "I'm worried. It's probably silly, but I am. Worried about someone."

Yvette was already charging across her office, gesturing that he follow her to the front desk. In a matter of moments, she had Paige's room number and a member of security with them heading for the elevators.

"When did you last see her?"

"Yesterday. She left Mariposa to come back here in the evening, and we agreed I'd pick her up this morning."

Yvette nodded as they reached the appointed room, knocking hard on the door. "Miss Barnes! This is the hotel management. Are you in there?"

When no answer came, Yvette rapped again, harder.

"Miss Barnes, if you don't answer, we have the authority to enter your room!"

After one more hard knock, Yvette nodded at the guard, who quickly unlocked the door. She walked in first, followed by the guard.

Adam didn't even need to clear the door when he saw the evidence that his fears hadn't been misplaced.

Paige was slumped over on the bed, her head hanging off the edge at an odd angle.

She wasn't moving.

Paige heard the commotion around her and felt the strong arms holding her before the blessed numbness of darkness took her under again. Her last thought was that she just couldn't keep her eyes open this morning when suddenly she was wide awake, the gentle eyes of an EMT holding hers as a second worked around her.

She wanted to ask questions but was suddenly conscious of a tube in the way and a weird numbness in her throat. Panic welled up, but the EMT talking to her spoke more firmly.

"Miss Barnes, you're going to be fine. We're here to help you. You've had an overdose and we're treating you."

Panic morphed into something even worse as she struggled to process the words and the commotion around her.

Overdose?

She caught snippets of conversation between the EMTs as well as the droning details from a morning-TV personality talking about the expected weather forecast for the day.

The soothing voice of the EMT continued as her partner worked efficiently, and Paige was held still as that terrible tube was removed.

"May I talk to her?"

Paige heard the voice over her shoulder and looked up to see Adam. She tried to say his name, but it came out as a hoarse whisper.

"Wha—"

He shook his head. "Don't talk. You're okay now."

He reached out, and his hand grazed hers before the EMTs blocked him, letting her know they were lifting her onto a stretcher.

The panic still wouldn't fully fade, but it had dulled a bit, and she focused on her breathing. Whatever had happened, she was getting help.

And Adam was here.

It was the last thought she had before her eyes felt unbearably heavy and she closed them, grateful for the darkness that took her under once more.

ADAM STAYED ON-SITE at Paige's hotel, speaking with Yvette as well as the police. He'd called Noah as soon as the EMTs left with her on the stretcher, and his brother-in-law arrived, knocking on the still-open door to Paige's hotel room.

"Adam. What's going on?"

A steady relief filled him—the first he'd had since seeing Paige passed out as he moved into the room behind Yvette and the security guard. "Paige overdosed."

"On what?" Noah asked.

"No idea. The security team's been in here, combing the bathroom and the rest of the space."

"What have they found?"

"Nothing, as far as I can tell."

He hated this feeling—all the questions that refused to calm swirling through his mind. He knew addiction was a disease, and individuals caught in its throes needed help and compassion, not judgment, but he still couldn't get over it.

Nothing about the past few days had suggested Paige was managing a drug problem.

Noah excused himself to talk to one of the police officers stationed outside the door. Adam briefly considered following but recognized Noah was likely to get far more one-on-one than he would if Adam interfered.

And still…

None of it made sense. The woman he'd known in college had been adamant she wanted nothing to do with the drug culture she was often exposed to on modeling gigs. And over the past few days, he hadn't gotten any sense that she was struggling with an addiction.

Yet regardless of what he thought, nothing could erase the horrific feeling that his arrival at the hotel and his fear that something was wrong had saved her from a fate far worse than simply having her stomach pumped.

"Adam."

Noah pulled him from the determinedly dark line of thinking. "The detective here spoke with the officer on-site at the hospital. Paige didn't have any food in her stomach, nor are the lab results turning up any standard street drugs."

"What does that mean?"

"The initial lab results suggest poison."

A harsh clanging filled his ears as Adam took in Noah's briefing.

Poison?

Someone tried to poison Paige?

"She's here on assignment. She's not even from here and hasn't had any incidents at home, by her own admission." He took in a sharp breath, realization dawning. "The near misses with those SUVs. She's been targeted."

"It looks like." Noah glanced around the room. "The EMTs said no food, though. What could she have had?"

Adam had observed his brother-in-law for a few months now and recognized Noah's police skills had been honed in the trenches. But it was something else to see how quickly he moved back into cop mode, his attention laser-focused on the room as he searched for clues.

His own gaze followed a similar path, drifting past the TV toward the expansive dresser that held the flat-screen. "The water."

He moved closer to the small stock on the counter, noticing everything from the hotel was still in its square tray, untouched. Noah stayed where he was, but that focus never wavered. "How many bottles are there?"

"Four."

"Have any been touched?"

"It doesn't look like it. We have a similar setup in our rooms. A small tray that holds the stocked amount."

"Then where did Paige get this identical bottle?"

Adam turned to see where Noah pointed to a nearly empty bottle, discarded by the side of the bed. A small amount of water was still in the base.

Noah pulled a handkerchief out of his back pocket and picked up the bottle. "I think we need to have this tested."

HER THROAT WAS on fire, and people thought she'd overdosed on drugs.

Those twin thoughts were all Paige could think as she lay in her hospital bed. The doctor had been in a few times, her smile gentle as she explained what had happened. How a stomach-pump procedure had been done and why her throat was not only in pain as the numbing agent wore off but how it would feel uncomfortable for a few days because of it.

Despite her hoarse protests that she hadn't taken any drugs, the doctor had encouraged her to rest and that they'd be back in to see her in a bit.

She wasn't sure why she was being treated like a child—

a silly, lying child—and that stung worse than the pain in her throat.

Why didn't anyone believe her?

She'd seen the destruction drugs caused firsthand, from her father's problems to many models she'd worked with through the years, and she wanted no part of it.

So being accused of using them despite her protests just seemed cruel, adding to the pain and confusion she already felt lying in a hospital bed. The hot prick of tears filled the back of her eyes, and she nearly gave into them before taking a hard—painful—swallow.

She wasn't going to wallow in this. She knew herself, and whatever people thought, she not only wasn't a drug user but she also had nothing in her room or in her baggage. Someone would see reason.

Someone had to.

That truth buoyed her, and she was about to ring to have the doctor come back when a soft knock sounded outside her door before Adam poked his head in. "Hey there."

"Adam!" His name came out on a deep whisper.

He came fully into the room, Noah on his heels. "I wanted to see how you were, and we also wanted to talk to you."

The seriousness that carved deep grooves into his face had her frowning, something sinking hard in her already-sensitive stomach. "What's wrong?"

Adam reached for her hand. "Try not to talk too much. I can tell it hurts."

She nodded, comforted by the gesture even as she was still confused by the oddness of having him and his brother-in-law in her hospital room.

"The doctor told us you have questions," Noah began.

"We asked her not to say anything until we could share what we know so far."

"Know what so far?" Each word felt like the stab of an ice pick in her throat from the inside out, but she refused to stay quiet. "What's going on?"

"First of all, just so we can rule this out..." Noah said. "Did you take any drugs in any form?"

"No! I didn't take drugs!" She pushed as much force into the word, regardless of the cut-glass pain it caused.

"I'm not saying you did. I'm ruling it out for a reason."

Noah's smile remained gentle, and she wasn't sure if she should be angry or concerned, but it was what came next that had raw fear racing through her body.

"We believe you were poisoned. Did you drink any bottled water?"

With startling clarity—the first she'd had that wasn't muzzled by confusion or the odd circumstances she'd suddenly found herself in—Paige nodded. "This morning. I got up, brushed my teeth, and came to the bed and turned on the TV."

"Where did you get it?"

"It was hotel water. I got it—" She stilled, recalling the evening before when she'd gotten back to her floor. A cleaning attendant had been coming down the hall with several bottles of water in her arms. "One of the hotel attendants gave it to me. Just as I was unlocking my hotel door."

Adam's grip tightened on her hand. "It wasn't on the credenza in the room?"

"No, she was kindly passing them out as she came down the hall and I took it. I didn't think anything of it. I..." The words died in her throat as she remembered the morning. "The lid came off really easily when I opened it. I nearly spilled it on myself."

"Paige," Adam said gently, his hand supportively still holding hers. "The water was drugged. Poisoned, most likely."

"Why would someone do that? She was a hotel employee."

"We're going to assume she wasn't," Noah said before gesturing with a thumb over his shoulder. "But I want to get to the officer working this so he can secure the video footage from the hotel."

Paige struggled to take it all in as she watched Noah walk out of her room. Drugged water someone deliberately gave her? Someone pretending to be a hotel employee?

And with that, an even scarier thought registered, more pieces falling into place. "The near misses with those SUVs. They weren't accidents."

"We're beginning to believe they aren't."

Without realizing the action until she'd done it, she pulled her hand from his before reaching for the controls on the electric bed to raise her position so she was fully sitting.

"Why would someone target me? I meant what I told Noah yesterday. I can't think of anyone who would hurt me. I haven't had any bad experiences or situations that would lead me to believe anyone I know or have met could do this."

It briefly flitted through her mind to tell him about her estranged relationship with her father, especially after all he'd willingly shared the past few days about his own family, but something held her back.

Her father wasn't part of this. He might be a miserable bastard, but he was gone. Dredging up those emotions and the soul-deep disappointment of that relationship wasn't going to help this situation or give any answers beyond putting a spotlight on him, and that was the last thing she wanted.

"I'm afraid you're being targeted because of me."

Whatever direction she was thinking, Adam taking ownership of this problem wasn't it. "Why would anyone do that?"

"The resort has had its share of problems. They've been aimed at others, but it's possible that now it's my turn."

"Your turn for what?"

"Mayhem. Distractions. Some sort of vendetta. Take your pick."

While she didn't understand it any better, she did recognize it might make sense. She didn't have anyone coming after her, and her life before coming to Arizona had been uneventful. Yes, her job kept her busy and traveling, but to say there was anything nefarious going on in her personal life simply didn't click.

"Who's responsible?" She hated to ask but pressed anyway. "Your father?"

"It doesn't play. He's desperate to save his own business and use Mariposa to do it, but he's not smart enough."

"It takes brains to hurt someone?"

"No," Adam shook his head before moving toward her guest chair, pulling it up close beside the bed before taking a seat. "What I mean is, my father's vindictive nature is more obvious. The takeover of Mariposa, for example, is just him taking what he believes to rightly be his."

"But it isn't his."

"Rationally, we both know that. My siblings know it, too. But he doesn't see it that way. It's like he convinces himself that something belongs to him, so it's okay to then take it."

Although Paige couldn't say she understood the sentiment or what Adam and his sisters and brother had experienced, he painted a picture that was hard to bump up against poison and attempted harm with a vehicle.

Those things felt personal.

And to use his word, vindictive.

They felt, Paige realized, cunning and sly. Hidden.

"Adam." She sat up, the light sheet covering her falling down to her waist. "Where is your stepmother? Where's Glenna?"

THE MOMENT PAIGE uttered his stepmother's name, Adam could actually visualize the pieces falling into place, like tumblers on a lock.

"Glenna's been behind a lot of things these past few months. Rightly or wrongly, I'd assumed she'd calmed down after her nephew, Matt, got together with Dani, but maybe not."

A memory of Matthew talking to him just before Laura and Noah got married returned in vivid details in his mind's eye. Glenna had asked her nephew to try to ruin the wedding—Matt had, of course, refused. He hadn't wanted to upset Laura at the time, but he'd confided the details to Adam.

"What has she done?"

He filled Paige in on the avoided disaster of the wedding but realized there were several other things Glenna had been behind.

"She also sabotaged the merger I tried to put together a few months ago to save the resort."

Paige looked surprised by that revelation. "You were going to give up Mariposa?"

"That's what I was trying to avoid, actually. But I thought if I could put together a merger, we'd salvage as much as possible and not lose the resort. It would have amounted to a fifty-fifty partnership with Sharpe Enterprises."

"What happened there? You said 'tried.' Did something derail the merger?"

"My father convinced them that the incidents at the resort were too much for Sharpe to want to take on. They were concerned about safety, obviously, but also that this was a risky investment."

"After being on the property, I can't see how anyone would think it was risky."

"Even for all the beauty of the resort and the costs of staying in that sort of luxury, we run on tight margins, just as much of the industry does. Missed room revenues or a few bad months can be more than an investor would want to take on."

"But they entered into talks with you, and from what you're describing, things got pretty far? Why walk away? Crimes happened but you had them handled, the perpetrators caught. It's unfortunate, but it's not like you've got a criminal running loose on the grounds."

She seemed to catch herself on that. "Or didn't have one until I went and proved that theory wrong."

The need to comfort her was nearly overwhelming, but Adam stayed where he was. He'd felt the way she'd pulled her hand from his earlier, and he needed to remember his place.

"You never know what can hurt a negotiation. Did someone get worried? Did their insurance company step in and posit an opinion? There was no way of knowing, but it all disintegrated after Laura's bachelorette party."

"What happened?"

"The women at the resort, many on Laura's team, threw

her a party in the hotel bar. Only, right in the middle of it, several women started getting sick."

Paige's eyes widened, and her voice was nothing more than a croak when she spoke. "More drugs?"

"Yes." He shook his head. "More or less, yes. It was ipecac in the punch."

"Was anyone hurt?"

"It was traumatic for everyone, and luckily all the women who got sick were ultimately okay. But we had to throw out all the liquor in the bar. We ultimately decided it had to be done for the benefit of our guests, but a loss that big was a financial hit we weren't prepared for."

"Of course not."

"My father and Sharpe got news of that, and they pulled the deal."

"So the poisoning had two benefits," Paige said, the subtle threads of fear receding as she grew thoughtful. "Cause trouble and pain for Laura *and* put the deal to save the resort at risk."

"You could look at it that way."

"It reinforces what I thought before. All of this feels very personal in the choices. Ruining large events like a bachelorette party and a wedding. Poison, even one only designed to make someone throw up, is a method of doing harm that takes planning and cunning but not a lot of up-close-and-personal connection to the harm done. Even the potential hit-and-run. That's hired muscle, nothing more."

Something dark swirled in his stomach as a raw cold swept through him.

Everything Paige described made sense. Worse, it had a certain sort of logic to it, especially when he bumped it up against the fact that his father didn't seem capable of anything like this. When Clive wanted something, he went after it. His play for Mariposa was front and center, not even remotely hidden in the shadows.

But Glenna had already proven she worked differently when she wanted something.

"Do you spend much time keeping your stepmother up to date on your life?"

"Hardly." Adam narrowly avoided the string of curse words that usually accompanied thoughts of his father's wife. "She pulls the family routine when she comes, always expecting a premium room and service that basically amounts to being constantly doted on, which we refuse. Basically, we're all happy when she's far away from here."

"Has she been here recently? I've only been here for a few days. If we play out the idea that she's responsible for this, how would she even know I'm here?"

"I don't know."

"Has she been seen anywhere near the resort since before the wedding?"

"No, and the staff is on alert to let us know if she does show up." Adam reached for Paige's hand, unable to stop touching her. He was gratified when her fingers closed over his, giving him a gentle squeeze. "But I think it's time to find out where she's been."

Chapter Eight

Adam had held her hand and stayed by her bed for a few hours, watching over her even when she drifted off to sleep. Yet no matter how often her eyelids drifted closed, each time she opened them, he was there. Paige didn't miss the worry stamped deep in his eyes, but his smile was gentle, and his touch was reassuring.

Each time she fell under, she dreamt of strange things. Swirling monsters in the bottom of a glass of water and dragons breathing so much fire at her that the acrid smoke made her throat hurt. Yet each time she awoke and gazed deep into those blue depths, the worst of the dreams faded.

She was starting to think the man could slay dragons if given a sword. She'd nearly said as much but she was fortunately saved from coming off moony when Laura knocked on her hospital room door late morning.

"I came to check on the patient." Laura held up a large to-go cup stamped with a local chain's insignia. "And I bring with me a restorative hot tea with honey and lemon, guaranteed to make your throat feel warm and cozy."

Paige looked over at Adam, nodding slightly. Her throat was still raw, and the words came out as little more than a whispery croak, but talking didn't hurt quite as much as it had earlier. "I know you wanted to go talk to Noah. Laura will keep me company."

He seemed to weigh the benefits of staying or going, but ultimately stood, gesturing his sister toward the bed. "Your husband around anywhere?"

"I saw him before I came in, pacing the waiting room lobby with his phone pressed to his ear, barking out orders."

Paige took an odd comfort in that description, and Adam seemed to as well when Laura waved him on. "Go on and talk to him. I'll keep Paige company."

Laura settled the cup down on the small serving table on wheels before moving it into place over Paige's lap. "I wanted to check on you and see how you're doing."

"I'm okay."

Laura's mouth turned down into a small frown before settling into a grim line. "You are now, thanks to some quick thinking and likely my brother's well-known impatience."

"Adam found me?"

"He pressed the front desk to take him up to your room out of worry. I'm glad he did."

Paige hadn't heard that part of the story, but now that she had, it made sense. What if they hadn't planned to meet today? Or worse, he hadn't insisted on driving into town and picking her up?

She'd already faced the fact that she could have died if the EMTs hadn't acted so quickly, but it was a harsh reminder of just how much danger she would have been in if she and Adam hadn't agreed to meet.

Laura glanced toward the empty doorway before turning back. "So how are you really doing?"

"Shaky," Paige admitted. "Scared. And increasingly coming to realize someone tried to kill me. More than once."

Laura frowned at that. "I'm sorry we've somehow gotten you mixed up in all this. I have to echo Adam's comments from yesterday. We could hardly hold you to this photo shoot commitment if you'd like to leave."

Although there was a small part of her that wanted to turn tail and run, a much bigger part of her wanted to see this through.

For no other reason than underneath all that fear, she was seriously pissed off.

It was that anger that she was determined to hold on to.

"No way. I'm in this now."

"Then I can tell you my husband strongly suggests you move into protective custody until he and the Sedona PD get to the bottom of this."

"That's silly."

"I wish it was." Laura leaned forward, her corporate face firmly in place. "In fact, I'm leaning toward making it a requirement of your contract. There's no way we can risk your life over what amounts to a few pictures." Laura held up a hand before Paige could say anything. "Photographs I have no doubt will be magnificent and a true testament to your talent, but photos all the same."

Paige wanted to be angry. Or at least a bit crusty at being given such a high-handed set of orders, but as she took a sip of the delicious and soothing tea, she realized she didn't have a lot to stand on beyond her principles.

And even those felt a bit weak.

Wouldn't she do the same if she were in the Coltons' shoes?

"Tell me more about this fight for Mariposa. I'd like to understand the dynamics here."

"The dynamics are simple, really. My father has run his legacy, Colton Textiles, into the ground, and he's decided he can sell Mariposa off to the highest bidder, using that money to save the textile company."

"His board has to know it's not that simple. Sure, it's a cash infusion, but every incident sabotaging the resort and its guests makes it less desirable to investors. Adam said the company you were looking to go in fifty-fifty with pulled out after the liquor incident."

"They did. And your point's a good one. The incidents piling up here have people nervous. But..." Laura's lips spread in a wry smile. "It hasn't done anything to the guests' interest in staying here. We're booked up solid. That's going to be appealing to some investors."

She was a photographer, not a hotelier, but even with the promise of scandal, Paige didn't understand how Mariposa would mean more to an investor with all the things happening here.

And if it was Glenna, sabotaging her own stepchildren's property, it didn't seem like that was going to go over well with anyone considering opening deep pockets.

It was something to think about—and she *would* think about it—but was interrupted from saying much more by the doctor's arrival. She looked less stressed than the last time she'd been in to do rounds, and Paige's earlier frustration at being kept in the dark vanished at the compassion that filled the doctor's face.

"Ms. Barnes. We have your lab results back. I'd like to discuss them with you." She glanced at Laura, but Paige beat her to the punch.

"Ms. Colton Steele and her husband, as well as Adam Colton, need to hear whatever it is you're going to tell me."

The doctor nodded as if resigned, and Laura stood from the chair. "Let me go get them both. They're just down the hall."

As Paige watched her go, she wondered at the sudden sense of calm sweeping over her.

Oddly, it felt similar to that last time she saw her father, dropping money on the table to cover the breakfast check.

Knowledge was power.

Information made you stronger.

And decisive action meant you were moving forward.

Only this time, she realized, she had something else.

Because, she was quickly coming to learn, having people to fight the battle with you made all the difference.

ADAM FOLLOWED HIS sister and brother-in-law down the hospital hallway back toward Paige's room. He hadn't wanted to be separated from her, but the time with Noah had given him much-needed information.

Including the scary news that whoever was determined to cause mayhem for him and his family had ratcheted up their efforts.

And put Paige in the crosshairs.

The poisoning had been confirmed by the hospital lab, and it was far more potent than what had been used at Laura's bachelorette party a few months ago. Noah had also been investigating Paige's two near misses with the SUVs, and those had a deadly air about them. If she hadn't been pulled away by the parking attendant at the hotel or by him at lunch, she'd most certainly have been hit.

Was Glenna actually capable of it?

Adam had never liked his stepmother, but he also hadn't seen her as a cold-blooded killer.

But these attacks on Paige suggested something else.

Something damn-near diabolical.

What if he hadn't gotten there in time this morning?

That thought had gotten progressively louder as he'd

talked with Noah and gotten updates from the man's near-continuous calls with the Sedona police.

And to think that he was irritated that Paige hadn't shown up.

Whatever other worries had gripped him, that assumption had once again forced him to evaluate what was driving him and what his life's focus had become.

He had already questioned that need for the upper hand yesterday when he'd arrived first for lunch. Then this morning he'd spent part of his time pacing her hotel lobby, annoyed she hadn't come down to meet him when she'd been fighting for her life upstairs.

Who was he?

Because while he might be willing to own and acknowledge all that had driven him for the past decade, he didn't like what he'd become in the heat of the proxy fight with his father.

He didn't like it at all.

And he was the only one who could change it.

Pushing it all to the back of his mind, Adam vowed to worry on it later. Right now, Paige needed their support. And while he couldn't—and wouldn't—sugarcoat what was happening, he didn't need to burden her with his concerns, either.

Or his turn at playing jackass of the century.

The only way to actually *be* better was to behave better, and that was starting right now.

He walked back into Paige's room, pleased to see how color had bloomed in her cheeks, replacing the sickly gray he'd seen earlier. Her pretty green eyes were still bloodshot, but there was a brightness to her demeanor that hadn't even been there a half hour ago when Laura had arrived with the tea.

Restorative, his sister had called the tea.

Paige gestured toward the doctor. "Dr. Wu has some details on my test results. I wanted you all to hear them as well."

The doctor was swift and efficient with her details, the information matching the same results Noah had gotten from his call with the Sedona PD detective.

Poison that was a hell of a lot more toxic than the vomiting medicine put into the punch at Laura's party.

Dr. Wu turned her attention toward him. "I understand you pressed the hotel management to check Ms. Barnes's room, Mr. Colton. You've likely saved her life with your insistence."

The doctor remained for a few more minutes, going over what to expect for the next twenty-four hours. Because they wanted to ensure her system had fully flushed any toxins, she would be kept overnight but should be ready to be discharged no later than the next afternoon.

When the four of them were left alone once more, Adam mapped out his plan.

"Paige, Laura and Noah will go over and collect your things at the hotel. After you're discharged tomorrow, I'll take you back to Mariposa myself. I've already spoken with security, and we'll make sure that you've got an escort no matter where you go for the duration of your stay here."

"I won't be a prisoner."

"I'm not suggesting—"

She cut him off before he could say anything further.

"I understand the need for protection. I'm not arguing that point. But I'm here in Arizona to do a job, and I won't be held like a captive at your resort."

Both the doctor's words about Paige's close call, as well as his own memories of seeing her passed out in her room, still had a hard grip on his nerves, and he met her frustration with his own. "Watching out for you isn't holding you captive."

"Marching in here and barking out orders doesn't really reinforce your argument."

In a move reminiscent of the day before in Noah's office, Laura and her husband shared a knowing look before interjecting into the fast-brewing fight.

"Why don't Noah and I head over to the hotel?" She made a point to speak directly to Paige. "I can collect everything for you, if you're okay with that."

"I'd appreciate that. I really don't want to go back to that room."

"Of course you don't." Laura patted Paige's arm. "We'll take care of it. I'll bring you a few things later so you're set overnight."

Once Laura and Noah had gone, the room felt unnaturally quiet, and Adam once again took the seat next to her bed. "I'm not trying to make you a captive. You have to understand that."

"I'm not sure I do. We've been at odds since I got here, Adam. It's ebbed and flowed, and I own my role in that, but I'm not your property and I'm not your concern. I deserve a say in what's happening to me and how it will be handled."

"We weren't at odds when we kissed yesterday."

"That was a moment of curiosity that's now been satisfied for both of us."

He leaned toward her, over the arm of her hospital bed, his gaze never leaving hers. "I won't deny the curiosity, but I'll be damned if one kiss is enough to satisfy me."

"If that's how you feel, then we shouldn't have done that."

"Then I guess we'll just have to agree to disagree on that point."

GLENNA HELD HER phone to her ear as Sasha gave her the latest updates from Arizona.

Commotion in the lobby...

Stomach pumped...

Rushed to the hospital...

The girl seemed determined to give her every damn detail except the ones she really cared about.

Did anyone suspect the motives behind Paige Barnes's poisoning?

Where was Adam in all this? By her bedside or pissed off she might not get the photo shoot done?

And most of all, why was Adam locked in his office with lawyers all day yesterday?

Those were the details she needed.

Instead, she had to parse through long, winding stories that, while lascivious and perhaps helpful if she eventually needed to blackmail anyone at Mariposa, weren't useful in her current situation. Because while she valued Sasha's intel—and paid handsomely for it—the woman's tendency to lean hard into the drama at Mariposa had been one of the most difficult things to manage.

It wasn't terribly useful to know that two of the bellmen were having a torrid affair and had been discovered in an empty bungalow by the head of housekeeping.

Nor was it at all helpful to know that one of the bartenders was rumored to have spent the night with an heiress who recently visited the property and was even now booked for three more consecutive stays, demanding a room closest to the bar.

And she really wasn't interested in knowing that the next big celebrity to arrive in a week was bringing his wife and his mistress and had already set them up in separate quarters with specific orders on how they were to be kept apart for the duration of the stay.

She needed to get her stepson off his game and unable to fend off her husband's advances for the resort, not bribe a few randy guests and employees.

"Has Adam returned to Mariposa?"

"No, not yet," Sasha said. "But Laura and Noah came through the main gates about ten minutes ago."

"The standard payment will be in your bank account this evening. Call me back when you get details."

Glenna hung up before Sasha could give her any more gossip or innuendo. The woman might be a chatterbox, but she *was* the best sort of accomplice—unwitting and compliant, so long as the money flowed.

After dealing with the payment necessities, she turned her attention to the problem at hand. While she wasn't keen on murder, Paige Barnes had seemed like an easy problem to solve. Now that the woman had survived the poisoning, there was a decision to be made.

Keep up the steady course of "accidents" or find a new way to manage Adam.

It would take a bit of strategy and planning and potentially a trip of her own to get the lay of the land. She'd spent the past several years building up a network in Sedona she could call on at a moment's notice.

Perhaps it was time to visit those contacts in person and map out a more thorough plan of attack instead of these hasty requests.

Glenna picked up her phone and dialed her husband. When she got him on the phone, he sounded as dull and distracted as he had for the past several months when his lack of business prowess had become evident in the deteriorating situation at Colton Textiles.

Although she wasn't expecting a fight, she figured a direct attack was best.

She'd made a solid marriage out of telling Clive what she had planned versus waiting for his input, feedback or opinions.

There was no reason to change the approach now.

"Clive, my darling," she cooed when he answered. Without pause, she pressed on, outlining her plans.

"I find I'm in need of a few days at the spa. I'll be heading out in the morning."

I'LL BE DAMNED if one kiss is enough to satisfy me.

Adam's words still hovered between them, as if captured in a thought bubble.

And right along with it, as persistent as that bubble, were the electric pulses of energy flipping beneath her skin as if she'd touched a live wire.

What had gotten into him?

Or worse, into her? Shouldn't she be resting and relaxing instead of having...*tingles*?

Paige wanted to be angry. Or frustrated. Or even a nice case of seriously furious would do right about now.

What she didn't want to be was hot and bothered and increasingly over-sensitized in her too-thin hospital gown, hooked up to beeping machines that had suddenly given away the racing speed of her heartbeat.

It was hardly fair.

Under any circumstances, it would be a problem, but when she looked far from her best, prone in a hospital bed with pumped-stomach breath that could likely fell a steer, it felt supremely unfair.

The man was lethal on a good day, with those all-American good looks, fit frame and a demeanor that had just the right amount of aw-shucks-ma'am sweetness to it.

He wasn't a pushover, and he wasn't always nice, but he was kind, damn it. It was appealing.

Adam Colton was a kind man.

And that meant something.

A lot of something, actually. It was one of the things she'd noticed right off about him. He was determined and driven and he lived in his head much of the time because of those traits. That focus often translated to brusque in his demeanor, but he wasn't nasty or mean.

He just knew what he wanted.

And when what he wanted was *you*, Paige thought, that focus was electrifying.

Because of it, she opted to ignore the kissing comment entirely and lean in on her bigger point. "I meant what I said before. I'm not willing to give up my independence. I'm committed to doing my job, and I want your commitment in return that you'll respect that."

"Then do me a favor."

If he returned to the subject of kissing, she vowed that she might actually dump what was left of her now-cooled tea in his lap.

Which made what he did say more of a surprise.

"Stay at my place. On-site at Mariposa."

Without warning, a memory she'd deliberately kept long buried rose up and nearly strangled her.

"Move in with me, Paige. We spend all the time at each other's apartments anyway. Let's make it official."

"I can't move in with you, Adam."

"Why not?"

"It's too fast."

"We spend all our time together. And it's been four

months. Besides, when it's right, there's nothing too fast about it."

"I—"

She struggled to come up with an argument but nothing surfaced beyond the internal squeals of Yes!

It was the force of that memory that had her words coming out sharper than she intended. "I can't stay with you."

"Of course you can. I have a two-bedroom bungalow with plenty of room. I also have strong security protecting my home, and I can ensure your privacy."

Modulating her tone and trying a new tack, she said, "Noah and Laura mentioned something about protection detail. I'm quite sure staying with you isn't what they meant."

He shrugged, obviously not caring about any impression his sister and brother-in-law might have given her.

"You'll have that during the day around the resort. We were already planning on having security at the shoot regardless, since the models are on-site along with the jewelry on loan. But I'd feel better if I could keep watch over you. I'm the one who got you into this, after all."

Unbidden, strains of "Someone to Watch Over Me" flitted through her mind, the line in that song that never failed to trip her up cycling through on a loop.

Adam *was* the big affair she couldn't forget.

For a decade.

And now she was actually contemplating staying in his home?

There were slippery slopes and then there were just plain stupid choices. How could she be even considering the latter after so little time back in his presence?

Hadn't she learned this lesson?

They'd barely moved in together in college, fully enmeshed in each other's lives, when he ended things. Even now, she could remember how their things, their homes and ultimately their lives had just sort of…comingled.

Hadn't that been one of the biggest factors contributing to the pain of their breakup? That abrupt ending he'd made—coming home one day and telling her he needed to go back to Arizona and was leaving New York—without any advance warning or even any sense he wanted out of the relationship?

She'd gone over it and over it in her mind and had never managed to find a new way of dealing with such an unexpected choice. So why was she even considering putting herself back in that position?

The fact it was only for a few days and she'd be a guest this time hardly seemed like the point.

He could argue it was for her safety or for his peace of mind, but was physical safety worth the price of her emotional protection?

Staying with him? Really?

And damn her foolish heart for leaping hard in her chest at the offer, yelling *Yes!* no matter how bad an idea it was.

"I don't think it's a very good idea."

"Of course it is. It's practical and it solves an immediate need, which is allowing you to do your job and ensuring you can do it without risk."

"I don't want to be an intrusion."

His patience never wavered, but she saw the humor flash in his eyes. He wasn't placating her, per se, but he was definitely enjoying having the upper hand.

And damn it, he did.

She didn't want to leave this job over some silly sense of fear, but she couldn't ignore three near-death misses in less than a day.

"I'm inviting you, Paige. And it's only for a few days. That's hardly an intrusion."

"Then we need to set ground rules."

"Who needs ground rules? You'll be a guest in my home. You can help yourself to whatever you'd like, my state-of-the-art individual-cup coffee brewer is always stocked and perpetually at your disposal, and you'll have an en suite bathroom."

"I mean about us. Especially since you're so—" she waved a hand at him and hoped her expression was stern "—*disagreeable* about the kissing."

His smile was broad and his gaze heated as he eyed her in the bed. "I think I'm quite agreeable."

"Incorrigible, more like it."

"Maybe so, but you know it's a good idea. The staying with me," he added with a cheeky wink. "Although the kissing is an inspired idea, too."

Paige fought the urge to rise to the sexy bait and vowed to stay on course.

Even if something hot and needy settled low in her belly at the idea of kissing Adam again.

And doing way more than kissing...

"It's a practical idea," she finally said on a slightly breathy exhale. "That's hardly the same thing."

"So it's a yes?"

Something way down deep kept her from using that word, no matter how loudly it pounded in her mind. So Paige just sighed and nodded.

"It's not a no."

Chapter Nine

A running loop of thoughts kept Adam company as he carefully drove Paige from the hospital to Mariposa. He'd hated leaving her overnight but had eventually left her to rest—with the security detail Noah had posted outside her door—and came home to make sure everything was in order.

And then he'd been right back at the hospital early this morning, even before she was awake.

The doctor had stressed how important rest was, both to get her system back in order and to give her throat time to recover from the trauma of having her stomach pumped. Paige had looked skeptical as she'd received a set of orders earlier from her discharge nurse, but healing must have won out, Adam thought with a small smile.

They'd barely cleared the hospital parking lot when he heard her soft snoring.

With her asleep, the questions that had kept him company since he'd insisted she stay with him kicked in once more.

Was his fridge stocked with anything she might need or want?

Did he have the coffee pods he blithely promised she could select from?

Would he kiss her again?

He passed through the entrance to the property, her steady, whirring breaths still light and even, when he caught himself cycling through those same questions yet again.

And with that realization came another.

He was nervous.

Especially because he knew damn well his fridge was perpetually stocked by the resort. He had a full selection of coffee no matter if she preferred caffeinated, decaf, flavored or even a strong tea.

And if he had a chance to kiss her again, he was damn well taking it.

It was the nerves beneath the questions that he had to own.

Paige was going to be a guest at his home.

It's not a no.

It had been an interesting way to say yes to his offer to stay with him, he reflected as he pulled up to his bungalow.

Would we call steamrolling over her wishes, wants and needs an offer, *Colton?*

He ignored that nagging worry that had kept equal time with the litany of questions on the drive.

Although it had come off heavy-handed, staying with him *was* the most practical option. He was responsible, even if indirectly, for the dangerous things that had happened to her. So it stood to reason that if she stayed with him, he'd be able to keep closer watch on her surroundings, know if anything was wrong and protect her.

And there might be that second chance to kiss her...

"I'm so sorry I conked out on you."

Her sleep-tinged voice interrupted the direction of his thoughts.

Just in time.

"You've been through a lot. Rest will go a long way toward making you feel better."

Her voice already held notes of improvement, less rusty and hoarse than the way she'd first sounded.

"I can't believe I'm about to say this, but I'm actually a little hungry. I didn't think I'd ever want to eat again, and all of a sudden I feel like I could eat a steer."

"I can fix that, and quickly."

She turned toward him, her surprise more than evident as he pulled into his garage. "You cook, Adam Colton?"

"I can..." He let his words trail off. "I can manage a mean order into the kitchen."

"Aha, that's more what I remember."

"You remember that?"

"That you could barely scramble an egg? Oh yeah, that memory is still surprisingly fresh. Max and I used to joke we could actually hear the little screams coming from the egg carton when you opened the fridge."

It was only as her joke sank in that he recalled the way she and Max would tease him mercilessly whenever he suggested he'd take over kitchen duties.

He'd blocked those memories and so many more, he admitted to himself. It was further proof that he might have made a choice a decade ago, but all his internal coping mechanisms had shifted into high gear to protect himself.

Especially now that he was forced to admit just how much he'd given up.

And how much he'd lost.

A loss that grew increasingly sharp with every moment in Paige's presence.

Once again pushing hard against those uncomfortable thoughts that now seemed determined to have their say, he tried desperately to find some levity.

"I do pop a mean bag of microwave popcorn."

"That's seriously sad, Colton. I would've thought by now you would have a few basics in your repertoire."

He reached for her hand, his fingers mingling with hers. "I haven't had anyone to cook for."

Although she didn't link her fingers with his, she didn't pull away, either.

"No one?"

"No."

"I'm not trying to call you a liar, Adam, but I find that hard to believe."

Although he dated, nothing ever progressed past a few evenings out along with a basic sating of needs. No woman he'd dated in the past ten years had found a more permanent place in his life.

And none of them had been to his home.

"Have you?" he finally asked, not quite sure he wanted to know.

"Have I what?"

"Cooked…for anyone? Or maybe more important, are you cooking for anyone now?"

A small smile tilted the edges of her lips, proof she'd seen through his curiosity on her personal life. "I've dated several men over the past ten years. Nothing that ever progressed to fully permanent, but I got pretty close to an engagement a few years after college."

"What happened?"

"Why does any relationship end?" She shrugged and slipped her hand from beneath his, unbuckling her seat belt. "In the end it wasn't right."

"And now?"

Adam wasn't sure why he was persisting in either the

idiotic metaphor *or* the line of questions, but he kept on all the same.

"Am I cooking for anyone?"

"Yes."

"Not that it's any of your business, Adam, but no, I'm not."

COOKING?

That's what passed for testing the waters on current and former relationships?

Paige might have felt sluggish when she'd left the hospital, but she was wide awake now. And done with that line of questioning. She dragged on the door handle and pushed open the door, only to hear Adam's "Whoa! Let me help you!"

She ignored the demand, managing to get herself out of the seat and beside the car when Adam reached her from the other side. "Please let me help you."

Paige would have ignored the offer—on some level, she wanted to—but her legs were more wobbly than she wanted to admit, so she reached for the hand he extended to her.

"Take it slow."

"I'm not an old lady."

He ignored it, continuing as he helped her toward the interior door into the house. "Laura and Noah dropped all your stuff off and set it in my spare room so you'll have your things."

Paige walked beside him, willing herself to calm down. Discussions about *cooking* aside, she needed to perfect an air of nonchalance and disdain.

It was the only way to get through this and shore up this ridiculous vulnerability that seemed insistent on having its day.

A feeling that would have been easier to stomach if she hadn't noticed that he made a point to close the garage door, waiting until it was fully down before closing and locking the entrance into the house. Once inside, he then showed her how to set the alarm before gesturing her toward the kitchen.

Adam kept a steadying hand on her as he filled her in on his home and what to expect for her stay. "Security walks the full property, and they'll add extra rounds to this part of the rotation."

"I do appreciate all you're doing."

And she did. Despite that suddenly awkward conversation in the car, she recognized just how much he was doing to keep her safe.

Now she just had to focus on avoiding the land mines that tripped up her heart.

Because really, what else was there to be done about it?

They *did* have a history. Pretending otherwise—or the fact that their shared history included some of the most wonderful moments of her life and its ending some of her worst—wouldn't change that reality.

The heavy ring of a doorbell echoed through the house and on back to where they still stood in the kitchen.

"Will you be okay while I go get that?"

"Of course."

Her legs were steadier already, and Paige took a seat in one of the leather stools that rimmed the high-topped edge of his marble counters.

Once seated, with Adam gone from the room, Paige gave herself the freedom to look around, taking it all in. Her photographer's eye had already cataloged the pristine laundry room that looked like it very rarely saw dirty clothes or items left out to dry, hanging from the cabinets that ran the length of the room.

Their walk into the kitchen had only reinforced the continued impression that his home was just a very pretty showpiece based on the acres of gleaming counter that had nothing on it beyond a silver paper-towel holder and a toaster oven tucked in the corner next to the fridge.

She already knew he wasn't a great cook, but the room was so austere she couldn't even imagine him fixing himself a bowl of cereal in here.

It wasn't fair of her to judge him, but what she'd seen of Adam's home so far only reinforced the discussion they'd just had.

He might not be figuratively cooking for anyone, but she didn't get the sense he was literally doing anything of the sort, either. Other than a place where he slept, it didn't appear as if Adam Colton lived here at all.

With that realization, another thought came quickly on its heels.

He'd given up their relationship—one he'd seemed as into and committed to as she was—in order to come back to this property and his family business.

But was he happy here?

Mariposa might drive him, but she didn't get the sense that it brought him all that much joy, and something about that idea bothered her.

While she would wholly own her emotions, including spending far too many years allowing the man to loom large in her thoughts, she had moved on to find happiness and fulfillment in her life.

And yes, even joy.

Her life might not have worked out exactly as she'd envisioned or planned, but she was happy with what she'd built and continued to build each and every day with work that mattered to her.

Her home was comfortable and messy and lived in, and *that* made her happy.

And her life was her own, with each and every decision one she wanted to make.

Was she glowing and ecstatic every day?

Maybe not, but she had found a path forward and she was proud of herself.

"Why don't you pat your own back a bit harder?" She muttered the words under her breath, catching herself from saying anything further by the loud booming voice coming from the direction of the front door toward the kitchen.

"Paige Barnes!" The voice was quickly followed by the arrival of a broad man with a big grin in a face she saw regularly on her TV *and* in her memories.

"Max!"

With swift strides across the kitchen, Max Powell had her wrapped up in his powerful arms, holding her tight. "How are you, Paigey?"

"I'm good." She clung to him, his familiar scent of cooking spices and aftershave one that nearly brought tears to her eyes.

Although she'd counted him as one of her closest friends in college, she'd admittedly lost ongoing contact with him after Adam had come back to Arizona. One more casualty in her grief over losing her relationship.

One that maybe she'd be lucky enough to make right over the next few days.

He pulled back and looked down at her, his tall frame more solid and hard than she remembered. The deep dimple that was one of his trademarks winked in his dark brown face, and she couldn't help but smile back.

"I've missed you."

He pulled her close once more, whispering into her hair. "It's been too long, Paige."

"I know. And—" she pulled back, a smile of her own tugging at her lips "—here I find out you came to Arizona and met someone. Tell me about her."

"Alexis."

She'd have sworn she saw little floating hearts rise up from his deep brown eyes to form a circling ring above his head.

"What can I say? She's incredible. She's the best concierge here at Mariposa, and for reasons that defy logic or good sense, she's happily working on making a life with me."

"That sounds like love to me." Paige reached up and pressed a hand to his cheek, the gesture natural and easy. "I can't wait to meet her."

"I can't wait for you to meet her, either. Which is why I'm going to take over this shameful kitchen tomorrow night with a home-cooked meal to welcome you to Arizona."

"What's this?" Adam asked from where he leaned against the doorway.

"I'm cooking in this monstrosity of a kitchen you have, which you never use."

Paige didn't miss Adam's pointed look from the doorway or the way he raised his eyebrows and wiggled them, a direct reminder of what they'd discussed in the car.

A flash of heat followed the wiggled eyebrows before it vanished as Adam pushed off the doorjamb and walked fully into the kitchen. "I make coffee. And a mean slice of toast."

"Yeah, yeah." Max waved a hand, his attention already

shifting back to Paige. "Alexis is on duty tonight, but she's off tomorrow and we'll make a night of it."

"That sounds amazing."

Max's gaze was careful on hers, his tone growing serious. "News travels fast around here, and I heard what happened to you. Be careful."

"I will."

Max glanced over his shoulder at Adam before those warm eyes came back to meet hers. "See that you do."

He hugged her once more before he said his goodbyes, full of promises for a proper catch-up with their dinner the next night.

"He's missed you," Adam said.

"I've missed him, too."

"You haven't talked to him much beyond a few holiday cards and emails." Adam moved closer into the kitchen. "He's told me as much."

"I saw him for dinner several years ago." Paige blew out a breath. "But we lost ongoing contact after college. His life has been on a very big upward trajectory with his restaurant and his TV show. I'm happy for him."

"He'd have made time for you."

"What's this about, Adam? Are you the friend police?"

"No." He shrugged before shoving his hands in his pockets. "I'm just sorry you weren't able to have a friendship with him after we broke up."

Paige wasn't sure where it came from, but the mix of fear from the day's events and the low-level ire at herself for these endless, ridiculous emotional swings finally spilled over.

"You mean after you left?"

"I mean when our relationship ended, Paige."

"Right." She nodded, still not quite able to modulate her response.

And as that ire built and built, like tinder catching fire, she found she didn't *want* to modulate her response.

Or hide the fact that he'd delivered one of the worst hurts of her life.

"The relationship we had that I'd believed was going somewhere and which you imploded with a few firm words and the confirmation you'd booked a one-way plane ticket home."

"I didn't implode—"

"Spare me your version of events, Adam. I was there." She slid off the stool, her legs now strong and firm as she stood. "I was a part of it. We were living together, and one day you decided to end it all to come running home. How has that worked out for you?"

Paige gestured at the immaculate kitchen, with its gleaming acres of counter space and bright, shiny appliances.

"Because all I see is a shell of a home, devoid of anything personal or happy or bright. I hope walking away and leaving me wondering for years what the hell happened or what I did was worth it."

Without giving him a chance to say anything in return, she headed out, confident she'd find whatever cold, spotless guest room he'd put her in on her own.

ADAM HAD NEVER believed in medicating his problems with alcohol, but every man had his limit, and he'd reached his. He'd taken a seat at the end of the bar in L Bar and was now nursing his second bourbon.

Neat.

The drink, that was.

Not a statement about his life.

The heat of the liquor still seared his throat with each swallow, but he'd managed to sip this one versus the first, which he'd basically tossed back.

None of it was helping.

He'd given Paige her space after she'd tossed that last relationship grenade his way and walked out of his kitchen, attempting to spend a bit of time catching up in his home office. There were several emails from his legal team that required follow-up and focus, and while he'd answered their questions, it had taken him about three times longer than it should have.

He also followed up on his promise to Paige while they were still at the hospital and did some digging on his stepmother. While he avoided calling his father's home whenever possible—a point only exacerbated by the current battle for Mariposa—he did have a few ins from his childhood.

Chief among them, the housekeeper his father had kept on staff since Adam was a boy.

Ingrid had greeted him warmly when he called, and after chatting a bit, him sharing a few details about his life and reiterating his ongoing offer for her to come to stay at Mariposa for an all-expenses-paid visit, he asked after his stepmother.

Only to discover Glenna had been at the Beverly Hills estate for the past few weeks.

He was well aware his stepmother's tentacles stretched far and wide, but it was hard to reconcile her as an overt problem when she was apparently busy with her own work and social calendar. It was more information he'd be sure to share with Noah, but it felt like a dead end all the same.

With two major items checked off his running to-do

list, his thoughts had inevitably drifted back to Paige and her accusations.

The relationship we had that I'd believed was going somewhere and which you imploded with a few firm words and the confirmation you'd booked a one-way plane ticket home.

No matter how many tentative steps they'd taken forward, that was still the prevailing belief she had about him.

And the worst part of it was that she wasn't wrong.

He did a quick check on her around eight, going to her room to see if she wanted dinner. When his soft knock went unanswered, he cracked the door to check on her, only to find her asleep on top of the covers in the guest room.

He closed the door, unwilling to disturb her but unable to spend one more minute in the house alone with his thoughts. After scribbling a quick note to help herself to anything she wanted and reminding her that the alarm was engaged, he'd slipped out and headed for L Bar.

Only to find he was still spending his time alone, despite the busy crowd and general hum of happiness that filled the room.

"I hope you realize pouting isn't a good look for the owner and general manager of an exclusive resort."

He looked over to find his sister standing there, a grim smile on her face. Laura requested a glass of her favorite cabernet when the bartender on duty hurried down the length of the bar to greet her, then took the empty seat beside Adam.

"I'm not pouting."

"Yeah, you are, but I'll call it brooding so it sounds more grown-up."

"I'm not—" He saw Laura's raised eyebrow and abandoned his argument.

"Honestly, I'm a bit surprised to see you here. I'd have thought you wouldn't want to leave Paige alone."

"She's resting, and I've got the house locked down with security keeping watch. I just needed to get out."

His sister did smile then, but there was something soft around the edges. "She's been through a lot."

"All because of us."

"All because of a bad actor trying to do harm. It's not the same, Adam."

"It might as well be. And the hell of it is, I can't just send her back home, because what if this problem follows her?"

"Noah's working as fast as he can. So is the Sedona PD."

"I know. I *know*," he reiterated, dragging a hand through his hair and tugging on the short ends. "But what I don't get is why this keeps happening."

"I'm forced to ask it, Adam. Do you think Dad's behind this?"

"He's so busy trying to take us over and keep his fingers in the Colton Textiles dam, do you honestly think he has the time or the smarts to do this sort of crap?"

Laura seemed to consider his words as she took a sip of the cabernet the bartender set before her.

"Aside from my general disdain for Clive Colton and all he stands for, our dear dad isn't quite the noob you make him out to be."

"No." Adam chose his next words carefully, their collective disdain for their sire not reason enough to dismiss Clive's possible role in all that was happening. "I don't want to be blindsided by what I think of his skills as a parent. But even putting that aside, it doesn't read like it's him."

"Tell me why."

"Think about all we do know of the man. He wants things free and easy. Anything that requires a degree of effort or work is beyond him. What's happened to Paige requires work. Planning."

"Effort." Laura nodded. "That's fair."

"And there was another point she made, which is how personal and calculating it feels."

Laura stopped with her drink midway to her lips. "How?"

"The cold, calculating nature of the crimes seems to be a part of it. And the poisoning. It's—"

"Powerful without needing physical power or strength. It's cunning and crafty," Laura added, considering. "Which is all a really smart way to look at it."

"Which is why I looked into Glenna. And because calculating is an adjective easily applied to her. I called Ingrid a few hours ago," he said, quickly filling Laura in on their beloved housekeeper. "She confirmed Glenna's been home in LA for the past few weeks."

"Calculating. Cunning. And a crime that doesn't require being there in person. I'm not so sure I'd count her out that quickly."

Adam had questioned that as well, but it still didn't explain how Paige had become a target. "I wondered the same, but then why Paige? She's not associated with Mariposa, and up until a week ago, when we finalized the photo shoot and the fact that she'd be on-site, no one would have even known she had any affiliation with us. How do you target someone you don't even know about?"

Laura's sudden interest deflated. "So what you're saying is that Glenna is the obvious and easy choice, but only obvious and easy."

"So it seems."

Laura's quiet sigh filled the air between them, along with the raw truth of her words. "While I'd be the first in line to skewer the woman, I'm not interested in making her a scapegoat, either."

"Make who a scapegoat?"

Noah came up behind Laura, his arms wrapped around her in a gentle bear hug. She glanced up at him, their mutual adoration evident, and Adam had a hit of jealousy so raw he felt like he'd been sucker punched.

Sort of like he'd felt in his own kitchen.

I hope walking away and leaving me wondering for years what the hell happened or what I did was worth it.

His father's takeover efforts combined with the problems at Mariposa had seemed overwhelming, and in that moment, he realized that part of the reason why was because he faced it all alone.

It was a path he'd chosen all those years ago instead of being mature enough or thoughtful enough to try to build a life in Arizona with the woman he'd fallen in love with.

And now it was too late.

Because Paige Barnes might be back in his life, but she'd moved on.

It was only having her back, long after he'd scorched the earth between them, that he realized just what an idiot he'd been.

One who had no hope in hell of ever getting her back.

Chapter Ten

Paige looked through her camera lens and framed up her shot, pleased when she saw the arc of sunlight curve around the edge of one of those distinctive red rocks. She snapped the image, capturing several more before resetting her position.

The stress of the past few days faded away as she worked, catching nature in all its morning glory. The models who'd be part of the shoot would arrive later, and she'd work on blocking with them once they arrived, but for now the time was hers.

Well, hers and the two security guards who watched from a discreet distance away.

She'd mentally tried out pairs of superhero names on them as a sort of internal joke to boost her spirits, but in the end defaulted to Doug and Kadim, since those were their names and they were nice guys.

With guns.

They were also here protecting her and ensuring that nothing would happen to her, and for that she was grateful.

It was the fact she needed them here at all that stung.

Vowing to put it out of her mind, she moved to her camera bag and pulled out a new lens she'd recently purchased. The incredibly high-powered lens would give her several majestic shots of the rocks and the way they formed a backdrop over the property, and she was excited by the possibilities, already envisioning the opening spread in the magazine article.

She'd share a few samples of what she captured each night with the photo editor, using real-time feedback to grab any additional images while here as well as any changes that might be needed.

Several of her colleagues hated that portion of the work, but she loved the collaboration and always had. It might have something to do with why she secured as many magazine gigs as she did—for Paige it had never been about money, always about the fun and excitement of collaboration.

Working toward something with others, where your collective inputs created something greater than the parts.

Something that...

She lowered her camera, an idea taking root.

Divide and conquer.

Wasn't that what had been happening here at Mariposa?

She had every sense that Adam and Laura were strong collaborators and business partners, not just siblings. She'd seen that firsthand in their interactions over the past few days. And while she'd only met Josh and Dani briefly as she'd moved all around the resort, she recognized that same bond there as well.

Yet none of it changed the fact that the things that had been happening here were meant to divide them and pull them apart.

Clive's attack on the business weighed heavy on Adam, pulling him in that direction.

The incidents on property—even her poisoning—were one more tug in yet another direction. If felt clinical and cold to think it, but if she'd died, Adam and Laura would have had a major distraction on their hands.

Oddly, surviving hadn't really alleviated the situation, either, she realized. If anything, it had only pulled their attention in yet another direction while they worked to help her and give her proper care and protection.

Her life-or-death situation—and she was grateful it was life—still dragged them away from the day-to-day at Mariposa and kept them busy and away from their other siblings.

Was that what these incidents were all about?

"Miss?" Kadim came a bit closer, his stoic expression offset by a small smile. "Are you all right?"

"Yes, I'm sorry. I got lost in thought."

"I got a call from Mr. Colton. He suggested you might want to meet him for breakfast on the patio by the pool if you were at a stopping point."

"Actually, his timing is perfect. I'm hungry, and I'd like to move to a different part of the property, anyway. Some photos of the pool are on my shot list for the day, so why don't we head that way?"

Doug joined them, and in moments, Paige was ensconced beside Kadim in the back of a large golf cart, her equipment loaded carefully in the back. Doug drove them toward the interior of the resort, and she watched each area they passed. The morning sun threw bright beams over the red rocks, and she toyed with ideas on how she might play with all that gorgeous light.

Speaking of gorgeous...

The cart came to a stop at the pool, mere feet from where Adam rose from his chair at one of the patio tables.

They'd spoken briefly the night before when he let her know that Doug and Kadim would be on her security detail today. Other than that brief, stilted conversation, she'd deliberately missed him this morning, choosing to get up early and leave a note on the kitchen counter with her plans.

It wasn't her finest moment, but at that point she was still smarting from their tense words in the kitchen after Max left, and she hoped some time with her camera and her thoughts would cool her down.

It's why she said yes to meeting Adam for breakfast.

A point that suddenly seemed silly now that she got a good look at just how devastating he was in his power suit and expensive haircut. The man looked every inch the powerful executive and she was surprised to realize just how enticing that was.

The Adam Colton who lived in her memory was a young man, living his life in jeans and T-shirts, with a lopsided grin that often poked through his serious demeanor.

But this adult male, with his aura of power and professionalism and responsibility, was something new.

A new view.

Or maybe she just had a new lens to view him with.

It was a reminder that she might still carry some pain from that time in their lives, but they *were* different. Time and age had done their work on them both, and maybe instead of continuing to focus on the past, she might be better off discovering the man he was now.

Perhaps it was the only way to not just put the past where it belonged, but actually leave it well and truly behind.

"Hi." She walked toward him, settling herself in the chair he held out for her.

Adam moved around to his own chair, giving Doug and Kadim instructions on where to place the golf cart and her equipment.

"Good morning so far?" Adam asked after he was settled.

An efficient waitress had already come up and filled

Paige's coffee cup and refilled Adam's while he was talking to the security team, and she doctored hers now with cream. "It's been a great morning. The sun rising over the red rocks was magnificent. Oh, and I met Dani and Josh, too. They're both really nice."

"I'm sorry I didn't introduce you sooner."

Paige waved it off, the steady hum of activity she'd observed all morning a clear sign that no one was sitting around Mariposa with nothing to do.

"It sounds like everyone's been busy, with Dani settling into her new role in the business. And Josh said he's had a full slate of guests taking his trail hikes."

"We're never quiet, but summer is always busy here."

She took a sip of her coffee, again marveling at the sheer beauty of the place. "I can't believe you get to see that every day. And this is coming from someone who lives in Southern California."

"What brought you there?" Adam asked.

It was an effort on his part to make conversation, and Paige realized it was a perfect chance to put her new approach to work.

Discussing who they were now was far preferable to their past.

They'd have a nice breakfast, getting to know each other, and she'd be sure to share her divide-and-conquer thoughts with him later.

"I continued modeling after college but knew that photography was what I really wanted. There's a huge photography community in New York, and I was making some inroads but ended up coming out to California for an intensive week long workshop. I made some contacts and landed a few jobs out of it and after a few trips realized that I loved being there."

"I think I've always associated Southern California a bit too much with my father and therefore never thought much of the place. But there's a lot to be said for the sunny weather and access to whatever you want, be it beach, mountains or culture with nothing more than an hour's drive."

"I'm sorry the relationship with your father is that bad." When he only reached for his coffee cup, Paige pressed on. "It's hard when the people whose love we're supposed to have unconditionally are the least dependable ones in our lives."

"That's a way to put it."

Paige considered what she was about to say, her normal hesitation about sharing her family life rearing up.

Divide and conquer.

It was a strategy to keep people feeling alone, and she didn't want to be in that place any longer. She and Adam were no longer a couple, but if she were lucky in this experience, they could become friends again. And telling Adam about her family would move them forward.

It was totally on her so many years ago that she didn't tell him then. And it was a reminder that, for all her feelings about him walking away, she'd been more than happy to take the thrill of each moment with him, never delving too deeply into what she'd lived through as a child.

Instead of continuing to hide her childhood, she could share it now. Do that hard work of putting her past *in* the past and allow him to know the woman she was now.

"I don't have a good relationship with my parents. With either of them, but it's the worst with my father."

"Then I'm sorry, too." Adam's deep blue eyes were sharp and assessing when he finally spoke. "You never said anything about him."

"I know. It's always been bad. Long before I knew you, in fact."

"So why say anything now?"

"I realize that I gave you a pretty tough time the other day for never having confided in me, but I've done the same. So maybe if I get a hold of my own emotional response and quit hiding the parts of myself I don't like, I might stop lashing out about us. About something that happened a decade ago now."

"You have a right to how you feel."

"Yes, I know that. But our breakup and that time in my life made me feel like I had once again lost control, and that's not on you."

She wasn't taking responsibility for Adam's choices, but it was time, Paige recognized, to take firm hold of her own.

FORGIVENESS.

Adam recognized that was what Paige was offering him. Or at least the path toward it.

He should say thank you and get on that path, but he struggled with how to accept it all. The past few days had made him realize that he bore far more responsibility for what had happened when he left New York than he'd ever allowed himself to believe.

But he also realized that in this moment, she was trying to share something with him. So, as his first step, he'd listen.

What came from there was on him to figure out.

"It sounds like your parents hurt you. I wish that could be different."

"I do, too. And I realize how much of my adulthood has been about trying to find a way past it all."

"It doesn't excuse the fact that I hurt you, too, Paige."

"No, it doesn't. But it may explain why I still have lingering feelings about that time. About our time together. I *have* moved on. I've built a life and I date or—" she smiled this time, a hint of deviousness flashing in her green eyes "—cook, as it were. But I'm still fundamentally living my life alone. That's not on you."

Their breakfast arrived, temporarily pausing their conversation, and it was only after their server delivered their omelets, toast and fresh rounds of coffee that Adam realized he had one more thing to say before she shared the details of her family.

"I want to hear about your parents. More than that, I want to keep hearing about whatever it is you need to say, even after you go back to California. I might have been talking about your relationship with Max yesterday, but I want to ask the same request of the two of us. I care about you, and I realize now that there has been a hole in my life since the end of our relationship. I don't want to lose you again."

"I don't want to lose you again, either."

"I've missed you, Paige. And I'm sorry it's taken having you come back into my life for me to tell you that. For me to realize that I should have had a better handle on my priorities before now."

She glanced around the covered area, the poolside seating spaced out so diners had discretion while they ate and talked, before her gaze resettled on him.

"This place is a part of you. I think I needed to see it for myself to understand that."

"Maybe too much a part of me."

Paige tilted her head at that. "Why would you say that? This was your mother's place. It's where you grew up. You said yourself, LA's tainted by the relationship with your father."

"The past few months have forced me to evaluate all of it. You coming back here has put it into sharp focus, but these feelings didn't just start with you coming to Arizona. They've been building over the past few months."

Adam stopped and shook his head. "And here I am doing it again. You were going to share something about your family, and I'm making this about me."

She leaned across the table then, her hand covering his. "We're talking. Sharing. I have a bad relationship with my parents. It's not going to get better or worse by waiting a few minutes to tell you about it. Talk to me, Adam. Tell me what's wrong."

It was a kindness he wasn't sure he deserved, but it was also an opening.

An act of friendship.

Support.

He hadn't realized just how badly he needed that.

"These past months have been nothing short of awful. They've forced me to reevaluate everything I thought I knew, and I'm not sure I like what I'm finding."

"What are you finding?" The question was spoken softly, the easy tone as comforting as the hand that still rested over the back of his.

"I've made this place my life. And as it's shown its cracks, from my father's attempted takeover to the crimes that have taken place here, I have to wonder what it's all for."

"You honored a memory by coming here. That means something."

"Yes, but I've made that memory everything. I think that's what I'm finally coming to grips with."

The words were bitter on his tongue, and he hated how

it sounded—like he somehow required pity for the choices he'd made. That was the last thing he wanted.

Especially from the person he hurt the most in the pursuit of those choices.

"Would you change it?"

"Would I change what?" Adam asked.

"Any of it. All of it." Paige shrugged. "Take your pick."

He'd considered that the other day and realized that his answer hadn't changed. "No. Much as I'm sorry for that, most of all the pain I caused, I wouldn't change it."

"Then all you can do is move forward. You can't regret the outcomes of something you not only can't change but wouldn't if you had the chance."

"Isn't that rather fatalistic?"

She tilted her head, her green gaze pointed, even as he clearly saw her compassion there as well. "If it were fatalistic, it would mean you can't change what comes next. But you can, Adam. You can make new choices moving forward if you don't like the ones you've made so far."

It was real and raw and likely the truth he needed to hear.

What it wasn't was a set of excuses.

Paige removed her hand from his and reached for her coffee. He felt an emptiness at the loss of her touch, and Adam recognized there were more choices to be made.

He didn't deserve her forgiveness, but she was giving it all the same.

The question for him now was what was he going to do with it?

He didn't deserve another shot at a romantic relationship with her. Nor did he have any right to ask her to change her very successful life.

But damn if he wanted to give her up after getting this time with her once again.

SASHA HIGHTOWER WAS a woman with a plan. She'd worked on it for some time now, finally finding her real shot at career progression in the form of Glenna Colton. The woman was a stone-cold bitch, but she was the exact ally and partner Sasha needed to make her dreams come true.

It was all in reach.

About damn time.

She might only be twenty-six, but she had plans. Goals. And she wasn't interested in waiting for them to happen someday. She wanted to make them happen now.

She'd always been adept at reading the subtext beneath whatever was happening. Throughout her life, she'd found a way to put that skill to good use.

Very good use, Sasha amended to herself as she considered the tableau playing out on the resort's patio.

Adam Colton had been difficult to read of late. Always a private person, that had only been more evident these past few months as he worked on his plans to save the resort from his father. Glenna had told her all about it when she propositioned Sasha to become her eyes and ears inside Mariposa.

But Adam had been the hardest one to track.

Oh, she saw his comings and goings. But it was the way he conducted his business—always in private—that had made gathering intel on him so difficult.

That had all changed a few days ago when Paige Barnes arrived.

It hadn't seemed like a big deal at first, the woman's arrival and details noted in the daily rundown the hotel staff received each day from Laura's office. She was here to photograph the grounds for an upcoming magazine article. Sasha had nearly ignored it all as nothing more than standard operating procedure until she overheard Max talking with Alexis.

"Max!" Alexis half moaned his name in a harsh whisper. *"You're going to get me in trouble trying to nuzzle my neck near the front desk."*

"We're behind the back office wall. And besides, I've missed you."

"You saw me two hours ago."

"That's one hour and fifty-nine minutes too long."

Sasha could hear them from where she stood at the front desk and was tempted to call them out at the byplay, her disdain for their pristine concierge nearly getting the best of her.

In the end, it was a good thing her common sense had won out.

"I've got to focus on work right now," Miss Goody Two-shoes said. *"We've got a big publicity shoot for the resort, and we need it to go off without a hitch. The photographer is on the helicopter now for her meeting with Laura and Adam."*

"If she's en route, you've got a few minutes."

"No, baby, I don't. She's got an excellent reputation. Used to be a model, apparently. I want everyone in their places when she gets here. This place needs to shine."

Although she couldn't see them, Sasha had heard a distinct change in Max's tone. "A former model?"

"Yes, Paige Barnes. She's a big deal and—"

"I know her."

"You do?"

"We used to be good friends..." Max's voice had trailed off before he seemed to rally. *"The best of friends, actually. She and Adam were hot and heavy in college."*

"They were?"

Sasha hadn't missed the interest in Alexis's voice, but she'd already hurried off to find a quiet corner to call Glenna with her news.

An ex of Adam's was big news and something Glenna needed to know.

And it was the overheard conversation that had springboarded yet another opportunity for her to prove to Glenna that she was an asset.

Glenna had already promised her a senior role running Mariposa once she got a hold of the resort out from under her husband's children. All Sasha needed to do was bide her time and keep feeding the information she was so adept at ferreting out. If she kept it up, that promotion and leadership role was hers.

It basically already was, she thought as she watched Adam stand, then move to Paige to help her from her chair.

The two walked off together, looking for all the world like two professionals wrapping up a business meeting over a meal.

Sure. Sasha smiled to herself. That's how they appeared. Only she'd seen the way they leaned in toward one another. Had seen the way Paige laid her hand over Adam's and kept it there.

Most of all, she'd seen the way Adam looked at the woman, a deep-seated longing in his gaze.

Adam Colton was a private man, rarely prone to showing anything personal of himself. But now that she'd seen him with Paige, Sasha knew the truth. Whether he fully understood it or not, Paige Barnes was his Achilles' heel.

Because he was still in love with the photographer.

She and Glenna could use that.

They *would* use it, Sasha vowed, as she found a private corner to make her phone call.

"Hand me that small bowl of chopped scallions, would you?"

Paige passed Max the requested bowl of fragrant green onions and despite standing in Adam's very large kitchen, she even now pictured the shots she wanted to take in Mariposa's industrial one.

She hadn't intended to go behind the scenes, but watching Max prep, chop, peel and now cook for the past hour had given her a few ideas.

It had also given her a chance to catch up with her friend. She had seen him a few times since college, but for all intents and purposes, they had roughly a decade to catch up on.

Not to mention getting all the wonderful details on Max's relatively new romance with Alexis Reed, Mariposa's head concierge.

"Wait till you meet her, Paigey. She's amazing."

"You're smitten."

"Smitten, gobsmacked, head over heels." Max looked up from where he sautéed the onions in butter. "And most of all, in love."

"I'm so happy for you."

"I'm happy for me, too. Especially since I nearly sabotaged it before anything had begun."

Paige took a sip of her wine, pleased when the cool sauvignon blanc Max had picked out slid down her throat with ease. For all the medical drama, she was feeling surprisingly well. Even her throat wasn't sensitive or scratchy any longer.

"I find that hard to believe."

"Believe it. I was my charming jackass self, which, as you know, means I was a rat bastard."

"What did you do?"

"I ran the woman ragged and had a lot of fun doing it. Adam had the bad foresight to put her at my beck and call while I was here, and I took full advantage."

"Why would you do that?"

"The woman claimed she didn't like good food and was immune to my charms. I had to retaliate in some way."

"Max!"

"It's true. Caveman instincts at their best." He glanced up, pulling his intense focus off the pan. "Or worst, really."

Before she could reply, his attention shifted to the entrance to the kitchen. A grin—one that was sort of goofy and all the way besotted—filled his face. "You're here."

"I am." Alexis moved quickly around the kitchen counter and pressed her lips to his in a warm kiss before turning to face Paige.

With an easy swat at Max's roving hands, Alexis dodged out of his range. "Don't get handsy with me. You'll burn that, and I'm starving."

"Woman, you cut me."

"I'll do more than that if you burn my dinner." She poured herself a glass of wine, all brisk efficiency, before stepping back to Max and giving him one more long, smacking kiss.

Her smile—all goofy and lopsided—made Paige's heart happy as she extended a hand. "You must be Alexis."

They made quick introductions as Alexis settled herself onto another one of the barstools that lined the counter.

The conversation flowed smooth and easy, Max and Alexis regaling her with their romance as well as the tense situation that had put Alexis in danger. Max hadn't been interested, but his disillusioned stalker had grown out of control, her anger and violence settling on Alexis as a way to hurt Max and exact revenge.

It was scary, Paige thought, even now with the danger well and gone, to listen to what they went through.

Sort of like your poisoning?

Paige fought an involuntary shiver and realized Adam hadn't arrived yet.

With that realization came another. Just how quickly she'd come to associate Adam's presence with safety and security.

"Where's Adam?" she finally asked, unable to hold off any longer. "I thought he was coming back with you."

"He sent me on so I wouldn't be any later and stayed back in the office to take a call with the lawyers."

"Another one?" Max asked, his frown conveying even more than the dour tone.

"They seem to be daily. Laura joined him for this one."

"That can't be good," Paige murmured, Alexis and Max nodding in unison with her.

"Which is why we're going to have a good meal and give him a chance to forget about it for a little while."

As if by unspoken agreement, they shifted their conversation to their respective jobs, Alexis peppering Paige with questions about photo shoots and her favorite exotic locales. Paige responded with as many celebrity questions as she could come up with.

By the time Adam walked in a half hour later, the three of them were on their second glasses of wine and Paige was still laughing about one of Alexis's better stories.

"The kitchen really prepared a full steak dinner at three a.m.?" Paige asked, trying to imagine starting up an entire hotel kitchen for one guest's demands.

"Steak, baked potatoes, brussels sprouts, and a divine

mac and cheese that might have made me weep when I snagged a spoon of leftovers in the pot."

"Are you telling tales about our rock star regular Maxim Wells and his crew?" Adam asked, quickly keying into the story as he joined them at the counter.

"You're not supposed to share names." Alexis gave him a good-natured swat on his arm.

"We're among friends." Adam winked at Paige as his hand snaked out and grabbed one of the bacon-wrapped dates Max had prepared as an appetizer. "Besides, the man's well-known as an indulgent snob. If you'd asked Paige to guess, I bet she could have pegged him in three guesses or less."

"I'd have gotten it in one." Paige smiled, rather sure she might have a few canary feathers lining her lips.

"No way!" Alexis said.

"Sadly, yes. I've met him before, and before you ask, my story also involves steak so raw it was still mooing and a visual I can't unsee with his girlfriend at the time."

Max and Adam groaned in unison before Max waved a spoon. "As someone who creates culinary art for a living, I do not want to hear this."

Paige tilted her glass toward Alexis in a light clink. "I'll fill you in later."

The laugher flowed as easily as the wine from there on out, the tension of the day vanishing as the four of them laughed over their wine and appetizers. Paige caught Adam's gaze several times across the counter, that magnetic blue drawing her in as it had so many years before.

Would she succumb to his charms once again? Or would she stand firm and resist that elemental pull that had flowed between the two of them from the start?

She was older and wiser, Paige reflected as she took a sip of her wine.

But some things even time couldn't erase.

Chapter Eleven

Adam finished pouring their after-dinner drinks at the small serving bar nestled off his kitchen. He so rarely entertained he'd had to wash out the fine glasses used expressly for this purpose.

The task had given him a bit of time to gather himself, their fun and lively dinner at odds with the sinking sensation in his gut that had kept him steady company.

How had he never realized just how much he missed Paige? Because now that she was back—now that they were in each other's company—he realized just how profound those feelings were.

And just how many of his own fleeting thoughts he'd ignored through the years.

How many times had he thought about calling her just to see how she was? It had happened after he'd first come back to Arizona, which was to be expected, but the sensation had continued through the years, catching him at odd moments.

When he was in one of his rare quiet moments outside the constant orbit of work, hiking the red rocks or driving somewhere, thoughts of her would whisper through his mind. Memories of things they'd done or jokes they'd shared coming back in full force in his moments of solitude.

And the music. How often had he thought of her when a particular song would come on, reminding him of the near-constant music she'd have on in their apartment, a sort of soundtrack to their relationship.

It all came flooding back, all the things he'd diligently dammed up so he wouldn't feel the loss of her so keenly.

Churning beneath it all were those words she'd shot at him yesterday, full of righteous anger and a world of hurt.

And truth, Adam admitted.

A hell of a lot of truth.

Because all I see is a shell of a home, devoid of anything personal or happy or bright. I hope walking away and leaving me wondering for years what the hell happened or what I did was worth it.

"You need some help with that?" Max asked, poking his head through the doorway of the serving bar.

"Yeah, sure." Adam shook his head, forcing a smile he didn't really feel. "I had to wash these glasses first."

Scrambling for something to say, he kept up a light patter as he poured out the cognac for Max and Paige, then the Irish cream for him and Alexis. "You outdid yourself on that meal."

"Thanks. It's a new twist I've been testing and decided to try out tonight. I'm thinking of making that one of the featured dishes next season."

"You'd better get ready to put it on the menu at your restaurant, too. It's—"

Adam broke off, his friend's dark gaze meeting his. When Max spoke, his voice was low but it didn't lessen the punch of it all. "Why are you hiding back here, man?"

"I'm not hiding."

"You've been hiding all night, right here in plain sight."

"This isn't the time."

"Probably not," Max said, reaching for two of the snifters. "But it needs to be said sooner instead of later. Go after her. Talk to her. Give this a chance."

"I ruined my chances."

"I don't know." Max tilted his head, considering. "I think you ruined something a long time ago. But I think Paige has a big enough heart and is a confident enough woman to look past it if you were sincerely willing to try again. To start fresh."

"Not gonna happen."

"Why not?"

How did he explain what he felt?

It wasn't the attraction or the heat that flowed between them. That part was easy. Elemental, even. And purely physical.

What he felt for Paige went so much deeper, and it was that bond he'd thrown away, without even telling her why.

There was no amount of groveling or apologies that could change that.

"Because I don't deserve it, Max."

"No, you probably don't. I certainly didn't." Max glanced back in the direction of the living room before he turned back with a rather somber gaze. "That's the beauty of love. It gives second chances even when we don't deserve them."

"Guests don't do dishes."

"Too late," Paige said with a shrug as she filled the sink with hot, soapy water.

She'd already loaded up the dishwasher with as much as possible, but she was doing Adam's high-end cookware and glasses by hand.

"Besides, it won't take long and then this job is done."

"The cleaning service can do it."

Paige shook her head, curious if that attitude was because he literally lived at his job or because he was rich.

Likely both, she ended up deciding, which was why she ignored his continued protests.

"So can I."

"Paige. Come on, you don't need to do this."

Paige threw her hand in the air to gesture that she was doing just fine when she realized her pinkie finger had caught on the washcloth she was using. The resulting spray—and sopping thud of the washcloths against Adam's shirt—had him jumping back like a cat.

"What was that for?"

"It was an accident, actually." She couldn't hold back the giggle. "With benefits."

Adam reached for a wad of paper towels and dried the big wet spot in the center of his chest. He had moved on to unbuttoning his cuffs and rolling them up when she caught sight of the way his shirt clung to his body. The outline of well-cut abs was highlighted by the wet shirt, and she fought the sudden wave of sexual need that nearly buckled her knees.

Serious benefits.

Willing her racing thoughts to subside, she focused on scrubbing one of the stainless-steel pans Max had used. Water sloshed around her rough movements before Adam's hand came into the water, stilling her.

"What did that pan ever do to you?"

"I think it's what Max did to the pan, actually. Genius is most definitely not tidy."

Adam's fingertips trailed along the back of her hand as he pulled it out of the water, and Paige fought another wave of need at his slick touch.

Get a grip, Barnes.

With his back to her as he rummaged in a nearby drawer for a fresh towel, Paige used the moment to catch her breath.

It had been a wonderful evening, with easygoing and often funny conversation as well as a few trips down memory lane. In deference to Alexis, they hadn't spent all their time talking about the past, but a few stories did come up, creating an intimacy she hadn't felt in a long time.

Not just with Adam, but with Max and Alexis, too.

She hadn't given Adam a line of BS at breakfast. She did date, and, by anyone's standards, successfully. She enjoyed the company of men and had an active social life. But very few of the men she'd dated over the years had managed to create that effortless intimacy where she felt truly understood.

The ex-model thing often stood in the way, she'd realized after a while. The term *model* left a certain impression, and she avoided bringing it up at all costs in the early days of dating. Unfortunately, that wasn't always easy when the inevitable discussion of how did you get into photography came up.

She refused to lie about her life, either. But also knew that revealing that information often changed her date's perspective of her.

Quickly.

It made the friendship she had with Adam and Max so much more. They'd known her at the beginning, just as the modeling gigs she'd used to get through school had begun to pick up. So it wasn't something special or extra—it was just a part of her.

"Max is doing some amazing things. Are you excited to have him shoot the next season of his show here at Mariposa?"

It might be more small talk, but it was also common ground and somehow that made a difference.

"I'm thrilled to have him. It's good to have him around, but it'll also bring a new and different dynamic to the resort. We've spent so long focused on exclusivity and privacy that I'm afraid we've become a little stodgy with it, too."

"How so?"

"I'm all for privacy. That's the core of what we offer, and I won't change that. But what I've also realized in this battle with my father and his takeover fight is that we haven't expanded or grown. Mariposa has offered the same promise for nearly a decade, and now it's time to also look at our own growth and expansion."

"And TV shows and magazine shoots are a way to do that?"

"Partially, yes. So is admitting there's a problem. Acknowledging that if you're not growing, you're dying." Adam had already dried the glasses she'd washed first and now took the clean pan from her hands.

"The near merger with Sharpe Enterprises made me see that. We've worked so hard on this property, but we don't have a lot else to offer. And a company looking to make an investment didn't have a lot of reasons to stick around once some of the bad things started happening here."

Paige rinsed out the small saucepan she'd cleaned, considering Adam's position. It only added to the picture he'd painted for her that morning over breakfast.

These past months have been nothing short of awful. They've forced me to reevaluate everything I thought I knew, and I'm not sure I like what I'm finding.

Whatever else she'd experienced since their breakup, she could always look at her life and feel it was moving forward. That her hard work and effort hadn't just found a landing pad but was actively changing and evolving.

That was a gift, she realized now. Her adult life was all about moving forward and Adam's...wasn't.

"Are you excited about the future?"

"I am. You were right yesterday, you know. I have been living in a strange sort of limbo in a shell of a home, and a lot of what's happening here is forcing me out of a place that's become entirely too comfortable."

Heat crept up her neck. "Adam, I'm sorry. My comments were harsh, and it was unfair of me to—"

He shook his head. "I don't need an apology, and I didn't bring it up to make you feel bad. You were right. Hell—" he tapped one of the glasses he'd set on the corner of the counter after drying them "—I had to wash those before I poured our after-dinner drinks because they haven't been used in so long."

A chagrined look crept over his face. "I think two of them might never have been used at all."

Her words the day before had been said out of frustration but she was surprised to see how Adam had internalized them. "What do you want to do about it then?"

"For starters, I guess I want to start having more dinner parties." His mouth quirked up in that lopsided grin she'd loved for so very long. "And I want to think about Mariposa, especially if we can get the time we need to evade this takeover attempt, as a place that's growing, not stagnating."

"What time do you need?"

"Dani has the shares we need to fight off my father."

"Adam, that's amazing. You can save Mariposa."

"It's not that easy. The shares were given to her mother by my father as a payoff after their affair. Dani's mother took them, always with the intention of giving them to her daughter, but she didn't trust anyone after my father's betrayal."

Paige had very little understanding of inheritance law, but if his sister had the shares, didn't that put them in a position to stave off the takeover?

"What did she do with them?"

"She willed them to Dani but left them in trust to her brother, Dani's uncle, Ken. He came here last month, scheming to keep them for himself."

Paige fought the involuntary shiver that rolled down her spine. There it was again—that continued swirl of danger around the resort.

"Scheming?"

"He tried to blackmail her first, but it escalated when Dani refused to buy into his ramblings about her mother's side of the family and how they have no money."

"But the shares are hers."

"Yes, they are. And no matter how much compassion she has for her mother's family, Dani was clear on that."

"How'd she manage through it?"

"An unlikely source." Adam smiled for the first time since launching into the story. "Glenna's nephew, Matt."

"Glenna your stepmother?"

"One and the same. Matt was here for Laura and Noah's wedding, and he and Dani hit it off, without him knowing of their connection."

"Adam, the magnitude of all that's happened here is mind boggling."

"It's been—"

"—a lot," she finished for him.

"That's one way to put it."

"So Glenna has been behind it?"

"Some things. When she found out Matt was invited to the wedding, she asked him to make trouble. He came to me straightaway and let me know, so we avoided any problems for Laura and Noah."

While she was happy nothing had marred the wedding, it all still seemed awfully incriminating toward Glenna.

"Oh! That reminds me." Paige couldn't believe she'd forgotten all about it. "The theory I had about her being behind what happened to me. Do you think it's possible?"

"I did some digging on that. She's been in California, staying close to home, and hasn't been anywhere near here."

"She could hire someone."

"She could, but how would she know you're here?"

"That's a good question."

Paige blew out a breath and reached for the stopper, letting the dirty water drain out. She heard the low, guttural gurgle as the last bit of water swirled down, a new idea taking root.

"Wait, though."

"What?" Adam looked up from where he hung the towel on the handle of the oven.

"If she doesn't live here, how does she know about anything happening here?"

Adam's mouth turned down in a frown. "She comes to visit often enough. Acts like she owns the place, playing up the family connection each and every time."

"Yes, but she's not family. Or not in a way that makes her a part of the inner workings of Mariposa. You said there was a poisoning at Laura's bachelorette party."

"Yeah."

"Why? Who would have any reason to do that?"

"Why do people do anything?"

Paige shook her head, an idea building in the back of her mind. "Glenna and your father are the only ones with motive, and you don't feel your father's up to the job."

"I really don't."

"Then go back to the obvious. Glenna could easily do things from afar." Paige turned toward Adam, gripping his forearms as it all fell into place. "Adam, she's got to have someone inside. Right here, at the resort. That's the way she knew I was here. It's how she knows what's going on."

"Like a mole?" His muscles flexed beneath her hands, a match for the one ticking in his jaw.

"Exactly like that."

"I need to call Laura and Noah."

"Let's go see them instead."

"ADAM, YOU DO realize what you're saying. What this means about our staff."

Laura's voice remained even and level, but he saw the sheer panic in his sister's eyes. Recognized it as a match for the same panic swelling and crashing in waves inside of him since Paige landed her theory in his kitchen.

Noah had put a pot of coffee on and was now distributing mugs as they worked through theories in their living room.

"We're not immune to staff troubles." He hated to say it, but it was a reality they were all too familiar with lately. They maintained a higher level of background checks based on their clientele, but in the end, bad actors could be found in every business. Even the ones who passed a deeper scrutiny into their lives.

"Yes, but someone here who's actively working to harm our guests? To harm us." Laura gestured between the four of them, and it wasn't lost on Adam how quickly Paige had become one of them.

Noah wrapped an arm around Laura's shoulders. "It does

give us something else to investigate with what's happened to Paige."

"And it reinforces why we were at such a loss as to why I was targeted," Paige added.

Adam wanted to reach for her, the same way Noah had reached for Laura, but he kept his hands to himself. He didn't have the same right.

Nor would he use the inherent fear and anxiety in what they were discussing as an excuse to make physical contact.

But oh, how he wanted to.

How he wanted to offer comfort and take it in return.

"Who do you think it is?" Laura asked.

"We'll need to increase surveillance. I can talk to Roland in security," Noah said, already thinking through immediate next steps. "He's our top man, and I have every confidence he'll be discreet."

Adam considered the implications. How were they going to run the resort if they were convinced a traitor was in their midst? "It can't go beyond us and Roland. And Josh and Dani."

"The circle stays small," Noah agreed. "But I think it's fair to assume at this point we have a mole."

"One who's feeding Glenna information." Adam hated to think it. Whatever he'd believed about his stepmother, he'd never put her in the category of someone who'd hire a contract killer.

But the crimes perpetrated against Paige couldn't be discounted.

Paige reached over and took his hand, linking her fingers with his.

It was unconditional support and the comfort he'd so

desperately wanted to give. And she innately understood the importance of that contact and freely gave it.

She humbled him and awed him, all at once, Adam realized.

It gave him strength and the recognition that he wasn't facing this alone.

"We need to consider who would be in a position to feed her information," he said. "We won't necessarily eliminate anyone yet, but I think we can downgrade Josh's activities team and the grounds staff."

"What about housekeeping?" Laura asked, even as Noah was already shaking his head.

"I think we need to keep them on the primary list. Anyone in and out of guest rooms has a prime opportunity to see things up close and personal."

"Same with resort staff. Wait staff, concierge, bell hops," Paige said. "Right?"

Noah nodded at that as well. "We'll start there. Front desk has the most access to information across the resort."

"I give a daily briefing," Laura added with a yawn. "In fact, I've got one in a little over seven hours. It's the big one, our Monday-morning team meeting."

"Why don't we get out of your hair? I'll join you for the briefing tomorrow."

Adam caught his sister's direct stare at his offer. "You never join me for the briefing."

"I do sometimes."

"When I'm not here," Laura argued. "Seriously, Adam, we can't make it look like we're acting differently."

Adam felt Paige's fingers tighten over his. "What if I took part? It's a Monday, which implies a fresh start. And I can make up a few remarks about the photo shoot. Tell them I want everyone to know where I'll be and if they know of any guest areas I need to avoid."

"That's a good one." Noah lit up at her idea, nodding. "I can make up a reason to be there, too. Something about security detail for the jewelry that's going to be on-site."

There it was again, Adam thought as he and Paige stood a few minutes later, leaving to go back to his place.

Just how quickly the four of them had become a unit.

And how easily Paige had become a trusted member.

Chapter Twelve

Paige reviewed her notes, flipping between her tablet and a small notebook. She carried both everywhere when she worked a complex shoot, especially one that encompassed multiple locations. She'd already committed the details to memory, but she wanted to review them once more to map out what she was going to say in the morning staff briefing she'd join with Adam, Laura and Noah.

"You're up early." Adam walked into the kitchen, clad in another of his power suits. She could still see the wet edges of his hair, fresh from his shower.

"I kept waking up. You know, that weird thing that happens when you know you have to be up, so you wake up over and over, convinced you'll oversleep."

"Ensuring you didn't get nearly enough sleep at all."

"Exactly." Paige smiled and pointed to her mug. "Which is why I've taken advantage of that fancy coffee maker of yours twice already this morning."

She saw something flash in his gaze just before he turned away from the table and headed for some morning fuel of his own. A big part of her knew she needed to leave him alone, their shared early-morning coffee conveying a sense of intimacy somewhat beyond what they actually had.

And yet she found herself standing and walking over to him all the same.

"Why are you upset?"

Adam turned from the growling single-pod coffee maker as it foamed its way through a cup and faced her. "I'm not upset."

"I saw it. That look you weren't quick enough to hide from me. What's wrong?"

That same look came into his eyes once more, a dark, dangerous flash of blue.

She thought he might shrug it off—actually expected he would—so it was a surprise when he spoke.

"What's wrong, Paige? How can you ask me that?"

Whispers of unrest layered beneath his words.

"I know there are things wrong in the macro sense. I'm asking what has upset you this morning."

"You, Paige! You!" Each word seemed ripped from his throat. "You're on lockdown in my home and are about to go to my staff meeting because we're looking for a traitor in our midst. I've brought that on you. I've put you in danger!"

"Adam. It's fine. We have a plan and we're handling it."

"Nothing about this is fine. Your life's in danger because one of the people in my employ is a traitor. That's on me. It's—"

Paige didn't give herself time to check the impulse. She simply acted.

Pushing forward, she wrapped her arms around his neck and moved in close, pressing her lips to his.

The same explosion of energy and frustration that had filled his words morphed and rechanneled itself into the kiss as Adam pulled her tight against his body.

Although it had grown increasingly difficult to ignore

the pulsing waves of attraction between them, Paige wasn't quite sure what had possessed her to kiss him.

She only knew how happy she was to have acted on the impulse.

His body was all lean muscle, and her hands explored the broad expanse of his shoulders as he deepened the kiss. Like a familiar memory *and* something entirely new and different, it was thrilling to wrap her arms around him and feel his around her waist, his hands drifting over her spine.

How she'd missed this.

For all her bravado of how much she dated, she rarely allowed a man to sleep over. Which meant there was nothing remotely sexy about her morning coffee.

But oh…

To wake up and be kissed like this every morning?

It was glorious.

He lifted his head and stared at her, that blue nearly drowning her in its intensity. "Why did you do that?" he finally murmured.

"Because you were entirely too far in your head. And if you walk into the conference room this morning with that level of anger, whoever is doing these things might realize you've figured them out. And…"

She trailed off as she lifted a hand to trace the hard line of his jaw.

"And I wanted to."

He pressed another kiss to her lips, softer than the heated one they'd just shared.

It was no less powerful.

But it was different.

It was about comfort. Camaraderie. Companionship.

Hadn't that been the hardest thing to reconcile all those years ago?

She and Adam had always had that. That punch of heat always underpinned by a mutual affection and support of one another that was rare.

Special.

And now that she'd had another taste of it, she was increasingly worried she'd underestimated just how powerful that combination really was.

ADAM WAS RARELY caught off guard.

Surprised, sometimes? Sure.

Even amazed when something unexpected happened. He'd own that, too.

But turned utterly upside down by something he never saw coming?

That just wasn't his life.

As a luxury hotelier, his entire world was devoted to minimizing or flat-out removing problems. That was what he offered his clients, and by running a well-ordered property, he removed many of them from his own life as well.

Add on that he catered to a minuscule segment of the population who often had more drama than most and he'd always believed he could handle whatever his work threw at him.

Until the past few months.

It had all begun when their yoga instructor and Noah's former foster sister, Allison Brewer, had been found murdered in one of their guest bungalows. The woman was a well-liked staff member, and her murder had scared them all.

They'd all been horrified to discover the manager of one of their celebrity guests had become obsessed with Allison.

While Adam knew they'd all live with those horrors for the rest of their lives, he also recognized it was a tragic event that had an ending and an explanation. He'd believed at the time that they'd move on. Never quite past it, but that things would go back to normal.

Only Allison's death had been the start of a series of problems that he'd never seen coming and had no experience handling.

More crimes.

A lingering sense of danger that wouldn't abate.

And now the idea that someone was helping it all happen from the inside?

Every one of those things would have been bad enough, but underlying it all was the battle with his father.

Clive's actions were the very definition of a problem Adam had never seen coming, and now he and his siblings had to figure out a way to fight off his father when the chips were stacked against them.

Clive had cheated his mother out of Mariposa at the height of her illness. If he could do that, his children were simply more collateral damage. It was also more indelible proof of what an absolute bastard his father was. One who believed his children—their dreams and livelihoods and their very homes—were expendable, too.

One surprise after another he'd never seen coming.

And then, without warning, Paige had dropped a different sort of surprise on him this morning that put a new spin on all of it.

There he was in the middle of building a head full of steam, feeling more and more out of control from his worry at what had happened to her since arriving in Arizona.

And she turned the tables and planted a kiss on him that singed him to his toes and had it all fading away.

Sure, those problems were there, but…

But somehow it all felt more manageable with Paige by his side.

He had no right to those thoughts and feelings. No right to put that sort of unspoken pressure on a woman he hadn't seen in a decade.

Most of all, no right to lean into it like a drowning man reaching for a lifeline.

Yet he felt it all the same.

Was he reaching for her because she was convenient? Because she was here?

However he'd treated his personal life a decade ago—and he'd certainly been clueless and careless—he wasn't a man who used women.

And he wasn't using Paige now.

But damn if he didn't feel something that was far deeper and more elemental than simple attraction or the memories of a better time in his life.

He missed *her*.

And if that scorching kiss this morning was any indication, he thought it was fair to think that she'd missed him in return.

He'd already taken a seat in the conference room, arriving early with Laura so they could watch staff coming into the room. Noah and Paige would come later once things started.

Adam had worked through the staging the night before, and Noah was quick to advance the strategy, rounding out a plan that would have him and Paige come later, looking for all the world like they'd mapped out her time at the resort.

"Let's hope this works," Laura leaned close, her voice a low whisper.

"Questioning your brother *and* your husband?" He couldn't resist the tease, especially because Laura's somber demeanor was at odds with her normally calm and personable approach to the staff.

"No questions, just an unexpected case of nerves," she murmured as the first few staff members strolled in. Two were already in a heated conversation about guests checking in later that afternoon. A third was on her phone, fingers flying as she tapped out a text message.

It all looked like business as usual, Adam thought as a few more team members floated in. Some had notebooks, others coffee cups in hand while others still strolled casually over to the sideboard and helped themselves to fresh mugs.

It was dependable and routine and while he didn't sit in on every morning meeting, leaving Laura to handle them most days, things looked normal to him as they greeted the anticipated twenty team members.

Front desk, restaurant and bar staff managers, and the head of housekeeping were all regular members, Adam mentally counted off in his head. So was concierge staff, the head of the bell desk and the head of the valet service.

As convinced as he was this was a good idea, he was starting to wonder as folks took their seats. He made a point to greet everyone, using those quick exchanges to size up each one of them, frustrated when nothing seemed...odd.

What were you expecting, Colton? Some supervillain rubbing their hands together like a TV cartoon?

Laura started the meeting promptly, the conversation in the room quieting at her obvious authority and command of the room.

Despite the show they were putting on this morning, Adam gave himself a moment just to take it in. He and his siblings had built something special here. Something they loved.

Yes, Mariposa had been a special place to their mother and to them growing up, but those had only been the roots.

He, along with Laura and Josh, had made something of Mariposa. Dani might have come to it a bit later, but her commitment to the place they loved was just as absolute.

This was what they were saving.

And in that moment, his earlier thoughts shifted and morphed.

Yes, they'd experienced some of the darkest days of their lives.

But with it, they'd gotten Dani back home in the US.

He'd gotten his friendship with Max back.

His siblings had found their life partners.

And, he thought as Paige and Noah chose that moment to walk into the conference room, he might have a shot at a second chance.

The trials they'd experienced had made them stronger. He fully expected they'd grow even stronger before this was all done.

The real question was who he wanted to be on the other side.

The man who'd spent his adult life building a place was no longer interested in just existing inside of it.

He wanted to build something real and lasting.

He wanted to thrive.

And he wanted to share it with another person.

PAIGE CAUGHT ADAM'S eye when she and Noah walked into the conference room, but other than that simple greeting, she'd kept her focus on Laura as the woman conducted her morning staff meeting.

Lists were reviewed and emails with status updates were

discussed. Then they moved on to each team member to give a quick rundown of their priorities for the day.

It was swift and efficient, and while she loved the fact that her job was far more free-spirited than the requirements outlined in the daily meeting, she could still appreciate all the work that went into making something look effortless.

Because whatever else she thought, the Colton siblings had created something that had an unbelievable number of moving parts yet they kept them all running seamlessly.

It was that quality, Paige realized on a start, that had allowed them to get infiltrated by a mole.

No matter how involved they were in the running of the resort, there was no way Adam, Laura or Josh could manage everything. You had to delegate and put trust in others.

Their traitor knew that and betrayed them with it.

One more aspect of a corporate job, Paige thought, that she had no experience with. Yet it also gave her a perspective Adam and Laura likely lacked.

They knew these people and had already put their trust in them.

How difficult would it be to have no inkling anything was amiss, yet you were now trying to seek that out in someone?

And there was still the small chance she and Adam were wrong. That all of them—even Noah, with all his police and security experience—were barking up the wrong tree.

"Paige," Laura said from the head of the table. "I'd love for you to introduce yourself and tell the team why you're here."

Paige took her cue, just as they'd rehearsed earlier. She told everyone who she was and why she was at Mariposa. With an added flourish, she fumbled her notebook slightly as she flipped to a page to read out what she was planning for her shot list.

"Have you considered the view from the helipad?"

A woman named Sasha, according to the small gold badge pinned to her chest, smiled from across the table as she made the suggestion.

"I hadn't considered that."

"Oh, you have to! The views are breathtaking, and that ride in by helicopter is something guests always remark on."

A few other people around the table nodded, caught up in the woman's exuberance, and Paige made a few notes. "Thank you. I'll definitely check it out and grab some shots up there."

A few more people asked questions about where she expected to be on property and around what times so they could make sure she wasn't bothered. The bar manager was kind enough to offer a selection of sparkling waters, sodas and teas set up in a few break areas.

After that, the team moved on to Laura's remaining topics, and before she knew it, the conversation had wrapped up and she was alone with Adam, Laura and Noah.

Rather than stay and risk anyone overhearing them, Adam and Laura filed out and Noah made a bit of a fuss about meeting her out in front with a golf cart.

Everything went just as they'd planned.

It was funny, Paige had to admit to herself as she gathered up her things and crossed to the sideboard to fix a to-go cup of coffee. She'd expected to pick out a problem employee straight off, but everyone was warm and congenial.

Maybe they were wrong.

Maybe she was only looking for someone to pin it all on

because the idea that she could have been randomly targeted was too scary to contemplate.

The thought kept her company as she crossed the conference room toward the doorway. The sound of voices filled the hallway, and she nearly walked out before thinking better of it.

If anyone came back in, she could say she was just getting the coffee. It wasn't exactly a lie, and to fortify it, she pulled her small notebook back out of her purse and quickly opened it up, pretending to read.

"That was a good idea, Sash," one of the team members said. "Suggesting the helipad location."

"Sure. Great." Sasha's voice sounded light, but there was something dark swirling underneath.

A point that paid off when she spoke next.

"Not like any of us ever get a shot at a helicopter ride in."

"It's called being the hired help," the guy said before making his goodbyes.

Paige held her breath, not daring to walk out too soon and risk discovery, but also panicked that the woman named Sasha might come back in.

So she waited, keeping her gaze focused on her notebook should Sasha walk back in and find her.

Instead of reading, Paige mentally counted off, backward from thirty. When she'd reached zero and was still alone, she took her first easy breath.

Stowing her notebook, she headed off to find Adam.

ADAM HELPED LAURA into the helicopter, then climbed in beside her. He had no interest in leaving Mariposa—even less, knowing it meant Paige was at the resort without him—but it couldn't be helped.

Their father had made good on his takeover threats and

initiated a fight that morning with a shady private equity group.

His phone went off and he glanced down to see a text from Paige.

TRIED TO FIND YOU. CAN YOU MEET FOR A QUICK LUNCH?

He responded quickly.

LAURA AND I WERE CALLED OFF PROPERTY. MORE DETAILS WITH THE LAWYERS. CAN WE DO DINNER INSTEAD?

He saw the dots come back almost immediately before he got her response. A silly smiling emoji, followed by one word.

YES.

"That's a happy, besotted grin."

"What?" He glanced over at his sister just as the helicopter lifted into the air. The heavy sound of the rotors blotted out a lot but it couldn't mute the clear-as-a-bell voice that filtered through his headset.

"Just because you're besotted doesn't mean the rest of us are."

"Oh, you're definitely besotted, big brother. And I'm having a grand time watching you work your way through it."

With only two years between them, Laura had been as much his lifelong nemesis as she was his most trusted business partner and confidante.

Even with that, he wasn't ready to talk about his feelings for Paige.

"I see that look. Where'd the happy go?"

Adam shot a meaningful glance toward the pilot, but Laura shut him down, tapping the headset and shifting their frequency.

"No one can hear us."

"Can it wait? We need to talk about Dad."

She looked about to argue but finally nodded, using the short twelve-minute ride to the helipad in Sedona to talk about the firm their father had brought in.

"Dude who runs it is shady, Adam. Every deal he's put together for the past two decades in hospitality has been nothing more than a chop job. He buys something, sells off the parts and rides the brand name for a bit until it dies because he's undercut what the brand actually means with customers."

Visions of all their hard work that had ensured Mariposa wasn't just a well-known name, but an experience flashed before his eyes.

Damn it, they needed Dani's shares, and they needed them fast. Because until she could produce them it looked like their father still had a way to take over with his ownership of the land Mariposa sat on.

They batted around a few ideas, just getting into it when the helicopter came to a gentle landing at the Sedona helipad just outside the airport. The car service they used was waiting for them, and in another few minutes they were ensconced in the back, heading to the lawyer's office.

"Okay. The partition is closed. We have privacy. What is going on with you and Paige?"

"And here I thought you'd forgotten about that."

Laura shot him a gimlet eye. "What sort of amateur do you take me for?"

He sighed, but it was more for effect than anything else. He knew damn well his sister wasn't going to let up and their conversation in the helicopter had only been a very short reprieve.

"Paige was my girlfriend in college. It's easy to fall back into old habits, especially when the habit is as wonderful and as easy to be around as Paige."

"A habit? Sure," Laura said, her glare only growing fiercer. "'Just what I want to be called,' said no woman ever."

"Oh, come on, I don't mean—"

"Nope. No way." Laura stopped him before he could make a total ass out of himself. "You're my brother, and I've spent my whole life knowing you, observing you and taking full sisterly advantage of your weak spots."

"A sibling skill I've returned in spades."

"Of course you have. I'd expect nothing less. But what it also means is that I know you, Adam. I know your heart and I know you're a good man. Don't dismiss what you and Paige have."

"I'm not dismissing it. I was a short-sighted idiot ten years ago. It doesn't matter that I'd like to have her back in my life. I don't deserve a second shot at that life."

"Of course you do."

"I left, Laura. With little warning and even less explanation. She deserved better."

"Yeah, she did."

"And I..." He trailed off as his sister's words caught up with him. "That's my point."

"No, I said *did* deserve better. Ten years ago, she deserved way better than you gave her. But it's ten years later. You're both older and wiser."

Laura's suggestions were tempting. The idea that somehow he and Paige could find a way past it all. But if he pushed too hard, was he really any better than his father?

Taking what he wanted, giving little thought to what anyone else wanted.

"I've never wanted to be Clive Colton, and I'll be damned if I start now."

"You're not!"

The genuinely shocked look on his sister's face had him realizing there were still times they could surprise each other.

"You want to sit there and tell me it isn't the same thing? The Clive Colton school of life has one principle: See something and take it for yourself, no matter the consequences. We're *living* it, Laura."

"Yes, we are. Which is why I know with utter certainty the man who sired us and who is currently making our professional lives a living hell has absolutely nothing to do with how you feel about Paige Barnes."

There was no one he trusted more than his sister.

But as the car pulled up to their law firm and he helped her out, Adam knew that her belief in him had blinded her to his point on this.

If he pursued Paige—if he at all thought he had a right to pick up where they left off—he was no better than his father.

On that point, he was frighteningly certain.

Chapter Thirteen

Although she'd spent the day thinking about that conversation between the two Mariposa staffers, it did fade as Paige focused on the photo shoot. She spent the morning capturing several of the shots she wanted, the play of summer sunlight over the red rocks giving her a magnificent canvas.

The models arrived at noon with their handlers, as well as the additional security team who was managing the jewelry rented for the shoot. She had it all planned out, but it still meant she had to manage through more logistics as well as doing way more setups for her shots.

It was a different animal, and on most days she enjoyed the contrast in styles. The carefully planned shots juxtaposed with the moments she could take a more freestyle approach.

Her plans for the magazine layout were good ones. She just hadn't banked on being so distracted with playing detective and attempting to hunt down a bad actor who wanted to do her harm.

Which, she almost laughed at herself, was sort of funny when you considered that real actors crawled the grounds of Mariposa regularly.

"Miss Barnes? Was this the equipment you wanted?"

"This is it." She smiled at Doug, well aware it would

be all too easy to get used to the extra pairs of hands. "Thank you."

Doug and Kadim were on her security detail again today. The three of them had gotten into an easy sort of rhythm with each other, and she liked to think she was behaving as a good subject. She hadn't tried to ditch them once, and she insisted on regular breaks, keeping them informed on her schedule and when they could expect she would need to move around the property again for a new set of shots.

It was only as they'd set up that she realized she'd left her new lens back at Adam's house. She could have waited and used it the next day, but the models had a great rapport and she had already gotten some phenomenal images of both of them.

Doug hadn't hesitated, heading off to get what she needed. And now she had it, not even needing to stop the work.

She'd already explained to her models how she wanted them draped over the pool-deck chairs. She'd get a few images of them lounging together and then a few with them in separate chairs but hamming it up. It was unlikely those would ever make it into the article, but she loved the possibilities that came from those unexpected shots.

There might end up being a gem in there she never expected, or she might be able to do something artistic with one of the shots in post.

Regardless of whether it made the final layout or not, the couple she was photographing had gotten comfortable with each other throughout the day, and it was the perfect time to have them start breaking out and putting that relaxation to good use.

Paige worked them through the planned shot list that

she'd already promised to the magazine's layout editor and then repositioned them for the fun stuff.

"Play with it. Feel the summer heat and the heat you generate together. Have some fun in the sun."

Her models took it to heart, and Paige used her new lens to capture them. Shot after shot, she kept calling out movements and positions to try. They complied, shifting effortlessly between poses until they got a real feel for what she wanted and were calling the shots themselves.

By the end of it, they were all laughing.

Paige knew she had a lot of stuff in the background she'd need to edit out, but the images were going to be a lot of fun. She already envisioned a few of them that she was going to put in the package for the photo editor, anyway, because she instinctively knew they worked.

Collaboration. She smiled to herself as she called time for the day. It was the siren's song of the job for her.

Forget stuffy conference rooms and business plans.

She'd take fresh air and laughing models any day.

Not that a stuffy conference room didn't look damn good on Adam, she thought to herself as she carefully packed away her new lens.

Of course, it was increasingly becoming clear that *everything* looked good on the man.

And what was she supposed to do about that?

It wasn't like she was staying. *Or that he's asked you to*, she quickly attempted to corral her own racing thoughts.

But memories of that kiss hadn't left her all day.

The impulse—and it was impulse to kiss him—had been met with pure, unadulterated male need.

And she'd reveled in every moment of it.

Did she push it further?

The heat and need they'd generated that morning in the kitchen had lingered all day, suggesting she should absolutely push for more. She was leaving soon, and the stakes were different.

They weren't the same people they'd been ten years ago.

And yeah, maybe it was the urgent, sexual need of the moment that was tormenting her right now, but even in spite of that, the past few days had given her a clarity she hadn't had before.

They were different.

Which meant that starting something new was different from picking up where they'd left off.

She wasn't the same person she was a decade ago, and neither was Adam. So it stood to reason that if they looked at the chemistry between them with fresh eyes, perhaps they could take a fresh approach, too.

Or you could just have sex with him and quit analyzing it all.

That last thought kept her company as she handed her equipment to Kadim, who stowed everything in the back of the golf cart.

It continued to haunt her as she settled into the guest room at Adam's home, freshening up after the long day outside.

And it swirled around her as she came down to the living room to meet him after he'd come back from a full day of meetings.

She didn't go to him this time as he stood inside his front door, even as the tired expression that carved deep lines on his face pulled at something deep inside her.

But she did watch in delight as that exhaustion faded as his gaze met hers.

As his smile spread, she finally walked toward him, extending a hand.

"Come on. I'll make you a drink and you can tell me all about it."

"Would I be a traitor to the cause if I asked for a beer?"

Adam watched Paige putter around his kitchen in bare feet, a fitted white T-shirt and a pair of very respectable-length navy shorts that still had his mouth watering at the gorgeous legs on display.

They'd decided to grill, and she was now inspecting his well-stocked fridge.

"Why does that make you a traitor?" she asked, straightening from where she pulled a package of premade hamburgers from the fridge.

"You offered to make me a drink, but I'm honestly not really a fancy cocktail guy."

A smile quirked her lips, and he felt his in response. "I'm not sure where you got *froufrou cocktail* out of my offer, but I can assure you my bartending skills don't extend much beyond opening a bottle and pouring it into a glass. I'm endlessly fascinated by the bartenders who keep a dictionary of drinks in their repertoire."

"You don't?"

"If it doesn't come straight out of a bottle and maybe mix with a carbonated beverage, I'm out of luck. What I'm more fascinated by," she said as she walked toward him, setting the package on the counter, "is the idea that you're not some fancy-drink snob."

"I'm a beer man all the way. Maybe wine with a steak."

She laughed at that, a deeply free sound that echoed around his kitchen. "I guess your power suit doesn't say everything about you."

It was fun and lighthearted, and as they laughed together Adam dragged at the knot of his tie, freeing himself from his corporate persona.

"Go change, and then I'm putting you to work for your beer. You can get the hamburgers going on the grill, and I'll make a salad. And I think I saw french fries in your freezer. We're having those, too."

"Now who's battling convention?" he asked, still laughing. "A model eating french fries?"

Her smile faded, something raw stealing over her face before she covered it up. If it were even a few days ago, he might have left it alone, but they were in a new place, and he was determined to be different.

Better than he was a decade ago.

"I overstepped there. I'm sorry."

She shook her head. "No, you didn't, actually."

"Then what is it?"

"Modeling is the box everyone reverts back to when it comes to me. It's a shackle I never expected when I did it all those years ago to pay for school."

"Does it bother you?"

"Not bother me, no." She shook her head, her gaze floating up as if she was trying to find the words. "It's just so present to others in a way it isn't for me. Often to the point no one sees anything else about me. Or maybe more to the point, can't shift to imagine something different about me."

"I see something different. I see a lot." Adam couldn't help but tease her a bit. "I imagine even more."

He could have stopped there, but the part of him that wanted no secrets between them—the part that wanted to make things right—kept on.

"But I've had to admit that I didn't see as much as I should have when I ended our relationship. I saw a beautiful woman who I assumed would move on quickly. Even knowing you, I put you in that box, too. I don't want to do that any longer."

"Thank you for telling me that. It might not change all that came before, but it does matter to hear it now. It matters a lot, Adam."

He moved around the counter to stand beside her, tracing the tip of his index finger down her cheek.

"Just because I've come to a better understanding doesn't mean I'll ever stop thinking that you're the most beautiful woman I've ever seen."

"That works nicely, then."

He bent his head, his lips hovering just near hers. "Oh?"

"I see the power suit and I like it. And I like all the facets of the man beneath it, too."

Adam closed that space of a breath between them and pressed his lips to hers.

She was sweet and so open and, in that moment, *his*. Adam knew what a gift that was and vowed to himself he would never take it for granted.

Even if their time together was limited.

A soft sigh echoed from the back of her throat, and he deepened the kiss.

God, she was amazing.

And while he owned what he'd said to her the other day—he wouldn't change the past decade—he was fully aware of all he'd missed.

The trick now would be to ensure he didn't waste the opportunity that he had.

It was only a few days, but he was determined to make the most of them.

No more misunderstandings. And no more comments that suggested he didn't see all of her.

And if a few more days was all he got, then he'd count himself the luckiest of men he'd had a chance to have her back in his life at all.

GLENNA COLTON HATED every hotel in Sedona. She was well aware her opinion was wholly her own—Sedona regularly made an endless parade of Top Ten travel lists each year—but she stood by her opinion.

Nothing was Mariposa.

The setting coupled with the exclusivity coupled with the extreme sense of style was beyond compare.

Which was why she'd have it soon.

Clive thought the resort was a means to an end to saving Colton Textiles, but she'd be damned if she allowed him to ruin it with his latest stunt with that private-equity slimeball.

Where did Clive find these people?

It was like her husband looked for someone who was the even greasier equivalent of the sludge you scraped out of the bottom of a barrel.

Well, she had far more important plans for Mariposa, and they didn't involve practically giving the resort away to another firm. Especially not one so utterly distasteful.

She'd also cultivated a few private investors she could bring in. To make those deals go through would mean stripping Colton Textiles for parts, but she'd deal with that—and her malleable husband—when the time came.

For now, she had to focus on destroying her stepchildren and lowering the asking price of Mariposa.

The rest would come in time.

Laura and Josh had proven challenging on that front. She had the utter misfortune of watching little Miss Perfect Laura end up with that creep of a cop, Noah Steele. Their mother was likely to be rolling in her grave at the thick, brutish build; heavy, bearish beard; and visible tattoos.

Josh was much too focused on the outdoors. He cared about the resort, but it was nature that truly fueled him. He'd be hurt if the family home was taken from him, but he had other loves. And hell, you could find a hiking trail anywhere you put your mind to it.

Dani had been the surprise. Clive's little secret, who was now grown-up and way more trouble than she was worth. Glenna had always believed she was the easy one, living in her brilliant mind and focused on her studies overseas in London. Until she'd decided to come home to Arizona and settle in, even hooking up with Glenna's nephew, Matt.

Ungrateful ass.

She'd pinned a lot of hopes on Matt. He was meant to ruin Laura's wedding, only he'd done the exact opposite, going to Adam and claiming that she was trying to make trouble.

It was a mess, and now it was time to end it all.

She was done depending on others to carry out her plans. Even more than that, she realized that she'd pissed around way too long.

She needed to end the game, and if she'd understood just how many things were going to be out of her control, she'd have started where she meant to finish.

Ending Adam.

Josh might love Mariposa, but Adam was the brains behind it. Laura kept the clients happy, but Adam ran the resort in a way that ensured there was something for them to be happy about.

Glenna listened to the message she'd received earlier from Sasha.

The message was way too chatty—seriously, get in and get out!—but she had intel Glenna could use.

Paige Barnes had gotten inside their staff meeting that morning. And while no one else seemed to give it much notice, Sasha had seen how often Adam's gaze drifted to the woman.

Between their poolside lunch and the morning meeting, the evidence was stacking up.

Paige Barnes meant something to Adam.

Which made killing her the perfect distraction to steal Mariposa right out from underneath him.

"THE PARMESAN ON the french fries was inspired." Paige stared at their empty plates and sighed. "And who knew the not-a-stuffy-businessman Adam Colton could grill a mean hamburger?"

"I'm a man of many talents."

She could attest to that, Paige thought. She kept it to herself, not wanting to show how utterly *un*cool she really was, but she was hardly unaffected.

Especially because the man had knocked the breath out of her and buckled her knees, all with the suave assurance of a well-placed kiss.

Or kisses.

Or hell, Paige amended to herself, hoping she wasn't turning bright pink, a kitchen make-out session so hot she was still trying to cool off.

A meal, two glasses of ice water and two cold beers hadn't managed it yet, but she was determined to keep trying.

"Ace hotelier. Man of business. Grill master. You come from good stock, Colton."

Paige mock saluted him as she reached for her water

glass and took a sip, needing something—*anything*—to take her mind off how amazing he was.

"Would it upset you to tell me more about your parents?" Adam asked.

The question was careful, with a thread of lightness beneath it that suggested she could easily say no. She was tempted to do just that, but the topic would go a long way toward re-centering her.

Her parents were a dismal topic on the best of days. Talking about them was bound to cool her off far more effectively than a glass of water.

But it was also a reminder that she'd promised during their lunch that she would share the details with him.

Time to pony up, Barnes.

"It won't upset me." She exhaled a long breath at that. "Well, it probably will, but not because you asked. Just because they're not a bright spot in my life."

"We can talk about something else."

"No, it really is okay. And technically, I already offered."

And it *was* okay. Even more than that, Paige realized, it was the last piece she needed to exorcize all that had come before between them.

So much of her hurt over their relationship had been about the two of them—she was clear on that. But she was equally clear that her unstable family relationships had only added to her sense of an accumulated hurt.

This was the last step to moving past all that had come before.

It was time, she thought, feeling a lightness at the mere idea of it.

Time to let it go.

"My father was—no, is," she clarified, "—a gambler who struggles with substance abuse. My mother has the misfortune of believing that he'll find some way past it and get better."

"Is that not possible?" Adam asked.

"I don't think so." Paige blew out a breath. "Not any longer. Maybe it might have been, once. And if I'm fair to my mother, I get why she's always wanted to believe in him. She loves him."

She shook her head, the sadness of her father's life weighing heavy on her heart, as it always did.

"But at this point I don't know if it's realistic anymore to believe he can change. That the disease that ravages him will ever let him go."

"Do you have contact with him?"

That awful day in the diner filled her mind. "Not anymore."

Since it did fill her mind, a lurking memory that often sat coiled, waiting to strike, she told Adam about it.

The request for money, not her father's first.

The unleashed anger, also not a first.

And the sheer dismissal of her value in his life if she refused to help him.

"Had he ever done that before?" Adam's voice was gentle, but his eyes had turned hard, glittering with anger.

"Not like that. He's asked for money through the years, but I could see something had changed for the worse this time. It's why I don't believe there's a way forward."

"Paige, I can see this is hard for you, so please forgive me for asking. But is it possible he's the one behind the things that have happened to you here?"

That day in the diner was still all-too present in her mind, the memories sharp and crisp. And although she could still conjure up the hurt, she remembered the other things as well.

How small and broken her father seemed. How empty, really, as if all his life essence had drained away from him.

"I wish I could say that he'd never do those things, but I can't. And I certainly believe it's possible if he was properly motivated. But he doesn't have the money to pull something like that off. He also has no access to my schedule."

Adam nodded at that, taking it in even as that crystal blue seemed to ice over.

"I hate this for you."

"I hate it for you, too. That your father isn't supportive of you. That he wants to get his hands on this place and all you've built."

"The people who should support us the most are active adversaries." His gaze never left hers, and in that intimacy, Paige saw yet another facet of their connection.

Their chemistry with each other had been there from the start, but so had that deeper sense of understanding each other.

Of supporting each other.

Even if they'd both hidden it when they were together in college, their family situations were still forces that had shaped them and drove them.

It made the idea of walking away again from someone she genuinely cared about so much harder, even as she felt better about their relationship than she ever had.

Their breakup had been devastating, but the past few days in Arizona had given her fresh perspective. On what motivated Adam and how deeply embedded that drive was inside him.

She'd also come to better understand his family dynamic, both the unbreakable bonds with his siblings, juxtaposed against the terrible, almost destructive relationship with his father.

With all of it, though, had come a separate marvel. One she had never seen coming: a deeper understanding of her own life. She'd always considered herself rather clear-headed about who she was and what she wanted, but there'd always been that lingering shadow of her failed relationship with Adam.

Now it was time to take accountability for allowing heartbreak to linger too long.

For *not* moving on.

Whether it was based on the time of her life when they were together or the dysfunction and sadness of her home life that colored her perspective, it didn't really matter.

What *did* matter was who she wanted to be moving forward.

A clarity Paige couldn't have imagined even a few weeks ago had settled inside her. With it, she knew the gift she wanted to give herself.

Not an echo of the past but a choice she could make freely, without those old memories tying her down.

Just as she had earlier when he'd come through the front door, Paige extended a hand to Adam.

"It's hard when the people who should support us don't. I've lived with that. You've certainly lived with it. What I don't want to live with any longer is feeling like the two of us are on opposite sides."

Adam's eyes filled with knowledge of what she offered, even as his mouth turned down in a slight frown.

"I can't, Paige."

"Because you don't want to?"

That frown morphed into a rueful smile. "*So* not because I don't want to."

"Then you're going to need to give me a better reason."

"I messed up my chance to touch you again. Like that,"

he added. "I ruined things, and I don't deserve to have you again."

"Seems like an odd perspective when I'm the one offering you exactly what you *can* have." She still held her hand there, even though he hadn't taken it yet. "You just need to take it."

"Paige."

Her name came out, a whispered sigh between them, and still she held her ground—and her hand—out to him.

"Let's put the past where it belongs and take what's here now."

His gaze drifted to her hand, his own reaching out to take hers in a firm grip.

"I don't deserve a second chance."

"Oh, baby, that's where you're wrong. We all deserve second chances. So please take this one for both of us."

She didn't have to ask again.

Not when he pulled her close, his arms coming tight around her. He buried his head in the curve of her neck, a deep, shuddering sigh feathering across her skin.

"I don't deserve you. But oh, how I want you."

And that, Paige knew, was enough.

Chapter Fourteen

Adam knew he should say no. Recognized he should resist.

But heaven help him, there was no force on earth that could pull him away from her.

He'd meant what he told her earlier. He'd never seen a woman more beautiful than Paige.

It was so easy to think it was simply because of her physical attributes, but she was so much more. Her beauty—her real beauty—came from all the things that she was.

Caring.

Generous.

Artistic.

And so much more.

He could have ten lifetimes with her and never discover all the beautiful things inside her. About her. With her.

But how he wanted to try.

He pulled her close for a kiss, only to realize his hands were shaking as he settled them on her lower back. One more sign of what this woman did to him.

She turned him upside down with need and gave space for all the vulnerable places inside him.

How had he never realized before what a gift that was? To feel so deeply powerful and utterly exposed, all at once.

He wanted to revel in it, but the urgency of being with her—of letting go and giving in—was rapidly taking over.

Their mouths met and merged, returning to each other with that familiar yearning that had somehow become new. It was endlessly fascinating to realize that he could remember the feel of her in his arms, the touch of her skin against his hands, yet acknowledge it was all different as well.

She was his miracle and she made him feel new, too.

Her fingers slipped beneath his T-shirt, her hands tracing the waistband of the joggers he'd changed into before grilling dinner. He was grateful for the looser clothes, especially as his need for her pressed hard against the stretchy material. And as her hand slipped beneath the waistband, Adam leaned into her, desperate for her touch.

He briefly worried things might be over too soon before giving himself up to her touch, not caring about anything but the tantalizing movements of her palm against his hard length.

Willing some control into the moment, he focused on the kiss, matching her strokes with the play of his tongue against hers. It was only as he felt his control slipping to the point of breaking that he finally pulled back, pressing his forehead to hers, his breathing heavy.

"I think the bed'll be a bit more comfortable."

"Are you feeling uncomfortable, Mr. Colton?" Humor filled that glittering green gaze, and if he weren't hanging on by a very slim thread, he'd have laughed at the taunt.

"I feel amazing."

She nipped at his jaw, her hand still pressed intimately against him. "Yes, you do."

"Which is why I can't end this before it's begun in the middle of my kitchen."

Her eyebrows quirked, the humorous light in her eyes

only growing. "And mess up our delightful metaphor about cooking?"

He did laugh at that, and the sheer irony that their tense words earlier in the week about their dating lives had suddenly morphed into a sexy sort of pillow talk.

Or counter talk, as it were.

He had no idea how she managed it, but even in her humor, she somehow demonstrated that she didn't hold a grudge. Or hard feelings.

She truly had the ability to move forward. To grant forgiveness and then find humor in the situation.

The raw, edgy need that coursed through his body shifted and changed.

Transformed, actually.

Because he still wanted her, his body strung like a taut wire, but it was no longer simply about the physical.

Maybe it never had been.

"Please," he whispered against her lips. "Let me take you to the bedroom."

"Let the record show," she sighed as she slipped her hand from his waistband, "I was more than willing to test out this very lovely marble counter."

"I'll hold you to that later. I promise. But right now, I want you in my bed, stretched out and naked, so I can kiss every inch of your skin."

He reached down and lifted her into his arms, holding her close as he headed out of the kitchen. Her arms wrapped around his neck, her lips pressed to the sensitive area beneath his ear.

"Well, when you put it that way, how can I refuse?"

Paige wanted to pinch herself. If she could stop touching Adam for a moment, she might have even tried it. But that would mean waking up from this amazing dream *and* not touching him any longer, and that wasn't acceptable.

She barely remembered getting from the kitchen to the bedroom, but in moments they were standing before each other, their clothing vanishing in a rush to feel each other.

I want you in my bed, stretched out and naked, so I can kiss every inch of your skin.

Adam's words had started a series of delicious shivers, and he pulled her close once they were both naked. Her breasts felt heavy and full, and she loved the feel of him.

The feel of being with him.

And how quickly they drove each other toward needing more.

Want and desire was a living, breathing thing between them, part of them yet a separate force, driving them on.

While she didn't want to bring the specter of other relationships into this, as Adam held her close, making good on his promise to kiss each and every inch of her, she recognized why things hadn't worked out with the other men who'd come into her life.

They'd all been good men. Kind, too. She'd never have progressed to something physical if she hadn't felt that. But in the end, the few men since Adam who she'd let into her bed hadn't made her feel *this*.

Incendiary and featherlight, all at once. Weighted with need yet practically flying as heat and light and sheer energy sparked between them.

It was a tall ask of anyone, Paige acknowledged, and something she'd never found outside of her relationship with Adam.

Which was why she'd take these stolen moments and not look back.

And never regret.

Everywhere he kissed was alight with the most delicious zaps of electricity, and she increasingly found it harder to form a complete thought through the building desire.

She felt him move and glanced over when he slipped a condom out of the bedside drawer, making quick work of it. And then he shifted back to her, and she opened herself fully to him, lifting her legs to hook them around his hips. His body was poised at the entrance to hers, but in that moment he paused and looked down at her.

Something heavy weighed against her heart, and it wasn't the physical weight of him.

It was so much more.

Laying a palm against his cheek, she felt how his muscles strained as he held himself still. Appreciated just how much that cost him. "I'm glad we found our way back here. Let's make something new together."

All she felt inside was reflected back in the depths of his blue gaze.

Need, yes, but so much more.

An inner vulnerability kept hidden from the world.

A personal solitude that longed for connection.

And a recognition that this was an endlessly safe and soft place to land.

He pressed his lips to hers, his kiss the voice of all they didn't say.

And then there was nothing but movement.

Pleasure.

And the light of a million stars.

She had no idea how they'd gotten here, Paige realized as pleasure crested in endless waves, but she knew she'd be forever grateful they'd found their way.

ADAM WOKE TO a physically empty bed, yet one that bore the distinct imprint of the night before. Paige's scent filled his senses, and the lingering warmth where she'd slept beside him was like a brand against his side.

The telltale sounds of a hair dryer echoed from down the hall, and he realized that she not only beat him awake but had also obviously won the morning while he lazed with all the speed of a sloth.

A well-sated sloth. He couldn't help grinning to himself. One who'd spent nearly all night making love to Paige. Their night together had been incredible.

Although he'd initially resisted, unwilling to take advantage of her, what had happened between them had been beyond his imaginings. A coming together that wasn't about the past at all.

Could it be about the future?

That thought hit him just as Paige walked into the room, fresh and ready to meet the day. She had on a loose-fitting white button-down shirt and jeans that molded to her curves. A trendy pair of sneakers completed the outfit, and he found himself caught, an image of waking up with her every day leaving no room for him to think about anything else.

"Shower's free."

When he only continued to stare at her, a cheeky grin lit up her heartbreaking face. "And no, I'm not getting back into bed with you."

"I—"

He stopped, sitting up and using the movement to try to gather his thoughts.

He what?

Wanted her to stay? After one incendiary night together, he was going to ask her to upend her life?

A life she'd created all on her own, building her future after he'd walked away.

"You what, Adam?" She moved closer, the smile fading as she took him in.

He forced a smile and hoped it was convincing. "I was only going to make a lame excuse that you hadn't actually read my mind but since you did…"

The lie didn't sit comfortably—at all—but neither did the idea of asking her to stay after this assignment was over.

So he went with it, hoping he hadn't made this brief morning-after interlude too weird.

"That's why we can pick up where we left off later." She bent down and kissed him, lingering a few moments over the kiss.

He reached for her, nearly wrapping her in his arms to pull her back down to the bed, but ended up pressing his hand at the base of her neck instead. The crisp material of her shirt against his palm was a reminder that she had things to do today.

When she lifted her head, her eyes reflected heat and sultry promise. "Kadim and Doug are waiting for me outside. I'll see you later."

"I can walk you to breakfast."

"No time." She was already on the move, clearly thinking about the day. "There's too much good morning light to catch to miss it with breakfast. I'll eat later."

And then she was gone, the essence of her lingering in the bedroom long after he heard the front door open, Kadim's morning greeting floating toward the bedroom.

Once he was awake, Adam never usually lay back down, but he did so this morning.

And stared at his ceiling far longer than he should have, contemplating just how empty his life was going to feel once Paige was gone.

PAIGE FOCUSED ON completing one more series of shots in front of a cabana that edged the property's infinity pool. Her models were draped over the cabana cushion, the male model holding his partner in a way that allowed the woman's hair to catch the light. The makeup crew had subtly oiled skin and hair to augment the morning sun's work, and Paige loved what she saw through the lens.

A romantic story that was over-the-top enough to be enticing and just the right side of attainable to make the fantasy feel real.

It was her business, Paige recognized. Understanding that very fine line so that someone could see themselves there instead of simply observing.

Or worse, tuning out because they didn't believe it was for them.

She'd tuned out a lot over the years, she admitted to herself as she called an end to the work and gave everyone a break for lunch.

The emotional noise of her parents' challenging lives. The clanging and often discordant cacophony that had been her modeling life. Even the melancholy over the end of her and Adam's relationship had simply become a subtle din of sadness that she'd forced to the back of her mind in order to focus on moving forward.

A fact of life or a way of dealing with it that wasn't healthy?

Maybe the answer to that, Paige thought as she packed up her equipment to move it to their next location, was what you did when the moment arrived when you had to tune back in.

She'd done so with her last conversation with her father. It had been painful and difficult, but she'd met him and done what she had to do. She wasn't going to support his problems by throwing money at them, no matter how hard it was to hear his vitriolic anger in return.

But she'd handled it.

Modeling had been the same. She'd kept the work in the right box in her mind, using it as a means to an end, not the definition of her life. On the back of it, she'd built a career that she loved. One that not only fulfilled her but also came from a part of her that was deeply rooted in how she saw the world.

And now you're dealing with Adam.

Last night had been incredible. Heat flushed her skin—a physical state she'd faced all morning as memories of the night before continued to assail her—and she figured anyone looking at her would have no problem figuring out how she'd spent her evening.

If that were all, she'd be fine, but Adam had caught her off guard this morning. The night had been perfect. Once she'd finally made him see that she wanted him—here and now, without any of the past interfering—he'd been in tune with her.

And then this morning she got the sense that a new day's clarity clouded how he saw the night before.

It didn't come off like remorse or a rush to get her out of the house. But she had seen something in his demeanor all the same. An expression she couldn't decipher no matter how many times she turned it over in her mind.

Was it regret?

Even as she tried it on, the idea didn't fit. He'd kissed

her before she left, a sort of melting into each other in a delicious blend of longing and promise.

Certainly *not* someone trying to give her the bum's rush out of the house.

Did he have lingering guilt?

Neither of them could change the past, but she would be forever grateful for these past few days. What had come before didn't have the power to hurt her any longer, and that was a miracle in itself.

A part of her had always believed the past would be firmly locked and shut when she moved on with someone else.

How amazing to realize she could close it all on her own. She knew herself and had come to appreciate all she'd built for the past decade. Add on that she'd gained an understanding of what had driven Adam so many years ago, and things had all fallen into place.

She was free from the past.

Which only brought her right back around to this morning.

What had put Adam in that odd, unreadable mood?

She'd left him sleeping when she went in to shower and get ready for the day. The move had been practical—she had to be down here by the pool for the first shots and waking him up to share the shower with her would definitely have made her late.

But it was also a bit of self-preservation, if she were honest.

The night before had been every form of magic, but it had also been…overwhelming.

And far more new and different than she ever could have imagined.

Had he sensed that?

Since all these questions interfered with her forward-thinking, embrace-the-present-and-forget-the-past attitude she was so excited about, she resolved to shrug it off. If Adam was bothered by something, he'd have to tell her.

No more mooning or worrying about things she couldn't control.

Since that evolved thinking felt fantastic, Paige headed for the business office, where they'd catered in lunch. Doug and Kadim had followed at a discreet distance, and not for the first time she thought it was a waste of resources that the two of them were stuck following her.

Adam wouldn't hear of reducing their schedules, but as Doug moved forward and scanned his badge to let them through a hidden gate that led to the business offices, she vowed to say something anyway.

She only had two more days here. Was it really necessary to keep them leaping to do her bidding?

Two more days.

That thought stuck an exceptionally hard landing. Between her thoughts of Adam and her focus on the shoot, she'd avoided thinking about leaving Mariposa, but her departure would be here soon.

And all her bright, happy, *forward-thinking* thoughts fled at the reality that she'd head home all too soon.

"Paige!" Noah called her name just as she stepped through.

She'd seen Laura's husband off and on throughout the shoot, either moving through the property with one of his team members or even a few times when he'd hung back quietly, observing her work.

The man seemed to have eyes everywhere. Add on his formidable tough-guy look and he left an impression. In addition to the stalwart Kadim and Doug, it was nice to know he was watching out for her.

She waited as he caught up to her, pasting on a bright smile. "I'm just heading into lunch. Why don't you join me?"

"You're actually the person I wanted to see. Let's grab a plate and head to Laura's office."

"You have an update."

"I do. And I wish it was a surprise, but it's not going to be." A fierce smile lit up his features, even if his next words were grim. "Glenna."

"Oh. But she wasn't here."

Noah gave a small shake of his head as they stepped into the business office. "Let's make up our plates, and we'll pick up in Laura's office. I already gave her and Adam a heads-up to meet us there."

"Of course."

If Glenna had orchestrated the various attacks on her life, it only reinforced the idea that Adam's stepmother had a mole inside the resort.

Which meant nowhere was safe from spying eyes.

Whatever ease she'd taken, settling in over the past few days, vanished as if it had never been.

The danger might have subsided momentarily, but it was still here and very much alive. Coiled and waiting to strike.

"WE'RE LIVING IN modern times," Laura fumed as she crisscrossed the length of her office for the fifth time. "Aren't we beyond the whole evil-stepmother thing?"

Adam let his sister have the floor, wishing he had any answer for her beyond no. He side-eyed Josh and Dani, who had pulled over several of her conference table chairs to join the briefing. Their faces were equally impassive, all of them a collective unit, fully aligned with Laura's ire.

"Hell, for a woman who thinks she's so glamorous and elegant, it's a damned cliché!"

He wanted to argue with his sister, but Noah's call earlier had him rushing to Laura's office from where he and Josh had reviewed a new sampling of trail markers. It wasn't normally a part of his work, as he trusted Josh to handle those sorts of things himself, but his brother had wanted his opinion on the aesthetic of the wooden plaques as well as to share some news.

And to show off the ring box he'd stowed in his pocket.

One more moment ruined, even inadvertently, by Glenna and her behavior, Adam thought.

"It may be cliché, but it's not a surprise," Adam pointed out. "So we need to focus on what comes next. She's got an informant here on property, and so far we've come up blank on who it could be. We need to redouble our efforts there."

"I've tried to ask questions," Dani said. "Not spending a ton of time here has given me a bit of a pass, and I've played the I'm-new card hard."

"That's a great point." Adam leaned into the fact that his sister had only decided to stay at Mariposa recently. Now she'd moved fully into a business role with the resort. "We're a bit stifled by the fact that we've known everyone for so long. You've got fresh eyes on the dynamics of the staff and the property."

"That may be true," Dani said, "but nothing's jumped out at me as particularly off. You've got a few odd folks, but so does everywhere. No one who seems like they're holding a grudge or causing problems."

There was a brisk knock before Noah and Paige came in, plates in hand.

Adam walked over to Paige, surprised to realize how much he just wanted to touch her. To feel her physical form and know she was okay.

"None of you are eating?" Paige asked as he walked up to her. She did settle a free hand on his arm, that gentle, supporting touch going a long way toward calming the steady drumbeat of anger that desperately wanted out.

"No one's that hungry."

"I'm not, either, but Noah wanted us to put on a show." Paige held up her plate. "I'm happy to share."

"I am hungry," Josh pointed out.

"I know it's maybe not the moment, but I am, too. And if we both go out, it'll lend an air of normalcy over lunch," Dani said before coming over to him and Paige. "I know we didn't get to talk much the other morning, but I just want say how sorry I am this is happening."

"Thank you for that." Paige's smile was gentle. "But you all have been dealing with this a lot longer than I have."

Dani's light brown eyes narrowed, and Adam saw that seriousness he always associated with his baby sister. "Noah's news is upsetting, but we're going to get to the bottom of this and root it out. Our father's pushed the takeover meeting up, and I think it's made Glenna sloppy. That's going to work in our favor."

Paige's surprise at that was evident as she turned to him. "Adam, what's this? The meeting was moved up?"

"To Friday."

"That's in three days. How are you going to fight this?"

"Dani's the owner of the shares. We can use that."

They'd have to use it. Especially because the red tape around inheriting them from her mother still meant she didn't have them in hand.

But she had them, he kept reminding himself. She was the rightful owner. They had the majority on their side.

"Let's focus on Noah's news," Laura cut in. "The lawyers are back this afternoon to work on our approach."

"You've got this, big brother." Dani gave him a quick hug, another sign their relationship had only grown deeper in the months since she'd been back in Arizona, before she slipped out of the office with Josh, firmly closing the door behind them.

Laura had already given him the broad strokes of what Noah had discovered, but Adam gestured Paige over to the chairs Josh and Dani had just vacated, taking the one next to her.

Noah stood beside Laura, his face set in stern lines as he settled a hand on her shoulder. "I spoke with the Sedona PD detective assigned to your case. They've traced the poison back to a supplier in Phoenix. From there, they put pressure on one of their local informants. The word among those in the know is that an elegant woman with a seemingly endless pocketbook is buying services in town."

Paige spoke first. "And you know for a fact it's Glenna?"

"She's been discreet, but the informant gave a description and then further confirmed her by name." Noah smiled. "It seems our Glenna doesn't just make trouble here at Mariposa for the staff. The informant spent a bit of time working one of the hotels in town as a barback. Glenna's got a reputation for being difficult, and he ID'd her to a T, along with prior stays, which the detective could match up."

Adam realized they all wanted answers, but it didn't change the fact that Glenna hadn't been anywhere near the resort for a few months. Add on the intel from his father's housekeeper and she hadn't been in Arizona at all.

"Much as she fits on motive, she hasn't been here. How's she doing all this?"

"Seems like her penchant for hiring people to poison others isn't new."

"My bachelorette party," Laura said on a heavy exhale. "She's responsible for that?"

Noah nodded, squeezing Laura's shoulder. "I'm afraid so, babe."

"What about the woman I thought was an employee of the hotel?" Paige asked. "The one who gave me the water bottle."

Noah nodded his approval at her perceptive question. "She's small-time and dealing with an unfortunate habit, but the informant tagged her, too. Sang her lungs out for leniency. Claims she wasn't paid off to poison you but that she was told to be hospitable. Got paid three hundred bucks by someone she doesn't know to make sure you had water."

"Giving away poisoned bottles of water?" Adam asked. He'd wanted the details, but even he recognized how diabolical it all was.

"The woman claims she didn't know," Noah said. "I think it stands to reason the three hundred bucks she was offered to hand out the water was seen as a boon, nothing more."

"What are we going to do about this?" Laura asked. "Everything the detective has found stacks up, but there still isn't anything to directly pin this on Glenna. It's not like she's paid for her deeds with a check."

"With this information, the detective's now working on finding records of wiring money," Noah confirmed.

Adam reached for Paige's hand, his fingers linking with hers. "We need to focus on finding the mole here at Mariposa. That's our link to solving this."

He had to keep faith in that. Even if finding the mole had remained elusive up to now.

Someone at Mariposa was feeding Glenna information.

They just had to hope that they found them before anything worse could happen.

Paige was leaving in two days. It had bothered him—weighing heavy all day—but now he saw it as a benefit. He'd known all along her visit had a shelf life and she had additional business commitments after her time here ended.

He'd miss her—far more than he ever could have imagined—but he'd have the confidence that she was far away from here. His admin had already booked the transportation for her, scheduling a helicopter out of Sedona to take her to Phoenix.

It felt like security overkill, but he wouldn't be too careful.

Not with Paige's life.

The most precious thing he'd ever been entrusted with.

Chapter Fifteen

"Taste it and weep."

Max offered her another one of his bacon-forward creations from a platter he held expertly in one hand.

"Weep?" Paige asked, unable to keep the tease off her lips as she reached for one of the small appetizers. "You're awfully confident in yourself, Mr. Powell."

Her friend's smile never wavered as he extended a cocktail napkin with his free hand. "I make magic with food. Confident doesn't mean a thing."

"He's so modest," Alexis joked as she came up beside Max, her hand landing casually against his back.

Paige loved seeing the two of them together. Max had always had that confident smile and nonchalant air, and he'd put them to good use as a playboy celebrity chef. Even when she knew him in college, he'd had a way with women. Always respectful, but also always casual.

With Alexis, it was obvious he was all in.

And in love.

He'd found that here, at Mariposa, even with all the horrors that had gone on around them.

It gave her hope, Paige realized, that good could come out of even the darkest moments in life. And yet…

Nothing could change the fact she was leaving tomorrow.

The clock had been ticking away and now here they were, at a small dinner Laura and Max had insisted on hosting for her. Laura as a thank-you and Max as a going away.

Her time with Adam was always going to have a shelf life. In fact, she'd designed it that way, intending to do the shoot and nothing more.

When things had progressed in a more personal direction, she'd hung on to the idea that she could keep everything in perspective, and she had.

Or she *was*, she amended to herself, keeping it all in perspective.

Even if she was increasingly worried that she'd fallen right back in love with Adam.

"Paige?" Max's dark eyes crinkled at the corners. "You with me?"

"Yes, sorry! Weeping over appetizers. Of course I'm here for it." She took one of the small bites he offered, biting into the tantalizing appetizer.

It was only as the flavors hit her tongue that she registered one more. "Oh my gosh! What's in here?"

"Manchego cheese."

She swallowed the little bite of heaven before leaning forward and pressing a kiss to Max's cheek. "I can hear the angels weeping above me. I will, however, avoid tears and keep my makeup dry."

"Once a runway goddess, always a runway goddess." Max turned to press a kiss to Alexis's neck. "The same is true for my beautiful concierge. Woman wouldn't deign to ruin her makeup for my food."

Alexis practically glowed beside him, her gaze as besotted as Max's. "You bet your sexy ass, Max Powell."

Paige could only laugh at the irony of it all as she took a sip of her wine. As recently as the other day with Adam, she'd chafed at the reference to modeling, but with Max it was different.

With her friend, it was a reminder of just how far they'd come.

Even if he actually *had* moved forward, both in his career and in his soul-deep love with Alexis.

It was only Paige who was still hanging out on the love sidelines.

"You still peddling your food by hand, Powell?" Adam came up behind her, wrapping his arm around her waist as he reached for an appetizer with a free hand.

"From the hand of a food god," Max shot back, the good humor between the two of them fun to watch.

Especially when Adam chewed, swallowed and then reached for another.

"Greedy much?"

"Just need a second one to make sure I'm right."

"About?" Max asked, watching Adam.

"How fast we're getting these babies loaded up on the restaurant's appetizer menu."

Alexis kissed Max once more before turning to Adam. "I need to deal with one last guest arriving and then I'll be back."

"Jeff's on shift right now," Adam said, notes of confusion still evident beneath his chewing.

"He is." Alexis nodded. "But he's not nearly as smooth as he needs to be when a big action star comes through the lobby. We're working on it, but I'd like to make sure he doesn't have a heart attack before he can get the man checked in."

"How far we've come," Paige murmured as Alexis headed off to handle her movie star.

Max was already slapping Adam's hand as he reached for one more small bite as both men turned to look at her.

"Far? Paigey," Max said, waving the pan in front of Adam. "We're just getting started."

Max had barely stepped away when Adam bent his head and pressed his lips to hers, the salty flavor of bacon still evident. He held back—the kiss was chaste by anyone's standards—but Paige felt exposed all the same.

Wary.

And she wasn't quite sure why.

Her time here had always had an expiration date. Forgetting that now was akin to being sad your birthday or Christmas had passed.

It didn't matter how much you enjoyed the day—it was eventually rolling into the next.

When Adam's gaze roamed over her face, obviously sensing her lingering discontentment, she scrambled for something to take those maudlin thoughts away. "Do you think that?"

"Think what?"

"That we're just getting started," she said.

"I'd like to think so. I'd like to think there's still so much more to come. In work. In life. But I can also appreciate all that's come so far. The experiences that ensure I might be on the right track."

Adam lifted a hand and traced the tip of his finger over her cheek. "Why do you look sad about that?"

"I'm not sad." *Liar.* "I'm melancholy. Reflective." Paige blew out a breath. "Yeah, okay. A little sad, too."

"The past week has been overwhelming in a lot of ways. And I'd never willingly put you in danger for any reason. But I can't deny that I'm happy you're here."

"Me too."

His gaze roamed over her face as he pulled her close. "It's going to be hard to say goodbye to you."

Paige nodded against his chest, well aware that it would be impossibly hard now that she'd had a taste of being with him again.

But it wasn't like Adam was making promises or asking her to stay, either.

It was that thought that carried her through as Laura and Noah stood at the front of the restaurant, glasses lifted in a toast to Paige in thanks for her contributions to Mariposa.

And it was that thought, Paige knew as she turned away from Adam's chest to lift her glass, that would keep her heart safe long after she was gone from here.

ADAM PULLED PAIGE tight against his chest, reveling in the feel of her pressed to him. Skin to skin.

They'd come back from Max's dinner and made love with a fervor he'd never known before, practically consuming each other before the front door had even closed.

It was unbearably sexy and hard to take, all at the same time.

Because it meant she was leaving.

He could paint their blistering need bordering on desperation any color he wanted, but he knew the real reason for the urgency.

And he knew she did, too.

She hadn't replied to him when he told her how hard it would be to say goodbye. Instead, she'd nodded, and then they were both carried up into the dinner festivities.

As was his trademark, Max had created an incredible dinner, and despite the heaviness hanging in the air, it had been a fun event.

But Adam also recognized both he and Paige had put on

bright, shiny faces. He suspected his siblings noticed, too, but everyone had been too kind to say anything.

Oddly, it had helped they were all so focused on Glenna. The dinner was a closed affair, Max and Alexis and the Coltons with their significant others the only ones in the room. It prevented any risk of observation by their mole, and it had also created an intimacy they didn't often find on the property.

Mariposa was about entertainment and escape for others, so it had been a novel experience to have the evening just for their party.

He'd even convinced Alexis to truly take the night off once she'd ensured their new movie-star guest was set for the evening.

"It was a nice night. Max outdid himself."

"He was in his glory," Adam agreed. "It's good to have him here. He brings an energy we didn't realize we were missing."

"You mean the walking party that is Max Powell?" She lifted her head, a soft smile on her face. "Even back in college, he commanded a room wherever he went."

"Those days keep coming up. College, I mean."

The smile faded. "There's been a lot to remember back on. We all knew each other well."

"And we know each other now."

"Is something wrong?"

"No." Adam blew out a harsh breath, well aware he was at immediate risk of ruining not only the evening but her entire stay. "I'm just conscious that you're leaving tomorrow."

"I know." She ran a hand over his chest, making abstract circles with her thumb. "When I got here last week, I didn't think the end of this assignment would come soon enough. And now it's here way too fast."

"I've liked having you here."

"I've liked being here, Adam. I'm glad we could move past college. Past all that came before."

"Is that all?"

Paige shifted away, sitting up and taking the sheet with her. "What are you looking for me to say?"

"The past few days have been different. Being together. As the people we are now. Not who we were all those years ago."

"It's been wonderful to have this time together. A chance to make new memories."

So stay.

The words were so close to spilling out Adam had to make a conscious effort to ensure they didn't slip.

Because he had no right to ask her to stay. Even less to press her when he knew she had to go on to her next work engagement.

"I like the people we've become."

It was the person he was before that he couldn't get past. He'd hurt her, and he didn't have a right to ask her to stay.

To ask her to change her life because, once again, he couldn't leave Arizona or Mariposa.

If they were successful against his father's takeover, Adam knew he needed to be here to see it through. Which brought him back to same place he was a decade ago.

Their relationship needed to exist on his terms.

Again.

And she deserved so much better than that.

So he wouldn't ask.

He'd just take the few hours he had left and show her what she meant to him.

That would have to be enough.

Paige wanted to be angry.

She wanted to yell and scream at the universe at how unfair it all was.

Even more, she wanted to tell him how badly she wanted to stay.

But she did none of that as she placed the last of her equipment in the back seat of the black car called to take her to the airport. Adam had already carried out her suitcase and her camera bag, leaving her to manage the padded case she carried with her most expensive equipment.

It's not passive aggressive, she assured herself as she stowed the case in the back seat. *Nor is it weak.* But she did have to hold her ground. Because if Adam wanted her to stay, he'd have said so last night.

And if, for some reason, he wanted her to stay but was unable to say it, the end result was the same.

She needed to be with someone who knew how to tell her what mattered to him. How to voice what was important.

She loved him.

There was no question in her mind about that, and more than a week in his company had only reinforced those feelings.

But she loved herself, too.

Standing firm was the only way to ensure she didn't end up back in that same dark place as after college.

Adam waited for her beside the open back-passenger door.

"Thank you for everything."

"Right back at ya, Colton." She moved into his arms, holding him tight, savoring these last moments with him.

She wanted to tell him they'd talk. That they'd remain friends and stay in each other's lives.

It might even be true.

But for now, she needed to walk away.

Lifting her face to his, she wrapped her arms around his neck and pulled him close for a kiss. The urgent desperation that had driven their joining the night before had burned out, leaving nothing behind but a soft sort of regret, pulsing beneath a chemistry that had never faded.

"Take care of yourself, Adam Colton."

"You too."

Paige slipped from his arms and slid into the back seat, avoiding looking at him through the darkened windows. But it was only after the driver pulled away and headed for the exit that she took her first easy breath.

Forward, Barnes. Focus on moving forward. He didn't ask you to stay.

Noah had vetted the driver who would take her all the way to the helipad at the Sedona airport. With nothing left to worry about regarding her safety, Paige settled back in her seat, resolved to focus on her work.

After slipping her laptop out of her workbag, she booted up and started the process of working through the photos she'd uploaded over the past few days.

Several shots had already gone to the layout editor, and she needed to send him another set today. The drive into Sedona was slow as the chauffeur navigated the twisting route through the red rocks, and she hoped focusing on work would offer a distraction.

Especially when all she wanted to do was ask the driver to turn around and take her back.

Deftly ignoring that sense of longing, she flipped through the photos she'd captured from different angles around the resort. The images she'd promised Laura would mainly come from this group, and the variety of shots she'd secured were going to look fantastic on the Mariposa website and in their sales materials.

Tagging a few that she wanted to save for Laura into one folder, then what she was sending to the photo editor in another, she switched gears to the more intimate shots she'd secured with the models.

"We're about ten minutes away, Ms. Barnes," her driver said to her over the partition window between them. "I know this is a slow, winding drive, but we'll be there soon."

His hangdog face was kind, but she'd already seen the body that went with it when he'd picked her up for the trip. Thick and fit, she had the definite sense that Hank could—and would—manage anything that got in his way.

"Thanks, Hank." She smiled at him through the mirror, pleased to know she'd be on her way soon.

While it wasn't the most efficient way to travel, the helicopter was private transport, which meant as soon as she was loaded up and seated, they'd take off.

No waiting around.

No more wondering if it was too late to ask Hank to turn the car around or to take her back to Mariposa.

Mentally calculating that she could flip through about twenty more photos before she needed to tuck her computer away, Paige opened the file with images near the infinity pool. She'd loved the way the sun arrayed over her couple and wanted to see them with a few days' passage of time.

Damn, but they were an attractive pair, was all she could think as she flipped through the images. If it were only their fit bodies draped in exquisite clothing and jewels that would be enough, but the two of them had a dynamic sort of chemistry as well.

Paige had seen it in person, but it came through in the photos as well, the images practically leaping off her screen.

Isabella was going to be happy with these, was all Paige could think as she tagged a few she'd also retouch and share with the models for their portfolios.

She flowed through the images effortlessly until something caught her attention. Slowing the rapid flip through the images, she was surprised to realize someone had walked into a few of her shots.

Leaning forward over her screen, Paige tried to remember when someone had gotten in their way. It had been a closed area, and she didn't remember an interruption, but she'd been distracted herself that day with the infinity pool shots.

She'd spent the night before making love with Adam and...

It was that woman, Paige realized. The one from the Monday-morning staff meeting whom she'd overheard complaining about the Coltons and what she perceived as the lack of perks at the resort.

Paige zoomed in and was pleased to see how clear the image remained, even as she got closer to a section. Score one for that new camera lens.

"Ms. Barnes, we're here."

The car had slowed, and Paige looked up as if surfacing.

"Are you okay?" A worried expression had settled over Hank's features, those long lines of his face going hard in concern.

"Yes, I think..." She trailed off. "I'm sorry, but could you just give me one more quick minute? I got my head into something and I want to wrap it up."

"Of course. I'll get your things."

She glanced out of her window to realize he'd pulled them straight up to the helipad. The helicopter that would take her to Phoenix loomed large out the window, and she could see her pilot walking around the edge of it, writing on a clipboard as he went.

She needed to be quick, but something nagged at her to finish what she was doing.

Tapping again, she used the zoom function to narrow in on the woman, who had a cell phone in her hand as she talked with buds in her ears. Although the photo had gotten slightly grainy, Paige was able to make out some key words on the face of the phone.

GLENNA COLTON

Paige nearly fumbled her computer off her lap at the realization of what she had.

Why was that disgruntled employee talking to Glenna?

Even as the question lanced through her thoughts, she already knew the answer.

That woman was the mole.

She had to be.

"Hank!" She slammed the laptop closed and scrambled out of her seat. "Hank! I'm sorry, but please put my things back. We have to go back to Mariposa."

"Ma'am? Why do you want to do that?"

The helicopter rotors had already started, and the end of his question faded off in the noise.

Willing him to understand, she screamed over the increasing whirl of the blades. "I'm sorry! I'll explain in the car! But I need to go back!"

"Miss, but we—"

Hank's words evaporated in the blink of an eye as the entire world exploded around them in an ear-splitting rumble.

It was Paige's last thought as the helicopter blew up in front of them.

Chapter Sixteen

"Adam. I need you to listen to me!" Noah's iron grip on his arms only added to Adam's panic, and he fought to shake his brother-in-law off. "You're not going to help her this way!"

Sound and light and anger and fear swirled around him in a raging cacophony against his senses.

Where was Paige? He had to get to Paige.

"Adam!" It was Dani's gentle voice that finally broke through. "The car's being brought around now."

He shook his head, speaking the first coherent sentence he'd managed since his sisters and his brother-in-law came into his office. "How the hell did this happen?"

The words came out on an agonized, nearly feral shout before he turned and marched for the exit. They'd worry about how it happened later. All that mattered *now* was that they got to her.

Although a part of him would have felt better driving himself, a desperate act of trying to retain control, he didn't argue when Noah took the driver's seat. Adam climbed in the back with Dani, and Laura joined Noah in the front.

"She's okay, Adam," Dani said, her words soft and soothing. "She's at the hospital for observation, but the feedback Noah has is that she's all right."

"I know." He reached for Dani's hand.

Their knowledge of the situation was tenuous at best, with bits and pieces coming in as calls to Noah. Hank was considered critical and taken straight to surgery, and the helicopter pilot was dead.

So he had to focus on the fact that Paige was okay.

He would see her again.

Could talk to her and tell her all he'd been too stupid to say earlier.

He'd spent the morning brooding in his office after saying goodbye to her. A million scenarios played themselves through his mind, each and every one ending with him asking her to stay.

Telling her he wanted her to stay.

Telling her he loved her.

And he'd lost his chance.

Who was he anymore?

The past few months had tested him beyond measure. At times, even worse than the period of his mother's illness and death. He'd been a child then, and in retrospect realized just how much she had kept from him.

But now?

Nothing was hidden away, and in that terrible light he was forced to assess himself, too.

He'd believed himself capable, battling against his father for Mariposa. He'd handled each and every grenade tossed at them, from murder to mayhem to corporate espionage.

And then Paige had arrived.

Like a second chance at everything.

With her.

With his life.

With the life they could make together.

And still, even with that fresh chance in front of him, he'd kept her at arm's length. Over what? Fear of hurting her again? Or the fear he wouldn't be enough?

Because now, at the reality that she could have been killed, he saw just how ridiculous it all was.

If she didn't want a relationship, that was fine. But sending her away without telling her he wanted one was unacceptable.

The drive into Sedona felt interminable. Laura provided the precious few updates as they got them, including the fact that Hank, the driver Adam had trusted to take Paige to the airport, was still in critical condition.

Dani was his rock, sitting beside him as the car crawled to the hospital.

It was that love and support that broke down the final wall between them. He'd always felt a distance between himself and Dani, and it was only now, in the face of her staunch support, that he realized yet another facet of his life that had been closed off.

Closed off and just plain stupid.

Josh had always had the closest relationship with her, and Adam had always felt that he came across as the stodgy older brother. But now, seeing her as a strong, capable adult beside him?

He was grateful to have his sister by his side. Even more grateful she was staying here with them permanently.

"Thank you for being here."

She leaned into him, placing her head against his shoulder. It was all he needed, and he tilted his head to rest on top of hers.

"Always, Adam. You all are my home now."

Home.

It's what he wanted with Paige and what he also wanted with his siblings.

The question now was if she wanted the same with him.

"Dr. Wu."

"Miss Barnes." The doctor smiled at her as she did another check of Paige's pupils.

"Is there any news on Hank?"

Dr. Wu stepped back, shaking her head. "I'm afraid not yet. He's still in surgery."

Paige nodded, happy to have gotten that much.

"What about the others? The pilot?"

Dr. Wu stepped back. "I'm sorry, I can't share more. The police have asked that they be the ones to convey details. They should be here soon."

Paige recognized an order when she heard it.

She also recognized an evasion.

The fact she'd been given a modest amount of information on Hank suggested to her the helicopter pilot hadn't fared as well in the explosion.

How could he have?

Even now, she struggled to process it all. One moment she was stepping from the car, and the next the world was a fireball before her eyes.

"You do have a mild concussion along with the cuts they cleaned up in the emergency room. I'm satisfied that's all you have, but I'd like you to stay off your computer and other electronic devices for a few days."

"My computer!" She sat straight up, her quick movements pushing Dr. Wu into action. The doctor stepped up, her hands firm against Paige's shoulders.

"Whoa, there. Hold on."

"My computer? Was it recovered?"

"I don't—"

Dr. Wu must have seen something in her gaze, because she nodded. "Let me ask someone to check on your belongings."

The doctor was barely out of the room when she heard the pounding of footsteps. Adam raced into the room, his gaze panicked and his hair standing on end from where he must have had his hands in it.

She'd never seen him look so disheveled or—

"Paige!"

He had her wrapped in his arms, gentle but insistent against her IV and various electronic cords.

"Adam." Her voice came out on a whisper, but it was the last coherent thing she said as the dam holding back a wall of tears pushed forth.

Whatever she'd managed to hold in check through the paramedics' arrival at the helipad and the race to the emergency room and the management of her cuts and bruises broke wide open. Adam held her close, murmuring nonsense words as the pain of all that had happened spilled over.

It was a long while later when she finally lifted her head. Her tears had subsided, but her throat was achy, and her eyes were dry from the crying jag.

"Oh, Adam!" Paige's gaze roamed over his chest. "You're soaked."

"It'll dry."

"I'm sorry, I—"

He stopped her words with a kiss. It was urgent and more than a little desperate, and she realized he was as shaken as she was.

"I'm the one who's sorry. I never should have let you go this morning. I never—" He stopped, shaking his head before standing and taking a few steps back from the bed. "I love you, Paige. All-the-way love. Don't-want-you-out-of-my-sight love. I was an idiot for not telling you, and I'm so very sorry it took you nearly getting killed for me to get my head out of my ass and tell you."

Her cheeks were still wet, and her hair smelled of bomb material and grease. The nurse in the ER had cleaned up her face, but there was a layer of grime that still covered her from head to toe.

And she would really like a toothbrush, since she kept tasting something gritty between her teeth.

Despite it all, Paige had never felt better.

"I love you, too."

"I CAN'T BELIEVE it's Sasha Hightower."

Paige sat on the couch in Laura and Noah's bungalow, huddled beneath a large blanket. Adam had his arm wrapped tight around her shoulders, a position he'd taken up since she'd come down from taking a shower in the guest bathroom.

Dr. Wu had been satisfied that she could recuperate outside of the hospital this time and had discharged her late that afternoon. Paige's visions of the cleansing shower had been delayed by the arrival of the police and a debriefing session in one of the hospital's conference rooms.

The local police were bandying about several theories about what was determined to be a bomb set on the helicopter, including a disturbing comparison to a recent Mob hit in the region. Noah had freely shared what they believed was going on at Mariposa and Glenna Colton's involvement. The lead detective promised to share additional details in the morning once the bomb squad had finished going over the wreckage.

It was only now, well into the evening, that Paige finally had a chance to pull the evidence for Noah to share with the police. Her computer had been blown to smithereens, along with much of the equipment Hank had pulled from the trunk. Fortunately, she'd uploaded all her images each evening and had everything in the cloud.

Noah had connected his laptop to his and Laura's large-screen TV and handed the computer to her to type in her details. In a matter of moments, she navigated to her files and the select list she'd uploaded from the infinity pool.

"Those are gorgeous," Adam breathed as Paige flipped for the one she wanted.

"I had an amazing canvas to work with," Paige said. "And I still need to retouch these."

"So they'll be even better?" Laura made a point of leaning toward the screen before turning to Noah. "You'd better put the hiring notices out tonight. Once that magazine article drops, we're going to be fighting people off with a stick to come here."

It was nice, Paige recognized, to have their support. Even in the midst of how terrible everything had been today, there was still a focus on the future.

I love you, Paige. All-the-way love. Don't-want-you-out-of-my-sight love.

A future she had now, too.

Adam's declaration had pumped through her, his words buoying her beyond all the residual fear from the day.

He loved her.

And they'd face whatever came next.

Together.

With that thought firm in her mind, she flipped through a few more photos and found the one she'd seen on her laptop. The wider canvas of the TV screen helped, and she heard Adam's low string of curses.

But it was Laura's raw, "Damn it, Sasha," that tugged hard at Paige's heart.

They needed answers, but this was a heavy betrayal. One that had come from a trusted member of their team.

"You can see it here." Paige made the adjustments in her photography program to blow up the quadrant of the image that featured Sasha and her phone.

"It's just the right angle," Adam said in wonder as Paige continued zooming in on the photo to produce the same result as in the car. "If she'd had the phone turned even another five degrees or if you'd shot just a few seconds later, we wouldn't have this."

"No, we wouldn't," she agreed.

Because right there, visible for all of them, was Adam's stepmother's name on the phone screen.

Paige made a copy of the image and sent it, as well as a copy of the base photo, to everyone's email. Which only left one detail.

How to fire Sasha.

There was risk to keeping her on, but there was equal risk to try to take her out early, and they worked through each and every scenario. It was only when Noah left to take a call from his contact at the Sedona PD that Adam pointed out their next steps.

"Much as I'd like to go after her right now, we need to let the police take the lead on this. She hasn't just betrayed us, Laura. She's committed several crimes, including accessory to murder with today's explosion."

Paige struggled to take it all in, the sheer magnitude of what had happened overwhelming her again.

All this over a resort?

A pile of bricks.

It was a full-circle thought and one she'd couldn't have imagined feeling even a week ago. Yet here she was.

Mariposa had taken Adam from her life and had somehow brought him back in.

And now there was a person so dark and destructive and so very determined to take it over that they'd resort to murder.

Noah came back from taking his call, and Laura filled him in on their discussion about drawing Sasha out.

"The Sedona PD want to put Paige in a safe house until this is all done."

"What?" Paige stood at that, the implications overwhelming. She had commitments. A job to get to. "But why?"

"Today's incident officially moves this from a menacing problem to a serious threat to civilians, most especially you, Paige."

"They can't make me. Why would I want to go away? Why—"

Adam had already stood up when she had and pulled her close. "Why don't we figure this out in the morning? It's a lot to take in, but I think it's worth taking the police department's guidance on this, Paige."

Guidance? Safe houses? Serious threats?

So far the only discussion she'd heard was protection for herself.

But all of this centered on the Coltons. Who was looking out for Adam and his family?

"I can't leave you all here to deal with this. What if Glenna just changes gears and comes after you all?"

"Then it'll be good you're well away from it."

Adam's care for her was admirable, but it did nothing

to assuage her concern that if she herself were out of the way, Glenna would simply shift targets.

And with the takeover meeting bearing down on them, the likely target was Adam.

ADAM PUNCHED IN the alarm code, locking down the house, and braced himself for a fight now that he and Paige were alone. She didn't want to go to a safe house and had made her point more than clear on that. Which meant he had to stay strong and persevere until he could convince her otherwise.

What choice did he have?

The short distance between Laura's home and his was traversed in a car with security detail.

Someone on Noah's team had already done advanced reconnaissance on his home, checking for bombs.

And that same guard assured him they were doing a full sweep of the business offices before work started the next morning.

What surrealistic nightmare were they living in?

One in which Paige needed to go to a safe house until this was all over and done with. Her stay wouldn't be for long. Not with the incriminating photos of Sasha and the proof the Sedona detective had found, linking Glenna to the poisoning.

Even if there was a hell of a lot of concern that the evidence was far too circumstantial for Glenna not to effectively lawyer up and stay out of jail free and clear.

Adam had even toyed with the idea of calling his father. Whatever he thought of Clive, he was hard-pressed to believe that his father's callousness extended to murder.

But what the hell did he know?

He'd never have expected his stepmother capable of that level of depravity, either.

"Adam?"

Paige stood in the middle of his living room, clad in one of Laura's outfits because all of hers had been destroyed in the helicopter explosion.

Something about the way she stood there tugged at him, and he crossed to her, pulling her into his arms.

"If you say you're sorry one more time, I may punch you." She said those words against his chest but lifted her head to stare at him. "And not feel bad about it."

"How about if I simply stress how important it is to me that you stay safe? And that I'll only feel better about it if I go with you and stay with you?"

"You want to go into lockdown?"

"I'm not sure that's what they call it."

"It's not out and about, walking freely," she quickly pushed back, obviously undeterred by his logic.

"It's only for a short while."

"An hour is too long." She blew out a hard breath. "But I get it. And I get why you're asking. But you can't do that for me and effectively prepare for the meeting with the lawyers."

"I'll find a way."

"And tip off the staff, too? You know Sasha's watching everything. How are you going to get that past her? Won't people want to know where you are?"

"We'll ensure that the people who actually know are limited. And it's no one's business where I go."

She didn't look convinced, but he saw a few cracks around the edges of her resistance.

Which meant he had to show a few cracks of his own.

"I know you don't want apologies, but please let me say

this. I'm so sorry I let you leave this morning. That I allowed you to walk away and not tell you how I feel about you."

"Why?"

It was a simple question, and in it Adam heard no censure.

It was also one she deserved an answer to.

And in that moment Adam realized all the running he'd done since he was twenty-one—whether valid or not—needed to stop.

There was nowhere else to go unless it was to her.

Why hadn't he understood that sooner?

"I don't deserve a second chance. Not at all, but certainly not when my life is upside down and my focus is on the very place that broke us up in the first place."

Paige only continued to stare at him, her expression inscrutable as she considered him and his words.

His heart beat hard in his chest, as if he'd had a long and taxing run, as he waited for her verdict.

And in the end, he should have known it would simply be perfectly Paige.

"You silly, stubborn man." She shook her head as she wrapped her arms around his neck. "Sometimes the moments that break us are when we most deserve a second chance. Not to mention—" she pulled his head down closer to hers, her lips tantalizingly close to his "—don't you think it's my choice to give one?"

He could hardly believe what she was saying. The generosity of spirit and the amazing feel of the past washing away.

"We've been apart too long, Adam. Let's not stay apart any longer."

"I love you." He whispered those words against her lips.

"I love you, too. Which is the very reason we don't need a second chance."

He lifted his head at that and stared down at her, the green of her eyes nearly swallowing him whole. "We don't?"

"No, my love. We need a fresh start."

As he pressed his lips to hers, Adam sank into the promise of what she was offering.

Something new and wholly its own.

NOAH DROVE AWAY from the safe house, bright sunshine just coming up over the red rocks. Now that he was satisfied Adam and Paige were settled it was time to get back to Mariposa and figure out how to deal with Sasha. He'd been a detective too long not to have a few tricks up his sleeve, and he figured he'd employ some of his well-honed professional mind games with their two-faced employee.

He considered how to play it, cycling through scenarios. The woman had a solid streak of entitlement, so the good-cop, bad-cop routine likely wouldn't have a ton of effect. Especially since Sasha knew him now and had gotten used to having him around.

He could dangle information, making her think he knew more than he did, but the woman was used to discretion in her job. She'd know how to play against that as well, waiting to confirm when he actually had details she knew to be true.

Which left one of his personal favorites.

Lean on the greed.

The big variable in all this was Glenna. Whatever power Sasha thought she had, it all sat with the payer-payee relationship she enjoyed with Laura's stepmother. That's where he'd push.

And that's what he'd use to draw her out.

He'd already begun thinking through the play, reaching for his phone to call Laura and get her buy-in on his approach.

His eyes on his in-dash screen, Noah abstractly registered a car passing him on the two-lane that led back to the safe house.

With a last tap on the screen, he called his wife. Laura answered on the first ring.

"How'd it go?"

"Hey, babe. Good. They're settled and I—"

Why was there a car driving the opposite direction?

Something hard burst in his chest as Noah slowed down, finding a place to turn the car around.

"Noah?"

"Call the police. Now!"

"Noah! What's going on?"

"I'm heading back to the safe house. A car just passed me heading in that direction. No one knows they're back there, and no one has a reason to go that way."

"Noah, wait for backup." Laura's voice was deadly calm as it settled over the car audio system, but he heard the panic all the same. "You can't go in there alone."

"Call the police, baby. Now. I can't leave your brother and Paige alone, either."

"Stay on the line. And you'd better still have the Kevlar on. I love you."

"It's on. And I love you, too."

Noah kept the line open and listened to his wife give rapid orders to the Sedona PD as he raced toward the safe house, bumping over the two-lane road.

He had to get there in time.

There was no other option.

PAIGE PACED THE small kitchen, one more attempted distraction in a morning full of restless, nervous energy.

She'd—of course—said yes to the safe house.

And it hadn't taken a night of making love to Adam to get her to say yes.

That had simply been the added bonus.

Deep down she'd recognized there was little choice in the matter, but after Adam promised to come with her, there wasn't any room or reason to keep arguing.

And she had to hand it to Noah, the man had quietly steamrolled through her objections, already setting things in motion with the Sedona PD.

A fact that had been clear when he'd arrived bright and early at Adam's bungalow, two officers beside him.

Since all her clothing had been destroyed in the helicopter explosion, it was deeply touching when he rolled a small suitcase out from behind his back and handed it to her. "A few things from Laura and I to make this a bit easier."

She'd nearly cried when she opened the suitcase after arriving at the small house about fifteen minutes outside of downtown Sedona. In addition to some new clothes, courtesy of the Mariposa boutique, there was a number of toiletries and shoes.

More proof that a woman understood the needs of another woman, and Laura's thoughtfulness in getting her a few items went a long way toward boosting her spirits.

If only she could appreciate it more.

Especially with a serious level of anxiety she couldn't seem to shake.

"Not like this is normal," she whispered to herself as she crisscrossed the room once more.

"What isn't normal?" Adam hovered at the entryway to

the kitchen, his shirtsleeves rolled up and the stress of his calls stamped on his face.

"This." She waved a hand. "Everything. All of it!"

Paige felt her voice rising and figured she was entitled to a modest freak-out.

"How do people live like this?"

"Fortunately, it's a temporary state." Adam remained calm, the voice of reason, as he stood there leaning on the doorjamb.

Paige looked around, wishing for some of that casual ease for herself.

"Temporary, maybe, but I have a heck of a lot more empathy for the celebrity clientele of yours. I've seen it through the years with my work but never registered it on this level. The entourage. The security measures. To have to live like this? Trapped in fear of someone in the outside world doing harm?" She crossed her arms, rubbing her hands just below her shoulders. "It's stifling."

"It's a choice. Max certainly experiences some of it."

"And he's not nearly on the level of some."

Adam did grin at that. Broadly. "I dare you to tell him that."

It was just what she needed to hear, and she felt her own laughter burst forth, breaking through some of the stifling anxiety. "Our dear friend does like the benefits of celebrity."

Adam pushed off the door and crossed to her, pulling her close. "It's only for a few days. Once the meeting happens, for good or for bad, it'll be done. And Noah is relentless on getting all the needed details on Glenna."

"I know."

She leaned her head on his shoulder, her gaze focused on the window as she reveled in his touch.

The large, soothing circles over her back.

The strong chest holding her up.

The simple miracle of being there with him.

It was all like a dream, the speed with which things had changed.

Her eyes were heavy, and she'd nearly closed them when something flashed outside the kitchen window.

Paige registered it, something discordant in the movement outside with the warm, soothing circle of Adam's embrace.

Fighting against the tender moment, she lifted her head from his chest and forced her gaze on the window.

Only to see the distinct shape of a man holding a gun, pointed directly through the window.

She pushed hard at Adam, her actions feeling like she was in the slowest motion, desperate to get away from the threat.

"Adam! Get down!"

He'd obviously registered her movements, his reflexes pushing against hers.

It was the last rational thought she had as his arms came around her, shielding her from the gunman and dragging her to the floor just as the window exploded.

Chapter Seventeen

"Stay down!"

Adam screamed the words as he felt a searing heat explode down his shoulder. He lay on top of Paige but knew they were still visible from the window, even though they were on the floor.

They needed to move.

Rolling them both to the side, he shifted until they lay flush against the cabinets beneath the sink. It wasn't much, and they'd have to move to get out of the kitchen, but at least they weren't visible to the gunman in the window.

"You've got nowhere to go!" the man screamed at them through the broken window. "Come on out."

They weren't coming out.

But, Adam admitted, they didn't have a hell of a lot of choices, either.

"Adam," Paige whispered against his ear. "Are you hurt?"

"It's my shoulder. It's fine."

Her lips trembled as she stared up at him. "You were shot?"

"I'm fine for now. We have to get you out of here. I'll cover you while you go to get help. My cell phone is on the end table by the couch. There's a gun in the workbag I brought with me. Back pocket. It's sitting against the couch."

He wasn't comfortable with guns, but a stay in the safe house had made him rethink that, and he'd packed the handgun he seldom took out of his safe just that morning.

"I'm not leaving you." Her arms banded even tighter around his waist where she held him.

"Get out of there, Colton!" the gunman hollered again. "Time's up!"

Another shot exploded through the window, striking the far wall. Adam registered the flying plaster and forced himself to ignore it.

To ignore the image of that same thing happening to Paige.

"I'm going to cover you, baby. We need help and we need that gun. You can do it."

"I can't go. He'll hurt you."

Adam knew she was right but also figured they had one small thing in their favor, assuming the man was alone.

If they stayed where they were, the gunman would have to move at some point to approach the door. He could cover Paige then and send her into the den to get the gun.

"You be ready to move as soon as he goes for the door." Adam whispered the words against her ear, hoping his voice didn't carry. "Get the gun."

"You can't—"

"Shhh." He pressed a hard kiss to her lips. "It's our only shot. He's not going to wait forever. As soon as he moves, you go."

One more shot exploded in the kitchen, and Adam realized it for the distraction it was when he heard the stomp of footsteps outside the window.

"Now! Go!"

He rolled off, his shoulder screaming in fiery agony, as he pushed her toward the living room. "You've got this. Go!"

She stayed low and scrambled for the exit.

He watched her go, taking his first easy breath just as a shot exploded through the glass of the back door, all while he lay there like a sitting duck.

Frantic, he glanced around for anything to use as a shield, spying the heavy case that Paige carried her lens in. Shoulder screaming, he pushed himself off the floor and toward the case, intending to use it as a shield to protect his chest.

He had the case in hand, lifting it up when another shot exploded from the door.

PAIGE DUG INTO Adam's workbag, the gun just where he'd promised in the back pocket. She wasn't big on guns, but she did know how to use one, and she was a fair shot.

She'd use it now to save Adam.

To save them both.

Two shots fired much too close together, and she screamed, leaping up from where she huddled over the bag.

She had to get to him.

That was her only thought as she fumbled with the safety, running back to the kitchen.

A million scenarios of what she'd find raced through her mind, one worse than the next, when she nearly fell over Adam's prone form on the floor.

"Adam!" She dropped to her knees, shoving at her big camera case when she heard a voice.

Trembling, she lifted her hands, the gun at the end of them.

"Paige!" Adam reached for her, shoving at her extended arms just as Noah walked through the door.

Again, that discordant sense of time slowing filled her, but something a lot like relief registered just as Noah hollered her name.

She tossed the gun, throwing it toward the sink and fell over Adam.

"Are you okay?"

"Shhh. It's all right." He lay flat on the ground, but his hands were on her face, smoothing her hair. "I'm okay."

"You're shot."

Noah moved fully into the room, dropping into a crouch beside them. His eyes were a little glassy with adrenaline and his voice was husky when he spoke. "You should see the other guy."

Paige reached out and took his hand, gripping him tight. "Thank you."

Noah nodded before ripping off his T-shirt and wadding it up, holding it tight to Adam's shoulder.

The three of them stayed there for several long moments before the insistent scream of police sirens echoed from a distance, getting louder with each second.

Noah dropped to a sitting position but never broke the contact between the three of them, one hand on Adam's shoulder, the other gripping her tight.

He finally moved when the paramedics came in to take Adam away, standing and helping her to her feet. And as Paige watched the paramedics take Adam out of the kitchen on a stretcher, she turned into Noah's open arms and let go.

"Ms. Barnes," Dr. Wu said. "Please take this the way I mean it, but I sincerely hope you're done taking advantage of this hospital's services."

The reserved doctor's comment was something of a surprise, and Paige laughed in spite of the circumstances. "I plan to follow your orders."

"Mr. Colton is resting in his room. He's incredibly lucky. The bullet passed through his arm cleanly, and we've debrided the wound fully. He's going to be fine."

Fine, Paige thought. Physically fine, maybe, but it would be a very long time—if ever—before she forgot the image of a hit man staring them down through that kitchen window.

"He has declined a sedative and refuses to stop asking when he can leave, so maybe you could go talk to him?"

The meeting!

Paige understood his urgency and, after thanking the doctor, headed to the room he'd been assigned.

She knew which it was without even seeing the number on the door, Adam's voice carrying down the hall from at least five rooms away.

"I need to leave."

"And you will, Adam. Calm down. The meeting's not for another three hours."

Paige walked in on a string of curses and a disgruntled Noah arguing with Adam.

"You were shot an hour ago."

"And I'm fine." Adam saw her coming through the door. "I need to get out of here."

She crossed to him, beyond grateful to see the color riding high in his cheeks. "You're setting off your machines in here. Quit being a bad patient and do as Noah says." She took his hand in hers. "Calm down."

"I need to get to that meeting."

"Oh, don't worry. Dr. Wu is more than happy to let you out of here."

Noah muttered something about stubborn, bullheaded

Coltons before heading out and leaving the two of them alone. Once he was gone, Paige leaned over the bedrail and laid her forehead against Adam's. "Thank you. For saving my life. And for making sure yours is whole and safe, too."

"Thank you for being whole and safe. I don't know what I'd do without you, Paige."

"Me either. Which is why each time a wave of panic hits me that you could have been hurt far worse, I try to reel myself back in. You're here and you're whole. And yelling at the hospital staff like an ogre."

"I'll double my annual donation to their charity dinner. I just need to get out of here."

"A point your sister is already managing with hospital administration. Imagine a Colton getting a free pass to the front of the line."

He had the good grace to look a bit chagrined but did seem to calm at the news Laura was getting him out of the hospital.

"Now all we have to do is get you home and changed and then head back into town for your meeting."

Adam eyed the pile in the corner. His outfit was a mess, with a hole from the gunshot wound and bloodstains on the front of the shirt and down to the pants.

Something dark and rather hypnotic came into his gaze.

"No, I think I'm all set with what I've got here."

Paige eyed the pile. "You sure about that?"

"Yes. I want my father to see what he wrought here with his greed. I want him to see what his wife set into motion."

"Not a chance at that," Noah said as he came back into the room, looking considerably more chipper than when he'd walked out.

"Oh?"

"Sedona PD picked her up twenty minutes ago. She apparently put on quite a show for the patrons of her hotel, kicking and screaming the entire way through the lobby."

"Imagine that," Adam said dryly.

"Yeah." Noah grinned. "Imagine. Which means I can now go make a call."

"To whom?" Paige asked, relieved beyond measure that Glenna was in custody.

"My security lead who's been discreetly keeping an eye on Sasha all day long with a plainclothes Sedona PD officer who's been keeping time in the lobby."

"It's the last piece," Paige murmured, turning to smile at Adam.

"Second to last." That blue gaze that saw so much narrowed in fierce determination. "It's time to go deal with my father."

ADAM WASN'T SURE how he'd expected the takeover meeting to go with his father, but arriving in a blood-and-gunpowder-stained shirt wasn't in his wildest imaginings.

"Adam?" Clive got up from the chair he'd occupied at the head of the conference room table at their law firm in downtown Sedona.

It didn't escape Adam's notice that his father moved slowly, a sign of his advancing age and overall poor health. The figure who'd loomed so large in his life for so long seemed...smaller, somehow.

Wasted.

He wasn't sure what it said about himself that he couldn't quite find it in his heart to be upset, but he could acknowledge the sheer sadness of it all.

If only things had been different.

"Clive."

"What happened to you?"

"I thought you should see it for yourself."

"See what?" Clive's normal bluster was nowhere in evidence as his gaze scanned over Adam's shirt.

"The way a man looks after stopping a bullet meant for the woman he loves. A bullet from a gunman, as a matter of fact—" Adam leaned in "—hired by the woman you love."

"What?" Clive stammered at that. "That's ridiculous."

"But true. Glenna's been behind any number of problems at Mariposa. Petty and small acts at first that have only grown in scale and scope." Adam sized up his father. "Were you aware of any of it?"

"How could you think that?"

"How could I not?"

Clive was about to say more when the conference room was suddenly flooded with noise and activity and what sounded like a stampede of feet.

Adam turned to find his sisters, their smiles wide, a thick envelope held high in Dani's hand. Josh pulled up the rear, following them into the conference room.

The shares.

Dani had gotten her shares.

In the end, Adam realized, that was all they'd needed to save Mariposa. The shares Clive had used nearly a quarter century before to buy off his lover had been his ultimate undoing.

Because his four children weren't going to let Mariposa out of their sights, nor would they allow him or whatever slimy partners he'd pulled in with him to take over Mariposa.

They would, however, gladly purchase his shares at a reduced rate to help fund the legal battles that were no doubt coming his way as a result of his wife's indiscriminate greed.

With the business finalized, Adam met his sisters and his brother and walked out of the conference room with them.

Maybe he'd be sorry one day that he didn't look back at the still-sputtering face of his father, but for now, all he felt was relief.

And elation when he saw Paige waiting for him.

She walked up to him, carefully wrapping her arms around his waist. "I wasn't privy to the inner workings of that room, but I heard the whooping and hollering out here. I can only assume that was a good sign."

"It was very good. But not nearly as good as knowing you were out here waiting for me." He leaned down and pressed his lips to hers.

She met him eagerly, and in that moment, Adam finally understood all he'd somehow reclaimed. What had started as a battle for Mariposa had become so much more.

Because he'd learned the most important lesson.

If things had gone differently today, if Dani had never gotten her shares and if his father had taken over the resort, he'd still be fine.

He had Laura, Josh and Dani.

He had his friends.

And now he had Paige.

The true gift—one of value and worth that would sustain him for the rest of his life—had finally come to rest on his shoulder, just like the butterfly Mariposa was named for.

He'd found love.

And he was the most fortunate of men.

Epilogue

"Speech! Speech!"

Max hollered those words from the end of the table where he was opening up a fresh bottle of champagne.

The reopening party for Mariposa was in full swing, and Adam had planned a small celebration for their inner circle in one of the hotel's conference rooms.

They'd spent the past three months healing and resting from the events of "the really, really hostile takeover" as Noah had begun to call those last days before defeating Clive, and now it was time to party.

It was Laura's idea to throw a reopening party, even though they'd technically not ever closed. But they had slowed down to focus on rebuilding.

And to bring some of those fresh, new ideas Adam was so determined to use as his North Star going forward.

That didn't mean he hadn't found time to play. He and Paige had taken a relaxing vacation to the Caribbean, followed by a week in Southern California packing up her home in Newport Beach.

She officially made her home base Arizona now, and he was beyond lucky she was willing to relocate.

"I know you have something to say," Paige whispered in

his ear as she stood next to him. "I caught you practicing in front of the mirror this morning. Remember?"

"Oh, I remember."

And he did, because they'd spent quite a while after she was done teasing him in other more exciting pursuits where he quite effectively put a new sort of smile on her face.

"Then you'd best get going before Max takes it upon himself to give the speech instead."

Since Adam knew his best friend just might do that, he took a few steps up onto the dais in the small ballroom they were using for their intimate family celebration.

As he took one of the champagne glasses Dani was passing around, Adam gave himself a moment to take it all in.

Laura and Noah were wrapped up in each other, and he saw his sister diligently trying to hold her champagne glass high enough not to spill it as Noah nuzzled her neck from behind.

Dani gave Matt a kiss as she handed off the last glass of champagne to him before moving into him and wrapping her arm around his waist.

Alexis was doing her level best to corral Max, and Adam laughed when she finally shoved his friend into a chair and plopped into his lap, obviously in an effort to hold him still.

Josh and Kelli stood arm in arm, Kelli's diamond sparkling under the ballroom lights while they talked to CJ and Erica, back visiting even though their executive assistant had taken some time off with her movie-star husband for the birth of her baby.

And then there was Paige, smiling up at him and, as she always did, making him feel as if he could do anything.

"I want to make a toast to all of us. To the past year that's made us stronger. To the past year that's given us all a future."

"Stronger together!" Laura hollered as she lifted her glass.

"Stronger together!" Adam said, toasting them all and taking a sip of his champagne.

It was only when it quieted once more that he lifted his glass, happy and, if he were honest, a little nervous.

Because this was the part of his speech Paige hadn't overheard this morning.

"If you'll indulge me, I have one more toast."

Everyone quieted as Adam stared out at all of them before turning his gaze fully on Paige.

"To Paige Barnes. The only woman I've ever loved. The only woman I will ever love." He lifted his glass to her. "Please make me the happiest of men and say you'll be my wife."

He belatedly realized that he still had her engagement ring in his coat pocket and quickly felt around for it.

But it hadn't mattered, he realized as she came up to him and wrapped her arms around his neck.

"In front of all these people, Adam?"

He smiled at her, well aware she was as happy as he was to declare their love publicly. "In front of all these people, my love."

"Then I guess there's really only one thing to say."

"What's that?"

"Yes, Adam. I say yes to you forever."

The room erupted in screams and shouts and clinking glasses, but it all faded away as he bent his head and met her lips in a kiss.

He'd never know how he'd gotten so fortunate to find her again, but Adam Colton wasn't one to argue with fate. Or luck.

Or the sheer brilliance that was a second chance at love.

* * * * *

COMING SOON!

We really hope you enjoyed reading this book.
If you're looking for more romance
be sure to head to the shops when
new books are available on

Thursday 17th July

To see which titles are coming soon, please visit
millsandboon.co.uk/nextmonth

MILLS & BOON

OUT NOW!

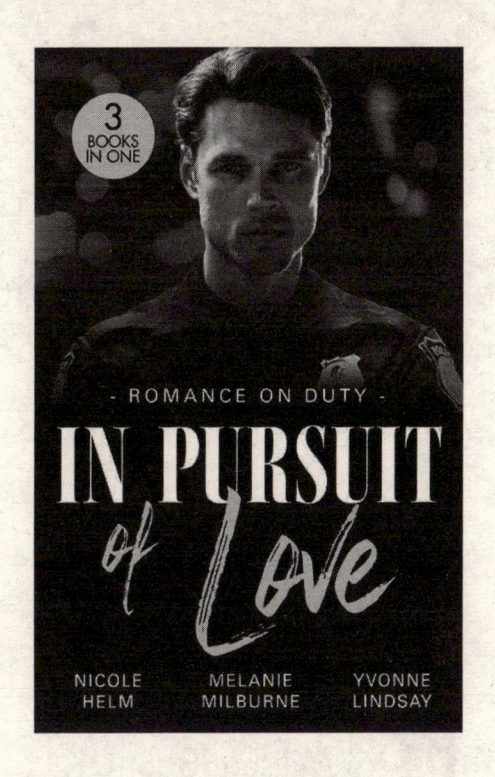

3 BOOKS IN ONE

- ROMANCE ON DUTY -

IN PURSUIT of Love

NICOLE HELM   MELANIE MILBURNE   YVONNE LINDSAY

Available at
millsandboon.co.uk

MILLS & BOON

LET'S TALK
Romance

For exclusive extracts, competitions and special offers, find us online:

- **f** MillsandBoon
- **X** @MillsandBoon
- **◉** @MillsandBoonUK
- **♪** @MillsandBoonUK

Get in touch on 01413 063 232

> For all the latest titles coming soon, visit
> millsandboon.co.uk/nextmonth